BATTLES HALF WON

BATTLES
HALF
WON

INDIA'S IMPROBABLE
DEMOCRACY

ASHUTOSH VARSHNEY

PENGUIN

VIKING

VIKING
Published by the Penguin Group
Penguin Books India Pvt. Ltd, 11 Community Centre, Panchsheel Park,
New Delhi 110 017, India
Penguin Group (USA) Inc., 375 Hudson Street, New York, New York 10014, USA
Penguin Group (Canada), 90 Eglinton Avenue East, Suite 700, Toronto, Ontario,
M4P 2Y3, Canada (a division of Pearson Penguin Canada Inc.)
Penguin Books Ltd, 80 Strand, London WC2R 0RL, England
Penguin Ireland, 25 St Stephen's Green, Dublin 2, Ireland (a division of Penguin
Books Ltd)
Penguin Group (Australia), 707 Collins Street, Melbourne, Victoria 3008, Australia
(a division of Pearson Australia Group Pty Ltd)
Penguin Group (NZ), 67 Apollo Drive, Rosedale, Auckland 0632, New Zealand
(a division of Pearson New Zealand Ltd)
Penguin Books (South Africa) (Pty) Ltd, Block D, Rosebank Office Park,
181 Jan Smuts Avenue, Parktown North, Johannesburg 2193, South Africa

Penguin Books Ltd, Registered Offices: 80 Strand, London WC2R 0RL, England

First published in Viking by Penguin Books India 2013

Copyright © Ashutosh Varshney 2013

Pages 403–04 are an extension of the copyright page

ISBN 9780670084289

Typeset in Minion by R. Ajith Kumar, New Delhi
Printed at Replika Press Pvt. Ltd, India

To Vibha and Kartik

Contents

III. Economic Development

List of Tables and Figures

Tables

Figures

Preface

For political science, which is my disciplinary home, India's democracy is a baffling phenomenon. Theories predicted democracy's demise in India, but that has not happened. Indeed, the opposite has transpired. Democracy is now firmly institutionalized. Elections are the only way to come to power; governments are openly and freely challenged by a whole host of actors, institutions, and organizations; incumbents routinely lose power in freely contested elections. Several inadequacies remain, but much has been achieved.

The aim of these essays is twofold. Not only do I seek to convey my understanding of why, in a highly counter-theoretical way, India's democracy has survived, but I also analyse the achievements and failures of Indian democracy. In the process, the interaction of democracy with caste, religion, language, and economy features widely in the book. India's democracy is shaped by these social and economic factors and, in turn, it influences them.

The essays presented here cover a period of twenty years of writing. With the exception of the first chapter, all chapters were originally published as articles, mostly in scholarly journals. While the original argument remains intact in each essay, all essays have been significantly updated for this volume. As far as possible, repetition has been avoided, though some foundational ideas are bound to figure prominently in several essays.

My understanding of Indian democracy has emerged out of a scholarly college formed seamlessly since my days as a student at Jawaharlal Nehru University (JNU) and Massachusetts Institute of Technology (MIT). At JNU, Sudipta Kaviraj, now at Columbia, greatly shaped my understanding, though I was never formally his student. At MIT, the late Myron Weiner mentored me with remarkable intellectual commitment and grace. Since starting my American career as a professor, my principal institutional homes—Harvard, Michigan, and Brown—have turned out to be stimulating intellectual sites, but they have not been my only sources of inspiration. As my career evolved, an invisible college of scholarly interaction emerged. Debating and critiquing in seminars and conferences, and reading drafts and published work, in addition to field research, generated new ideas.

For the arguments presented in this volume, I would especially—and thankfully—like to acknowledge intellectual exchanges over the last two decades with Amit Ahuja, Kanti Bajpai, Jagdish Bhagwati, Marshall Bouton, Kanchan Chandra, Pradeep Chhibber, Anis Dani, Jorge Dominguez, Sumit Ganguly, Anna Grzymala-Busse, Joshua Gubler, Stephan Haggard, Robert Hardgrave, John Harriss, Patrick Heller, Ronald Herring, Stanley Hoffmann, the late Samuel Huntington, Christophe Jaffrelot, Niraja Jayal, Rob Jenkins, Stathis Kalyvas, Atul Kohli, Margaret Levi, Daniel Levine, Roderick MacFarquhar, Scott Mainwaring, James Manor, Pratap Mehta, Uday Mehta, Mick Moore, James Morone, Ashis Nandy, Deepa Narayan, Phil Oldenburg, Robert Putnam, Swati and Ramesh Ramanathan, Biju Rao, Sanjay Reddy, Lloyd and Susanne Rudolph, Jeff Sachs, Teresita Schaefer, James Scott, Amartya Sen, Rajath Shourie, Bhrigu and Prerna Singh, Eswaran Sridharan, Alfred Stepan, Ashley Tellis, the late Myron Weiner, Rina Williams, and Yogendra Yadav. Not all are, or were, India specialists, but their intellectual curiosity and questioning contributed to greater rigor, or greater breadth, in arguments.

At Penguin, this volume went through several editors. Finally, Kamini Mahadevan's wisdom, tenacity, and meticulous reading brought the volume to fruition and significantly influenced its final shape. It has been a pleasure to work with her. Poulomi Chakrabarti's research assistance has been exemplary. My heartfelt thanks!

Providence, Rhode Island
1 October 2013

I

Democracy

1

The Odyssey of
an Improbable Democracy

Independent India was born with multiple projects. Three projects were especially important: securing national unity; bringing dignity and justice to those at the bottom of the social order; and eliminating mass poverty. These were by no means the only projects of the founding fathers, but they were viewed as critical. Freedom was not simply to be intrinsically valued, though there was some of that to be sure. A free India would also allow its citizens to achieve some cherished and worthy goals.

In and of themselves, these three missions—national unity, social justice, and elimination of mass poverty—were not unusual. Indeed, with some variations, these were familiar themes on the political agenda of many other countries that became independent after the Second World War. The uniqueness of the Indian experiment lay in the political framework within which these projects had to be pursued. India's founding fathers committed themselves to a universal-franchise democracy. Vote was not to be based on differentiations of gender, class, or ethnicity. Universal franchise came to the West after the Industrial Revolution—that is, after incomes had reached a substantially high level. India was to practise

3

it at a very low level of income, long before an economic revolution
had come about.

In other newly decolonized nations, too, democratic
commencements were common, as many instituted the vote
and political freedoms. But democracy was not a primary, or
an unwavering, commitment elsewhere. If the Asian, African,
Latin American, (or even Southern European) elite thought that
democracy was coming in the way of achieving the objectives of
national unity, social justice or prosperity, in many places it was
tossed aside in favour of an authoritarian, quite ardent, embrace.
By the 1960s, country after country had abandoned its democratic
pledge.[1] In contrast, with the solitary exception of nineteen months
during 1975–77, India's democracy survived.

Fifteen national elections and many more state-level elections
have been held till now. The probability of a democratic collapse is
minuscule. Democracy has become the institutionalized common
sense of Indian politics: no one thinks any longer that there is any
other way of coming to power. Comparative evidence, examined at
length below, makes it clear that, *for the first time in human history,
a poor nation has practised universal franchise for so long*—already
for over six decades.

The long swathe of democratic experience allows us to answer
some important questions. Has India's democracy aided, or
impeded, the pursuit of national unity, dignity and justice, and
elimination of poverty? The essays in this book, written over a
period of two decades and now revisited, argue that the battles
are half won. Keeping the nation together is perhaps the greatest
achievement of Indian democracy, though democracy alone has
not made that happen: a combination of force and persuasion has
been used to quell insurgencies and riots. Democracy has seriously
attacked caste inequalities in the South, but in the North the process
has only recently acquired force. Mass poverty remains the greatest
failure of Indian democracy. Since 1991, the rate of decline in

poverty has accelerated, and a real measure of prosperity has reached the middle classes for the first time in modern Indian history. But, anywhere between roughly one-fourth and over one-third of India—depending on what measure is deployed—remains trapped in various forms of poverty. Begging bowls, hungry faces, emaciated bodies—young and old—continue to greet the rising curve of prosperity. In recent years, corporate players have enthused a great deal over India—indeed, signs of business dynamism have been all too evident. But those who look at poverty, primary and secondary education, and public health find economic growth figures entirely, or substantially, unsatisfactory. They bemoan India's social lag.[2]

What accounts for these partial successes? And how, in turn, can we understand the surprising longevity of Indian democracy? The essays presented in this book seek to give an account. Since the essays are mostly about how democracy has affected the pursuit of the larger ends—national unity, social justice, poverty, and economic welfare—I will touch on them only briefly in this opening chapter.

My main focus here will be on the origins, the longevity, and the unfinished quests of Indian democracy. The statistical sophistication of recent democratic theory presents the exceptionalism of India's democracy with stunning clarity. It is clear that India's democratic longevity is less a consequence of some objective characteristics of Indian society, culture, or economy—the factors normally invoked. Rather, India's democratic success is primarily a consequence of politics. Leaders and political organizations, going back to the freedom struggle in the first half of the twentieth century, have played a salutary role. Without centrally bringing their role into our analysis—especially those from the pre-independence and early post-independence period—India's democratic longevity cannot be understood. The leaders and their organizations did not carry larger impersonal forces of history. They made democracy.[3]

The quality of Indian democracy generates a great deal of

concern, and rightly so. The desire to improve the ethical and civic fibre of democracy is a feeling shared by a large number of Indian citizens, and the intellectual and political energy that has time and again gone into a moral or civic enhancement is substantial. 'Argumentative Indians' have often debated and critiqued the existing democratic practices. Movements expressing dissatisfaction with the democratic process have repeatedly emerged.

But a prior question needs to be posed and explored. Comparative experience, in retrospect, suggests that India's democracy was unlikely to be stable. A Pakistani- or Indonesian-style political history was more likely. Both these nations were, like India, desperately poor at the time of independence, and both were unable to stabilize democracy in the first half-century, or more, of their post-independence history. We need to ask why Indian democracy has lasted so long, as much as what is wrong with it.

National Projects: What Was to Be Done?

Let us, however, begin with a brief overview of the three great national projects—national unity, dignity and social justice, and elimination of mass poverty. Why were they so important?

The first project was principally focused on keeping India's linguistic and religious divisions in check. India was linguistically and religiously so diverse that liberation from what the leaders repeatedly called 'fissiparous tendencies' was absolutely necessary. The immensely violent partition of India on grounds of religion had only served to underline how important the creation of a national feeling was. Both joy and agony had attended India's freedom. The British left after nearly two centuries, but India's partition led to hundreds of thousands of deaths. And, in search of safety, millions had to leave their homes and become migrants. National unity, as a consequence, became an abiding concern in politics. Unity simply could not be assumed.

The second project—dignity and social justice—called for attacking the inequities of the caste system, a lasting feature of Hindu society which constituted over 80 per cent of the country after partition. An independent and modern India could not possibly live with the notion that, depending on the caste in which one was born, a human being's rights and responsibilities would be different; that discrimination would continue to be practised as in the old days; and that roughly one-fifth of the Hindu community, whose touch would pollute those hierarchically above, could be called 'untouchable'. A modern polity could not accept radically different bundles of rights based on birth.

The third project sought to bring basic material comforts—food, clothing, health and shelter—to the millions of Indians living in shocking squalor and deprivation at the time of independence. When the British left India after ruling different parts of the country for a century and a half to nearly two centuries, a mere 15–17 per cent of India was literate and, though reliable poverty statistics do not go as far back as 1947–48, it will not be implausible to suggest that at least half of the nation's population was below the poverty line and millions above it were also quite poor.[4] The enormity of the problem required a concerted and systematic attack.

How do we know that these objectives were central to national political life? In modern times, a nation's fundamental missions are normally enshrined in its Constitution. But, relying on legal exactitude, constitutions have a way of lending a prosaic touch to missions that are conceptualized as grand, enduring, and politically and emotionally compelling. Constitutions are not sites of splendid rhetoric rendered in captivating metaphors. Able and imaginative political leaders often construct such rhetoric, representing the heroic idealism of founding moments.

As it turned out, Jawaharlal Nehru, India's first prime minister and a leader next only to Mahatma Gandhi in the freedom movement, was remarkably capable of delivering national missions and political aspirations in prose fitting the spirit of the moment. In a speech delivered on the stroke of midnight, just as India was about to be free of British rule, a speech famously entitled 'Tryst with Destiny', this is how Nehru began:

> Long years ago we made a tryst with destiny, and now the time comes when we shall redeem our pledge, not wholly or in full measure, but very substantially. At the stroke of the midnight hour, when the world sleeps, India will awake to life and freedom. A moment comes, which comes but rarely in history, when we step out from the old to the new, when an age ends, and when the soul of a nation, long suppressed, finds utterance.[5]

Having thus sketched the historic significance and depth of the moment of freedom, Nehru, in less rousing prose, began to lay out the principal projects of modern India:

> The future beckons to us. Whither do we go and what shall be our endeavour? To bring freedom and opportunity to the common man . . . to fight and end poverty and ignorance and disease; to build up a prosperous, democratic and progressive nation, and to create social, economic and political institutions which will ensure justice and fullness of life to every man and woman.

Towards the end of the speech, he turned to religion that had so tormented India's freedom movement and led to the birth of two nations, India and Pakistan. He did not wish to speak of the violence that had already broken out, and that had also kept Mahatma Gandhi, the father of the nation, away from the capital. While India was celebrating freedom, Gandhi was making valiant attempts to restore peace in Calcutta, a city of great political significance to modern India, but one awfully torn by Hindu–

Muslim riots. Formulating the problem of Hindu–Muslim relations more generally, Nehru said:

> All of us, to whatever religion we may belong, are equally the children of India with equal rights, privileges and obligations. We cannot encourage communalism or narrow-mindedness, for no nation can be great whose people are narrow in thought or in action.

All selections of prime national goals tend to have an element of subjectivity. The listing above is no exception. Based on the Constitution, major speeches and the basic political disputes of post-independence politics, the identification of national unity, social justice, and elimination of poverty as India's fundamental national projects reflects my understanding of what was central. Other listings may be different, at least partially.

In particular, some will point to national security and India's international standing as a major national objective. Though Nehru was intermittently India's defence minister,[6] he always kept the portfolio of external affairs. For seventeen years, Nehru was not only prime minister, but also India's secretary of state, as it were. Nehru clearly attached a great deal of importance to foreign policy. He even invented the concept of non-alignment in international affairs, seeking to stay away from the encircling blocks of the Cold War.

The significance of defence or foreign policy is beyond doubt. But both have been important primarily to India's elite politics, not to the nation's mass politics.[7] Both have indirectly helped or hindered mass welfare, but neither has directly determined election results in India. As India's power grows, the direct political significance of defence or foreign policy might well change but, as of now, they have not played the same role in mass politics as religion, caste, or poverty. As Tellis puts it, India has always viewed itself as a developmental state, hoping the problem of national security would go away: national energies have never quite concentrated on security or foreign affairs.[8] Even after the terrorist attacks in Mumbai in 2008, the incumbents did not lose power in 2009. That is in part because villages continue to have a preponderant weight in election politics, and neither national security nor foreign policy is an issue of overriding importance in rural politics. Until India is significantly more urban, this situation is unlikely to change dramatically.

Defining Democracy

On what grounds can we claim that India is a democracy? To many, this might appear to be an unnecessarily pedantic matter. Is it not obvious that India has been democratic for over six decades, holding regular elections, allowing freedom of press, judiciary, faith, association, and movement? The matter is not so straightforward.

Critics of India's democracy have often called it a procedural, not a substantive, democracy. Indeed, there has been a long tradition of inquiry going all the way back to Karl Marx, which critiques elections, elected institutions, and freedom to elect as being wholly inadequate. This tradition insists that democracy should be defined in terms of some larger goals—for example, economic equality. If citizens are not relatively economically equal, the freedom to elect can only be illusory. Following this tradition, Jalal has argued that even though Pakistan—often ruled by the military—has had very few elections, and India has always had elections and civilian rule, there is no fundamental difference between the polities of India and Pakistan. Both societies are highly unequal, which makes elections deceptive and unreal.[9]

This view is implausible for two reasons. First, greater equality deepens a democracy, but inequality does not make it impossible. The *deepening* of democracy and the *presence* of democracy are analytically separable. Following this reasoning, Heller has argued that the state of Kerala has a deep democracy, whereas other states of India—let us say, Rajasthan and Madhya Pradesh—are not so deep.[10] But democracy exists both in Kerala and Rajasthan.[11]

Second, and more generally, even if we claim that democracy is not about elections, but about some larger goals, we cannot escape the necessity of the elective principle. For how do we know which goals a society really wishes to strive for? Some may prefer freedom; others, equality; still others, dignity for all. Unless societal objectives are subjected to an elective principle, they will necessarily be chosen in an authoritarian manner. Lee Kuan Yew's goals for Singapore— prosperity, equality, a merit-based society—are laudable. Singapore has also achieved them quite substantially, but the goals he chose have never been seriously questioned or debated in elections. As a result, Singapore cannot be, and has never been, called democratic.

Given that a hierarchy of goals is very hard to establish *for society as a whole*, as opposed to individual life, democratic theory embraces an institutional or procedural definition of democracy. Indeed, Dahl's twofold principle—contestation and participation—has become the classic definition of democracy. Contestation signifies the freedom with which the ruling party—which normally has control over the police and bureaucracy—can be challenged in an election. Participation covers franchise—whether all citizens have the right to vote and can effectively vote.[12] Dahl argues that such polities have existed mostly in Western societies, but notes that 'a leading contemporary exception . . . is India, where (democracy) was established when the population was overwhelmingly agricultural, illiterate and . . . highly traditional and rule-bound in behavior and beliefs.'[13]

The Improbability of Indian Democracy

The improbable success of India's democracy has been talked about for a long time.[14] But the newer concepts and the statistical evidence provided by Przeworski and his colleagues allow us to see India's democratic exceptionalism in a fresh light.[15] The biggest surprise about Indian democracy is income-based.[16]

The claims of Przeworski *et al.* are based on the most comprehensive data set ever constructed on democracies and dictatorships. The data set covers 141 countries between 1950 and 1990. In this period, there were 238 regimes—105 democratic and 133 dictatorial. Of the 141 countries, only 41 experienced a regime transition from democracy to dictatorship, or vice versa. The remaining 100 countries—67 dictatorships, 33 democracies—witnessed no change.

Of all the patterns that Przeworski *et al.* have identified, the following have special relevance for India:

1. Income is the best predictor of democracy. It correctly predicted the type of regime in 77.5 per cent of the cases; only in 22.5 per cent, it did not.[17] No other predictor—religion, colonial legacy, ethnic diversity, international political environment—is as good on the whole.

2. India is in the latter 22.5 per cent set. Indeed, if we consider only decolonized countries, the claim for India can be made even more specific and precise. Democracies that emerged from decolonization survived only in India, Mauritius, Belize, Jamaica, Papua New Guinea, Solomon Islands, and Vanuatu. Of these, the most surprising case is India, which 'was predicted as a dictatorship during the entire period' (1950–90). 'The odds against democracy in India were extremely high.'[18] All other poorer exceptions had higher income than India.

3. Some other countries have defied the pattern on the obverse side. They were rich enough to be democratic earlier. Those that became democracies later than their income levels would have predicted include South Africa, Taiwan, Chile, Portugal, and Spain. Income would also have predicted Mexico to be a democracy in the early 1950s, not in the late 1990s. And

Singapore 'had a 0.02 probability of being a dictatorship in 1990', but it is still authoritarian today.[19] If India is the biggest exception on the low-income end, then Singapore is the biggest surprise on the high-income side.

4. A relationship between growth rates and the probability of a democratic breakdown can also be ascertained. Democracies that grow at rates lower than 5 per cent per annum collapse at a higher rate than democracies whose economies grow at rates faster than 5 per cent per annum.[20] Again, India is a big exception, but for a specific period. India's economic growth rate has been higher than 5 per cent per annum since 1980 but, in the period 1950–80, Indian economy grew at only 3.5 per cent per annum. This larger statistical relationship, too, would have predicted a collapse of Indian democracy between 1950 and 1980. Had Indira Gandhi's Emergency lasted longer than eighteen months (1975–77), India would actually have followed the larger trend.

A new conceptual framework undergirds these statistical patterns. Przeworski *et al.* draw a sharp distinction between the 'endogenous' and the 'exogenous' conceptions of democratization. The endogenous view is that democracies are more likely to emerge as countries become wealthier. The exogenous explanation distinguishes between emergence and survival. Democracies can be established for any number of reasons, but they are likely to last mostly at higher levels of income.

Przeworski *et al.* challenge the endogenous view.[21] They argue that wars, the death of dictators, economic crises, foreign pressure, or the end of colonial rule can all lead to the establishment of democracies. However, evidence shows that democracies tend to collapse in poorer countries, but survive in wealthier countries. This view, called the exogenous view, distinguishes birth from longevity, emergence from survival. Essentially, the origins of democracies are not economic, but survival mostly is.[22]

Why this should be so is unclear. The analysis of Przeworski *et al.* is not causal, it is only about identification of patterns. But they do partially rule out the validity of one explanation: education. At higher levels of income, education levels tend to be higher, and it is sometimes suggested that a more educated citizenry is more tolerant of dissent, leading to an acceptance of democratic values. '*At each level of education*,' they find, 'the probability of democracy dying decreases with income.' Hence, for reasons that are not easy to identify, 'wealth does make democracies more stable, independently of education.'[23]

While scholars continue to investigate the reasons why democracies are so hard to sustain at low levels of income, a couple of hypotheses are worth entertaining.[24]

In poor societies, governments tend to be heavily involved in the economy, either as direct producers or service providers, or as regulators. Political power can greatly enhance one's economic chances and those of the group associated with the winner, while loss of power can spell doom. It is not uncommon for this doom to include imprisonment and forms of extreme vengeance. In contrast, at high levels of income, opportunities can be pursued in many sectors which are not controlled by the government. Political defeat does not entail a rapid and comprehensive closure of opportunities. Defeats are easier to accept when they do not lead to painful economic sunsets or harsh punishments.

Of course, economic reasons alone do not exhaust the explanations for why politics in poor democracies become such a do-or-die contest. Group persecutions may also take place on religious or cultural grounds. For its beliefs, the small group of Ahmedis was declared non-Muslim in Pakistan by an elected regime in the 1970s. In a currently democratic Indonesia, too, Ahmedis are being targeted for their religious doctrines. Such a problem especially affects minorities. In India, the Muslim minority in Gujarat was targeted in the 2002 riots and the Sikh minority in Delhi, in 1984. The police and civil service can sometimes nakedly represent majoritarianism, believing that majoritarian feelings should brook no legal obstacles. The majoritarian logic of democracy can thus undermine its liberal logic, hurting minorities and dissenting groups and individuals. Richer democracies are not entirely above this problem, but countervailing power—through the media and courts—can be created with less difficulty.

Be that as it may, India's democratic surprise is now much clearer than before. By their very nature, statistical arguments tend to be probabilistic, not deterministic.[25] They establish the odds, not certainties. India's democracy was highly improbable, but not impossible. We need to ask: What made the improbable so real?

Explaining Longevity

The reasons for the survival of Indian democracy—some of which are examined in Chapter 2—are both structural and political. The structural reasons essentially deal with some enduring features of Indian society; the political reasons have to do with the way leaders and organizations dealt with those enduring features, constructed strategies, and developed institutions. In the account given below, leaders will play a central role.

Keohane has remarked that scholars have been silent, erroneously, on the role of leaders in bringing about change.[26] The concentration has been on the economy, culture, and society. Focusing on India, Kohli echoes Keohane and has come closest to the argument developed below:

> Indian democracy is ... best understood by focusing, not mainly on its socio-economic determinants, but on how power distribution in that society is negotiated and renegotiated. A concern with the process of power negotiation, in turn, draws attention to such factors as leadership strategies, the design of political institutions, and the political role of diverse social groups.[27]

The Identity Structure of Indian Society

On the whole, class cleavages, class coalitions, and class conflict have been historically regarded by scholars as the main structural reasons for democratization.[28] Certain types of class structures and coalitions impede the evolution of democracy; some other types promote it. Economic inequalities are often the centrepiece of such analyses.[29]

Of late, ethnic or communal cleavages—as opposed to class cleavages—have received a lot of attention. Dahl did present some early thoughts about the links between cultural cleavage patterns and democracy,[30] but these links remained underexplored. The new thinking is that even in the birth of democracy in Western Europe, religious and ethnic cleavages and structures can be shown to have played a significant role.

> Rather than class being the single variable that explains how and why democracy came about, scholars can see how religious conflict, ethnic cleavages, and the diffusion of ideas played a much greater role in Europe's democratization than has typically been appreciated.[31]

The idea of the impact of ethnic or communal cleavage structures on democracy has obvious relevance to India. For decades, it has been a familiar trope of scholarship on Indian politics that class has played a secondary role in determining political patterns and struggles; language, religion and caste have been far more influential.

What is the relationship between identity-based cleavages and democratic longevity in India? India's identity structure is dispersed, not centrally focused; and the identities cross-cut, instead of cumulating. Such structural features have political consequences.

Dispersed and Cross-Cutting Identities

Horowitz proposed the seminal conceptual distinction between *dispersed* and centrally *focused* ethnic structures.[32] Identities in dispersed systems tend to be locally based and many such identities exist. Centrally focused systems tend to have fewer salient identities, which have a nationwide resonance. As a consequence, conflict tends to escalate throughout the system. In dispersed ethnic structures, ethnic conflict remains localized and does not have a national spillover. The Centre can handle one group at a time in one part of the country without worrying about the nightmare of having the entire polity get affected.

Sri Lanka's Sinhala–Tamil conflict has a centrally focused quality, as does the Malay–Chinese conflict in Malaysia, and as did the East–West conflict in pre-1971 Pakistan. In India, all identity-based cleavages are regionally or locally concentrated. Most major languages have a geographical homeland in the federal set-up. Linguistic conflicts are thus typically confined to one part of the country or another. Religious cleavages are not too different. The Sikh–Hindu religious cleavage is confined basically to the state of Punjab and to some other parts of North India; the Hindu–Muslim cleavage rarely affects the South in a violent way;[33] the insurgency in Kashmir remained confined to the Kashmir Valley and did not spill over to include all Muslims. The 'sons of the soil' movements in Assam, Mumbai and Telangana, remained region-based or city-based. Even the caste system is local or regional in character. Castes typically split state politics, generally not allowing any given state to become a cohesive and united political force against the Centre.

Analytically separable, but equally important, is the cross-cutting nature of Indian identities. Cumulative cleavages create greater potential for conflict escalation; cross-cutting cleavages tend to dampen conflict.[34] Sri Lanka is a classic case of cumulative cleavages.

Tamils are not only religiously, but also linguistically and racially, distinct from the Sinhalese.

India's four principal identities—language, religion, caste, and tribe—tend to cut across one another. Depending on the location, the first language of a Muslim could be Urdu, Hindi, Gujarati, Bengali, or Malayalam, to name a few. The same characteristic marks the Hindus. Moreover, the Hindus are split into thousands of castes.

Despite the many diversities of India, insurgencies have been few and far between.[35] Conflicts, of course, keep simmering, sometimes creating the impression that the political system is breaking down. Yet, violence dies before long, and democracy returns to normalcy. If the battle had been between keeping democracy alive and letting the nation break down, perhaps India's democracy would have faced sterner tests. A centrally focused and cumulative identity structure would have created much greater concerns for national integrity. A dispersed and cross-cutting identity structure may generate many more conflicts, but the intensity of conflict rarely reaches a level constituting an existential threat to the entire nation. As a consequence, India cannot easily become a Yugoslavia (which did not have a democracy in the first place).

The question of nationhood is important in yet another important sense: political. It was not merely the dispersed and cross-cutting structure of identities which prevented a deadly clash between democracy and nationhood. It is also that democracy benefited from the construction of nationhood during India's freedom struggle. India was not only an unlikely democracy, but also an unlikely nation.[36] The construction of nationhood—made possible by the national movement and led by Gandhi—was a political enterprise; as was the consolidation of the nation after independence, led by Nehru, through political practices and institutions, especially the Constitution.

Nationhood and Democracy

Two kinds of historical discourses are relevant to a discussion of Indian democracy: one, a theoretical claim that nationhood is a prerequisite for democracy; and two, a conventional observation that India's radical diversities made nationhood virtually impossible. Since India could not be a nation, it followed as a syllogism that it could not be a democracy either.

Let us examine this through the arguments put forth by John Stuart Mill, often viewed as the father of modern liberalism; John Strachey, a leading administrator of colonial India; and Mark Twain, a literary giant, whose reflections about the impossibility of Indian nationhood were stimulated by his visit to India. The focus, then, shifts to how the Gandhi-led freedom movement sought to deal with such important claims, and how politics overcame arguments about structural or theoretical improbability.

Mill's Assertion

John Stuart Mill was among the first to argue that democracy was not possible without a national feeling. 'It is in general a necessary condition of free institutions that the boundaries of governments should coincide in the main with those of nationalities.'[37] Mill thought linguistic diversity was a special, virtually insuperable, 'hindrance to nation-making'.[38]

Mill's proposition can be translated into today's language. Regular democratic elections are about who should run a government of the nation, not about whether one should accept the nation at all. The latter can be decided by *referendums*, but *elections* are analytically distinct. If regular elections turn into battles over sovereignty, they are likely to be bloody, might unleash unmanageable passions, and render considered voting judgements virtually impossible. For periodic elections to have meaning, the basic political unit should not be in question. That is why national feeling is a prerequisite for democracy to function.

Mill, of course, had another argument about who could have—or who deserved—representative government. He spoke of 'two classes' of colonies: 'Some are composed of people of similar civilization to the ruling country: capable of, and ripe for, representative government: such as British possessions in America and Australia. Others, like India, are still at a great distance from that state.'[39] If so, what sort of government should 'Others, like India' have? A 'vigorous despotism is in itself the best mode of government for training the people in what is specifically wanting to render them capable of a higher civilization.'[40]

There are, thus, two arguments here. One, nationhood is a prerequisite for a democracy; and two, colonies with a European ancestry, such as Canada and Australia, could have a democracy, but Indians came from an inferior civilization, and only when they reached an advanced state under British tutelage could they attain democracy.

In recent times, Mill's second argument has been subjected to detailed intellectual scrutiny.[41] And it is less relevant to our discussion here.[42] The civilizational or cultural arguments are not taken seriously by students of democracy any longer.[43] In the 1950s and 1960s, cultural arguments enjoyed their heyday.[44] But empirical evidence now is stacked against cultural prerequisites. Stepan shows that even predominantly Muslim countries—often viewed as entirely inhospitable to democracy—have had democracies outside the Arab world.[45] And as already mentioend, Przeworski et al. show that income predicts more than 75 per cent of democratic instances. Culture plays a very small role.

The more important of Mill's two arguments is that nationhood is a prerequisite for democracy. Could India develop a national feeling, or was it simply an assemblage of inveterate localities, each locality speaking a different language? Language, according to Mill, was key to nationhood.

Strachey's Observation, Twain's Anxiety

Whether India could become a nation was also often debated by the powerful bureaucrats of the British Empire. John Strachey, a member of the British Governor General's Council, was one of the most prominent official voices in the late nineteenth century. In his oft-cited words, written in 1888, 'there is not, and never was an India, or even any country of India possessing, according to any European ideas, any sort of unity, physical, political, social or religious'; and 'that men of the Punjab, Bengal, the Northwestern Provinces and Madras, should ever feel that they belong to one Indian nation, is impossible. You might with as much reason and probability look forward to a time when a single nation will have taken the place of the various nations of Europe.'[46]

This argument essentially proposes that India was a civilization like Europe, not a nation. Just as Europe has so many nations, the various units of India could conceivably become nations, but India could not be a single nation. A civilization is a cultural construct and does not require political unity. Building a nation—to use Gellner's famous words that will mark several essays in this volume—is 'to endow a culture with its own political roof'.[47] That roof, Strachey argued, could not be built over all of India.

Roughly similar claims were made by Mark Twain. After travelling in India in 1896, Twain was filled with admiration for India, but also concluded that Indian unity was impossible:

India is the cradle of the human race, the birthplace of human speech, the mother of history . . . India had . . . the first civilization; she had the first accumulation of material wealth; she was populous with deep thinkers and subtle intellects; she had mines, and woods,

and a fruitful soil. It would seem as if she should have kept the
lead, and should be today not the meek dependent of an alien
master, but mistress of the world, and delivering law and command
to every tribe and nation in it. But, in truth, there was never any
possibility of such supremacy for her. If there had been but one
India and one language—but there were eighty of them! Where
there are eighty nations and several hundred governments, fighting
and quarreling must be the common business of life; unity of
purpose and policy are impossible . . . patriotism can have no
healthy growth.[48]

From Improbability to Reality: Gandhi's Construction

It is this challenge—turning a civilization into a nation, generating
patriotism and unity of purpose—which the freedom movement,
under Mahatma Gandhi's leadership, accepted as its own. It sought
to build what came to be called 'unity in diversity'. This project
was hugely political. In 1920, a freedom movement, which came to
mobilize millions against British rule across the length and breadth
of India, was launched. A mass movement would construct a nation,
despite the odds.

In and of itself, conceptually speaking, the construction of
Indian nationhood was not a novelty at all. As Chapters 4 and 6
argue, the new literature on nation-making, born nearly a hundred
years after Strachey and Twain, shows that *all* nations are politically
constructed. Path-breaking work by Weber demonstrates that a
conscription army and a public school system turned peasants
into Frenchmen over the course of many decades in the nineteenth
century.[49] At the time of the French Revolution, very few spoke
French outside Paris. In an equally seminal work on British
history, Colley argues that four factors—shared Protestantism, a
Catholic enemy in France, search for commercial opportunities

and Empire—transformed a troubled Union of England, Scotland and Wales into a British nation over a period lasting more than a century (1707–1837).[50] The relationship between Scotland and England was especially conflict-ridden.[51]

Gandhi and most of his colleagues basically began to see that European-style nationhood was not conceivable in India.[52] If they sought linguistic uniformity—a requirement in Mill's conception of nationhood—it would only lead to destruction and violence. In India, diversities were far too rooted, historically. Not only linguistic but other forms of diversities would also have to be accepted as natural. Instead, *a second layer of all-India identity would be created*, leading to what we call hyphenated identities today. Indians would be Gujarati Indians, Bengali Indians, Muslim Indians, Hindu Indians, so on and so forth, not undifferentiated Indians. To paraphrase Immanuel Kant, a straight line could not be created out of the crooked timber of India. Erasure of diversities would destroy India, not make it stronger.[53]

In particular, unlike Europe, language was systematically delinked from the concept of nation. Multiple languages and multilingual leaders were seen as an inevitable part of nation-building in India. If citizens could learn several languages, communication and fellow feeling were possible.

It is entirely conceivable that if the leaders of India's freedom movement had insisted on a 'one language, one nation' formula, there would have been as many nations in India at the time of British departure, as there are in Europe today. But that was not to be. In a radical formulation, Gandhi even accepted English as an Indian language. When asked whether English would continue in a free India, despite its association with the British, Gandhi famously argued:

> I do not want my house to be walled in on all sides and my windows
> to be stuffed. I want the cultures of all the lands to be blown about

my house as freely as possible. But I refuse to be blown off my feet
by any. I refuse to live in other people's houses as an interloper, a
beggar or a slave.[54]

Gandhi also delinked nation from religion. 'If the Hindus believe
that India should be peopled only by Hindus, they are living in a
dreamland. The Hindus, the Muslims, the Parsis and the Christians
who have made India their home are fellow countrymen.'[55] And in
another radical formulation, he argued that the British could be
part of a hyphenated India: 'It is not necessary for us to have as our
goal the expulsion of the English. If the English become Indianized,
we can accommodate them'.[56] A layered or hyphenated concept
of national identity made such conceptual formulations possible.

It is with these ideas that the political roof over the long-lasting
cultural configuration called India was politically constructed.
Peasant armies—or the public schools—were not the principal
institutional vehicles of nation-making, as in France. Rather,
the Congress party played a functionally equivalent role. The
Congress party became the organizational centrepiece of the
freedom movement. After Gandhi's rise, as early as 1920, the party
was conceptualized as a federation of linguistic units. District and
provincial offices of the party were opened, a membership drive
was launched, cadres and an institutional presence were developed
all over India during the 1920s. By 1937, the party had won power
in seven out of eleven provinces, though admittedly in limited-
franchise elections. Between 1920 and 1937, the party managed to
penetrate much of India.

The Congress party called itself an inclusive, umbrella-like party,
to which all were welcome so long as the basic principles of the
nation attracted them. However, the Congress was unable to win
over the Muslim community fully. In the end, a significantly large
proportion of Muslims embraced the Muslim League, which led the
movement for Pakistan. But it is noteworthy that when the British

left India, only two nations emerged, not many. Mill, Strachey and Twain would have been surprised if they had lived till 1947. It was a substantial, if not full, victory of a concept of nationhood that did not insist on singular identities, but allowed layered or hyphenated identities.

It is noteworthy that Gandhi himself was not very fond of representative government. His ideal polity was one that had local village republics, more in line with direct—not representative—democracy.[57] But the freedom movement he led built a nation that established the foundations of post-independence democracy. In retrospect, without the freedom movement, India's nationhood is inconceivable. Perhaps, there would have been many nations. How many would have had democracy is a question too radically speculative and, therefore, unanswerable.

Be that as it may, viewing diversity as national strength, not as a source of national weakness, turned out to be critical. Politics, thus conceptualized and executed, created the Indian nation, against all odds. And democracy became a possibility, once a nation was constructed.

From Improbability to Consolidation: Nehru's Nurturing

The next huge political act was the consolidation of democracy after 1947. Here again, political leadership, especially the role of Nehru, was critical. Though more can surely be said, the Nehru period (1947–64) of Indian democracy is well researched.[58] My own view is presented in Chapter 2. Others too have written in detail.[59]

It is not clear how many early post-independence leaders, other than Nehru, were intensely committed to the democratic project.[60] Perhaps many were but, because of how much Nehru has been researched, we understand him better than we do the others. 'Our democracy is a tender plant,' said Nehru, 'which has to be nourished.'[61] It is perhaps no exaggeration to say that if Gandhi is the father of Indian nationhood, Nehru is the father of Indian democracy. Their colleagues and the organizations they built were indeed most valuable, but *someone had to lead.*

In India's contemporary public discourse, there are passionate arguments about Nehru's role. A large part of the debate is influenced by the way the Nehru dynasty came to occupy the highest rungs of Indian polity. In modern times, a family-domination of political parties is never viewed with unalloyed joy. However relevant dynasties might be to shoring up political organizations in the short-to-medium run, they are inherently anti-modern. They generate strong reactions.

But, whatever the view of practitioners and activists, scholars clearly need to separate Nehru's role from that of his family, especially since the family acquired its current status only after his death. In retrospect, it is clear that there were four keys to India's democratic consolidation: the unique position of the Congress party, elections, the primacy of the Constitution, and minority rights. Nehru played a vital role in each.

Modern democracy is inconceivable without political parties. But what do we know about the role of political parties in the early—as opposed to the later—stages of a democracy? Huntington, Kohli and Weiner have made the significant point that, when a democratic polity begins to get institutionalized, it helps if there is at least one political party which feels confident about winning power.[62] Early democracies with too many contenders for power find it hard to institutionalize themselves. India's ruling coalitions since 1998 have sometimes had twenty political parties or more. Had that been true in the 1950s, democracy could well have died. The fact that the Congress party had no effective challengers to its power right through the Nehru years paradoxically strengthened democracy. There were intense political disputes, but they were primarily inside the party.[63] As the Congress party further penetrated villages and districts after independence, such disputes were natural. But because they were contained within the framework of the party, their intensity did not generate unbearable pressures in the polity. Kothari's term, 'Congress System', best represented the management properties of the polity under Congress dominance.[64]

A commitment to elections also set important norms. Described as a leap in the dark, India's first general elections in 1952 were the biggest elections in history. There were 173 million voters, of whom 75 per cent were illiterate. Hence, party symbols—bicycles, lamps, lanterns, flowers, animals—were put on the ballot. The elections took almost six months. A million officials were deployed.[65] 'Nearly 81 million votes were cast in around 1,32,600 polling stations . . . In 1952 this was a particularly dramatic assertion of India as a democratic nation. No other Asian or African part of the British Empire had yet gained its freedom, and here was India proving itself to be the world's largest democracy, despite earlier assumptions that India was unfit or unready for democracy, or that democracy could never take root in Indian culture and society.'[66] Two more elections, in 1957 and 1962, before Nehru's death, both contested freely and vigorously, deepened the legitimacy of the electoral process in Indian consciousness. Yadav reminds us:

> Within two decades of the inauguration of democratic elections based on universal adult franchise, the phenomenon of elections had ceased to surprise the students and observers of Indian politics . . . It is therefore worth remembering that historically this apparently natural, taken for granted, world of elections is a recent import and quite extraordinary development in the Indian society.[67]

Constitutional primacy was tested in several ways. There were repeated clashes between the executive and the judiciary over land reforms. Nehru was committed to land reforms in agriculture, but the courts kept identifying the right to property as inviolable. Instead of attacking the judges and appointing pliant ones, Nehru went through the constitutionally assigned process of overturning judicial verdicts: namely, getting a super majority—not a simple majority—of the legislatures to approve the legislation contested by courts. Battle lines at the highest levels of the polity were constitutionally drawn. When an unchallenged and hugely charismatic leader adheres to constitutional rules—despite many inconveniences and despite the fact that he could get away with violations—important norms get institutionalized. This Weberian insight is very relevant in understanding Nehru's significance. By attaching his charisma and authority to constitutional rules, Nehru made them stronger. His constitutional record is not unblemished, but it is very substantial.[68]

The relationship between minority rights and democracy was also central. Irritating many in his own party—including his deputy prime minister—Nehru relentlessly argued that democracy could not be equated with majoritarinism in a multi-religious, multilinguistic society. A majority of seats was the key to running a government in a parliamentary democracy, but a government so elected had to be responsible for the security and rights of all, especially those of the minorities. An 'insidious form of nationalism', argued Nehru, 'is the narrowness of mind that it develops within a country, when a majority thinks itself as the entire nation and in its attempts to absorb the minority actually separates them even more.'[69]

Given that Pakistan had already emerged as a homeland of Muslims and that India's partition was hugely violent, anti-Muslim sentiment had reached the highest reaches of his party and administration.[70] If the Hindu minority in Pakistan was being massacred, should not India, a Hindu-majority nation, take revenge, asked some . Faced with an awful situation that contesting nationalisms have repeatedly produced, Nehru never tired of arguing that defence of the Muslim minority in India did not depend on how the Hindu minority was treated in Pakistan. India's founding principles were simply different. India was committed to a multi-religious nationhood. It could not be made Hindu majoritarian, just because Pakistan, a nation made for Muslims, was not unfailingly committed to the welfare of non-Muslim minorities.

> Whatever the provocation from Pakistan and whatever the indignities and horrors inflicted on non-Muslims there, we have to deal with this minority in a civilized manner. We must give them security and the rights of citizens in a democratic state. If we fail to do so, we shall have a festering sore which will eventually poison the whole body politic and probably destroy it.[71]

This was, then, a claim that Hindu majoritarianism was a threat to both national and democratic survival. Without a steadfast commitment to minority rights, India's democracy would be in serious peril.

After Nehru

Nehru died in 1964. Nearly half a century has passed since then. How do we understand Nehru's legacy? An understandable response would be that the first seventeen years of Indian democracy required meticulous nurturing. If democracy had failed then, a restoration would have been hard. The highly probabilistic linkage between democracy and income would have become a reality.

This response, while not entirely untrue, is not exhaustive. A legacy can be ruptured. Indeed it was, by no other than Nehru's daughter, Indira Gandhi, in 1975, when an internal emergency was announced; the Constitution was suspended; opposition leaders were jailed; press freedoms were taken away; judicial independence was compromised; strikes were outlawed; and the slogan, 'India is Indira and Indira is India', was made to reverberate in many corners of India.

Either it was sheer miscalculation that Indira Gandhi called elections in 1977 and managed to lose them, or India's most un-Nehru-like prime minister had somehow internalized a basic democratic norm—that electoral legitimacy was required for continued rule. The announcement of the 1977 elections remains shrouded in ambiguity.

Be that as it may, the post-Nehru survival of democracy may only in part have to do with the institutionalization of norms. Nehru's role in stabilizing the early democratic years is absolutely critical, but the same significance cannot be extended to later years.

In India, it is widely argued that the democratic integrity of the last two decades has been, most of all, preserved by two of India's premier and independent institutions of oversight—the Supreme Court and the Election Commission. Both have repeatedly fought the predatory instincts of politicians, whenever such instincts have surfaced in politics. As India spent more and more years under democracy, these institutions began to take their constitutionally assigned role increasingly seriously. They have repeatedly emerged as two of the most popular institutions in polls.[72] The Election Commission, in particular, has developed substantial mass legitimacy. Armed with that knowledge, it has made sure that elections are not stolen in India. Incumbents, who have often rigged elections in many other polities, are repeatedly defeated in Indian elections.

To this popular and correct explanation, one more needs to be added, especially for the last two decades. Despite the many criticisms that can be made, India's political parties have become the mainstay of democracy. There are so many parties in power—at the state and the central level—that a multilateral balance of power has come about. At any given point, half or more state governments are run by parties that are not part of the ruling coalition in Delhi. As a result, if the ruling party—at the state or central level—becomes dictatorial or predatory, enough countervailing power is available in the system to oppose it. Parties can easily mobilize citizens, initiate court challenges and launch press campaigns. It is not that power cannot be abused in India today, but that its outer limits get clearly defined. Democracy just cannot be easily suspended any more. All political parties accept that, some willingly, some not so willingly, but all in substantial measure.

In the 1960s and 1970s, a hyper-mobilized society was often viewed as a threat to democracy.[73] Huntington famously argued that an excessively demanding society could outrun the capacity of polities to respond, making democratic breakdowns likely.[74] India is hyper-mobilized, much of it by political parties. Hyper-mobilization might make Indian democracy very noisy, even chaotic, but in many ways, it also keeps democracy going.

The Unfinished Quests

Some of the unfinished quests of India's democracy concern the three great post-independence projects: national unity, dignity and social justice, and the elimination of mass poverty. Others have become important of late.

National Unity

After India's independence, the problem of national unity had three dimensions: linguistic divisions, religious differences, and insurgencies. Linguistic and religious heterogeneity was not to be erased, but accommodated in a capacious national framework. Insurgencies had to end, or insurgents made part of the democratic political process.

Of the three, managing linguistic diversity has been India's greatest success. Language was a very divisive issue right through the 1950s and 1960s, causing a great deal of mobilization and violence, so much so that some thoughtful observers of Indian politics were willing to argue in the early 1960s that language-based conflicts might lead to India's break-up.[75] In contrast, in some circles today, India's language policy is viewed as a model worthy of emulation in multilingual countries.[76]

As Chapter 6 argues, by assigning a state to each major language, a linguistic federalization of India took the sting out of language-based disaffection and hostilities. The three-language formula, by making educated Indians multilingual, also made interstate communication and national consolidation possible. Stepan, Linz and Yadav have used the concept of state-nation to explain India's linguistic success.[77] The concept, essentially, means that India did not erase regional linguistic identities; rather, by accommodating them and by creating national-level institutions in which people from varied backgrounds could participate, the polity deepened the national feeling.

Some problems of federalism do remain—for example, the states' demand for a larger share of the national revenue, as well as demands for new states. But language has more or less lost its conflict-mobilizing potential. Cities of great inward migratory flow might in future see language-based conflict, but it is unlikely to be a state-level conflict. A city-level conflict is less dangerous.[78] New states would now be formed mostly on grounds of governance or regional underdevelopment, not on claims of linguistic disregard and discrimination.

Religion remains a matter of concern for India. The fact that, despite India's partition on religious grounds and the countless partition-related deaths and migrants, India was able to accommodate its Muslim minority in the polity was, in large measure, a tribute to Nehru's policy towards minorities. Anti-Muslim hysteria in parts of North India required resolute state conduct, at least at the highest levels of the polity. Had Nehru given in, India could have become a Sri Lanka–style polity, with minority rights as a 'festering sore', a phrase Nehru often used.

But, as Chapter 4 argues, problems remain. Hindu nationalism is a great force in Indian politics today, and some of its basic impulses continue to be anti-Muslim. Moving forward, a key question is whether ideological purity, or the coalition-making requirements of Indian democracy, inducing ideological moderation, would dominate the thinking and actions of Hindu nationalists, especially the Bharatiya Janata Party (BJP). Chances are that democracy would triumph and the anti-Muslim core of the ideology would be moderated, as it was when the BJP-dominated coalition ruled India (1998–2004). But if ideological purity, for some unexpected reason, comes to rule Hindu nationalists, another terrible chapter will reopen in Indian politics.

Riots have reduced in frequency and intensity, but have not entirely disappeared. But an attack on minority rights, should it happen, will make terrorism, not riots, more likely today.[79] In addition, India's democracy has to continue to think about how to fight quotidian anti-Muslim prejudice. It is not a unique Indian problem. Many societies have had to find ways of dealing with prejudice and discrimination against minorities. India will have to find its own solutions, especially as it grows richer and more resources become available to groups for organizing their politics and interests. As Indian power grows, the way Indian democracy deals with its minorities will also be watched closely by the international system.

On insurgencies, too, the glass is half-full. As Chapter 6 argues, India has always had a three-pronged policy with respect to insurgencies: an armed counter-insurgency campaign; a bigger allocation of resources for areas of insurgency; and an invitation to insurgents to participate in elections and, if they win, to let them run the state government. On the whole, given its size and diversity, India has witnessed very few insurgencies. A Maoist insurgency in Central India has surfaced of late. The Lokniti data shows it is not as widespread as was assumed. Indeed, it is highly locality-specific.[80] No American-style civil war has ever taken place. But the three constituents of the policy, noted above, have not always been combined well. What the judicial mix is in each case remains a problem that India's democracy has not fully resolved. Counter-insurgency sometimes gains a quite unproductive upper hand over the two other components .

Dignity and Social Justice

Given the enduring and deep inequalities of the caste system, covering a little over 80 per cent of India that is Hindu, the problem of providing dignity and social justice to citizens has primarily been conceptualized as a problem of affirmative action: of providing reservations—legislative, educational or administrative (in the public sector)—to the lower castes: the other backward classes (OBCs), the scheduled castes (SCs, or Dalits), and the scheduled tribes (STs, or adivasis).[81] Initially, nationwide reservations were only for the SCs and STs in the legislatures, education and government services. OBC reservations were left to the states. But by the early 1990s, OBC reservations in government services became nationwide and, by the middle of the last decade, OBC reservations in higher education, too, became nationally mandatory.[82]

What have been the results? Has dignity been delivered to those who were deprived of it? Has social justice?

First, as Chapter 3 argues, the dignity gains of Indian democracy are substantial. The daily degradation of the lower castes that traditionally accompanied the caste system has declined, though not altogether disappeared. Rudolph and Rudolph were the first to note the changing trends in South India in the 1950s and 1960s,[83] and even today, as argued in Chapter 7, the change is greater in the South than in the North. But there are gains all around. The emerging research on elected local governments, now in existence for over a decade and a half, reinforces this claim.[84]

It is also evident that the political empowerment of the lower castes has primarily brought this about. When political parties representing the interests of the lower castes come to power, or become powerful players in the polity, extreme prejudice and overt maltreatment, if detected, can be vigorously punished. Indian politics has undergone an OBC revolution.[85] In some parts of India, Dalit empowerment is also appreciable, though, on the whole, the OBC gains are much greater than the Dalit gains.[86] Prejudices may continue to operate at a subtle level, but political power has begun to correct the most awful aspects of the caste system, so widely documented by scholars and activists. As Chapters 3 and 7 argue, India's democracy has become a great ally of the lower castes.

Second, however, the economic effects of political empowerment remain ambiguous. The OBCs do not have legislative reservations, and their administrative and educational reservations were confined to the Southern states until the 1990s. But, as Chapter 8 argues, their share of the small business sector—where millions of Indians are occupationally located—is by now quite close to their estimated population share. Economic results for the OBCs appear to have paralleled their political rise, at least to some extent. But the SCs and STs, despite having legislative, administrative and educational reservation all over India since 1950, have continued to lag economically. Though there is some evidence of increases in their economic consumption,[87] the political empowerment of SCs (and STs) has not translated into substantial economic entrepreneurship. The recent rise of SC millionaires is a remarkably slender exception.

Third, let us examine what in North America has come to be called the politics of civil rights—access to public spaces and institutions, and the struggle against discrimination. Such politics in India is called the politics of dignity (*sammaan ki raajniti*). Adapting the philosophical arguments of Rousseau and Tocqueville for India, Mehta has argued that in a society of deep-seated and enduring inequalities, the politics of dignity can often degenerate into the politics of retribution (*badle ki raajniti*), both in terms of policy and behaviour.[88] Politics starts to devalue collective projects of national interest, privileging narrower projects of group interest. When lower castes come to power, upper castes can be targeted in all kinds of ways—in government appointments, educational admissions, public contracts. The new lower caste political bosses can also treat upper-caste civil servants quite shabbily, mirroring to some extent, though not wholly, how they themselves had been historically treated by the upper castes.

There are two issues here that need to be separated: ethical and psychological. Ethically, retributive shabbiness in human conduct is entirely undesirable. But, psychologically, it is possible to locate a short- and a long-term dynamic here. When lower groups rise in a deeply hierarchical society, short-term behaviour can be quite insulting, as they avenge earlier violations of their dignity by the upper castes. But once the psychological needs of gratification have been met, a new equilibrium can set in, lacking the earlier aggression and offensiveness.

South India epitomizes such a divergence in short- and long-run dynamic quite well. In the 1950s, anti-Brahmin agitations routinely insulted 'Brahmin gods' in the most offensive manner and the rhetoric had an unsettling adversarial shrillness about it.[89] But as lower castes became confident of their power, the shrillness receded and many Brahmins eventually became part of lower caste parties. Something similar may well be under way in parts of North India.[90]

Similarly, public policies can also move from entirely group-based to those that represent, or build, cross-group alliances, especially as political parties and leaders look for breadth in support for gains in electoral competition. Generally speaking, beyond defence and foreign policy, it is hard for public policy to cover all interests, not only in India but in all democracies, but how many groups it can represent normally depends on electoral calculations. And such calculations do not remain static. Retributive policy and behavioural aggression are best viewed as a problem of transition to a new order.[91]

Poverty

The inability to conquer mass poverty remains the single greatest failure of Indian democracy. But in what way it represents a failure requires analysis.

As Chapter 9 argues, democracy does not eliminate poverty; economic policies and processes do. The question, therefore, is whether India's democracy came in the way of economic policies that could have attacked poverty better. More than half of India's population might have been below the poverty line at the time of independence but, even today, depending on the measure one adopts, about a fourth to over a third of the population suffers from poverty.[92] China's poverty profile in the late 1940s was not significantly different, but it has had significantly greater success in dealing with poverty.[93]

It is customary to split the discussion of poverty in India into two phases: the years 1950–80, when central planning operated, and the three decades since then, when economic policies began to embrace markets. Chapter 10 presents available evidence to show that no appreciable dent in poverty was made in the first period, whereas the second period has witnessed a considerable decline in poverty. In many circles today, therefore, central planning is blamed for India's unimpressive poverty-alleviation record. During 1950–80, India's per capita income grew at a little over 1 per cent per annum whereas, in the three decades thereafter, the per capita income grew at over 4 per cent per annum, roughly four times the earlier rate.

The argument about the failure of central planning is not wrong, but incomplete. For it is noteworthy that in the 1950s and 1960s, no models other than planning held sway in policy and economic circles. As Hirschman has argued, due to the Great Depression of the 1930s and the extraordinary success of the Soviet Union in transforming itself into an industrial giant in three decades through central planning, markets held little attraction for the newly decolonized countries.[94] Sachs and Warner also show that at the time of their independence in the 1950s and 1960s, only eight developing countries could be called open economies. The list included Singapore and Malaysia. All others were centrally planned.[95]

The key question, then, is: Could India have moved vigorously towards a market-led economic growth model before the 1990s?[96] Did democracy delay India's embrace of markets?

That is indeed the case, substantially if not wholly (Chapter 10). In poor democracies, direct methods of poverty-alleviation tend to be much more politically attractive than the indirect market-based ones. An argument about income redistribution—a direct method—works better in election campaigns and mass politics than an argument that a higher growth rate—made possible by markets—might benefit the rich now, but would also help the masses later. The irony, of course, is that, without high growth, enough resources to run redistribution programmes cannot be easily generated.

The incentives and constraints of mass politics in a poor democracy, thus, tend to be aligned against the markets, a problem that continues to hobble the onward journey of market-oriented reforms in India. Economic reforms resonate well in India's elite politics, but not in mass politics, where arguments about mass welfare, however constructed, hold sway.

These constraints can be overcome with imaginative political leadership and commitment. Just as the post-1947 political leadership did not wait for India to reach the right level of income to institute democracy, a more sustained push for markets could also be made. The key is to argue that markets can enhance mass welfare. Of course, markets alone may not attack mass poverty sufficiently rapidly and some other measures, including investments in mass literacy, public health, and anti-poverty programmes, may be necessary, but without a growth-enhancing embrace of markets, mass poverty cannot easily be attacked, nor can resources for education, health, and anti-poverty programmes be generated.[97] India has still not witnessed a national-level mass politician, who can make a *political* claim on behalf of markets and integrate it as part of an election campaign.[98]

Elections and Accountability

As already stated, Indians have deeply internalized the idea of elections. 'Like tea, cinema or cricket, there is something about elections that makes it appear like an age-old Indian passion,' even though elections are 'a recent import'.[99] Further, defying democratic theory, which says the poor tend to vote less than the rich, by now India's poor often vote more than the non-poor do.[100] Ahuja and Chhibber show that the poor think of voting as a dignifying right.[101]

If electoral competitiveness and people's participation in elections were the only yardsticks to judge a democracy—as the democratic theory discussed above says—India would qualify as a great success.[102] Over the last two decades, the incumbents have repeatedly lost elections. Since incumbents can control the state machinery, which conducts elections, it is clear that elections are genuinely competitive and, popular will, barring individual exceptions, is clearly expressed.

What happens between two elections, however, can be very different. India's democracy has become Janus-faced. Political power is used at the time of elections to please citizens. Between elections, it is often used to treat citizens in an unfeeling manner. Empowered at the time of elections, the citizen often feels powerless until the next elections arrive.

No one fully understands how to restore greater accountability in Indian democracy. A great deal of intellectual effort in the coming years will almost certainly be spent thinking about it. Comparative cases—how other societies have dealt with the problem of routine accountability—will be probed for instruction. Greater accountability of government and politicians would make democracy deeper.

Meanwhile, three dimensions of the problem are worth registering: freedom of speech, gender, and corruption. All three are connected to the idea of electoral issue salience: political parties respond only to those issues that have a clear electoral salience regardless of how important the other issues may be on some other grounds.

Democracies are routinely guided by the twin imperatives of popular sovereignty and freedom of speech. The two can come into conflict, as they historically have in many democracies,[103] but the fundamental commitment to both in principle must be kept. Over the last many years, considerations of popular sovereignty have repeatedly trumped freedom of speech in India. Since freedom of expression is critical to liberalism, an argument that India's democracy, while electorally vibrant, is becoming increasingly illiberal is gaining ground.

Thus, Salman Rushdie can be forced to cancel his participation in a literary festival because it would hurt Muslim sentiments; a cartoon of Ambedkar can land authors—who use it in a school textbook—in trouble because it would harm Dalit feelings; scholars can be threatened for writing research tracts or articles that go against Hindu nationalist beliefs; remarks by a leading intellectual that lower caste political parties can be quite corrupt when in power can lead to a demand by lower caste politicians and intellectuals that he be legally prosecuted for insulting lower castes.

In each of these cases—constituting only a few of the many over the last two decades—an argument about ascription of injury to an electorally important group curtailed freedom of speech. Sometimes, of course, the principle of free expression can be attacked even when no group is 'hurt', but more often than not, the grounds for truncating freedom of expression are the assumed—or actual—sentiments of a group considered putatively important to electoral outcomes.

Similarly, some other issues of vital importance to citizens can be ignored because their electoral relevance is unclear, in doubt, or negligible. Like race in American democracy right up to the Second World War, when lynching of Blacks was not uncommon,[104] gender violence in India has acquired alarming proportions. However, the response of Indian democracy has been quite inadequate. Quite illustrative was the politics following the brutal rape of a young woman in the nation's capital in December 2012. The rape galvanized thousands of citizens, both men and women, leading them to weeks of protest. Though legislative action was initiated later, no political party came forward to express solidarity in the first weeks of the protest. The underlying calculation was that gender violence was irrelevant to rural vote, which continues to constitute more than two-thirds of India's total vote. It is not that gender violence does not take place in the villages, but such violence does not swing votes in rural India. An issue of great relevance to women, thus, continues to be marginal to mass politics.[105]

A final set of issues concerns corruption. As India has become richer, corruption too has grown. The problem has two dimensions: the routine corruption of the street-level bureaucracy and the spectacular corruption in the higher decision-making circles. Both reduce the quality of Indian democracy.

Entry into schools and treatment in hospitals may often depend on whether a politician or a bureaucrat can call on a citizen's behalf, or whether the citizen has resources for a bribe. The police may not register a case of crime unless a bribe is paid or someone in a position of power makes a phone call. Corruption also marks the issuance of driving licences, property registration, enrolment in the employment guarantee scheme, and the payment of wages. The list can go on.

Spectacular corruption concerns 'rent seeking' provision of licences and permissions to businessmen by government decision-makers, both politicians and bureaucrats; or alternatively, the entrance of politicians and bureaucrats into the world of business, to provide illegal—or unethical—benefits to businessmen as well as themselves.

Some of these problems are generic to high growth. Whether it is India or China today, or the US during the Gilded Age (1865–1900), the first sustained flush of high economic growth is often accompanied by large-scale corruption.[106]

Consider some of the details of the Gilded Age corruption in the US. They read like the many stories of corruption reported from India in recent years. In Washington, during the administration of Ulysses Grant (1869–76), the vice-president, the treasury secretary, the attorney general and Grant's private secretary, among others, were indicted for financial misconduct. At the state level, 'I wanted the legislatures of four states,' declared railroad baron Jay Gould, 'so I made them with my own money.' New York's customs house was a den of corruption; and so was Tammany Hall, the seat of the city's government. In a famous passage, George W. Plunkitt, a legendary oft-elected 'boss' of New York's Tammany Hall, said:

> Everybody is talking these days about Tammany men growing rich on graft, but nobody thinks of drawing the distinction between honest graft and dishonest graft. . . . Yes, many of our men have grown rich in politics. I have myself, but I've not gone in for dishonest graft—blackmailing gamblers, saloon keepers, disorderly people, etc. . . . There's an honest graft . . . Let me explain by examples. My party's in power in the city, and it's going to undertake a lot of public improvements. Well, I'm tipped off, say, that they're going to lay out a new park at a certain place. I see my opportunity and I take it. I go to that place and I buy up all the land I can in the neighborhood. Then the board of this or that makes its

plan public, and there is a rush to get my land, which nobody cared particularly for before. . . . Or supposing it's a new bridge they're going to build. I get tipped off and I buy as much property as I can that has to be taken for approaches. I sell at my own price later on and drop some more money in the bank. . . . Wouldn't you? It's just like looking ahead in Wall Street or in the coffee or cotton market. It's honest graft, and I'm looking for it every day in the year.[107]

While the problem of corruption may have generic properties, polities have to seek their own corrective solutions. Through the legislative process, India's democracy is beginning to respond, but a very important aspect of the problem—campaign and party finance—remains unresolved. India's political parties are primarily, if not entirely, financed by businesses, but not in a manner that can be called legal or ethical.[108] Without a reform of campaign finance, the problem of corruption in India's democracy cannot be fully tackled.

An interconnected problem is the lack of intra-party democracy. Inter-party competition is vigorous, but intra-party competition is not. Party officials are appointed by the leaders, not elected by party members. During 1920–73, the Congress party used to have regular internal elections, a practice dropped since then. Most other parties followed the post-1973, not the pre-1973, Congress model. Scholars have argued that campaign finance and lack of internal democracy are interlinked.[109] Be that as it may, internally democratic parties will undoubtedly make India's larger democracy deeper.

Conclusion

Reflecting on the gap between the ideals of democracy and the actual political practices in the US, Huntington wrote: 'Critics say that America is a lie because its reality falls so far short of its realities. They are wrong. America is not a lie; it is a disappointment. But it can be a disappointment only because it is also a hope.'[110]

With the exception of 'disappointment', the same lines can be written about India's democracy. Surveying a history of two centuries, Huntington was disappointed, though he remained rooted in the hope of further reform. India is in its seventh decade under democracy. A deeply hierarchical and poor society has come quite far. But it needs to go much further. A battle for deeper democracy is under way.

2

Why Democracy Survives

The previous chapter contains my latest thinking on the longevity of Indian democracy. This chapter introduces some of my early attempts at explanation. Those not interested in the evolution of ideas may wish to turn directly to Chapter 3.

As already stated, India has long baffled theorists of democracy. Democratic theory holds that poverty and a deeply hierarchical social structure are inhospitable conditions for the functioning of democracy.[1] Yet, except for nineteen months during 1975–77, India has maintained its democratic institutions since independence in 1947. Over those five decades, there have been fifteen parliamentary elections and many more state assembly elections. Since 1967, the parties that ruled in New Delhi have *not* ruled in nearly half of the states. Since 1977, incumbent governments have been repeatedly defeated in elections, both at the central and state levels. The press has remained vigorous and free. It is unafraid to challenge the government. Television, too, has become free since 1991. The judiciary, despite pressure from the executive branch, maintains institutional autonomy. Election turnouts have exceeded the levels typical in several advanced Western democracies. Having started at 45.7 per cent in the first general elections (held in 1952), turnouts are now regularly close to 60 per cent, if not higher, including in the most recent parliamentary elections in 2009.

Predictions of an imminent collapse of India's democracy were common after the death of Nehru in 1964. When Prime Minister Indira Gandhi suspended democracy in June 1975 and declared a state of emergency, it seemed that India was finally starting down the path that most of the world's poorer democracies had already travelled. Yet, democracy returned nineteen months later, and emergency rule proved to be a conjunctural aberration rather than an emerging structural trend.

To be sure, problems continue to exist. When unpopular ruling parties are thrown out, the hope that the new incumbents will govern wisely and well gives way, quickly and too often, to anguish, marked by troubling questions. How long can democracy survive, some ask, if public trust in India's political leaders continues to decline? How long will short-term benefits—rather than long-term insight—determine the behaviour of politicians? Some scholars have written about the governability problem of India's democracy, saying India's democratic health is not what it was in the 1950s and 1960s.[2]

But one should not expect a textbook model to work if there has been a serious rise in political participation and a near-breakdown of the caste hierarchy that had long acted as glue for the social order. Indeed, rising participation by once-marginal groups, such as the 'lower' castes is, at one level, a sign of how much the democratic process has succeeded. Theory and historical experience suggest that rising political participation—its desirability on grounds of political inclusion notwithstanding—nearly always comes with the risk of substantial disorder.[3]

Therefore, the yardstick for judging India's democratic health today should not be derived from the glory days of the 1950s. 'Lower' castes, tribes, minorities, women, and citizens' groups are all exercising their democratic rights to a degree that was unheard of in the 1950s and 1960s. That India is still practising democracy is, in and of itself, unique and theoretically counter-intuitive.

Among developing countries, the closest parallels in terms of democratic longevity seem to be those of Chile (1932–73), Venezuela (1958–98), and Costa Rica since 1948.[4] All three have been much richer than India and, therefore, less anomalous in the view of democratic theory. Given all this, as noted in Chapter 1, it is hardly surprising that no less an authority than Dahl cites, as a leading contemporary exception to democratic theory, 'India, where polyarchy was established when the population was overwhelmingly agricultural, illiterate . . .'[5] Diamond, Linz, and Lipset come to the same conclusion in their multi-volume survey of Third World democracies.[6]

Finally, the historical novelty of Indian democracy was also noted by Barrington Moore as early as 1966:

Economically [India] remains in the pre-industrial age. . . . But as a political species, it does belong to the modern world. At the time of Nehru's death in 1964, political democracy had existed for seventeen years. If imperfect, the democracy was no mere sham. . . . Political democracy may seem strange both in an Asian setting and one without an industrial revolution.[7]

Why has Indian democracy survived amid these unfavourable conditions? Building in part on work done by a number of prominent scholars of Indian democracy,[8] I would frame the answer to this question in four parts. The first part is *historical*, and seeks to draw out the democratic implications of the processes of party formation and nation-building that went on during the period of the independence movement. The second is *economic*, and suggests links between India's strategy of economic development and its democracy. The third connects the structure of India's *ethnic configuration* to its democracy, while the fourth and final part looks to the crucial role of *political leadership* in the period just after independence, when democratic norms were institutionalized even though taking democratic rights away from certain parties and citizens would have been relatively easy.

A 'Post-Postcolonial Reconstruction'

In the 1950s, any suggestion that British colonial rule had facilitated postcolonial Indian democracy would have been dismissed as preposterous. However, as time passed and the 'post-postcolonial' era set in, more dispassionate analyses became possible. Writing in 1985, Weiner pointed out that 'an impressive number of erstwhile British colonies', including India, 'have maintained British-style democratic institutions for all or most of their post-independence history,' while 'not a single former Dutch, Belgian, or French colony currently has democratic institutions'.[9]

Seeking to account for democracy's success in India, Weiner cited the political experience that indigenous leaders were able to gain as they were allowed greater governmental participation during colonialism's last phase, as well as the characteristics of the leading political party that emerged during the national movement. Weiner was correct on both counts, but recent comparative scholarship on the topic of nationalism suggests a third reason. Between the 1920s and 1940s, as noted in Chapter 1, the independence movement, under the leadership of Gandhi, Nehru and the Congress party, turned what had previously been only a cultural unit (as summarized by the concept 'Indian civilization') into a cultural-political unit—a nation.[10] Without this transformation, Indian democracy would have been stillborn: There has to be a political unit before there can be a democracy.

Bringing nation-building into the picture changes the argument about the links between British rule and Indian democracy. It was not the British legacy per se, but rather the strategic interactions that took place between British authorities and national-movement leaders that laid the foundations of democracy. No historical explanation can be complete unless it takes the 'agency' of India's freedom movement into account.

The British began local-level experiments with partial self-rule in the 1880s, and turned over provincial governance entirely to indigenous politicians in 1937. Between 1937 and 1939, and again in 1946, the Congress party was able to add state-level governance to its long experience in local governance. Thus, when the Congress finally came to power at all levels of government in 1947, it had some years of invaluable seasoning under its belt, giving India an advantage unknown to many other decolonized nations.

The Congress itself had changed in significant ways since its founding as an urban, upper-middle-class grouping in 1885. Gandhi transformed it into a mass party in the 1920s, in the process giving it what Weiner identifies as the institutional groundwork of a competitive political party. It began opening district and provincial offices to spread its message and organization more widely across the vast subcontinent; launched membership drives to augment its ranks; and held intra-party elections for leadership positions. Because of Congress's popularity and its rule-based internal functioning, no competitor with a similar nationwide mass base ever arose to challenge it for the leadership of the national movement, with the partial exception of the Muslim League after 1946. On the whole, the Congress felt safe, and the Indian national movement was spared the intense internecine conflict—possibly, even open warfare—that would scar several national movements in Africa and cripple democratic functioning after the advent of independence in the early 1960s.

Previous governing experience and security of rule were not the only reasons for the ease with which the Congress party embraced democratic procedures. India's history after 1920 also demonstrates the political relevance of the distinction between a civilization—which is a cultural unit—and a nation—in which are merged the cultural and the political. As Ernest Gellner famously put it, nation-building requires the alignment of culture and polity, that is, 'to endow a culture with its own political roof'.[11] India has not always had such a roof: when the British conquered the subcontinent in the eighteenth and nineteenth centuries, they had the help of many local allies. The Crown's suppression of the North Indian mutiny of 1857 caused no great repercussions or uprisings in the South.

This began to change in early twentieth century under the leadership of Gandhi, as mass mobilization took place through the instrument of a cadre-based party. In 1920, the civil disobedience that followed the massacre at Amritsar in the province of Punjab was not just regional but India-wide. By the 1930s, Congress was establishing and deepening its presence in most parts of India. Embracing the idea of a free and united country, millions came out to protest, and thousands went readily to jail.

India as a nation was conceived and constructed in opposition to the British. The independence movement was at the same time a nation-building movement. Just as schools and the army had turned 'peasants into Frenchmen',[12] the Congress party under the leadership of Gandhi and Nehru not only protested British rule, but also quite successfully sought to turn locally and regionally oriented folk into Indians.[13]

The immensely painful partition of 1947, ironically, helped democracy by mooting the Muslim League's demands for separate electorates; communal quotas in representation and administration; a one-community, one-party arrangement; and other hallmarks of consociationalism.[14] The Congress party was committed to minority rights, but insisted on the framework of an adversarial, liberal democracy. The creation of Pakistan effectively ended the clash within India between consociational and liberalism democracy in favour of the latter.

Even if British rule facilitated Indian democracy by providing a framework of parliamentary institutions, the notion that democracy is a British legacy is a mistake. Pakistan has the same background, but has been under implicit or explicit military rule for more than half of the period since its independence. How does one explain this variation?[15] The strategies and commitments of India's national movement constitute an important intervening factor. Along with the British authorities (and after 1940, the leaders of the Pakistani movement), the leaders of the Indian national movement were key players in politics. They were not acting out a British script, but writing their own.

When Indians launched their struggle for greater democratization and self-rule, the British need not have responded by inviting Indians to run local and provincial governments, or by allowing the Congress party to function, or, to put it bluntly, by letting Gandhi and Nehru stay alive. That the British rulers were not more ruthless, however, was more a systemic consequence than a result of an inherent generosity. The national movement's deliberate embrace of non-violence made the idea of using force to crush it counterproductive and unacceptable to many British people themselves.[16] None of this would have been true if the national movement had turned violent, when the British would have had few qualms about using lethal force to crush it. Instead, the most they could do was throw people in jail, which was hardly enough when hundreds of thousands were willing to go.

Moreover, the British had long enjoyed pointing to the legitimacy of their institutions—a mere 150,000–60,000 colonial officials were after all ruling almost a quarter of a billion Indians in the early 1920s. How could the British in the end deny self-rule to Indians, who were actively affirming the value of Britain's free and democratic political institutions by demanding that the institutions be kept in place, but with Indians ruling India through them? As a democracy trying to run an empire, Britain found that its liberalism was increasingly coming into conflict with its imperialism. The Indian national movement highlighted this contradiction just as self-consciously as it adhered to non-violence. Thus, an understanding of the strategy chosen by the Indian leaders is necessary for understanding why the British acted as they did. Democracy was fought for by Indians, not just given on a platter by the British.

Industrialization, Agriculture, and Democracy

Economic arguments about democracy have been of two types. Lipset first proposed an intuitively simple correlation between wealth and democracy.[17] Though this largely remains true, it is not helpful in understanding India, which is one of the exceptions. A second kind of argument was made by Moore,[18] who probed economic history to unearth the processes that generated democracies. He was more successful in explaining why India was unable to achieve economic modernization than he was in accounting for its ability to become a democracy before undergoing industrial development.

Modern democracies, Moore observed, emerged *amid the process* of European and American industrialization. Both industrialization and democratization were transformations without precedent. Democracy subverted the hereditary principle of rule; industry transformed what had been essentially rural societies. Moore's analysis led him not only to his famous dictum 'no bourgeois, no democracy', but also to a second dictum that can be summed up as, 'yes peasants, no democracy'. For, while the emergence of a bourgeoisie can bring about industrialization, it cannot by itself bring about democratization. The latter also depends on what happens to rural society in the process of industrialization—or, as Moore put it, on whether agriculture is commercialized, and how.

Why is commercialization of agriculture necessary? Nobel Laureate Arthur Lewis provided an answer.[19] If a society is predominantly rural—as all societies are in the early stages of

industrialization—then, most, or all, of the surplus necessary
for industrialization must come from the countryside. A
commercialized, as opposed to a stagnant, agriculture can provide
the necessary surplus: a *labour surplus* to man the new working class
in the industrial sector; a *food surplus* to feed the working classes in
emerging towns; and a *savings surplus* to fund industrial investment.

Commercialization of agriculture means the disappearance of
the peasantry as a class, for peasant-dominated agriculture and low-
productivity agriculture have generally been synonymous. Moving
from economic to political analysis, Moore concluded that 'the
elimination of the peasant question through the transformation
of the peasantry into some other kind of social formation appears
to augur best for democracy.'[20] Over two centuries, the enclosures
in Britain forced peasants into cities and turned them into an
urban proletariat. The United States never had a peasantry, only
a commercial farming class. The peasantry survived in the Soviet
Union, China, Japan, and Germany—and all four countries
experienced dictatorship during the course of their industrialization.

What makes India an exception is that democracy has survived
even though the peasantry has not disappeared. One reason, surely,
is the advent of the Green Revolution, which boosted agricultural
productivity so effectively that India, often threatened by food
shortages in the 1950s and 1960s, started experiencing food
surpluses after the late 1970s. In brief, technology has made peasant
agriculture productive enough to blunt the contradiction between
industrialization and the existence of the peasantry.

This explanation is fine as far as it goes, but India had been
a democracy for two decades by the time the Green Revolution
arrived in the late 1960s. The 1950s, moreover, saw the initiation,
under Nehru's leadership, of a state-led heavy industrialization
programme. Were the resources for industrialization extracted
from the countryside?

In fact, Nehru and his planners struggled with precisely

this problem. Among the solutions that Nehru proposed were nationalizing the foodgrain trade; gathering small peasant farms into larger cooperatives; and compulsory government purchases of foodgrain 'at fixed and reasonable prices'. However, Congress party leaders at the state level, who were much better informed about the political realities of rural India, persuaded Nehru to abandon the first two measures and to scale back the third substantially.

In effect, Nehru chose democracy over development (or, at least, the model of development that he was initially inclined to favour). Guided by the advice of Congress cadres from various states, he realized that one could not give suffrage to rural India and, at the same time, extract huge quantities of food from it at below-market prices. By not forcing the issue, the Congress avoided putting democracy at risk. For the first twenty years of planning, resources for industrialization did not come primarily from agriculture.[21]

Although the Green Revolution, by finally solving the problem of shortage of foodgrains, deserves some credit for the preservation of democracy, credit must also go to Nehru and other political leaders of the 1950s and 1960s, who resisted the urge to force the pace of industrial development when peasant agriculture was stagnant. Settling for a slower road to industrialization during this period was vital to the maintenance of democracy.

The Ethnic Configuration

Ethnic rather than class conflict has been the most persistent, visible, and virulent source of political violence in the developing world, with the qualified exception of Latin America.[22] It has been behind democratic breakdowns in Lebanon, Nigeria, and Sri Lanka, among other countries.[23] India has hardly been spared, having suffered from (among other things) Hindu–Muslim riots; caste-based strife; insurgencies in Kashmir and the North-east; 'sons-of-the-soil' movements in Assam, Telangana, and Maharashtra;

and language-based riots in the 1950s and 1960s. Yet, democracy has endured.

Scholars who have studied ethnic conflict in different societies suggest a valuable distinction between *dispersed* and *centrally focused* ethnic configurations.[24] In a dispersed configuration, there is a plethora of locality- or region-specific identities; the centrally focused configuration features a small number of identities that cut across the whole country. In the dispersed systems, generally speaking, ethnic conflict remains localized; the Centre can often manoeuvre between the fighting groups while seeming to stand outside the conflict. In the centrally focused system, the ubiquity of the cleavage tends to foster heightened conflict throughout the system, threatening the integrity of the Centre. Sri Lanka's Sinhalese–Tamil conflict has a systemic quality; so do the Malay–Chinese relations in Malaysia; and so did the East–West conflict that eventually broke up Pakistan and spawned Bangladesh. In Sri Lanka, democracy was badly eroded all over the country after the early 1980s, and a nasty civil war ensued, lasting two and a half decades. In Malaysia, after the ethnic riots of May 1969, the political leadership deepened the pro-Malay character of the polity, regulating the Chinese minority more than before, including its role in the economy. By extending quotas to the private sector, Malaysia became even more consociational than it had been at the time of independence.

In India, all ethnic cleavages except one are region- or locality-specific. The Sikh–Hindu cleavage is basically confined to Punjab and other parts of the north. The Muslim insurgency in the Vale of Kashmir has never spilled over to include all Indian Muslims; likewise, violence in the North-eastern state of Assam killed hundreds in the early 1980s but rarely went beyond state borders, and so on. As a result, Punjab and Assam burned while life in the rest of India went on more or less as usual. Even the all-pervading caste system—so intrinsic to the entire Hindu society—has a local character. Caste riots in one part of the country do not necessarily affect other parts. In Tamil Nadu, an anti-Brahmin movement forced a large number of Brahmins out of that Southern state, but Brahmins in the North were unaffected. Indians speak over twenty languages and many more dialects. There are numerous tribal groups, but altogether they form only 6 per cent of the population and are widely dispersed over Central and Eastern India.

When dispersed ethnic conflicts keep breaking out, it is easy for observers to get the false impression that the system is breaking down, even when the Centre is holding. Parties mobilized around ethnic issues may cause turmoil in one state, but nowhere else. In a dispersed system, even an insurgency gets bottled up in one area; democracy may be suspended there while the rest of the country continues to function under more or less routine democratic processes with no threat of systemic breakdown. Federalism also helps, for, as the case of Sri Lanka shows, in a unitary state, all grievances wind up aimed at the Centre. It is not surprising that the years during which the leaders of the post-Nehru Congress party were striving to centralize an essentially diverse and federal polity also saw the advent of such severe stresses as the insurgencies in Punjab and Kashmir.

The only cleavage that has the potential to rip India apart is the divide between Hindus and Muslims. History bears awful witness to the hatred, violence, and disruption that can surround this split: though exact numbers are not known, the partition that created Pakistan in 1947 cost the lives of between 200,000 and 500,000 people, and forced about 12 to 15 million more to migrate. In 2001, India was home to a little over 138 million Muslims[25] (see Table 2.1). Though accounting for only a modest 13.4 per cent of the country's total population, these numbers give India the fourth-largest Muslim population in the world (after Indonesia, Pakistan, and Bangladesh), and form the largest group of Muslims in any country where Muslims are not a majority. The geographic distribution of

India's Muslims, moreover, magnifies their political significance. According to the 2001 Census, they were a majority in the northern state of Jammu and Kashmir; made up about 31 per cent of Assam and 25 per cent of West Bengal in the East; formed 18.5 per cent of Uttar Pradesh and 16.5 per cent of Bihar in North-central India; constituted 10 per cent of Maharashtra and 9 per cent of Gujarat in the West; and in the South, made up roughly 25 per cent of Kerala and 12 per cent of Karnataka.[26] In a number of cities throughout the country, they constitute considerably more than 20 per cent of the local populace. Thus, unlike the Hindu–Sikh problems confined to Punjab, a serious worsening of Hindu–Muslim relations anywhere could harm such relations all over India.

TABLE 2.1: INDIA'S RELIGIOUS PROFILE

Religion	Percentage
Hindus	80.5
Muslims	13.4
Christians	2.3
Sikhs	1.9
Buddhists and Jains	1.2
Others	0.6

Source: Census of India, 2001

During the first two decades of independence, Hindu–Muslim conflict was dormant because the migration of millions to Pakistan had rendered India's Muslim community leaderless, and because Congress under Nehru's resolutely secular leadership maintained a multi-religious character. Since the mid-1970s, however, a Muslim middle class has emerged, while the Congress party, watching its pre-eminence recede, often compromised on its once-firm secularism for the sake of electoral calculations.

Finally, Hindu nationalism added new anxieties to Hindu–Muslim relations. Hindu nationalism saw its most virulent expression in the demolition of the Baburi Mosque at Ayodhya in December 1992 and in the Gujarat riots of 2002. According to Hindu nationalist ideology, India's secularism has degenerated into a pandering of minorities, with the state being held hostage by assertive religious minorities. Especially worrisome to Hindu nationalists is what they call Muslim disloyalty to India. Hindu nationalists understand India as a Hindu-centric country, and at least the ideologically pure Hindu nationalists would like to see a reassertion of 'Hinduness' in politics and society.[27]

If the BJP ever manages to execute its ideology fully, India will leave the democracy-friendly realm of what Dahl called 'subcultural pluralism' and enter the more dangerous one of 'cultural dualism', with a Hindu majority lording it over a non-Hindu minority. If, at that point, India's minorities were to accept Hindu political dominance, India would be set on the Malaysian path (a regulated democracy with the bounds of political competition laid down by the dominant group). Minority restiveness, on the other hand, could bring about a Sri Lankan scenario. Bitter Hindu–Muslim hostility thus holds great potential for damage.

By and large, Muslims have so far chosen electoral and democratic means of opposing the BJP; caste differences within Hindu society still often take precedence over Hindu unity; and powerful institutions, such as India's courts, argue that secularism is a basic principle of India's Constitution and, as such, beyond change by ordinary legislation. In 1998, the BJP managed to assemble a broad alliance of parties and come to power, but only after dropping key Hindu nationalist demands, such as the construction of a new temple on the site of the razed Ayodhya mosque; the adoption of a common civil code to supersede all the 'personal laws' of the religious minorities; the termination of the special status of Jammu and Kashmir (India's only Muslim-majority state). India's pluralism has induced the BJP to scale back its anti-Muslim rhetoric; to build coalitions across caste, tribal, linguistic, and religious lines; and to seek alliances with regional parties in states where a Hindu nationalist ideology makes no sense. Given that ideological moderation carried the BJP to power in 1998 and 1999, while ideological extremism would have kept it in a pariah status, there is reason to expect that the BJP will now avoid becoming radicalized. As a result, the deep concerns raised by Hindu majoritarianism in the early 1990s have declined. However, if Hindu majoritarianism were to revive for some unexpected reason, the challenge to democracy would re-emerge. During the anti-Muslim violence of 2002, Gujarat seemed to turn back the tide, but the pendulum has on the whole swung back towards moderation. The tension between purity and moderation is unlikely to disappear fully.

Institutions, Ambitions, and Ideology

Comparative studies of democracy have noted the key role of leadership.[28] Ferdinand Marcos in the Philippines, Syngman Rhee in South Korea, Sukarno in Indonesia, Zulfikar Ali Bhutto in Pakistan, Sirimavo Bandaranaike in Sri Lanka, and Indira Gandhi in India—all undercut democracy by suspending freedoms, jailing political opponents, rigging elections, prolonging their rule through constitutional manipulations, and promoting the powers of the executive branch at the expense of the legislature and the judiciary.

A democracy cannot function if the institutional logic of the system is made subservient to the personal ambition or the ideological predilections of political leaders. Leaders must accept institutional constraints on their decision-making. In a parliamentary system, this means accepting the sovereignty of Parliament, working within the constitution of one's party, opposing adverse court rulings only through proper constitutional channels and, if the system is federal, respecting the degree of autonomy afforded to state governments.

In many postcolonial societies, the leaders who came to the fore during the independence struggle enjoyed so much prestige that, far from being compelled to subject themselves to democratic norms, they could easily reverse the process and fix or change norms and procedures according to their own personal preferences. India was fortunate that its first generation of post-independence leaders resisted such temptations, and displayed instead a remarkably democratic temper.

For the sake of analytic convenience, let us view Nehru as representing this entire group of leaders. When his colleagues in the Congress party disagreed with him on key policies or programmes (such as the introduction of agricultural cooperatives; the reorganization of states along linguistic lines; the role of the public sector in the industrialization drive), Nehru did not expel the dissenters, but let intra-party forums resolve the dispute. When the courts turned down his land reform programme on grounds that the right to property was a fundamental tenet of the Constitution, he did not attack the judiciary itself. Rather, he went through the constitutionally provided amendment process, seeking the approval of two-thirds of Parliament and a majority of the state legislatures in order to gain the authority he needed to enact his plan. Nehru did not appoint state-level party chiefs or state chief ministers, leaving them to be elected instead by the Congress party units in each state.

Nothing illustrates Nehru's regard for democratic norms better than his handling of the language controversy in the early 1950s. Indians speak more than twenty different tongues. Even before independence, Congress had committed itself to language as the underlying basis of federalism. However, Nehru's private correspondence after independence clearly reveals that he was deeply ambivalent about these plans, in part, if not entirely, because he regarded unfinished tasks like poverty-alleviation, economic development, and national consolidation as far more urgent.

However, when popular linguistic movements arose, he finally gave in and returned to the prior commitment of the party.

One result of Nehru's democratic predilections was the manageability of the political system. Since the state leaders were elected—not appointed by Delhi—the elective principle within the party regularly produced leaders who had stature, a base of their own, and considerable command in the state. They could manage regional political disorders. In a later decade, when Indira Gandhi went against the Nehruvian principles and sought to centralize the party, she only succeeded in ensuring that disputes and disorders from every state became Delhi's problem. A top-heavy Central government was unable to manage a continent-sized and culturally diverse polity. Disorder and democracy came to coexist, along with a considerable erosion of democracy.

Let us now drop the assumption that Nehru represented an entire generation of leaders, and that they were all strongly for democracy. In several ways, Nehru's emergence as the topmost leader was a monumental fortuity. In the womb of post-independence Indian history, lay two other tendencies. At various times in the 1930s and 1940s, Subhash Chandra Bose and Vallabhbhai Patel were both serious competitors to Nehru. Calling a democratic and non-violent national movement too weak, and admiring the strength of fascism, Bose turned to Japan and Hitler's Germany as allies in an attempt to overthrow British rule by force. Although Patel's pre-1946 political career showed no sign of frustration with Muslims, he became disenchanted with secularism in his later years, and openly demanded that any Muslims wishing to stay in India after the formation of Pakistan should take a loyalty oath. He was also given to the use of force, or to what Hindu nationalists today call 'the full assertion of state authority'. Bose died in 1945, Patel in 1950. Given their political trajectories, one shudders to think what kind of political system India would have evolved into if they had dominated the 1940s and 1950s. In fact, of course, neither was able to displace the top leadership of the national movement and change the party's basic commitments, which says something about Congress's democratic leanings of the time. Nonetheless, it is good to recall Bose and Patel, if only to underline the point that, had some accidents changed the nature of the elite, the challenges to India's democracy would be even more serious.

   Much scholarly writing on democratization has discussed the post-transitional 'honeymoon', when new democratic leaders enjoy maximum freedom of action. The standing of national liberation leaders as fathers of the nation made their honeymoon longer and their political autonomy greater. Bold choices shaping new structures could be made. The democratic temper of India's first-generation leaders contributed handsomely to building up the system's democratic base. Once such a solid base was in place, it became hard to undermine the democratic edifice completely, as Indira's Gandhi's failure showed. Her attempt to centralize politics and suppress dissent in formal politics only led to a flowering of political activity in civil society, as groups, who felt marginalized, formed organizations outside the state and mobilized the people, thus exerting democratic pressure on the state.

Liberal Hypocrisy?

In the late 1970s and early 1980s, Weiner often argued that the biggest threat to India's democracy came from the deinstitutionalization of the party system—in particular, the decay of the Congress party and the inability of opposition forces to provide a cohesive and effective alternative. The logic of this argument was simple: How could representative democracy continue to function without solid and stable parties?[29] In the late 1980s and early 1990s, a long-forgotten factor—religion in public life—posed another big threat. The BJP, a disciplined party with a solid organization, emerged as a political alternative to Congress. The new party thus partially filled the organizational vacuum, but its Hindu nationalism brought religion explicitly into public life.

The first generation of postcolonial leaders had maintained a plausible distinction between religion and the public realm. There was an element of 'liberal hypocrisy' to this for, in a deeply religious society, all kinds of religious symbols, if not appeals, were used at the time of elections anyway. There was, however, a consequentialist rationale for the distinction: no party could think of turning religious antagonism into an *explicit* plank of its ideology, or into the ideological basis of state governance. Implicit use of religion was not as threatening as its explicit use in politics.

This liberal hypocrisy was frontally challenged as Hindu nationalism rose in the late 1980s and early 1990s. That India's democracy has moderated the ideological inclinations of Hindu nationalism shows how deeply ingrained the democratic tradition has become. The BJP came to power in 1998, but it did so in alliance with several mainstream parties. Since then, the moderates within the BJP have on the whole had the upper hand, and the odds that an ideologically pure Hindu nationalism can win remain low. If, in the future, the ideology of Hindu nationalism were somehow to triumph at the polls, the hard work of the first generation of leaders and the many structural strengths of Indian democracy would be seriously tested.

3

Is India Becoming More Democratic?

How should one characterize India's political developments since the late 1980s? There is, of course, a consensus that the Congress party—a towering political colossus between 1920 and 1989—has unambiguously declined. It may be in power, but not entirely on its own, a dramatic contrast from its earlier fortunes. We cannot, of course, be sure that the decline of the Congress party will continue to be irreversible, but it is clear that much of the political space already vacated by the Congress has so far been filled by three different sets of political forces. The first force is Hindu nationalism, extensively discussed in the literature.[1] The second force is regionalism, also well analysed.[2] A third force covers an array of political parties and organizations that encompass groups normally classified under the umbrella category of 'lower castes': the so-called 'scheduled castes'; the 'scheduled tribes'; and the 'other backward classes' (OBCs).[3] How should we understand the politics of parties, which represent these groups? How far will they go? What are the implications of their forward march, if it continues, for Indian democracy?

In an attempt to answer these questions, this chapter compares political developments in Northern and Southern India. My principal claim is that our judgements about contemporary North Indian politics would be wrong if we did not place South India at the centre of our analytic attention. In the twentieth century, the South experienced caste-based politics much more intensely than the other regions of India. If the Hindu–Muslim cleavage has been a 'master narrative' of politics in North India for much of the twentieth century, caste divisions have had the same status in Southern India.[4] Partly because electoral politics was organized around caste lines in the South and not around a Hindu–Muslim axis, non-Brahmin castes, constituting an electoral majority, came to power in virtually all southern states by the 1960s. Our analysis of North Indian politics since the 1970s and 1980s will be deeper if we appreciate how the empowerment of lower castes took place in the South.

The major South Indian conclusion about caste is culturally counter-intuitive but politically easily grasped. Socially and ritually, caste has always symbolized hierarchy and inequality; however, when joined with universal-franchise democracy, caste can paradoxically be an instrument of equalization and dignity.[5] Weighed down by tradition, lower castes do not give up their caste identities; rather, they 'deconstruct' and 'reinvent' caste history; deploy in politics a readily available and easily mobilized social category ('low caste'); use their numbers to electoral advantage; and politically fight prejudice and domination. It is the upper castes, beneficiaries of the caste system for centuries, which typically wish caste did not exist when a lower caste challenge appears from below.

North India today, and in the future, may not follow in South India's footsteps entirely, but the rise of lower caste politics in the North bears several similarities. Its power is beyond doubt. Even Hindu nationalism—though fundamentally opposed to lower caste politics in ideological terms—has not been able to dictate terms to northern lower caste politicians. By implication as well as intention, Hindu nationalism stands for Hindu unity, not for caste consciousness. Lower caste parties are against Hindu unity. Arguing that Hindu upper castes have long denied power, privilege, and even dignity to the lower castes, they are advocates of caste-based social justice and a caste-based restructuring of power. Such has been the power of lower caste politics in recent years that it has forced Hindu nationalists to make ideologically distasteful but pragmatically necessary political coalitions.

For the sake of power, the Hindu nationalists—in the 1998 and 1999 parliamentary elections, respectively—had to team up with other parties, several of whom were based among the lower castes. The latter, as explained in the previous chapter, ensured that the ideologically pure demands of Hindu nationalism—the building of a temple in Ayodhya; a common civil code and no religiously based personal laws for minorities; abolition of the special status of Jammu and Kashmir, the only Muslim majority state of Indian federation—were dropped and a programme more acceptable to the lower caste parties was formulated.

Thus, in their moment of glory, even as the Hindu nationalists rose to power during 1998–2004, Hindu nationalism as an ideology did not. They ended their political isolation, but did not achieve an ideological victory.

Hindu nationalism is majoritarian in impulse. In its ideological purity, it is deeply threatening to non-Hindu minorities, who constitute over 18 per cent of the country's population. Ideologically, lower caste politics also endeavours to be majoritarian but, much as working-class politics was in late nineteenth century Western Europe, its ideological aim is to put together a plebeian, not a religious, majority. It is essentially non-threatening to religious minorities and inclined towards the socio-economically disadvantaged.

More than ever before, we need to pay greater attention to the determinants and dynamics of what may be called India's plebeian politics. As is becoming increasingly clear, lower caste parties may not be able to come to power on their own, but their share of votes and seats has been substantial, presenting certain implications for India's political landscape.

The Larger Picture: From a North–South Divide to an Emerging Southernization of North India

Let us begin with a brief comparison of the caste composition of Indian politics today with the situation soon after independence. In the 1950s, India's national politics was dominated by English-speaking, urban politicians trained in law. Most politicians came from the upper castes, and many leaders had been educated abroad. Lower down the political hierarchy, an agrarian and 'vernacular' elite dominated local and state politics,[6] but even the lower-level political leadership tended to come from the upper castes in North India.

South India was different. Southern politicians were not only 'vernacular' but, as the 1950s evolved, they were also increasingly from the lower castes.[7] By the 1960s, substantial parts of South India had gone through a relatively peaceful lower caste revolution: the Dravida Munnetra Kazhagam (DMK) came to power in Tamil Nadu as an anti-Brahmin party in the 1960s, and the Communist party, first in power in Kerala in 1957, was primarily based in the Ezhava community, a low caste of traditional toddy-tappers engaged in the production of indigenous liquor.[8]

The social indignities inflicted on the Nadars of Tamil Nadu, another toddy-tapping caste of traditional South India, are all too well known.[9] To appreciate how much the state of Kerala has changed, it would be instructive to get a sense of the humiliations, which the Ezhavas routinely suffered until the early decades of this century:

They were not allowed to walk on public roads. . . . They were
Hindus, but they could not enter temples. While their pigs and cattle
could frequent the premises of the temple, they were not allowed to
go even there. Ezhavas could not use public wells or public places.
. . . An Ezhava should keep himself at least thirty-six feet away
from a Namboodiri and twelve feet away from a Nair. . . . He must
address a caste Hindu man, as Thampuran (My Lord) and woman
as Thampurati (My Lady). . . . He must stand before a caste Hindu
in awe and reverence, assuming a humble posture. He should never
dress himself up like a caste Hindu; never construct a house on the
upper-caste model. . . . The women folk of the community . . . were
required, young and old, to appear before caste Hindus, always
topless. About the ornaments also, there were restrictions. There
were certain prescribed ornaments only which they (could) wear.[10]

By the 1960s, in much of the *public* sphere of Southern India—
not only in Kerala—such egregious debasement and quotidian
outrage were radically curtailed, if not entirely eliminated. A
democratic empowerment of the lower castes was the catalytic
agent for the social transformation. The lower castes were always
numerically larger than the Brahmins, but were unable to use their
numbers before the rise of universal franchise.

A classic distinction between horizontal and vertical political
mobilization proposed by Lloyd and Susanne Rudolph[11] captured
the essence of North–South political differences at the time.
In South India, lower castes had already developed their own
leaders and parties by the 1950s and 1960s—a case of horizontal
mobilization—whereas in North India the model of mobilization
was top-down, with the lower castes dependent on the upper
castes in a clientelistic relationship. The latter represented vertical
mobilization. At the national level, the Congress party aggregated
horizontally, as it brought together different linguistic and
religious groups, but at the local level, it was a typical clientelistic

party, building a pyramid of caste coalitions under the existing social elite.[12]

In the 1980s and 1990s, southern-style plebeian politics rocked North India. The names of Mulayam Singh Yadav, Lalu Prasad Yadav, Kanshi Ram, and Mayawati—all 'vernacular' politicians who came up from below—repeatedly made headlines. They were not united. Indeed, great obstacles to unity—both vertical and horizontal—remain, and a political or programmatic unity is unlikely to come about in the future. Vertically, though all lower castes are below the upper castes/*varna*s (Brahmins, Kshatriyas, and Vaishyas), there are serious internal differentiations and hierarchies among them. In the traditional caste system, the OBCs were placed above the Dalits. Their alliance cannot come about easily because of their internal differences, even if the upper castes cease to be the political adversaries. Similarly, under the umbrella OBC category, there are some castes which are ranked higher, others lower. Such sub-hierarchies also impede unity.

Horizontally, even though the *caste system* is present all over India, each *individual caste* has only a local or regional meaning, making it hard to build extra-local or extra-regional alliances. There are Brahmins and Dalits all over India, but South Indian Brahmin castes (Aiyar, Ayengar, etc.) are quite different from their North Indian counterparts (Shukla, Mishra, etc.). Indeed, few North Indian Brahmins know what the South Indian Brahmin castes are, and vice versa. The caste system is nationwide in concept, but castes are local or regional in operation. Thus, horizontal caste mobilization tends to be primarily region- or state-specific, not nationwide.

Nonetheless, since 1989, lower caste leaders have often made or broken coalitions in power. In the five national elections held between 1996 and 2009, the various parties explicitly representing lower castes, in the aggregate, received between 17 and 21 per cent of the national vote, as against 18 to 25 per cent for the BJP, and 23 to 38 per cent for the Congress party.[13] Their total vote share thus continues to be lower than that for the Congress and the Bharatiya Janata Party (BJP) respectively, but it is large enough to force concessions from the two largest parties.

Disunity at the level of political *parties* notwithstanding, lower caste *politics* has come to stay. The power of the new plebeian political elite is no longer confined to the state level, though that is where it is most prominent. Central government policies and programmes have also been substantially reconfigured. An enlarged affirmative action programme is by far their most striking national success. An extra 27 per cent reservation for the lower castes has been added to Central government jobs and educational seats. In the 1950s, only 22.5 per cent of such jobs were reserved, and more than three-fourths were openly competitive. Today, these proportions are 49.5 and 50.5 per cent, respectively. At the state level, the reserved quota has been higher for a long time in much of Southern India.

Indian politics thus has a new lower caste thrust, now prevalent in much of the North as well as the South. Democracy has been substantially indigenized, and the shadow of Oxbridge has left India's political centre stage. Does the rising vernacularization mean that India's democracy is becoming more participatory and inclusive, or simply more chaotic and unruly? Or, are such developments mere cosmetic changes on the surface, a political veneer concealing an unchanging socio-economic structure of power and privilege?

To understand what the rise of lower castes can do to politics, state institutions, and policy, we need to understand the twentieth-century history of South India, where the lower castes have exercised remarkable power since the late 1950s and early 1960s. Plebeian politics in South India was primarily conceptualized in terms of caste, not class. Even the ideologically class-based Communists in the state of Kerala found it necessary to plug into a discourse of caste-based injustice in the 1930s and 1940s, and they relied heavily on the traditionally depressed Ezhava caste for their rise.[14]

Indeed, with isolated exceptions, caste rather than class has been the primary mode of subaltern experience in India. The rising middle class of a low caste has customarily had to fight social discrimination and disadvantage. For contesting hierarchy and domination, therefore, the emerging elites of the lower castes have every reason to use caste identities in politics. Whether this strategy means that, in the long run, caste itself will disappear remains unclear. What is clear is that, relying on a horizontal mobilization, a large proportion of the lower castes would rather fight prejudice here and now, whatever the consequences in the long run.

The Scheduled Castes (SCs), the Scheduled Tribes (STs), and the Other Backward Classes (OBCs) in North India

The aggregate profile summarized above can be separated into three different, and historically underprivileged social groups in North India:[15] the ex-untouchables, officially named scheduled castes by India's Constitution, and now politically called the Dalits; the adivasis, known as 'scheduled tribes' in official terms since 1950;[16] and the other backward classes (OBCs). Technically, the term OBC incorporates two different disadvantaged communities—Hindu and non-Hindu. Of these, Hindu OBCs are the low castes whose traditional social and ritual status has been above that of the scheduled castes, but below that of the upper castes (See Figure 3.1 and Table 3.1). Hindu OBCs overlap mostly, but not entirely, with the Sudra varna of the traditional hierarchy, a category consisting mainly of peasants and artisans.

According to the 2011 Census, the scheduled castes (SC) constitute about 16.6 per cent of India's population, and the scheduled tribes (ST) 8.6 per cent.[17] Because no full caste census has been taken in India since 1931 statistical exactitude on the OBCs, Hindu or non-Hindu, is not possible. We do have approximate

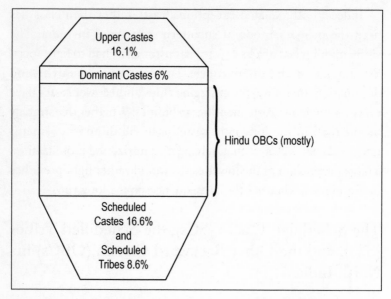

FIGURE 3.1: ALL-INDIA HINDU RITUAL HIERARCHY

Note: 1. The OBC figures are at best guesses. Beyond the scheduled castes and tribes, a caste census has not been taken since 1931. These best guesses, however, are widely viewed as statistically reasonable, if not statistically exact.

           2. Since a fraction of scheduled tribes is Christian, the numbers above add up to more than 82 per cent.

Source: 1. For scheduled castes and tribes, Government of India, *Census of India,* 2001

           2. For other castes, Government of India, *Report of the Backward Classes Commission* (The Mandal Commission Report), First Part, Vol. 1 (1980)

figures, however. The Mandal Commission, the only nationwide source available on the OBCs, suggests that Hindu OBCs constitute about 43.7 per cent of the total population.[18] These three groups constitute a majority of India's population and electorate.[19]

Until recently, the scheduled castes have primarily supported the Congress party in India. Though the leaders of the Congress

TABLE 3.1: INDIA'S CASTE COMPOSITION

Group	Percentage of Population
Upper Castes	16.1
Lower Castes	43.7
Scheduled Castes	16. 6
Scheduled Tribes	8.6
Non-Hindu Minorities	17.6

Note: Since no caste census has been taken since 1931, these figures should be seen as best guesses, not exact estimates. However, they are sufficient to show the overall magnitudes. It should be noted that when political parties strategize about which groups to target for political mobilization, the relevant calculation is at the state, not national, level.

Source: 1. Government of India, *Report of the Backward Classes Commission* (The Mandal Commission Report), 1980, First Part, Vol. 1, p. 56
　　　　2. Government of India, *Census of India*, 2001, Series A, Table 00–005

party typically came from the upper castes, they were able to get scheduled caste support partly because the Congress party was the first architect of the affirmative action programme, and partly because traditional patron–client relationships in villages were on the whole alive and robust. In 1984, a new political party of the scheduled castes—the Bahujan Samaj Party (BSP)—was launched. Receiving 4.7, 4.2, 5.3 and 6.2 per cent of India's vote in the 1998, 1999, 2004 and 2009 national elections, respectively (up from 1.8 per cent in 1991), the BSP may not yet be a powerful force in the national Parliament. However, on the basis of the share of national vote, it has by 2009 become the third largest party in India, following the Congress, the BJP, and ahead of the Communist Party Marxist (CPI [M]).[20]

More importantly, the BSP has developed a substantial political presence in almost all North Indian states, especially Uttar Pradesh

(UP), Punjab, Haryana, and Madhya Pradesh (MP). In UP, India's largest state, the party was in power entirely on its own during 2007–12. By 1996, the BSP had started receiving a whopping 20 per cent of UP's vote, crippling the once-mighty Congress in its citadel of great historic strength. In the 1996, 1998, 1999, and 2004 national elections, the Congress party's vote in UP was considerably below that of the BSP.[21] Well until the mid-1980s, such scenarios for the Congress in UP were altogether inconceivable.[22]

How did the BSP break the dependence of the scheduled castes on the Congress? Chandra[23] provided the first exhaustively researched answer by taking research down to the constituency level.[24] Chandra argued that the BSP's success in replacing Congress was built upon two factors.

First, affirmative action for the scheduled castes led to the emergence of a middle class among them. The new middle class is made up almost entirely of government officers and clerks. Despite experiencing upward mobility, these officers continued to face social discrimination. Endured silently earlier, such discrimination led to a firm resolve to fight for respect and dignity. Second, the scheduled castes within the Congress experienced what Chandra calls a 'representational blockage'. Most of the district committees of the Congress had been dominated by upper-caste politicians. Scheduled-caste leaders were mere tokens and symbols in the party structure. By the early 1990s, such meagre rewards of clientelism were considered largely insufficient by the newly mobile scheduled castes in several states.

The new middle class eventually took over as local BSP leaders. Their strategy was to argue that *humiliation*, rather than economic deprivation, was the main problem of the scheduled castes, and that greater political representation—instead of material advantage—was the principal solution. The scheduled castes had to be horizontally mobilized, had to have a party of their own, and had to win assembly seats. Financed initially by the new middle class, the BSP took off in much of North India and developed a large group of cadres.

However, as the BSP has progressed further, new political realities have dawned. In no Indian state do the scheduled castes constitute even 30 per cent of the population, nor are they geographically concentrated, nor for that matter do all scheduled castes vote for the BSP, but a large proportion does.[25] As a consequence, the BSP cannot capture power, unless it incorporates other groups or develops alliances with other parties. This is what finally happened in Uttar Pradesh when the BSP came to power in 2007. It sought to develop an alliance with the upper castes, especially the Brahmins, in an attempt to defeat the Samajwadi Party (SP).[26]

The need for alliance-making has led to a moderation in the BSP's rhetoric. Still, such moderation is different from being a client in the Congress hierarchy. In a fragmented political space dominated by no single party, the BSP has the political muscle to strike bargains over legislative seats, appointments, policies, and material goods. In the past, benefits were not bargained for, but handed top-down by the Congress party and assumed to be sufficient.

Unlike the scheduled castes, the scheduled tribes are geographically concentrated. For example, prior to the division of the state of Bihar, they lived mostly in the South.[27] Since 1981, Corbridge's fieldwork among Bihar adivasis has repeatedly taken him from some of the state's urban centres—where most of the adivasi government and public sector employees work—to three adivasi villages, from where they come. Corbridge is able to compare systematically the situation of adivasis in government jobs with their rural backgrounds. He argues that both affirmative action and democracy have offered new opportunities to adivasi communities. They have made possible material advancement for many, and led to a new awareness of politics and power for the whole group.[28]

One consequence of affirmative action is that the tiny middle class of the scheduled tribes has become considerably larger. And one result of democratic politics is that an adivasi-based political party headed a movement for a separate state in the Indian federation, where the adivasi population would be in a majority. This movement met with partial success, as it led to the creation of the state of Jharkhand; however, the geographical boundaries of the new state were smaller—because of political considerations—than those proposed by the movement. Consequently, even while their representation has increased, adivasis remain a minority in Jharkhand. Additionally, as appropriation of adivasi lands for industrialization continues apace, and calls for improved land rights among poor Jharkhandis remain ignored, scepticism about the real benefits of statehood is increasing among the adivasis.[29]

The OBCs are different from the other two groups. As already noted, compared to the scheduled castes and tribes, the OBCs command much larger numbers: according to the Mandal Commission, Hindu OBCs constitute about 43.7 per cent of India's total population. Being mostly Sudras, the OBCs have faced many social and economic disadvantages, but the fit between the two categories—OBC and Sudra—is not perfect.

If one goes by the all-India classification of castes—a national-level abstraction—the picture that emerges is unable to capture the many regional variations in dominance and power. Sociologists and social anthropologists construe the term Sudra to include the so-called 'dominant castes': the Jats, Reddys, Kammas, Patels, Marathas, and others, which the category of OBC on the whole excludes. The notion of 'dominant castes' was coined by Srinivas (1966) to specify those groups which, in a ritualistic or formal sense of the all-India caste/varna hierarchy, have been termed Sudras. But the ritualistic usage of the term is vacuous because these groups have historically been substantial landowners and rather powerful in their local or regional settings. In any realistic sense, the term Sudra cannot be applied to them, nor are they always included among the OBCs.

Jaffrelot[30] argues that the rise of the Janata Party to national power in 1977 was a turning point for the OBCs. Since then, the share of upper-caste legislators in North Indian assemblies and the national Parliament has, by and large, been declining and that of the OBCs going up, the state of Rajasthan being the only exception. In the first Lok Sabha (1952–57), Jaffrelot calculates, 64 per cent of North Indian members of Parliament (MPs) were from the upper castes and only 4.5 per cent from the OBCs; by 1996, the former proportion had declined to 30.5 per cent and the latter, risen to 24.8 per cent. Since 1996, too, these trends have held.[31]

Jaffrelot also shows how the contradictions within the sprawling Sudra category have produced two different kinds of plebeian politics in North India. For political mobilization, an urban versus rural ideology was proposed by the redoubtable Charan Singh, and an upper versus lower caste construction by Lohia. Charan Singh's was a sectoral world view: it subsumed the lower castes in a larger political category of the rural sector, in which the lower castes were a clear majority. Charan Singh's main demands were economic: higher crop and lower input prices in agriculture, and greater public investment in the countryside.[32] In contrast, since both cities and villages have lower castes, Lohia's ideology cut through the urban–rural sectors as well as Hindu society. Affirmative action for the lower castes, says Jaffrelot, was Lohia's principal thrust, and a social restructuring of state institutions—especially the bureaucracy and police—his primary objective.[33]

After several ups and downs, the biggest votaries of sectoral politics have been defeated in electoral politics. Non-party politics is now their principal arena of functioning, and caste has trumped sector in plebeian politics. If demands for higher agricultural prices are expressed today, it is the *lower caste* parties that primarily do so, not *rural* parties.

Checking the further rise of OBCs, however, are two countervailing forces: Hindu nationalism and the disunity among the OBCs. With an ideological stress on Hindu unity rather than caste distinctions, the Hindu nationalists seek to co-opt OBCs in the larger 'Hindu family'; and new distinctions are also getting institutionalized between the *upper* OBCs—such as the Yadavas—and the *lower* OBCs—such as the Telis and Lodhas. These differences have already undermined the OBC cohesion evident at the time of the Mandal agitation of the early 1990s. The rise of Nitish Kumar in Bihar and the defeat of Lalu Prasad Yadav in two successive state assembly elections (2005 and 2010) demonstrate the divisions within the OBCs.[34]

Whether or not the OBCs can come together in North India—it is very unlikely that they will—a re-establishment of upper-caste dominance is now most improbable in North Indian politics. Political power in North India has moved downward. Even Hindu nationalists—the biggest proponents of Hindu unity—are increasingly caught between giving a greater share of internal power to the OBCs and emphasizing Hindu unity over caste considerations. The latter tendency, traditionally unquestioned in Hindu nationalist politics, is no longer unchallenged. Fighting it is an ideological posture, termed 'social engineering' at one point and proposed by some party ideologues, who would rather give the OBCs more power and visibility within the BJP. 'Social engineering' was not another expression of vertical clientelism organized under upper-caste leadership, but an attempt to build Hindu unity by incorporating lower castes more equally.

The New Plebeian Upsurge and Democracy

In what ways has the rise of lower castes in the North, now added to their empowerment in the South, changed Indian democracy? Many would argue that India's democracy has become more inclusive and participatory.[35] Yadav has argued that India is going through a 'second democratic upsurge'. The first upsurge, for him, was the beginning of the end of Congress dominance in the mid-1960s. In a century-long perspective, however, it would perhaps be fair to say that this is the fourth democratic upsurge in India. The rise of mass politics in the 1920s under Gandhi's leadership was the first, and the universalization of franchise after independence the second.

Such judgements, of course, have not remained uncontested. Even those who agree that power has decisively moved down the caste hierarchy are unsure about what it means for the country's democratic health or longevity. Some issues keep appearing again and again: how the language of politics has become more coarse and the style more rough, compared to the sophistication of political dialogue and conduct under Nehru; how men of 'dubious provenance' have taken over electoral politics; how the governmental stability of a previous era has given way to unstable and unruly coalitions, in which mutual differences quickly turn into unseemly bickering and intemperate outbursts; how the politics of dignity that lower caste parties represent often becomes the politics of retribution; and how an emphasis on caste is impeding the rise of an all-India citizenship.[36] A democracy moving downwards may well be a poorer and shakier democracy.

Such anxiety is genuinely felt and should not be lightly dismissed. It is not simply the swansong of an anglicized, globally linked, upper-caste elite. We do, however, need to put the anxiety in perspective.

A large number of political theorists today—not only the so-called communitarians—lament the decline of moral values, or 'civic virtue', in *all* liberal democracies. No democracy currently functioning in the world seems to have institutions or mechanisms in place to ensure a durable moral or civic enhancement of political life. Democratic politicians, say these theorists, are increasingly turning politics into a marketplace, paying attention merely to the utilitarian calculus of routine politics: winning elections regardless of what it takes to do so; making promises to citizens that cannot be fulfilled; 'misbehaving' while in office but seeking the cover of legal principles and technical formalities. If the quality of goals pursued in politics becomes immaterial, these political theorists contend, even procedurally correct democratic politics can only weaken the moral and civic fibre of nations. Democracies today are ceasing to be 'civic republics'; they are becoming 'procedural republics'.[37]

Lest it be believed that such lament is confined only to the insulated ivory towers of universities, consider some of the popular discourse, reflected in the press. 'How low can they go?' bemoaned *The Wall Street Journal* in its editorial, highlighting the corrupt electoral practices followed in some parts of the US:

> (V)oter fraud is slowly undermining the legitimacy of more and
> more elections. . . . Since almost all states don't require a photo ID,
> it is fairly easy to vote in the name of dead people, vote if you are
> an illegal alien, falsify an absentee ballot or vote more than once . . .
> Two years ago, groups using federal funds registered hundreds of
> non-citizens in Orange County, California. The House Oversight
> Committee . . . came up with the name of 1499 voters who should
> be removed from the rolls, but election officials claim it is too late
> to purge them for today's election. This month, the Los Angeles
> County registrar identified 16,000 phony registrations submitted
> by two groups aligned with the Democratic Party.[38]

Unvirtuous politics, in other words, is not specific to Indian democracy. A decline in morality and a debasement of political practices and language are indeed significant problems for every society, as they have been for India. But, unless they totally invalidate citizen preferences, they do not amount to a negation of democracy. Fortunately, the latter is not the conclusion of the critics of caste-based politics. It is a call for correction—which we may all share—not an argument that democracy in India has become meaningless. It may also be worth recalling a famous argument about democracies, made by Huntington, which goes roughly along the same lines:

> Elections, open, free and fair, are the essence of democracy, the inescapable *sine qua non*. Governments produced by elections may be inefficient, corrupt, shortsighted, irresponsible, dominated by special interests, and incapable of adopting policies demanded by the public good. These qualities make such governments undesirable but they do not make them undemocratic.[39]

Democratic Authoritarianism?

A second challenge to the view that India's democracy is becoming more participatory is rather more radical in conception and thrust. Simply put, its principal claim is that India's democracy is a sham. In Jalal,[40] we have the most detailed statement of this view, though some others have also written in a similar vein.[41]

According to this view, changes at the level of elections and elected institutions are of little consequence so long as the social and economic inequalities of civil society remain unaltered, and the non-elected state institutions—especially the bureaucracy and police—continue to act in an authoritarian manner vis-à-vis the citizens, much as they used to when the British ruled. For democracy to function in a *real*, not *formal*, sense there has to be greater prior equality among its citizens. A deeply unequal society cannot check the authoritarian functioning of the state structures and, therefore, cannot have a polity that is 'really' democratic.

'Democratic authoritarianism', Jalal argues, is the best way to describe India's polity, and there are no fundamental differences between India, Pakistan, and Bangladesh, except at the level of political superstructure. All have profound socio-economic inequalities and all have inherited insensitive, colonial state structures in which the non-elected institutions easily trump the elected powers-that-be:

> The simple dichotomy between democracy in India and military authoritarianism in Pakistan and Bangladesh collapses as soon as one delves below the surface phenomena of political processes. . . . (P)ost-colonial India and Pakistan exhibit alternate forms of authoritarianism. The nurturing of the parliamentary form of government through the meticulous observance of the ritual of elections in India enabled a partnership between the political leadership and the non-elected institutions of the state to preside over a democratic authoritarianism.[42]

Thus, even when meticulously observed, elections are basically a 'ritual'. At best, they combine 'formal democracy and covert authoritarianism'.[43] If societies are unequal, the poor will inevitably be manipulated by the political elite:

> Unless capable of extending their voting rights beyond the confines of the institutionalized electoral arenas to an effective struggle against social and economic exploitation, legal citizens are more likely to be handmaids of powerful political manipulators than autonomous agents deriving concrete rewards from democratic processes.[44]

In its theoretical anchorage, we should note, this kind of reasoning is not new. Commonly associated with Marx, Lenin, Gramsci, Mosca, and Pareto, it has a long lineage lasting over a century. The arguments of Gramsci and Mosca are the most elaborate.[45] Gramsci[46] reasoned that so long as the economically powerful had control over the cultural means of a society—its newspapers, its education, its arts—they could establish a hegemony over the subaltern classes and essentially obfuscate the subaltern about their own interests. And Mosca[47] argued that in democracies—given their many inequalities—domination by a small elite was inevitable.

For our discussion about caste and democracy, there are two levels at which the claim about the emptiness of Indian democracy compels attention: theoretical and empirical. The key theoretical issue is: Should we consider socio-economic equality a precondition for democracy? And since a change in the social base of parties— to reflect a closer correspondence between party politics and India's caste structure—and a change in the composition of state institutions through affirmative action—to make the state respond better to the needs of the deprived—are the two principal aims of lower caste politicians, the key empirical questions are: Is the rise of lower caste parties only formal, not real? And is affirmative action illusory?

Is Socio-Economic Equality a Precondition for Democracy?

A theoretically defensible notion of democracy is not possible based on the example of South Asia, a region in which only two countries—India and Sri Lanka—have had the institutions of democracy, formal or real, in place for any substantial length of time. Any reasonable sense of testable theory should mean that we cast our net wider, especially if the larger universe is where most of the actually existing democracies have historically existed. Either South Asian materials can be interpreted in the framework of a larger, more historically embedded, democratic theory, or their empirical specificities can be used to modify the broader insights of democratic theory. In and of themselves, South Asian instances of democracy cannot make democratic theory, if most democracies exist outside South Asia. For a theoretical assessment, we need to turn to democratic theory, which has a long tradition in political science.

In the leading text of democratic theory,[48] as summarized in Chapter 1, the two basic criteria of democracy have been contestation and participation. The first principle, in effect, asks how freely does the political opposition contest the rulers. The second inquires how many groups participate in politics and determine who the rulers should be. The first principle is about liberalization; the second about inclusiveness.[49]

Contestation and participation do not require socio-economic equality; they may affect, or be affected by, inequality. Democratic theorists expect that if socially or economically unequal citizens are politically equalized, and if the deprived constitute a majority of the electorate, their political preferences would, sooner or later, be reflected in who the rulers are and what public policies they adopt. By giving everyone equal vote irrespective of prior resource-endowments or social standing, universal franchise creates the potential mechanisms for undermining vertical dependence. In Europe, labour parties pushing for workers' interests emerged in politics, once franchise was extended to the working class.

Another well-known theoretical point is germane to a discussion of inequalities and democracy. If inequality—despite democratic institutions—comes in the way of a free expression of political preferences, such inequality makes a polity *less* democratic, but it does not make it *un*democratic. So long as contestation and participation are available, democracy is a *continuous* variable (expressed as 'more or less'), not a *dichotomous* variable (expressed as 'yes or no'). Variations in degree and dichotomies should be clearly distinguished. In the classic formulation of Dahl, the United States was less of a democracy before the civil rights revolution of the mid-1960s, though it can in future be even more democratic if inequalities at the level of civil society come down further.[50] Similarly, by allowing a great deal of contestation but restricting participation according to gender and class, England in the nineteenth century was less democratic than it is today, but it was democratic nonetheless, certainly by nineteenth-century standards. *Given contestation and participation, greater equality certainly makes a polity more democratic, but greater equality, in and of itself, does not constitute democracy.* There is no democracy without elections.

These claims are empirical, not normative. They are not a defence of inequalities, nor do they imply that having universal franchise is better than having equality. Relative economic equality, for example, may well be a value in itself, and we may wish to defend it as such. But we should note, for example, that economic equality and democracy are distinct categories. Societies with high levels of economic equality may well be quite authoritarian: South Korea and Taiwan until the late 1980s, China under Mao, and modern Singapore come to mind. And societies with considerable economic inequality may have vibrant democracies: India and the US are both believed to have a Gini coefficient of 0.4–0.45, as opposed to a more equal Gini coefficient of 0.2–0.25 for the pre-1985 and authoritarian South Korea and Taiwan.[51] Precisely because economic equality and democracy are analytically distinct, some people may quite legitimately be democrats but not believers in economic equality; others may believe in democracy as well as economic equality; and still others may be democrats but indifferent to the question of economic equality. A similar argument can also be made about social inequalities.

In light of this theoretical discussion, let us now turn to India. Has Indian democracy become more inclusive or not? And hasn't greater inclusion reduced inequalities? In case inequalities have come down as a consequence of the political process, it will, in the theoretical terms proposed above, make India *more* democratic, even though an inability to reduce inequalities will not make India's polity *un*democratic.

Are the OBCs an Elite Category?

If the OBCs are in many regions the 'better-off farmers and peasant proprietors who benefited from the abolition of *Zamindari* (absentee landlordism) in the fifties',[52] their rise would indeed not constitute a significant change in the patterns of 'social and economic exploitation'.[53] An old set of 'exploiters' would simply be replaced by a class only slightly less rich and privileged. Are the OBCs an elite group in the latter sense of the term?

To call the OBCs 'better-off farmers and peasant proprietors' is a serious conceptual and empirical error, for it conflates the OBCs with the 'dominant castes'. Most OBCs are *not* dominant castes. The latter term, as already stated, represents those groups which, in the national-level abstraction of a varna/caste hierarchy have been incorrectly termed Sudras but, for a whole variety of regional or local reasons, this term makes no sense for them. Their power and status have far exceeded anything that the term Sudra implies.[54] The all-India hierarchy was simply irrelevant for groups of substantial landowners, such as the Jats, Patels, Kammas, Reddys, Nairs, and Marathas. They have been much too powerful and rich, even if they were not Brahmins, Kshatriyas, or Vaishyas, the customary upper three Hindu varnas/castes. Many of these castes did indeed benefit from the abolition of the Zamindari system if it prevailed in their areas.[55]

The dominant castes and the OBCs have some intersections—for example, the Okkaligas and the Lingayats in Karnataka count as both—but the two are not overlapping sets (Figure 3.2). *By and large, the category of OBCs is equal to the Sudras minus the dominant castes.*

Can the argument about the relative élitism of the OBC category be extended to any OBCs at all? The upper OBCs, such as the Yadavas, are indeed peasant proprietors and also beneficiaries of the abolition of Zamindari. Much like the Patels in Gujarat at the

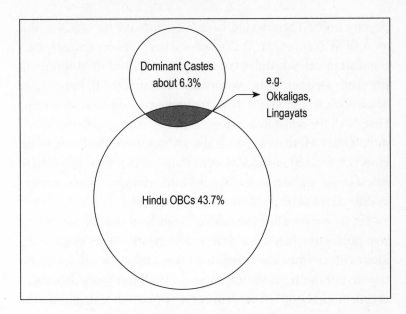

FIGURE 3.2: OBCs AND DOMINANT CASTES

turn of the century, the Yadavas have achieved sufficient upward mobility since the Green Revolution, and have used their numbers to considerable effect in a democracy. One can indeed say that they are fast becoming a dominant caste, and will in all probability be viewed as such in the coming decades. But the lower OBCs, such as the Lodhas, Pals, Malis, Telis, and Mauryas, are not as privileged.

This bifurcation of the OBC category raises an important question: What proportion of the OBCs can be called economically deprived? Though landholding data for castes has not been collected for decades and therefore precise estimates cannot be given, simple calculations—combining the separate caste and landholding statistics in an empirically defensible way—can show that a majority of the lower OBCs are most likely to be marginal farmers (owning less than 2.5 acres of land) or small farmers (less than 5 acres).

Let us work with an example. In 1993–94, using the prevailing measures of poverty, about 36 per cent of India was below the poverty line.[56] There would have been virtually no OBCs in this group if we assume that (a) all scheduled castes (16 per cent of India's population); all scheduled tribes (8 per cent); and all Muslims (12 per cent) were below the poverty line; and that (b) all upper-caste households were above it. Both assumptions, we know, are wrong. First, both the scheduled castes and tribes, as argued above, have a middle class. Moreover, there is also a Muslim middle class in India, especially in Southern and Western India, from where migration to Pakistan was minuscule, and also in Northern India where a Muslim middle class has reappeared after the late 1960s.

Let us suppose for the sake of argument that of the 36 per cent population below the poverty line, nearly 30 per cent (of the total) comes from the scheduled castes, tribes, Muslims, and a tiny percentage from the upper castes. With this more reasonable supposition, about 5–6 per cent of the population falling below the poverty line would consist of the OBCs.

Since the poverty line is primarily, if not entirely, nutritional in the developing world—meaning that below the line one could not buy enough food to get enough calories[57]—another 15–20 per cent of the country's population, if not more, would also be quite poor. In some statistical accounts, this latter proportion—poor but not below the absolute poverty line—is larger,[58] but even if we worked with the more restricted figure, the OBCs would constitute 20–25 per cent of the population that is below, or just above, the poverty line. That, in turn, would make up 50–55 per cent of Hindu OBCs (constituting, as they do, 43 per cent of the Indian population).

We also know that marginal farmers with less than 2.5 acres of land constitute about 50 per cent of all landed households in India.[59] Thus, putting the caste and landholding data together, we can safely infer that marginal farmers constitute an overwhelming proportion of OBC households. Even after the Green Revolution, the level of productivity in Indian agriculture has not reached such a level that we can justifiably call these latter classes 'peasant proprietors or better-off farmers'.[60] In agrarian political economy, the terms 'peasant proprietors' and 'better-off farmers' do not signify debilitating economic disadvantage, but rather considerable advantage. These are terms that cannot, by and large, be applied to marginal and small farmers.

In short, to say that peasant proprietors or better-off farmers benefited from the abolition of Zamindari is correct; but to conclude that peasant proprietors and better-off farmers are by and large OBCs is a non sequitur. Many lower OBCs are not only socially subaltern but also economically so, and only slightly better in both respects than the scheduled castes. That is why an older question continues to be politically relevant: Can the lower OBCs be incorporated with the scheduled castes in a political coalition (as opposed to a coalition led by the upper OBCs)?

Is Affirmative Action Illusory?

Theoretically speaking, it is possible that affirmative action leads to the co-optation of a tiny lower caste and scheduled-caste elite into the existing vertical structure, without any widely dispersed welfare-gains for their castes. After all, India's affirmative action concerns only government jobs, not the private sector. In 2011, of the nearly 487 million people in the workforce, only 17.3 million were in the public sector.[61] One can, therefore, say that affirmative action in the public sector will directly benefit only a small proportion of the deprived, and one can, in principle, suggest that 'access to education, government employment and state patronage based on reservations may, in fact, have hampered rather than strengthened the autonomy of the more privileged and talented members of the scheduled castes and tribes'.[62]

Is there evidence that this theoretical possibility holds up empirically? This question can, in turn, be broken down into two parts: (a) affirmative action for the OBCs (in addition to the scheduled castes), which has taken the form of quotas in much of South India since the 1960s; and (b) affirmative action for the SCs, implemented all over India since 1950, to which the OBCs have been added outside the South only after 1990. Clearly, it is far too early to evaluate the impact of affirmative action for the OBCs beyond Southern India. For the scheduled castes, however, our empirical judgements can be national in scope.

In South Indian states, over and above the scheduled caste quota, close to 50 per cent of state government jobs have been reserved for the OBCs in the state of Karnataka since the 1960s; in Tamil Nadu, the OBC quota was 25 per cent to begin with, and was increased to over 50 per cent later; in Kerala, the OBC quota has been 40 per cent; and in Andhra Pradesh, 25 per cent. What has been the impact of such large-scale reservations? Have the non-elected state institutions changed?

No detailed breakdown of state bureaucracies, according to caste, is available for South India, but there is no mystery left about the results. It is widely known that a lot of Brahmins migrated out of South India as the OBC quotas were instituted. Once access to government jobs—their traditional stronghold—was substantially reduced, some Brahmins went into the private sector, becoming businessmen for the first time, but a large number migrated to Delhi, Mumbai, the United Kingdom, and the United States. Indeed, so large was the flight and so capable were the Brahmins of getting jobs anywhere that their migration to, and rise in, Mumbai led to a serious anti-southern movement in the late 1960s and early 1970s.[63] By now, bureaucracies of southern states have become remarkably, though not entirely, non-Brahmin.[64] Moreover, though systematic empirical studies have not been undertaken, it is also widely recognized that the South is governed better than the North. Large-scale affirmative action in bureaucratic recruitment does not appear to have undermined governance in the South.

Let us now turn to the impact of reservations for the scheduled castes. Before his death, Kanshi Ram, the founder of the BSP, argued that affirmative action had 'done enough for the scheduled castes', noting that in the state of UP, of the 500 officers in the elite Indian Administrative Service, 137 were at that time from the scheduled castes.[65] However, Kanshi Ram added, affirmative action was 'useful for a cripple but a handicap for someone who wants to run on his own two feet'; instead, the scheduled castes, he said, should focus on winning power through elections, for 'the capture of political power will automatically transform the composition of the bureaucratic elite'.[66]

Following this logic, some years after Kanshi Ram's death, his party did come to power in Uttar Pradesh. One term in the government (2007–12) might not change the ground realities radically, but should the BSP return to power, it would be interesting to observe the results. In any case, compared to the theoretical possibility of affirmative action leading to co-optation, notice how different the claim of the founder of the BSP was. Affirmative action, in his judgement, was an inadequate tool for empowerment; it was time to play the game of democratic politics more equally. Finally, his politics was premised upon the assumption that non-elected institutions did not trump the elected institutions; rather, capturing elected institutions would transform the bureaucracy and police much more fundamentally. It is the elected institutions of India that set the tone for the non-elected state institutions of bureaucracy and police, not the other way round.[67]

After all is said and done, the most telling evidence of the impact of affirmative action on the scheduled castes may well be *indirect*, not direct. Affirmative action has produced a new counter-elite, which has started leading political mobilization. Chandra[68] shows that scheduled-caste government officers—the beneficiaries of affirmative action—were the early BSP leaders. Rather than leading to a vertical co-optation, affirmative action, by producing a scheduled caste elite, appears indirectly to have facilitated horizontal mobilization. A hampering of autonomy follows directly from vertical client–patron links, not from horizontal mobilization.

Deeper, but Unfinished

None of the above should be construed to mean that India cannot be made still more democratic. There is no doubt that many battles for social dignity and equality for the lower castes still lie ahead, even in South India;[69] and so do struggles for the rights of women and minorities. The continuing hostility between the upper OBCs and the scheduled castes in several parts of India is another example of an unfinished social transformation. However, we have enough evidence that democracy has already energized India's plebeian orders.[70] They have challenged the traditional forms of clientelistic politics and started fighting for more power.

Whether or not *economic* inequalities have gone down, *social* inequalities certainly have, even for the scheduled castes.[71] This is a serious achievement. If, in South India, it was not possible for Ezhavas to walk on public streets; if it was impossible for Nadar women to cover their breasts when walking in front of higher caste Hindus; if scheduled castes in much of India could not traditionally have access to schools, public transport, and public wells, then, the emergence of the notion of basic dignity among, and for, the lower castes in the public sphere must be taken extremely seriously, even though economic inequalities may not have lessened to the same degree. The battle for social dignity is being increasingly won in the public sphere.

By all accounts, India's democracy has made such social victories possible. In India, unlike in many other democracies in the world, the incidence of voting by now is higher among the poor than among the rich, among the less educated than among the graduates, in the villages than in the cities.[72] The deprived seem to have greater faith in Indian's elections than the advantaged. Unless we assume short-sightedness, the subaltern seem to think that the electoral mechanisms of democracy can be used to serve at least some of their purposes.

It should also be noted that many scholars who accept these claims have nonetheless been quite critical of some other aspects of Indian polity. But we should specify how their criticisms differ from the claim that India's democracy is a sham. The three most common criticisms are:

1. that a crisis of ungovernability has arisen due to increasing political participation and the inability of the state to respond adequately to the rising groups and demands;[73]
2. that India's political elite has focused far too much on narrow identities on the one hand and purely economic goals on the other, but far too little on using public policy to expand educational and health opportunities for the deprived;[74]
3. that there is nothing unnatural about politicians making use of identities in democratic politics, but that does not explain why India's politicians have paid such inadequate attention to issues of public policy in general, both concerning education and health on the one hand and incomes on the other.[75]

Nothing in India's democracy precluded a switch from *dirigisme* to a market orientation, as was demonstrated in 1991, nor does democracy rule out a greater effort at universal primary education and public health, as Sri Lanka and some Indian states show. The failures of public policy may have less to do with democracy per se, more with the *ideology* and mindset of India's political and bureaucratic elite.[76] Quite different ideologies have been, and can be, pursued in a democracy.

Moreover, sensible welfare-enhancing public policies do not always have to wait for popular pressures to build up; they can emerge with an ideological change from above.[77] The shift in

India's agricultural policy in the mid-1960s is an example;[78] so is affirmative action enshrined in India's Constitution. Both came into force without a popular movement in favour of either. Though the subaltern, through the electoral process, have on the whole so far pressed India's decision-makers less for better incomes, education and health, and more for everyday dignity and respect, such a lack of pressure on the former objectives did not dictate relative inaction, or lack of boldness, on the part of the government. India's greatest failure is one of imagination and awareness on the part of the political and bureaucratic elite.

Notice the implications of the third critique. It accepts that elections have a real, not simply formal and ritualistic, value and yet it claims that *if popular demands were different or if the state responses were*, the results of India's democracy would be so much more impressive. The admittedly unremarkable functioning of the Indian state in enhancing economic, educational and health opportunities for its masses is not as a negation of democracy, but a problem analytically separable and one attributable to elite ideologies. For a balanced record, such failures must be contrasted with the success of India's democracy, reflected in rising participation and inclusiveness and victories at the level of social dignity and respect. By privileging numbers and allowing freedom to organize, democracy has become the biggest enemy of the hierarchies and degradations of India's caste system.

Conclusion

Instead of arguing that only relative equality can produce a democracy, a much more empirically grounded claim would be that democracy can help reduce inequalities, at least social if not economic. Understanding how this happened in South India in the 1950s and 1960s is increasingly a necessity for a deeper understanding of contemporary North India. Not only have social humiliations gone down significantly in the South, but there is a consensus that South India is on the whole less unequal today than the Hindi-speaking North (as well as better governed).

It is clear that the rise of lower castes to power between the 1950s and 1960s has had a great deal to do with the transformation of South India since then. Whether the North will replicate the South is still an open question: the proportion of the upper castes, for one, has always been substantially higher in the North, and lower caste movements in the South, for another, did not have to contend with Hindu nationalism. Thus far, the lower caste parties of North India have also not emphasized education and health as much as their counterparts in South India. However, should the northern outcomes even approximate southern outcomes in the coming years, the votaries of both the liberating potential of democracy and of reducing inequalities will have much to cheer about. Democratic power is increasingly moving downward.

II

Religion, Language, and Caste

4

Contested Meanings: India's National Identity, Hindu Nationalism, and the Politics of Anxiety in the 1980s and 1990s

This chapter concentrates on the rise of Hindu nationalism in the 1980s and 1990s. Hindu nationalism has been around for decades, arguably longer, but it is only in the 1980s and 1990s that it became a significant force in Indian politics.

Three arguments are made. First, a conflict between three different varieties of nationalism marked Indian politics of the 1980s and 1990s: a *secular* nationalism; a *Hindu* nationalism; and two *separatist* nationalisms in the states of Kashmir and Punjab. Hindu nationalism was a reaction to the other two nationalisms. In imagining India's national identity, there was always a conceptual space for Hindu nationalism. Still, it remained a weak political force until the 1980s, when the context of politics changed. The rise of Hindu nationalism can thus be attributed to an underlying and a proximate base. Competing strains in India's national identity constitute the underlying base. The proximate reasons were supplied by the political circumstances of the 1980s. A mounting anxiety

99

about the future of India resulted from the separatist agitations of the 1980s and from a deepening institutional and ideological vacuum in Indian politics. The Congress party, India's key integrative political institution since 1947, went through a profound organizational decay, with no centrist parties taking its place. And secularism, the ideological mainstay of a multi-religious India, looked pale and exhausted. Claiming to rebuild the nation, Hindu nationalists presented themselves as an institutional and ideological alternative.

Second, India's secularism looked exhausted not because secularism is intrinsically unsuited to India and must, therefore, inevitably come to grief. That was the principal claim of the highly influential writings by T.N. Madan[1] and Ashis Nandy.[2] Insightful though their arguments were, Madan and Nandy did not sufficiently differentiate between different varieties of secularism. The secularism of Indira and Rajiv Gandhi was not a logical culmination of the secularism of Nehru. Each practised secularism differently. The politics of the 1980s discredited the kind of secularism practised by various regimes in the 1980s. It did not discredit secularism per se.

Third, Hindu nationalism, though a reaction to separatist and secular nationalisms, posed the most profound challenge to the governing principles and intellectual maps of independent India. Hindu nationalism had two simultaneous impulses: a commitment to the territorial integrity of India as well as a political commitment to Hinduism. Given India's turbulent history of Hindu–Muslim relations, it was unlikely that Hindu nationalism could realize both its aims. To push Hindu political dominance was also to court incalculable violence and national fissures; and to preserve national integrity required moderating the ideology of Hindu nationalism. Especially because of threats to the nation's integrity—the most serious since independence—Indian politics, for roughly a decade after the mid-1980s, was experienced by a large number of Indians as an anxiety, as a fear of the unknown and, on occasions such as the demolition of the Ayodhya mosque, even as a loss of inner coherence. A yearning for re-equilibrating designs that could impose some order on anxieties was unmistakable. To many, Hindu nationalism appeared as a solution to their anxieties about national integrity and to others, the biggest challenge to national integrity.

The Context: Three Contesting Nationalisms in India

India, wrote Naipaul in 1990, was 'a country of a million little mutinies', but, he added that, 'there was in India now what didn't exist 200 years before: a central will, a central intellect, a national idea. The Indian Union was greater than the sum of its parts.'[3] While one may disagree with Naipaul about whether a 'national idea' existed in India in earlier times, he is rightly pointing to a paradox: both little mutinies and a 'central' or 'national idea' were concurrently present in the 1980s. As disintegrative tendencies deepened, a sense of pan-Indian nationalism also grew. The two tendencies—the mutinous disaggregation and a national resurgence—fought it out, with no clear victor at that time. The narratives of the time, especially the journalistic ones, concentrated mostly on the disintegrative tendencies. The merit of Naipaul's position lay in recognizing that the political tendencies were dualistic, not unitary. It was also the kind of duality for which direct evidence, privileged in the social sciences, could not then be provided. Evidence from large-scale surveys did not exist at that time; as reported in Chapter 6, the survey evidence that did subsequently emerge supported Naipaul. Following the method of a writer, Naipaul travelled, talked, heard, and saw. Social science surveys later substantiated his insights.

Separatist nationalisms in Kashmir and Punjab were the most powerful expressions of the disintegrative tendency.[4] The two other varieties of nationalism—secular and Hindu—were committed to India's territorial integrity, though they sought to do it in different ways.

Unsurprisingly, the three nationalisms did not have the same conception of the nation. Separatist nationalists claimed that Sikhs and Kashmiris were not part of the Indian nation. They were nations by themselves. Their point was not simply that there was something distinctive about the Sikh and the Kashmiri identities that separated them from India; rather, to use Gellner's words again, 'the political and the national unit should be congruent'.[5] A nation is not merely a cultural configuration; it means investing a cultural community with sovereignty.[6]

These movements, then, were not mere ethnic assertions. Ethnicity as a term designates a sense of collective belonging, which may be based on common descent, language, history, or even religion (or some combinations of these).[7] An ethnic group may function without a state of its own; a nation implies bringing ethnicity and statehood together. In principle, this congruence may be satisfied in a federal arrangement, in which case the concerned nationalism becomes a form of sub-nationalism. The larger federal entity, then, has the highest claims on that group's loyalty. Alternatively, one may opt for nothing short of sovereignty. That is what Sikh and Kashmiri nationalists aimed at. A Bengali can be both a Bengali and an Indian, so can a Gujarati also be an Indian. Bengalis and Gujaratis are ethnic groups; for separatists, Sikhs and Kashmiris were nations. For Indian nationalists—both secular and Hindu—the Sikhs and the Kashmiris were simply ethnic groups, not nations.

Unlike separatist nationalisms, secular nationalism—the official doctrine of India's national identity since independence—seeks to preserve the geographical integrity of India. In principle, it includes all ethnic and religious groups in its definition of the nation, and respects their beliefs and cultures. Giving security to the various ethnic and religious groups is considered part of nation-building. One can be a good Muslim or a good Bengali and a good Indian at the same time.

That, to Hindu nationalists, is the opposite of nation-building. A salad bowl does not produce cohesion; a melting pot does.[8]

Hinduism, to Hindu nationalists, is the source of India's identity. It alone can provide national cohesiveness.

This claim inevitably begs the question: Who is a Hindu? Savarkar, the ideological father of Hindu nationalism, explains: 'A Hindu means a person who regards this land . . . from the Indus to the Seas as his fatherland as well as his Holyland'.[9] The definition is territorial (the land between the Indus and the Seas); genealogical ('fatherland'); and religious ('Holyland'). Hindus, Sikhs, Jains, and Buddhists can be part of this definition, for they meet all three criteria. All these religions were born in India. Christians, Jews, Parsis, and Muslims, however, can meet only two criteria. India is not their 'Holyland'.

Can non-Hindu groups be part of India? Yes, but only by assimilation, say the Hindu nationalists. According to Hindu nationalists, of those groups whose holyland is not India, Parsis and Jews are already assimilated, having become part of the nation's mainstream.[10] With the departure of the British, Christianity also lost its political edge, being no longer associated with foreign rulers; but if Christian missions converted the Hindus, then proselytization would bring Christianity into conflict with Hindu nationalism.

Ultimately, however, Muslims became the principal adversary of the Hindu nationalists, partly because of their numbers, but also because a Muslim homeland in the form of Pakistan had caused India's partition in 1947. Twenty-five per cent of pre-1947 India was Muslim. Even after the formation of Pakistan, Muslims remained the largest minority, constituting about 13 per cent of the country's population today. This explains, in part, the enormous attention given to Islam by the Hindu nationalists.

The Hindu nationalist claim is not that Muslims ought to be excluded from the Indian nation. While that may be the position of Hindu extremists,[11] the generic Hindu nationalist argument is that, to become part of the Hindu nation, Muslims must agree to the following: 1) accept the centrality of Hinduism to Indian civilization; 2) acknowledge key Hindu figures, such as Ram, as civilizational heroes, and not regard them as mere religious figures of Hinduism; 3) accept that Muslim rulers in various parts of India (between roughly 1000 to 1857) destroyed the pillars of Hindu civilization, especially Hindu temples; and 4) make no claims to special privileges, such as the maintenance of religious personal laws, nor demand special state grants for their educational institutions. They must assimilate, not maintain their distinctiveness. Through *Ekya* (assimilation), they will prove their loyalty to the nation.[12]

It is interesting to note that some Muslim politicians, though only a few, did accept this argument. Sikander Bakht, a Muslim, was a vice president of the BJP when the Baburi Mosque was torn down in December 1992. He did not resign.[13] Even today, the BJP has a Muslim vice president.

Hindu nationalism has two simultaneous impulses: building a unified India as well as 'Hinduizing' the polity and the nation. Muslims and other groups are not excluded from the definition of India, but inclusion is premised upon assimilation, on acceptance of the political and cultural centrality of Hinduism. If assimilation is not acceptable to the minorities, Hindu nationalism becomes exclusionary, both in principle and practice.

Created in 1925 in the state of Maharashtra, then part of the Bombay Presidency of British India, the Rashtriya Swayamsevak Sangh (RSS, National Voluntary Corps) is the institutional core of Hindu nationalism.[14] The ideological trend, however, goes much further back. Viewed as a means to resurrect India's cultural pride, Hindu revivalism in the second half of the nineteenth century was a response to British rule. This revivalism preceded the national movement headed by the Congress party in the first half of the twentieth century, but it could not dominate the movement itself.[15] There were two principal modes in the national movement: Nehru's secularism and Gandhi's Hinduism. Nehru's opposition to religion is well known. Even a devoutly religious Gandhi could not be called a Hindu nationalist. He was a Hindu and a nationalist, not a Hindu nationalist. Gandhi's Hinduism was inclusive and tolerant. Being a good Hindu and having respect for other religions were not contradictory.[16] Inclusion of non-Hindus in the Indian nation followed as a corollary of this position. Gandhi argued: 'If Hindus believe that India should be peopled only by Hindus, they are living in a dreamland. The Hindus, the Muslims, the Parsis and the Christians who have made India their home are fellow-countrymen.'[17]

Gandhi's love for Muslims even during the formation of Pakistan was, for Hindu nationalists, incomprehensible. In 1948, when a Hindu fanatic assassinated Gandhi, Hindu nationalism was set back by decades. In popular perception, Hindu nationalists killed the Mahatma, the father of the nation.[18] Many in the immediate post-1948 generation were told by their parents to keep a safe distance from Hindu nationalists.

Hindu nationalism began its political ascendancy in the late 1980s (see Table 4.1). That something as inconceivable as the mass demolition of a protected mosque could be undertaken and executed as a political project demonstrated, in and of itself, the new mobilizing capacity of Hindu nationalism.[19] The assassination of Mahatma Gandhi in 1948 was the last politically critical act of Hindu nationalism, but that was neither a manifestation of its organized strength nor an expression of its capacity to mobilize the masses. It was the insane act of an angry individual who was motivated by the ideology of Hindu nationalism.[20]

Three Strains and Two Imaginations: India's National Identity and Hindu Nationalism

Who is an Indian? The question, deceptively simple, is hard to answer, as indeed it is with respect to several other nations in the world.[21] Literature on comparative nationalism suggests that national identities have historically been based on several principles

Battles Half Won

TABLE 4.1: INDIAN NATIONAL CONGRESS (INC) AND
BHARATIYA JANATA PARTY (BJP) NATIONAL ELECTION
RESULTS, 1952–2009

| | Percentage of National Vote | | Seats Won in the Lok Sabha | | Total |
	INC	BJP	INC	BJP	Seats
1952	45	3.1	364	3	489
1957	47.8	5.9	371	4	494
1962	44.7	6.4	361	14	494
1967	40.8	9.4	283	35	520
1971	43.7	7.4	352	22	518
1977	34.5	-	154	-	542
1980	42.7	-	353	-	542
1984	48.1	7.4	415	2	543
1989	39.5	11.5	197	86	543
1991	36.5	20.1	232	120	543
1996	28.8	20.3	140	161	543
1998	25.8	25.6	141	182	543
1999	28.3	23.8	114	182	543
2004	26.5	22.2	145	138	543
2009	28.6	18.8	206	116	543

Note: Until 1980, the BJP was known as Bharatiya Jana Sangh (BJS). The BJS
merged with the Janata coalition in 1977 and 1980, making it impossible to
derive good estimates of its popular vote.

Source: 1. David Butler, Ashok Lahiri, and Prannoy Roy, *India Decides:
Elections 1952–1991* (New Delhi: Living Media India Limited,
1995) for 1952–91 data
2. Election Commission of India, *Statistical Report on General
Elections, Various Issues* (*National and State Abstracts and Detailed
Results*) for 1996–2009

of collective belonging: language (much of Europe); race (Japan,
Germany); religion (Ireland, Pakistan, and parts of the Middle
East); ideology (successfully in the United States, unsuccessfully

in the former Soviet Union and Yugoslavia); and territory (Spain, Switzerland, and a number of developing countries).[22] One should note that the territorial idea inevitably becomes part of all nation-states, but territory does not have to be the defining principle of national identity.[23]

Moreover, in some cases, there may be no clear principle of collective belonging. Rather, competing notions of identity may exist, one of which becomes dominant at one time, the other at another time. As Hoffman argues, there are two competing views about French identity. One is based on the French Revolution and the principles of freedom and equality, which bring French national identity quite close to the definition of the American nation. A second one is based on quasi-ethnicity (conceptualized as history and heritage) which, in French history, leads to the Vichy regime and to Le Pen in recent times.[24] In the United States, as Huntington has argued, the key constituents of the 'American creed'—liberty, equality, individualism, democracy, and the rule of law—have not always existed together, nor can they possibly, for they do not form a coherent logical set.[25]

What turns on the distinctive principles of national identity? Their political implications vary. Some of the most passionate political moments of America have been over the issues of freedom and equality, just as those of Germany have been over race. Similarly, competing strains in national identity open up distinctive political logics. Excessive drift in one direction brings forth a reaction, and competing strains begin to acquire political momentum. A significant number of French people have of late felt threatened by the increasing ethnic diversity of France, which is conceptualized by some as a mono-ethnic society, a conception opposed by others as too narrow and destructive of the principles of the French Republic.[26] In American history, as Huntington has argued, 'Conflicts easily materialize when any one value is taken to an extreme: majority rule versus minority rights; higher law versus popular sovereignty; liberty versus equality; individualism versus democracy'.[27]

Since the rise of the Indian national movement, three competing themes about India—territorial, cultural, and religious—have fought for political dominance. The territorial notion is that India has a 'sacred geography', enclosed between the Indus River, the Himalayas, and the Seas, and emphasized for twenty-five hundred years since the time of the Mahabharata.[28, 29] The cultural notion is that ideas of tolerance, pluralism, and syncretism define Indian society. India is not only the birthplace of several religions (Hinduism, Buddhism, Jainism, and Sikhism), but in its history it has also regularly received, accommodated, and absorbed 'outsiders' (Parsis, Jews, and 'Syrian' Christians, the followers of St Thomas, who arrived as early as the first century, whereby Christianity reached India before it reached Europe). In the process, syncretistic forms of culture and even syncretistic forms of religious worship have emerged and become part of India.[30] Apart from syncretism—which means a coming together and merging of cultures—pluralism and tolerance have also existed with different communities finding their niche in India and developing principles of interaction.[31] *Sarva Dharma Sambhava* (equal respect for all religions) is the best cultural expression of such pluralism. Finally, the religious notion is that India is originally the land of the Hindus, and it is the only land, which the Hindus can call their own. India has the Hindu holy places (Varanasi, Tirupati, Rameswaram, Puri, Haridwar, Badrinath, Kedarnath) and the holy rivers (Cauveri, Ganga, Yamuna, and the confluence of the last two at Prayag). Most of India is, and has been, Hindu by religion[32]—anywhere between 65 to 70 per cent in the early twentieth century and roughly 80–81 per cent today. A great deal of ethnic diversity may exist within Hindu society: a faith in Hinduism brings the diversity together. India viewed in this fashion is a Hindu nation.[33]

The three identity principles have their political equivalents. In political discourse, the territorial idea is called 'national unity' or 'national integrity'; the cultural idea is expressed as 'political pluralism'; and the religious idea is known as Hindutva,[34] or political Hinduism.[35] The political notion of pluralism itself has two meanings, dealing with the linguistic and the religious issues. The principle of federalism was developed to respect the linguistic diversity of India: not only would the states be organized linguistically but the ruling party would also be federally organized, leaving enough autonomy for state-level party units. The political principle about religion has two levels. In general, religion would be left untouched so that religious pluralism could exist, but if the state did have to intervene in religious disputes, it would do so with strict neutrality. The state would maintain a posture of equidistance, a principle that came to define India's secularism.

These three strains have yielded two principal imaginations about India's national identity—the secular nationalist and the Hindu nationalist. The former combines territory with culture; the latter, religion with territory. For the secular nationalist construction, the best source is Jawaharlal Nehru's *The Discovery of India*. Syncretism, pluralism, and tolerance are the main themes of Nehru's recalling of India's history:

Ancient India, like ancient China, was a world in itself, a culture and a civilization which gave shape to all things. Foreign influences poured in and . . . were absorbed. Disruptive tendencies gave rise immediately to an attempt to find a synthesis. Some kind of a dream of unity has occupied the mind of India since the dawn of civilization. That unity was not conceived as something imposed from outside, a standardization . . . of beliefs. It was something deeper, and within its fold, the widest tolerance of belief and custom was practiced and every variety acknowledged and even encouraged.[36]

Notice that Nehru, unlike Hindu nationalists, finds unity in culture, not in religion.[37] He has no conception of a 'holyland'. Ashoka, Kabir, Guru Nanak, Amir Khusro, Akbar, and Gandhi—all syncretistic or pluralistic figures, subscribing to a variety of Indian faiths[38]—are the heroes of India's history in *The Discovery of India*, while Aurangzeb, the intolerant Moghul, 'puts the clock back'.[39]

Perhaps the best way to illustrate the difference between culture and religion is to cite Nehru's will. Nehru wanted his ashes scattered in the Ganga, not because it was religiously necessary but because it was culturally appropriate:

> When I die, I should like my body to be cremated . . . A small handful of (my) ashes should be thrown in the Ganga . . . My desire to have a handful of my ashes thrown into the Ganga has no religious significance . . . I have been attached to the Ganga and Jamuna in Allahabad ever since my childhood and, as I have grown older, this attachment has grown . . . The Ganga, especially, is the river of India, beloved of her people, round which are intertwined . . . her hopes and fears, her songs of triumph, her victories and her defeats. [40]

To religious Hindus, the river Ganga is sacred. To Nehru, it was part of India's culture, and equally dear. The sacredness was not literal, but metaphorical. Similarly, India's geography was sacred, not literally but metaphorically. The emotions and attachment generated by the geography were equally intense. To draw a parallel, one does not have to be a religious Jew to celebrate and love the land of Israel. Secular Jews, too, can do that. Consider how Nehru narrates the geography of India—as territory and topos, not as a holyland:

> When I think of India, I think of broad fields dotted with innumerable small villages . . . of the magic of the rainy season which pours life into the dry parched-up land and converts it suddenly

into a glistening expanse of beauty and greenery, or greater rivers
and flowing water . . . of the southern tip of India . . . and above
all, of the Himalayas, snow-capped, or some mountain valley in
Kashmir in the spring, covered with new flowers, and with a brook
bubbling and gurgling through it.[41]

As discussed earlier, multiple strains of a national identity have
their own political implications. An excessive shift towards one
of the strains produces a reaction. Let us take secular nationalism
as an example. If secular nationalists violate the principle of
pluralism—let us say, by attacking federalism on the argument
that too much federalism weakens national unity—they undermine
a serious principle of the nation itself, and begin to generate a
reaction. Such attacks do not correspond to the concerned state's
view of national identity, which has a place for regional identity as
well. A man from Tamil Nadu is both a Tamilian and an Indian.
Sometimes the reaction takes the form of separatist agitations. And
these agitations, in turn, generate concern about territorial integrity.
The centralizing solution thus worsens the disease. Indira Gandhi
repeatedly undermined federalism on grounds of 'national integrity',
only to generate separatist nationalisms.

On the other hand, one can also go too far when protecting
pluralism. Kashmir was given a special status in the Indian
Constitution. Delhi was to be responsible only for foreign affairs,
defence, communications, and the currency; the state government
would handle the rest. Other Indian states had fewer powers. The
Kashmir arrangement, thus, had the potential for contradicting
the territorial principle if the Kashmiris claimed that they were
still unhappy. Nehru was instrumental in shaping its special status,
but he himself had to deploy force to quell Sheikh Abdullah's
vacillations between India and Kashmiri independence. A second
form of pluralism deemed excessive and therefore harmful for
national integrity concerns 'personal laws'. Should the various

religious groups be under a common civil code or under their distinct religious laws? If secular nationalists claim that separate personal laws destroy national unity, they generate a reaction in the religious community whose personal laws are at stake. If, on the other hand, they promote personal laws with the argument that such concessions make minorities secure, they can set off a reaction in the majority community that the state might have gone too far towards 'minority appeasement', opening up fissiparous tendencies and undermining national unity.[42]

Since the territorial principle is drawn from a belief in ancient heritage, encapsulated in the notion of 'sacred geography', and figures in both imaginations, it has acquired political hegemony over time. It is the only thing in common between the two competing nationalist imaginations. Therefore, just as America's most passionate political movements concern freedom and equality, India's most explosive moments concern its 'sacred geography', the 1947 partition being the most obvious example. Whenever the threat of another break-up, another partition, looms, it unleashes enormous passions in politics. Politics based on this imagination is quite different from what was seen when Malaysia and Singapore split from each other in the 1960s, or when the Czech and the Slovak Republics separated in 1992. Since territory was not such an inalienable part of their national identity, these territorial divorces were not desecrations. In India, however, they become desecrations of the sacred geography.

If national identities are imaginations (though not unreal for that reason),[43] an important counterfactual question remains to be answered. Why did secular nationalists not put the ideas of pluralism, tolerance, and syncretism at the heart of India's definition, so that the territorial idea was displaced? Why could it not be a purely cultural imagination of tolerance, pluralism, and syncretism, which, in principle, could be a solution for the tensions between territory and culture? Mahatma Gandhi, the father of the nation, embodied these ideas in his person and politics.[44] That, however, was a source of strength as well as an impediment. Gandhi, a devout Hindu both in his private and public life, used religion to mobilize the masses in the national movement, turning a movement confined to the educated and anglicized upper middle classes into a mass movement in the 1920s and 1930s. Given Gandhi's religiosity, these ideas got inextricably entangled with Hinduism, making them suspect in the eyes of many Muslims. For Jinnah, the founder of Pakistan, Indian nationalism under Gandhi was Hindu nationalism. The non-violent, inclusive, mass movement created a nation and shook the British, but the religious foundations of mass politics led also to Hindu–Muslim riots.

Because pluralism, syncretism, and tolerance became associated with Gandhi and his Hinduism, the secularists in their construction of national identity sought to escape the religious trappings. The political challenge consisted of putting these ideas at the heart of India's dominant political discourse without linking them to Hinduism—that is, explicitly defending them as inalienable parts of Indian culture common to all religious traditions and communities of India. It is conceivable that a secular Nehru and his colleagues might have undertaken this challenge. They did not. Nehru sought instead a solution in modernity and economic development: big dams became 'temples of the modern age'. Believing that all interpretations of India's past would generate controversy, that creating a national idea in terms of India's past was inherently problematic, he tried to make modernization and economic development the basis for national identity, something on which presumably everyone could agree. National identity, on this reading, could dissociate itself from a common past or from common origins and gravitate towards a common future or a common purpose. Let us forget the traditional past, let us build a modern future: this in effect became Nehru's political refrain. State policy, institutions, and ideological discourse, Nehru thought, would deepen the nation's commitment to modernity. As a consequence, the historically derived ideas of pluralism and tolerance became the implicit idiom of Nehruvian politics: while they informed his political conduct, they were not *explicitly* articulated as the basis of India's national identity. Politics since Nehru has paid even less ideological attention to the principles of pluralism and tolerance.

From Religion versus Culture to Religion as Culture

Finding a blending of territory and pluralism insufficient, the Hindu nationalists argue that politics, laws, and institutions do not make a nation. Emotions and loyalty do. Pluralism in the secular view is embodied in laws (such as personal laws and the protection of minority educational institutions) and in political institutions (such as federalism). According to Hindu nationalists, laws can always be politically manipulated, and a proliferation of pro-minority laws has not led to the building of a cohesive nation.[45] Instead, 'fissiparous tendencies' have regularly erupted. Rather than running away from Hinduism, which is the source of India's culture, one should explicitly ground politics in Hinduism, not in laws and institutions:

> In short, the Hindu *rashtra* [nation] is essentially cultural in content,
> whereas the so-called secular concept pertains to the 'state' and is
> limited to the territorial and political aspects of the nation. [T]he
> mere territorial-cum-political concept divorced from its cultural
> essence can never be expected to impart any sanctity to the country's
> unity. The emotional binding of the people can be furnished only
> by culture and once that is snapped then there remains no logical
> argument against the demand by any part to separate itself from
> the country.[46]

In their conception of Hinduism, Hindu nationalists fluctuate between two meanings of Hinduism—Hinduism as a culture (as the quotation above suggests), and Hinduism as a religion. 'Hindu is not the name of a religious faith like the Muslim and Christian; it denotes the national life here.' In the same vein, Advani once argued that, since 'Hindu' is the description of the nation, Muslims could be called 'Muslim Hindus', Sikhs could be called 'Sikh Hindus', and Christians could be called 'Christian Hindus'.[47]

However, when Hindu nationalists made speeches for the liberation of Ram's birthplace in Ayodhya, the campaign was imbued with religious imagery, and the rituals were *sanatani* (religious in an idol-worshipping sense). It is not at all clear what the intended distinction between religion and culture is for Hindu nationalists. While they are correct that the term Hindu—in its original meaning—meant those who lived in Hindustan (the everyday term for India in much of the North), over the past few centuries the term 'Hindu' has become a religious term, and 'Indian' has replaced 'Hindu' for the civilizational, and later national, meaning.[48] Labels acquire new meanings in history.

For a secular nationalist, the two terms—religion and culture—are clearly separable: syncretism and tolerance are the properties of all religions and communities in India, not simply of Hinduism. A celebration of Indian culture does not require one to be a Hindu. For Hindu nationalists, the two terms—India and Hindu—are synonymous. They make no special attempts to incorporate Muslim symbols into their conceptions of culture. The Hindu nationalist attitude to the great Moghul monuments, such as the Taj Mahal, remains unclear. Many object even to the Muslim names of North Indian cities: Aligarh, they say, should be called Harigarh; Allahabad, Prayag; and Lucknow, Lakshmanpur.[49] In Hindutva, the cultural and religious meanings of Hinduism blend into each other and the distinction, so critical for the secular nationalist, disappears.

The Hindu nationalist discourse on Islam has been selective and ominous. In India, Islam developed two broad forms: syncretist and exclusivist. Syncretistic Islam integrated into the pre-existing Indian culture. Exclusivist Islam may be a personal faith, or may also enter the political sphere, becoming an ideology, sometimes displaying fundamentalist qualities.[50] Syncretistic Islam has produced some of the pillars of Indian culture, music, dance, architecture, poetry, and literature. In 1940, Maulana Azad, a devout Muslim who, during the freedom movement, never embraced the demand for Pakistan but remained committed to the Congress party, of which he was one of the leaders, put the matter thus:

> I am a Muslim and proud of that fact. Islam's splendid traditions of thirteen hundred years are my inheritance. . . . In addition, I am proud of being an Indian. I am part of the indivisible unity that is Indian nationality. . . . If Hinduism has been the religion of the people here for several thousand years, Islam has also been their religion for a thousand years. Just as a Hindu can say with pride that he is an Indian and follow Hinduism, so also we can say with equal pride that we are Indians and follow Islam. . . . Eleven hundred years of common history have enriched India with our common achievement. Our languages, our poetry, our literature, our culture, our art, our dress, our manners and customs, the innumerable happenings of our daily life, everything bears the stamp of our joint endeavour. . . . This joint wealth is the heritage of common nationality and we do not want to leave it and go back to the times when this joint life had not begun.

It is not possible to conceptualize India's culture—both popular and classical—if Muslim influences are completely excluded. Moreover, Indian Muslims have also fought wars against Pakistan. By generating an anti-Muslim discourse, Hindu nationalists embittered most of India's 130 million Muslims in the late 1980s and 1990s, including those syncretistic in their religiosity and culture, and also those for whom Islam is a faith, a way to sustain troubled private lives, but not a political ideology. One might argue that the political and ideological battle of nationalists was against Islamic fundamentalism and Muslim separatism. How could it be against all those who profess faith in Islam? In the Hindu nationalist discourse of the 1980s and 1990s, these distinctions were easily blurred. An anti-Muslim hysteria resulted.

It should now be clear why secular and Hindu nationalism are ideological adversaries, and have remained so for decades. In an ingenious way, Mahatma Gandhi sought to combine the two. Tolerance and pluralism, he argued, stemmed from his belief in Hinduism. Being a Hindu and having respect for Muslim culture could easily go together. Frequently referring to his appreciation of Christianity, Buddhism, and Jainism, he never defined India as a Hindu nation. The nation, he argued, should incorporate all religions; being a Muslim in no way excluded one from being an Indian.

Gandhi, of course, succeeded and failed. India acquired independence, but he was unable to dissuade Jinnah and the Muslim League from creating Pakistan. Gandhi's failure to prevent the partition of India sent out two signals. For the secular nationalists, it highlighted the antinomy between religion and Indian nationalism. For the Hindu nationalists, it reinforced their belief in the complementarity between Hinduism and the Indian nation on the one hand, and a basic antinomy between Islam and Indian nationalism on the other. Since then, Hindu nationalists and secular nationalists have been locked in a conflict for political power and for the ideological shaping of India.

Has the 'Secular Project' Unravelled? The Organizational Decay of the Congress Party

In twentieth-century India, the principal organizational embodiment of secular nationalism was the Congress party. Once a powerful organization associated with the founding and building of the nation, by the 1980s the Congress party was a rusty, clay-footed colossus. Nations, as we know, are politically created; they do not naturally exist. As already argued in Chapter 1, just as peasants were turned into Frenchmen over the course of many years,[51] a serious attempt was made by the Congress to turn an old civilization into a nation in the first half of the twentieth century. Of the other large multi-ethnic countries in the world,[52] the Communists in the Soviet Union and Yugoslavia also sought to create nations, but not on the basis of conciliation and democracy. Because their nation-building was based on coercion, it was not clear how deeply a Croat felt for Yugoslavia, or how ardent a Georgian or a Balt was for the Soviet Union.[53] The Congress party mobilized the masses into a national movement, generated pride and belief in India, and, most of all, maintained an ideology of non-violence, an ideology that emphasized that even the British were to be politically defeated, not killed. While violence erupted periodically, it was not the cornerstone of the national movement.

The mobilization lasted almost three decades. As a result, the idea of India as a nation reached most parts of India. By the 1930s and 1940s, Gandhi, Nehru, and the Congress party had penetrated the far-flung countryside, not simply the urban centres. The emergence of Pakistan was the greatest failure of the Congress. The Muslim League could not be won over. However, nor could the Muslim League win over all Muslims in the subcontinent, in good part because the inter-religious idea of India so painstakingly promoted by the freedom movement and the Congress party held considerable attraction. It is noteworthy that after partition, very few Muslim artists, dancers, poets and musicians left India for Pakistan.

Under Indira Gandhi (1969–84) and Rajiv Gandhi (1985–91), the Congress declined as an institution. Electoral success coexisted with organizational emaciation. The organizational decay of the Congress coincides with Indira Gandhi's rise to unquestioned power by the early 1970s. As argued in Chapters 1 and 2, Nehru had used his charisma to promote intra-party democracy, not to undermine it, strengthening the organization in the process. Indira Gandhi used her charisma to make the party utterly dependent upon her, suspending intra-party democracy and debate, and weakening the organization as a result. Nehru's ideological positions were openly debated in party forums, and sometimes rejected. Indira Gandhi imposed her positions on the party. She would suspend state-level leaders if they dared to oppose her; she would not allow the state unit to elect its leader. Since this could not be done in a party that elected its office holders, she finally did away with party elections. She also tried to suspend national elections, but that attempt succeeded only for nineteen months.[54]

Secularism as a Modernist Ideology

It is not modern India which has tolerated Judaism in India for nearly 2,000 years, Christianity from before the time it went to Europe, and Zoroastrianism for more than 1,200 years; it is traditional India, which has shown such tolerance . . . As India gets modernized, religious violence is increasing . . . In the earlier centuries, inter-religious riots were rare and localized . . . [S]omewhere and somehow, religious violence has something to do with the urban–industrial vision of life and with the political process the vision lets loose.[55]

Social analysts draw attention to the contradiction between the undoubted, though slow, spread of secularization in everyday life, on the one hand, and the unmistakable rise of fundamentalism, on the other. But surely these phenomena are only apparently contradictory, for in truth it is the marginalization of faith, which is what secularism is, that permits the perversion of religion. There are no fundamentalists or revivalists in traditional society.[56]

With these words written by Nandy and Madan, respectively, a powerful argument against secularism emerged in India in the 1980s. India's secularism was in crisis, according to the anti-secularism view, not because it had not gone far enough, but because it had gone too far. Secularism was a victim of its official success.

The anti-secularist argument proceeded at two levels—a larger theoretical level and an India-specific level. The theoretical attack on secularism was embedded in the generic critique of modernity so common in the disciplines of anthropology, literary criticism, and history (especially of the developing world).

Secularism, in this view, is a necessary concomitant of the project of modernity, science, and rationality. Modernity is viewed as facing serious political difficulties all over the world, leading to religious (and ethnic) revivals. The basic flaw of modernity, according to this view, is that it mocks the believer for his morality, but it provides no alternative conception of what the purpose of life is, what the good life is, or how we should conduct ourselves in our families and communities. Politics founded on such a modernist, secular vision suffers from irremediable defects. No means are considered detestable enough so long as they facilitate the realization of political ends. Holding nothing sacred, lacking an alternative source of ethics, and having no internal restraints on political behaviour, modernity and secularism denude politics of morality. Because human beings cannot live without notions of right and wrong, the secular and modernist project creates increasing popular scepticism. Moreover, because it also generates condescension towards religion, secularism puts the believer on the defensive, setting off a religious reaction.

Pointing to the origins of secularism, the anti-secularists also argue that it is a Western concept with foundations in the Enlightenment and the Reformation. The Enlightenment heralded the supremacy of reason over belief, and, by making the individual responsible for his salvation without the intermediation of the Church, the rise of Protestantism made the separation of the state and the church possible. Secularism became embedded in Western culture. There is no similar civilizational niche for secularism in India. Religion was, and remains today, the ultimate source of morality and meaning for most Indians. Communal riots never took place in traditional India, for traditional religiosity allowed for principles of religious tolerance and coexistence. Modernity, however, has led to two results in the realm of religion and politics. Because of the link between secularism and amoral politics, communal riots in India have increased with the advent of modernity. And because secularism places the believer on the defensive, fundamentalism and secularism have become two sides of the same coin. Principles of tolerance will have to be derived from traditional India in the manner of Mahatma Gandhi, not from modernist secularism as Nehru did.

This is not the place to engage in an argument about the relationship between modernity and morality. For purposes of this chapter, the application of 'modernist logic' to Indian politics is more pertinent. It would suffice to note that the view that modernity and secularism lead to a moral and spiritual vacuum in human life is philosophically grounded in the Counter-Enlightenment. The themes of the Counter-Enlightenment continue to reverberate in several fields of knowledge: literature, philosophy, social sciences, and, surprisingly, even in the natural sciences.[57] Moreover, several leading students of rationality accept the claim that rationality is morally quite neutral. As Albert Einstein argued, science and rationality are essentially about 'is', not about 'ought'. Unless morally grounded, rationality can indeed be destructive. Embedded in moral ends, however, it can make a remarkable contribution to human life. Nuclear energy, according to Einstein, is the best example of this reasoning.[58]

The anti-secularists may indeed be right that modernity is morally neutral. It does not follow, however, that modernity (or secularism) therefore leads to intolerance and violence. Given contrasting conceptions of truth, religiously driven men may also be intolerant and violent, notwithstanding the morality of each religious system. Moral men do not necessarily make a tolerant society if there are multiple and exclusive conceptions of morality.

The anti-secularists do not distinguish between different types of tradition, or between the various types of modernity. Akbar, the tolerant Moghul ruler, and Aurangzeb, the intolerant one, were both products of medieval India. Akbar built bridges across communities; Aurangzeb destroyed them. Not only did he repress 'infidels' (non-Islamic religious groups), but he also sought to impose religious purity within the Muslim community, targeting 'heretics' and 'apostates', and killing his own brother, Dara Shikoh, in the process. Shikoh's crime was heresy: he used Islam to justify his attempt to combine features of Islam and Hinduism. Religion and tradition can thus be tolerant as well as brutally violent.[59]

Varieties of Secularism: Tolerance, Arrogance, and Innocence

Similarly, modernity and secularism can come in various forms. Two trends marked the behaviour of India's secular politicians in the 1980s. One may be called secular arrogance; the other, secular innocence. Secular arrogance was best exemplified by Indira Gandhi, secular innocence by Rajiv Gandhi. Both these variants are very different from Nehru's secularism, which can be called secular tolerance.[60] Nehru, a modernist, might have held strong reservations about religion, but his private beliefs did not translate into an arrogant abuse of religion in public life. It is principles in public life, rather than cosmologies governing private life, which are the issue here. In their private lives, Nehru, Indira, and Rajiv Gandhi may have all been a-religious (though there are indications that Indira Gandhi turned to religion in the last years of her life). In their public life, however, they were profoundly different. Secular

arrogance and secular innocence, associated with Congress politics
in the 1980s, fit the Nandy–Madan view best. It was not preordained
that, over time, tolerance would degenerate into arrogance and
innocence.

Secular arrogance is the idea that political power may be used
either to co-opt the believer, or to subdue him. The believer is viewed
not only as an object of modernization/secularization—an aim with
which a number of modernists including Nehru agreed—but also
as a pawn on the political chessboard, which modernists like Nehru
never thought appropriate. In its worst form, secular arrogance
combines two drives: the use of the believer by the politician for
secular, political purposes, and the wish to crush him.

This kind of process was initiated by Indira Gandhi. Her
political dalliance with Sikh religious extremism in the late 1970s
was dangerous. To defeat the Akali Dal—a moderate Sikh party
which competed with the Congress in Punjab, she used a religious
leader, Sant Bhindranwale. Religious preachers, like Bhindranwale,
felt that the Sikh community was losing its soul, in part due to the
modernity and economic prosperity that the Green Revolution
had brought about. Indira Gandhi would not concede the secular
demands of the moderate Akali factions (a greater share of river
waters, or a larger share of federal fiscal resources), but she
conceded several demands of the religious extreme (declaring
Amritsar a holy city, banning smoking there, and allowing Sikh
religious broadcasts over the state-controlled radio).[61] That was in
striking contrast to the situation in the late 1950s and early 1960s
when religious issues figured in Punjab politics. Nehru refused
to legitimate the Master Tara Singh faction associated with a
religion-based politics. Instead, he strengthened the Sant Fateh
Singh faction associated with *linguistic* demands, defeating the
religious faction in the end.[62] He would neither trifle politically
with religion—despite his opposition to religion—nor would he
legitimate religious leaders in politics.

Indira Gandhi used religion for political purposes; Bhindranwale used politics for his religious pursuits. She achieved a dubious success in the end. The moderate Akali factions—her rivals in party politics—were weakened, but the preacher and his men went out of control. Seeking to restore piety, Bhindranwale and his followers targeted the heretics and apostates, then, the 'infidels'. They eventually took shelter in the Golden Temple and conducted their religious mission from there. Indira Gandhi finally ordered the army to invade the temple.[63]

The army's desecration of the Golden Temple was a transformative event of contemporary Indian history. It led to Indira Gandhi's assassination by her Sikh bodyguards. June 6, 1984 (the attack on the Golden Temple) and October 31, 1984 (Indira Gandhi's assassination) began a cycle of desecration and revenge. Even the most patriotic Sikhs felt violated by her desecration. A large part of the Hindu middle class was equally revolted by the action of her Sikh bodyguards. Amoral, Machiavellian statecraft was known to be Indira Gandhi's hallmark. Weakening the moderate Akalis was her goal; the legitimacy of means was not an issue for her. Given her notion of politics and power, in all probability she imagined that state power would ultimately subdue Bhindranwale; that even after a mighty desecration, the enticements of power would either co-opt the Sikh community, or crush its 'pretensions'. She paid for this arrogance with her life, and it took a long while before the Hindu–Sikh wounds were healed.

Secularism as innocence can also spell danger. In India, secularism is not defined as a radical separation between the church and state.[64] The founders argued that in the Indian context, keeping the state equally distant from all religions and not letting it favour any one in public policy was the best solution.

Unlike the clarity entailed in a radical church–state separation, secularism as equidistance is a nebulous concept. *Equal distance* can also be translated as *equal proximity*. If it is alleged that the state is moving towards one particular religion, the state, to equalize the distance, can subsequently move towards other religions. Each such equalizing step may be aimed at soothing religious communities. But the state gets steadily more embroiled in religion. An unstable equilibrium results, breeding distrust all around, for no one is quite sure what the state will do next. Under Nehru, equidistance was not turned into equi-proximity. Under Rajiv, it was.

The turning point was the Shah Bano case in the mid-1980s. Shah Bano, a Muslim woman, filed for maintenance after being divorced by her husband. The husband argued that maintenance was not required under Islamic law. Shah Bano sought protection under the country's civil law, not the Islamic personal code. The Supreme Court argued that the country's civil law overrode all personal laws. Faced with a Muslim furore, Rajiv Gandhi first supported the Court. Then, to soothe Muslim feelings, he ordered his party to pass a law in Parliament that made the Shariat (Islamic personal law) superior to the civil law in matters concerning the maintenance of divorced Muslim women. He argued that secularism required giving emotional security to minorities. A Hindu storm consequently erupted. The Temple–Mosque site in Ayodhya, closed for years, was opened to Hindu pilgrimage and worship. The largest demonstration of Muslims seen in Delhi followed, with riots breaking out. Ostensibly trying to equalize the distance between religions, the government became more entrapped in religion.[65]

Twisted Meanings, Embattled Symbols

The Shah Bano case gave Hindu nationalists a remarkable opportunity to press their claims on the disputed Temple–Mosque site. Hindu belief about the birthplace of Ram, argued Hindu nationalists, was enough for the construction of a Ram temple. Courts, they said, could not pronounce judgments on matters of faith. The government's response that civil laws were above religious faith (or religious laws) had become a contradiction in terms. In the Shah Bano case, after all, the government had affirmed the superiority of religious faith over civil laws, and the Supreme Court had been overruled. The secular contention about the superiority of law over faith could not possibly apply to only one community.

After agitating for and getting a faith-based legislation, Muslim leaders could not, without contradiction, claim the mosque. Their arguments were either religious or legal. The religious argument was that a mosque was always a mosque even if it was not in use—as the disputed mosque had been for several decades. And the legal argument was that, as a mosque, the building was their community property and could not be destroyed. By the time Lal Krishna Advani led the mobilization to rebuild the Ram temple, these arguments were becoming part of the political process where a different logic operated. Arguments were not only to be made; they also had to be made acceptable to the masses in general. The arguments had to be political.

It is in the political realm that the secular as well as the Muslim leadership showed a lack of imagination, thereby playing into the hands of Hindu nationalists. So long as the issue was presented as mosque versus temple, the dispute remained religious, and could not generate a movement. But when it also became a Ram versus Babur issue—which is how the BJP simultaneously presented it—it took on nationalistic overtones. In Indian history, Babur is viewed as an alien conqueror; Ram is not. Babur, of Turko-Mongol descent, had invaded India with an army and founded an empire. Though several of Babur's descendants, especially Akbar, blended into India's culture, Babur himself remains an outsider in popular imagination. On the other hand, though no Hindu god is uniformly popular all over India, out of Hinduism's pantheism, Ram is one of the most popular. His popularity has made him both a religious and a cultural figure. The Ramayana (the tale of Ram) is one of the most popular epics, especially in North India. An annual and popular enactment of the tale of Ram (*Ramlila*), in which many Muslims have traditionally participated, makes Ram part of popular culture in much of India. In India, one does not have to be religious to experience the Ramayana culturally.

Muslim and secular leadership dwelled on the religious meaning of Ayodhya, and refused to encounter the second, nationalistic meaning. The various mosque action-committees (and the secular historians) initially argued that Ram was a mythological figure; there was no historical proof either for Ram's existence or for his birthplace. This was a gratuitous argument. Core beliefs of many religions flourish without proof. How can one *prove* that Prophet Mohammed's hair was brought to a mosque in Srinagar? Muslims of Kashmir believe it. Similarly, how can one prove that Buddha left his tooth in Sri Lanka, or that Jesus was born of a virgin? Religious belief does not depend on rational evidence. If the Shariat was the word of God for which no proof was required, as the Muslim leaders had claimed in the Shah Bano controversy, how could proof be sought for a Hindu belief?

The problem was compounded by three more facts. First, it is widely known that the disputed mosque had not been used for the last several decades. Second, mosques are known to have been removed in the past, even in Muslim countries. By repeatedly attacking an article of faith over a mosque not used for decades, the mosque action-committees and Muslim leadership gave the appearance of utter intransigence. Was Babur so much more important than Ram in India? The question was repeatedly asked by a large number of Hindus, many of them non-religious.[66]

Finally, while the Muslim leadership was conducting its struggle to save the Baburi Mosque, some of the most visible leaders of the Muslim community, for example, Syed Shahabuddin and Imam Bukhari, gave a call for the boycott of India's Republic Day. The aim, according to them, was to draw attention to their demands.

This strategy was symbolically disastrous not only for Hindu nationalists, but for a large number of secular Indians. The fight was presumably with Hindu bigotry, not with India as a nation. The Republic Day was a matter of pride for the entire nation, not only for the Hindus. Some of India's Muslim leaders did indeed reject the call for a boycott. Unfortunately, the most visible leaders continued undeterred.

As argued above, Indian Islam has taken a syncretistic as well as a separatist form. Most Muslims are syncretistic in their culture. The Muslim leadership at that time did not reflect the cultural syncretism of Indian Muslims but instead chose dangerous symbolic politics.[67]

The context thereby provided muscle to the BJP's critique of the actually existing secularism in India. Secularism in India, Advani argued, was pseudo secularism; it meant excessive appeasement of minorities, or what he called 'minorityism'. The argument was both right and wrong, but the wrong side was scarcely noticed in the politics of the late 1980s.

Muslims, Sikhs, Christians, and Buddhists, added to the scheduled castes and the scheduled tribes (non-religious minorities, nonetheless viewed as minorities), constituted more than 37 per cent of India's electorate.[68] In a 'first-past-the-post' British-style parliamentary system, a 40 per cent vote can translate easily into 50 to 60 per cent of the legislative seats. Since, according to conventional wisdom, the fractious majority community does not vote as a block but the minorities do, there is a temptation in the system of power-seeking centrist parties to develop pro-minority programmes. Purely in an electoral sense, therefore, India's political system does indeed gravitate towards the minorities, though the minorities may feel that this is not enough, and there is some justice in that claim.

Whatever the objective truth—if there was, or can be, one—the problem of perceptions dominated the discussion. Minorities are visible in India's upper political, bureaucratic, and cultural layers.

Roman Catholics and Sikhs have led the armed forces of India. General Jacob, a famous Jewish general, led India to victory in the 1971 India–Pakistan War. Muslims have regularly occupied positions in the Cabinet. The man who produced India's first medium-range missile is a Muslim. Muslims have led the national cricket team, a sport that generates national hysteria. They are among the leading classical musicians of the country. Muslim film stars have been role models, even for Hindu youth. Minority educational institutions have legal privileges and enjoy special grants from the government. Finally, in 1986, the government, on political grounds, overruled the Supreme Court by declaring that Muslim personal law was superior to the country's civil law in matters of marriage and divorce. If Muslims remain unhappy, many secularists and Muslim politicians argue, the state ought to do more.

The same set of facts, however, was used to present the BJP story. Muslim film and sports stars, musicians, and scientists are proof that talent matters irrespective of religion and that a largely Hindu society may not be unfair. This argument has a serious flaw. The BJP forgets that Muslims, despite these special provisions, are among the poorest and the least educated community in the country. Often, they have also been the object of police brutality in riots.

The problem of perceptions boils down to how many concessions to the minorities are sufficient. There is no objective answer to this question, in India or elsewhere. Muslim politicians and secularists point to the economic backwardness of Muslims and argue for greater assistance. The BJP pointed to the visibility of minorities in India's political and cultural life, saying that enough was enough.

When secularism was equated with secular tolerance and legitimated by Nehru's principled behaviour, arguments could be openly made that it was the responsibility of the majority community to make minorities secure.[69] Despite such open arguments in favour of minorities, Hindu nationalists were not able to win against Nehru. When principled secularism—not legitimating religion in political mobilization but maintaining a concern for minority welfare—was replaced by unprincipled secularism, the secular project began to weaken.

This weakening did not disprove the worth of secularism as a political principle, as Nandy and Madan argued. Morality and meaning in politics, first of all, do not have to emerge from religion; they can also emerge from a modernist, liberal conception of ethics. Nehru was moral as well as a-religious. Moreover, non-religious ethical behaviour can also be politically legitimated, even in societies marked by intense religiosity. Thus, secularism by itself does not make one amoral or unethical. If this was how secular politicians of the 1980s behaved, it is not what secularism as a principle entails.

As already indicated, the Nehruvian secular project relied on ideas of political liberalism and modernity. Nehru did not make a case for his project in terms of India's civilization, for which *The Discovery of India* has laid the groundwork. He wanted Indians to leave their past and become modern. That can be called a mistake. The more pertinent issue is: How does a nation reconstruct its past? Which traditions should be revived, and which ones dropped? Since a nation's past is not undifferentiated, contesting visions are generally available. The ideological task is to retrieve that which is valuable, and to make this selective retrieval a political reality. An England could not have been, and cannot be, created in India; only a future consistent with one of India's several pasts is possible.

Strictly speaking, Nehru's political pluralism and his opposition to religion are separable. One does not depend on the other. It is possible to re-conceptualize secular nationalism, by combining Nehru's political pluralism with his understanding that India's history is marked by cultural pluralism. One does not have to defend political pluralism and tolerance in terms of a modernist liberal theory; one can also defend it in terms of India's historical and cultural traditions. A pluralist democracy and secularism can thus be civilizationally anchored. This vision of politics requires recalling the pluralistic and syncretistic heroes of India's past, explicitly defending a politics and ideology of secularism in cultural terms, and mobilizing the people on that understanding.

Conclusion

In the 1990s, it became clear that India's future depended on who ruled India and what the ruling ideology was going to be. Hindu nationalists had, and have, a moderate faction and an extremist faction. The moderate faction emphasizes *dialogue* with the Muslim community and the secularists.[70] Against the moderates, the right wing of the movement staged a coup in Ayodhya.[71] Many of the cadres were galvanized into action by the promise of a Ram temple and wanted that promise to be kept, regardless of the political implications.

At the national level, four future possibilities presented themselves in the 1990s: 1) a continuation of Congress rule, though with a changed, pro-market economic ideology; 2) the rise of the BJP to national power with the centre right in command; 3) the rise of the BJP with the right wing in command; and 4) a non-Congress coalition, or a coalition of the Congress with other anti-BJP parties.

Since 1996, India has realized three of the four possibilities above. The third possibility—the rise of the BJP with the right wing in command—never materialized. It says something about the basic idea of India that is multi-religious, pluralistic, and syncretistic. It also speaks of the realities of democratic politics. No political party can come to power without putting together multi-religious, multi-caste, multilingual coalitions. Barring entirely unpredictable shocks to the system, a right-wing takeover of Indian politics is inconceivable.

5

Ethnic Conflict and Civil Society:
India and Beyond

Generally speaking, ethnic or communal violence is not uniformly spread across the length and breadth of a country. It tends to be highly locally concentrated. In Uttar Pradesh (UP), for example, Aligarh has been a riot-prone town, but neighbouring Bulandshahar has rarely witnessed Hindu–Muslim riots. The same is true of Meerut and Saharanpur in UP; Ahmedabad and Surat in Gujarat; Hyderabad and Warangal in Andhra Pradesh. In each of these combinations, the first city has a history of riots, the second one of peace. Many more examples can be given, both from India and elsewhere.

How does one understand and explain local concentrations of violence? This chapter argues that there is an integral link between the structure of civic life in a multi-ethnic society, on the one hand, and the presence or absence of ethnic or communal violence, on the other. To illustrate these links, two interconnected arguments are made. First, interethnic or inter-communal and intra-ethnic or intra-communal networks of civic engagement play very different roles. Because they build bridges and manage tensions across groups, interethnic networks are agents of peace, but if communities are

132

organized only along intra-ethnic lines and the interconnections with other communities are very weak or even non-existent, then, ethnic or communal violence is quite likely. I shall also specify the conditions under which this argument may not hold.

Second, civic networks—both intra-ethnic and interethnic— can also be broken down into two other types: organized and quotidian. This distinction is based on whether civic interaction is formal or not. I call the first *associational forms of engagement* and the second *everyday forms of engagement*. Business associations, professional organizations, reading clubs, film clubs, sports clubs, NGOs, trade unions, and cadre-based political parties are examples of the former. Everyday forms of engagement consist of simple, routine interactions of life, such as whether families from different communities visit each other, eat together regularly, jointly participate in festivals, and allow their children to play together in the neighbourhood. Both forms of engagement, if robust, promote peace; if not, their absence or weakness opens up space for ethnic violence. Of the two, however, the associational forms turn out to be sturdier than the everyday forms, especially when confronted with attempts by politicians to polarize people along ethnic lines. Vigorous associational life, if it cuts across group boundaries, acts as a serious constraint on politicians, even when inter-group polarization is in their political interest. The more the associational networks cut across group boundaries, the harder it is for politicians to polarize communities.

This chapter also briefly considers how interethnic civic organizations developed in India. Much of India's associational civic structure was put in place in the 1920s, a transformative moment during the freedom movement against the British, when a new form of politics emerged under the leadership of Mahatma Gandhi. After 1920, the movement had two aims: political independence from the British and social transformation of India. Gandhi argued that independence would be meaningless unless India's social problems—lack of Hindu–Muslim unity, the abolition of untouchability, self-reliance, women's uplift, tribal uplift, labour welfare, prohibition, and so on—were addressed. The associational structure of India before Gandhi had been minimal, but the Gandhian shift in the national movement laid the foundations of India's associational civic order. In the process, between the 1920s and 1940s, a host of new organizations came into being.

Historical reasoning, therefore, requires that we draw a distinction between proximate and underlying causation. The role of inter-communal civic networks has been crucial for peace at a proximate level. Taking the long view, however, the causal factor was a transformative shift in national politics. Once put in place by the national movement, the civic structures took on a life and logic of their own, shaping the behaviour of politicians in the short-to-medium run.

The first section of this chapter clarifies three key terms whose meanings are not self-evident: ethnicity, ethnic conflict, and civil society. The second section deals with the puzzle that led me to discover the relevance of civil society for ethnic conflict. The third section summarizes how the puzzle was resolved and shows how ethnic conflict and civil society are linked. Empirical evidence in support of the latter is presented in the fourth section. The fifth section considers whether my argument sufficiently distinguished the causes from the consequences. The final section suggests a possible set of conditions under which the basic argument about interethnic and intra-ethnic engagement is unlikely to apply.

Clarifying Concepts and Terms

The terms 'ethnic', 'ethnic conflict', and 'civil society' mean different things to different people. To pre-empt misunderstanding, we need to specify the meaning that we have in mind.

There are two distinct ways in which the term 'ethnic' is

interpreted. In the narrower construal of the term, 'ethnic' groups mean 'racial' or 'linguistic' groups. This is the sense in which the term is widely understood in popular discourse, both in India and elsewhere. For example, when describing politics and conflict based on religious groupings, Indian scholars, bureaucrats, and politicians since the time of the British have used the term 'communal', not 'ethnic', reserving the latter term primarily for linguistically or racially distinct groups.

There is, however, a second, broader definition. As Horowitz argues, all conflicts based on *ascriptive* group identities—race, language, religion, tribe, or caste—can be called ethnic.[1] Under this umbrella usage, ethnic conflicts cover: (1) the Protestant–Catholic conflict in Northern Ireland and the Hindu–Muslim conflict in India; (2) the black–white conflict in the United States and South Africa; (3) the Tamil–Sinhala conflict in Sri Lanka; and (4) the Shia–Sunni troubles in Pakistan. In the narrower construction of the term, (1) is religious; (2) is racial; (3) is linguistic-cum-religious; and (4) is sectarian. In the past, the term 'ethnic' was often reserved for the second and, at best, the third conflicts, but would not be extended to the first and the fourth.

Proponents of the broader usage reject such distinctions, arguing that the form which ethnic conflict takes—religious, linguistic, racial, tribal—does not seem to alter its intensity, duration, or relative intractability. Their emphasis is on the ascriptive and the cultural core of the conflict, and they distinguish it primarily from the largely non-ascriptive and economic core of class conflict. Ethnic conflict may indeed have an economic basis, but that is not its core feature. Irrespective of internal class differentiation, race, language, sect, and religion tend to define the politics of an ethnic group. On the other hand, class conflict tends on the whole to be economic, but if the class into which one is born is also the class in which one is trapped until death—and this is true for large numbers of people—then, class conflict takes on ascriptive overtones. Following

Horowitz, it is now well understood that the latter characteristic—
the interchangeability of ethnicity and class—applies not to ethnic
systems in general but to *ranked* ethnic systems such as America
during the period of slavery; South Africa during apartheid; and
India's caste system. Ranked ethnic systems merge ethnicity and
class; unranked ethnic systems do not.

The larger meaning, one might add, is also increasingly becoming
the standard meaning in the social sciences, even if that is not yet true
of politics and activism. I will use the term 'ethnic' in this broader
sense. In other words, I may distinguish between communal (that
is, religious) and linguistic categories, but I will not differentiate
between 'communal' and 'ethnic'. Ethnicity is simply the set to
which religion, race, language, and sect belong as subsets.

Does 'ethnic conflict', our second term, have a uniquely
acceptable meaning? On the whole, existing literature has failed
to distinguish between ethnic *violence* and ethnic *conflict*. Such
conflation is unhelpful. In any ethnically plural society that allows
free expression of political demands, some ethnic conflict is more
or less inevitable, but it may not necessarily lead to violence.[2] When
there are different ethnic groups that are free to organize, there are
likely to be conflicts over resources, identity, patronage, and policies.

The real issue is whether ethnic conflict is violent or waged
via the polity's institutionalized channels. If ethnic protest takes
an institutionalized form—in parliaments, in assemblies, in
bureaucratic corridors, and as non-violent mobilization on the
streets—it is conflict, not violence. Such institutionalized conflict
must be distinguished from a situation in which protest takes violent
forms; rioting breaks out on the streets; and, in its most extreme
form, civil war ensues or pogroms are initiated against some ethnic
groups with the complicity of state authorities. Given how different
these outcomes are, explanations for institutionalized conflict may
not be the same as those for ethnic riots, on the one hand, and for
pogroms and civil wars, on the other. Ethnic peace should, for

all practical purposes, be conceptualized as an institutionalized channelling and resolution of ethnic demands and conflicts: *as an absence of violence, not as an absence of conflict.* The world would arguably be a happier place if we could eliminate ethnic and national conflicts from our midst, but such a post-ethnic, post-national era does not seem to be in the offing in the near term. Indeed, many postmodern conflicts, even in richer societies, are taking ethnic forms on grounds of authenticity of living styles and distinctiveness of expression.[3]

Though highly popular and much revived in recent years, the concept of civil society also needs to be examined closely. According to conventional notions in the social sciences, 'civil society' refers to that space which (1) exists between the family, on the one hand, and the state, on the other; (2) makes interconnections between individuals or families possible; and (3) is independent of the state. Many, though not all, of the existing definitions also suggest two more requirements: that the civic space be organized in associations that attend to the cultural, social, economic, and political needs of the citizens; and that the associations be modern and voluntaristic, not ascriptive. According to the first requirement, trade unions would be part of civil society, but informal neighbourhood associations would not. Following the second requirement, philately clubs and parent–teacher associations (PTAs) would be civic, but a black church or an association of Jews active on behalf of Israel would not.

Should we agree with the latter two proposals? Can non-associational space also be called civic or part of civil society? Must associations, to constitute part of civil society, be of a 'modern' kind—voluntaristic and cross-cutting—rather than ascriptive and based on ethnic affiliation?

The modernist origins of civil society are originally attributed to Hegel's nineteenth-century theoretical formulations.[4] In recent years, however, it has often been suggested that the revival of a modernist notion of civil society derives from debates in Eastern Europe and the English translation of Habermas's *The Structural Transformation of the Public Sphere.*[5] Because the concept of civil society has been so important to the field of political philosophy, it is mostly political philosophers who have explored it in recent times.[6] In comparison, empirical work has not been as voluminous,[7] though the need for it should be quite clear. Only by a systematic empirical investigation of the associational and non-associational forms of civic life can we determine whether the functions and forms attributed to civil society in normative literature exist as more than simply theoretical propositions.

As an illustration of the modernist bent in the definitions of civil society, consider the theoretical arguments of Ernest Gellner, whose writings on civil society have been plentiful as well as influential. 'Modularity,' argues Gellner, 'makes civil society,' whereas 'segmentalism' defines a traditional society.[8] By modularity, he means the ability to transcend traditional or ascriptive occupations and associations. Given a multipurpose, secular, and modern education and given also the objective availability of plentiful as well as changing professional opportunities in post-traditional times, modern man can move from one occupation to another, one place to another, one association to another. In contrast, traditional man's occupation and place were determined by birth. In traditional society, a man born into a carpenter's family would be a carpenter, whether he liked it or not, and all his kinsmen would be carpenters. He would also generally not be involved in associations; and if he were, the association would most likely be an ascriptive guild of carpenters. An agrarian society, argues Gellner, might be able to avoid the tyranny of the state. That is because the power of the state could not reach all segments of a traditional society, given the decentralized nature of production structure, the low level of communication technology, and the relatively self-sufficient character of each segment. But that does not mean that such a society would be 'civil' for, instead of the 'tyranny of state', it would experience the 'tyranny of cousins'. Civil society, concludes Gellner, is not only modern but also based on strictly voluntary associations between the state and the family, not on ethnic or religious considerations.[9]

Such claims can be empirically challenged. First, a remarkably large number of studies shows that ethnic and religious associations combine ascription and choice. Not all Christians have to be members of a church in a given town, nor do all blacks members of a black church. Moreover, it has also been widely documented that ethnic associations can perform many 'modern' functions such as participating in democratic politics, setting up funds to encourage members of the ethnic group to enter newer professions, and facilitating migration of ethnic kinsmen into modern occupations and modern education.[10]

A similar objection can be raised with respect to the requirement that associations be formal. In much of the developing world, especially in the countryside and small towns, formal associations do not exist. That does not mean, however, that civic interconnections or activities are absent. If what is crucial to the notion of civil society is that families and individuals connect with other families and individuals—beyond their homes—and *talk about matters of public relevance* without the interference of the state, then, it seems far too rigid to insist that this must take place only in 'modern' associations. Whether such an engagement takes place in associations or in the traditional sites of social get-togethers depends on the degree of urbanization and economic development, as well as on the nature of the political system. Cities tend to have formal associations; villages make do with informal sites and meetings. Further, political systems may specify which groups may have access to formal civic spaces and establish organizations, and which may not. Nineteenth-century Europe provided the propertied classes with access to a whole range of political and institutional instruments of interest articulation; trade unions for workers were slower to arrive.

Some of the spirit of these remarks is conveyed in the commentary generated by Habermas's distinction between the 'lifeworld' and the 'system' in *The Structural Transformation of the Public Sphere*. In its original formulation, the distinction indicated a radical rupture between the significance of everyday interaction and that of interaction made possible by institutions and organizations. The latter, according to Habermas, was associated with a modern public sphere. Everyday interaction made life, but organized interaction made history.[11] The new history of popular struggles launched by those not formally admitted to the public sphere in much of nineteenth-century Europe and America— women, peasants, workers, minorities—suggests the limited utility of the original Habermas distinction.[12] Indeed, in his more recent positions, Habermas has all but dropped his earlier, radical distinction.[13] Street-corner activity can now be viewed as a serious civic form if more organized and institutional civic sites are not available—whether generally or to some particular groups.

The point, of course, is not that formal associations do not matter. One of the arguments of this chapter is that they do. But, at least in the social and cultural settings that are different from those of modern-day Europe and North America, if not more generally, the purposes of activity, rather than the forms of organization, should be the critical test of civic life. Tradition is not necessarily equal to a tyranny of cousins, and capitalist modernity does not always make civic interaction possible. At best, such dualities are ideal types or based on normatively preferred visions. Empirically speaking, tradition often permits challenging the cousins when existing norms of reciprocity and ethics are violated.[14] Similarly, even capitalist modernity may be highly unsocial and atomizing, if people in America stay home and watch soap operas on TV, instead of joining PTAs and other civic organizations.[15] Both informal group activities and ascriptive associations should be considered part of civil society so long as they connect individuals, build trust, encourage reciprocity, and facilitate the exchange of views on matters of public concern—economic, political, cultural, and social. That they may have very different consequences for conflict or peace is an entirely different matter. The latter is an argument about what type of civil society is better for governance and peace, not whether civil society per se is endowed with benign possibilities.

Why Civil Society?

The use of civil society as a lens for the study of ethnic conflict is relatively new. Therefore, how it emerged as a cause of peace or violence requires a brief explanation.

A striking empirical regularity marks the phenomenon of ethnic violence. Despite ethnic diversity, some places (regions, nations, towns, villages) manage to remain peaceful, whereas others experience enduring patterns of violence. Similarly, some societies with an impressive record of ethnic peace suddenly explode in ways that surprise the observer and, very often, the scholar as well. Variations across time and space require explanation.

How does one account for such variations? Until recently, the standard research strategy, with some exceptions,[16] had been to seek the commonalities across the many cases of violence. Although this approach will continue to enlighten us, it can give us only the building blocks of a theory, not a full-blown theory of ethnic conflict. The logic underlying this proposition is simple, often misunderstood, and worth restating.[17] Suppose, on the basis of commonalities, we find that (a) interethnic economic rivalry, (b) polarized party politics, and (c) segregated neighbourhoods explain ethnic violence (X). But, can we be sure that our judgements are right? What if (a), (b), and (c) also exist in peaceful cases (Y)? In that case, violence is caused by the intensity of (a), (b), and (c) in X; or, there is an underlying factor or contextual element that makes (a), (b), and (c) conflictual in one case but not in the other; or, there is yet another factor (d) that differentiates peace from violence. It will, however, be a factor that we did not discover precisely because peaceful cases were not studied with the conflictual ones.

The necessity of studying variance leads to another important methodological question: At what level must variance itself be studied? Should the unit of analysis be nations, states, regions, towns, or villages? What methodologists call a large-N analysis can help us identify the spatial and temporal trends in violence and allow us to choose the appropriate level for analysing variance. This study, therefore, considered all reported Hindu–Muslim riots in the country between 1950 and 1995.[18] For purposes of identifying larger trends, two results were crucial.

First, villages constitute a remarkably small portion of communal rioting. Between 1950 and 1995, rural India—where the majority of Indians still live—accounted for a mere 3.6 per cent of deaths in communal violence. Hindu–Muslim violence turns out to be primarily an urban phenomenon. Second, in urban India, too, Hindu–Muslim riots are highly locally concentrated. Eight cities[19] accounted for a hugely disproportionate share of communal violence in the country—nearly 46 per cent of all deaths in Hindu–Muslim violence (Table 5.1, column d). As a group, however, these eight cities represented a mere 18 per cent of India's urban population (and about 5 per cent of the country's total population, both urban and rural). Put otherwise, 82 per cent of the urban population was not 'riot prone'.

Given such high local concentrations in urban India, the large-N analysis clearly establishes town/city as the unit of analysis. India's Hindu–Muslim violence is city-specific, not state-specific, *with state (and national) politics providing the context within which the local mechanisms linked with violence are activated.* To understand the causes of communal violence, we must investigate these local mechanisms.

Following this reasoning, I selected six cities—three from the list

TABLE 5.1: HINDU–MUSLIM RIOTS IN 28 INDIAN CITIES, 1950–95*

Minimum of 15 Deaths in 3 Riots over 2 Five-Year Periods (a)	Minimum of 20 Deaths in 4 Riots over 3 Five-Year Periods (b)	Minimum of 25 Deaths in 5 Riots over 4 Five-Year Periods (c)	Minimum of 50 Deaths in 10 Riots over 5 Five-Year Periods (d)	Total Deaths 1950–95
Bombay	Bombay	Bombay	Bombay	1,137
Ahmedabad	Ahmedabad	Ahmedabad	Ahmedabad	1,119
Aligarh	Aligarh	Aligarh	Aligarh	389
Hyderabad	Hyderabad	Hyderabad	Hyderabad	312
Meerut	Meerut	Meerut	Meerut	265
Jamshedpur	Jamshedpur	Jamshedpur		198
Bhiwandi	Bhiwandi			194
Surat				194
Moradabad	Moradabad			149
Baroda	Baroda	Baroda	Baroda	109
Bhopal	Bhopal	Bhopal		108
Delhi	Delhi	Delhi	Delhi	93
Kanpur	Kanpur	Kanpur		81
Calcutta	Calcutta	Calcutta	Calcutta	63
Jabalpur				59
Bangalore	Bangalore	Bangalore		56
Jalgaon	Jalgaon	Jalgaon		49
Sitamarhi				47
Indore	Indore	Indore		45
Varanasi	Varanasi	Varanasi		42
Allahabad	Allahabad	Allahabad		37
Nagpur	Nagpur	Nagpur		37
Jaipur	Jaipur			32

Table 5.1 (*continued*)

Minimum of 15 Deaths in 3 Riots over 2 Five-Year Periods (a)	Minimum of 20 Deaths in 4 Riots over 3 Five-Year Periods (b)	Minimum of 25 Deaths in 5 Riots over 4 Five-Year Periods (c)	Minimum of 50 Deaths in 10 Riots over 5 Five-Year Periods (d)	Total Deaths 1950–95
Aurangabad	Aurangabad	Aurangabad		30
Srinagar	Srinagar	Srinagar		30
Ranchi				29
Malegaon	Malegaon			23
Godhra				18

Notes: * The total number of deaths from riots for all of India, 1950–95 = 7,173, of which 3.57 per cent of deaths took place in rural India.
  (a) The total number of deaths from riots in these cities = 4,706. This is approximately 66 per cent of deaths from riots throughout India and 69 per cent of all deaths in urban riots during these periods.
  (b) The total number of deaths from riots in these cities = 4,359. This is about 61 per cent of deaths from riots throughout India and 64 per cent of all deaths in urban riots during these periods.
  (c) The total number of deaths from riots in these cities = 3,887. This is about 54 per cent of deaths from riots throughout India and 58 per cent of all deaths in urban riots during these periods.
  (d) The total number of deaths from riots in these cities = 3,263. This is 45.5 per cent of deaths from riots throughout India and 49 per cent of all deaths in urban riots during these periods.

of eight riot-prone cities and three peaceful ones—and arranged them in three pairs. Thus, each pair consisted of one city where communal violence was endemic and one city where it was rare or entirely absent. To ensure against comparing apples and oranges, roughly similar Hindu–Muslim percentages in the city populations constituted the minimum control in each pair. The first pair—Aligarh and Calicut—was based on population percentages only. The second pair—Hyderabad and Lucknow—added two controls to population percentages, one of previous Muslim rule and the other of reasonable cultural similarities. The third pair—Ahmedabad and Surat—was the most tightly controlled. The first two pairs came from the North and the South. The third came from the state of Gujarat, sharing the same history, language, and culture but not endemic communal violence.

Why was similarity in demographic proportions chosen as the minimum control in each pair? Both in India's popular political discourse and in theories about Muslim political behaviour, the size of the community is considered to be highly significant. Many politicians—especially those belonging to the Hindu nationalist Bharatiya Janata Party (BJP)—have argued that the demographic distribution of Muslims makes them critical to the electoral outcomes. Muslims constitute more than 20 per cent of the electorate in 197 out of a total of 545 parliamentary constituencies in India. In a first-past-the-post system, where 30 per cent of the vote is often enough to win a seat in multiparty contests, these percentages make the Muslims electorally highly significant.[20] The higher the number of Muslims in a given constituency, argue BJP politicians, the greater the inclination of mainstream political parties to pander to their sectional/communal demands and, therefore, the lower the incentive for Muslims to build bridges to Hindus. Thus, according to this argument, appeasement of Muslims, based on their large numbers in a democracy, is the cause of communal conflict and violence in India.[21]

That Muslim demography has political consequences is, however, not an argument confined to the Hindu nationalist BJP. Several Muslim politicians also make a demographic claim, but with the causation reversed. The higher the number of Muslims in a city or town, they argue, the greater the political threat felt by the leaders of the Hindu community, who react with hostility to legitimate Muslim anxieties about politics and identity. An unjustified, even self-serving, opposition on the part of Hindu leaders, they argue, is the source of communal hostilities.[22] Both extremes of the political spectrum thus rely heavily on demography for their explanations.

These popular arguments are shared by social scientists as well, although their reasoning is different. It has been argued, for example, that when a city/constituency has a Muslim majority or plurality, Muslims typically prefer Muslims-only confessional parties to centrist inter-communal parties.[23] Muslims support centrist parties when their share of the population/electorate is small in a town/ constituency. Smaller numbers make it rational to seek the security of a large and powerful mainstream party.

Can one find cases—cities or constituencies—where similar demographic distributions lead to very different kinds of outcomes? As described above, I compared three pairs of cities where a rough similarity in demographic proportions coexists with variance in political outcomes—peace or violence.

Resolving the Puzzle: The Role of Civil Society

The pre-existing local networks of civic engagement between the two communities stand out as the single most important proximate explanation for the difference between peace and violence. Where such networks of engagement exist, tensions and conflicts are regulated and managed; where they are missing, communal identities lead to endemic and ghastly violence. As already stated, these networks can in turn be broken down into two parts: associational forms of engagement and everyday forms of engagement. Both forms of engagement, if inter-communal, promote peace, but the capacity of the associational forms to withstand national-level 'exogenous shocks'—such as India's partition in 1947 or the demolition of the Baburi Mosque in December 1992 in the presence of more than 300,000 Hindu militants—is substantially higher.

What are the mechanisms that link civic networks and ethnic

conflict? And why is associational engagement a sturdier bulwark of peace than everyday engagement?

One can identify two mechanisms that connect civil society and ethnic conflict. First, by promoting communication between members of different religious communities, civic networks often make neighbourhood-level peace possible. Routine prior engagement allows people to come together and form organizations in times of tension. Such organizations, though only temporary, turn out to be highly significant. Called peace committees and consisting of members of both communities, they police neighbourhoods, kill rumours, provide information to the local administration, and facilitate communication between communities in times of tension. Such neighbourhood organizations are difficult to form in cities where everyday interaction does not cross religious lines, or where Hindus and Muslims live in highly segregated neighbourhoods. Sustained prior interaction or cordiality facilitates the emergence of appropriate crisis-managing organizations.

The second mechanism also allows us to sort out why associational forms of engagement are sturdier than everyday forms in dealing with ethnic tensions. If vibrant organizations serving the economic, cultural, and social needs of the two communities exist, the support for communal peace tends not only to be strong but also to be more solidly expressed. Everyday forms of engagement may make associational forms possible, but associations can often serve interests that are not the object of quotidian interactions. Inter-communal business organizations survive because they connect the business interests of many Hindus with those of Muslims, not because of neighbourhood warmth between Hindu and Muslim families. Though valuable in itself, the latter does not necessarily constitute the bedrock for strong civic organizations.

That this is so, at one level, is a profound paradox. After all, we know that at the village level in India, everyday face-to-face engagement is the norm, and formal associations are few and far between.[24] Yet, rural India, which was home to over 80 per cent of India's population in the early 1950s and still contains two-thirds of the country's population, has not been the primary site of communal violence. By contrast, even though associational life flourishes in cities, urban India—containing about one-third of India's population today and less than 20 per cent in the early 1950s—accounts for the overwhelming majority of deaths in communal violence between 1950 and 1995.

Why should this be so? Figure 5.1 presents a formal resolution of the paradox. It depicts diagrammatically the relationship between size and civic links, holding the level of civic engagement constant. Moving from circle 1 to 4, we can see why associational engagement is necessary in cities if we answer the following question: How many links will have to be made if we wish to connect each individual with every other individual as we move from villages to cities? Let

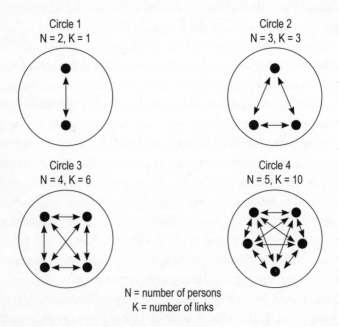

N = number of persons
K = number of links

FIGURE 5.1: EVERYDAY ENGAGEMENT IN VILLAGES AND CITIES

N represent the number of persons in a village or city, and K the number of links that must be made if everybody is to be connected with everyone else.

The four circles in the diagram increase the size of the local setting. In circle 1—our diagrammatic representation for a small village—there are only two individuals ($N = 2$); to connect them, we need only one link ($K = 1$). In circle 2, there are three individuals ($N = 3$); we need at least three links ($K = 3$) to connect them all. This circle can represent a small town. Circle 3, in which we have four individuals ($N = 4$), can be called a city. To connect one with all, we need six links ($K = 6$). In circle 4—our diagrammatic substitute for a metropolis—there are five individuals ($N = 5$), and at least ten links ($K = 10$) are needed to connect each of them to everybody else. Thus, *for a given level of civic density* (*in this case, each person connected to everyone else*), K rises faster than N.

This whole relationship can be written as: $K = N (N - 1)/2$.

This formula essentially means that, as we move from villages to towns and from towns to cities, we need many more links to connect people than the increase in population. Cities naturally tend to be less interconnected; some degree of anonymity is inevitable.

We can now understand what associations do, when village-like intimacy is no longer possible. Since each association can represent a lot of people, organizations end up reducing N in cities and making a lower K viable. That is why everyday engagement may be effective in villages, with fewer Ns, but not in cities, with more Ns. Therefore, to maintain the same level of civic engagement in cities as in villages, one needs associations, rather than informal and everyday interaction.

The explanation above is deductive. It explains why everyday engagement has very different meanings in rural and urban settings, but it still does not tell us how exactly associations prevent or mitigate communal conflict when they do. That is an empirical question, to which we now turn.

Organized civic networks, when inter-communal, not only do a better job of withstanding the exogenous communal shocks—like partitions, civil wars, and desecration of holy places—but they also constrain local politicians in their strategic behaviour. Politicians who seek to polarize Hindus and Muslims for the sake of electoral advantage can tear at the fabric of everyday engagement through the organized might of criminals and gangs. All violent cities in the project showed evidence of a nexus of politicians and criminals.[25] Organized gangs readily disturbed neighbourhood peace, often causing migration from communally heterogeneous to communally homogeneous neighbourhoods, as people moved away in search of physical safety. Without the involvement of organized gangs, large-scale rioting and tens and hundreds of killings are most unlikely, and without the protection afforded by politicians, such criminals could not escape the clutches of law. Brass has rightly called this arrangement an institutionalized riot system.[26] In peaceful cities, however, an institutionalized peace system exists. Countervailing forces are created when organizations, such as trade unions, associations of businessmen, traders, teachers, doctors, and lawyers, and at least some cadre-based political parties[27] (different from the ones that have an interest in communal polarization) are communally integrated. Organizations that would lose from a communal split fight for their turf, alerting not only their members but also the public at large to the dangers of communal violence. Local administrations are far more effective in such circumstances. Civic organizations, for all practical purposes, become the ears and arms of the administration. *A synergy emerges between the local wings of the state and local civic organizations, making it easier to police the emerging situation and preventing it from degenerating into riots and killings.* Unlike violent cities, where rumours and skirmishes— often strategically planted and spread—quickly escalate into riots, the relationships of synergy in peaceful cities nip rumours, small clashes, and tensions in the bud. In the end, polarizing politicians either do not succeed or eventually give up trying to provoke and engineer communal violence. Figure 5.2 represents the argument diagrammatically.

This argument, it should be clarified, is probabilistic, not lawlike. It indicates the odds but should not be taken to mean that there can be no exceptions to the generalization. Indeed, lawlike generalizations about ethnic violence may not be possible at all. Upsetting the probabilities, for example, a state which is bent on inciting ethnic pogroms and deploying its police or the armed forces may succeed in creating a veritable ethnic hell. My argument, therefore, would be more applicable to *riots* than to *pogroms* or *civil wars*. A theory of civil wars or pogroms would have to be analytically distinguished from one that deals with riots.

Indeed, perhaps the best way to understand the relationship between civic life and violence is via a geological analogy. If the civic edifice is interethnic and associational, there is a good chance it can absorb ethnic earthquakes that register quite high on the Richter scale (a partition; desecration of a holy place); if it is interethnic and quotidian, earthquakes of smaller intensity can bring the edifice

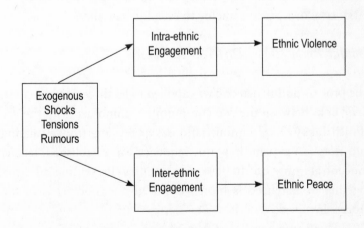

FIGURE 5.2: CIVIC LIFE AND ETHNIC CONFLICT

down (defeat of an ethnic political party in elections; police brutality in a particular city). But if engagement is only intra-ethnic, not interethnic, small tremors (unconfirmed rumours; victories and defeats in sports) can unleash torrents of violence. A multi-ethnic society with few connections across ethnic boundaries can be very vulnerable to ethnic disorders and violence.

How Civil Society Matters

To establish causality, the technique of process tracing was applied to each pair of cities. The technique of process tracing works back from the outcome—peace or violence—step by step, looking to identify what led to what.[28] In each pair, we looked for similar stimuli that led to different outcomes in the two cities and then identified the mechanisms by which the same trigger produced divergent outcomes. Civil society emerged as a causal factor from such comparisons. If we had studied only violent cities, where interconnections between Hindus and Muslims were minimal or absent in the first place, we would not have discovered what inter-communal civic links can do. A controlled comparison based on variance allows process tracing to establish causality.

Similar Provocations, Different Responses

The process outlined above was applied to all three pairs of cities. Civic links between the two communities, combined with the use of such links by local administrations, kept tensions from escalating into riots. To explain how this sequence was established, let me concentrate only on the first pair of cities. Presenting all cities together in a stylized fashion will not give a good sense of the process involved.

The first pair consists of Aligarh and Calicut. The former is a riot-prone city in Uttar Pradesh (UP) and the latter, a peaceful city in the state of Kerala. Calicut has not had a single riot in this century; Aligarh figures in the list of the eight most riot-prone cities (Table 5.1, column d). Both cities are roughly 36–38 per cent Muslim, with the remaining population overwhelmingly Hindu.[29] Between 1989 and 1992, when the Hindu nationalist agitation to destroy the Baburi Mosque in Ayodhya (hereafter Ayodhya agitation) led to unprecedented violence in much of India, both cities experienced rumours, tensions, and small clashes. But the final outcomes were very different. In Calicut, the local administration was able to maintain law and order. Unfounded rumours circulated in the city that pigs had been thrown into mosques. Similarly, there were rumours that Muslims had attacked the famous Guruvayur Temple, a site greatly venerated by Hindus in the state. Such rumours often led to riots in several cities in India and frequently did so in Aligarh. In Calicut, the peace committees and the press helped the administration quash the rumours. The storm of the Ayodhya agitation, the biggest since India's partition and one that left hundreds dead in several cities, skirted Calicut and left it unharmed.

In contrast, the city of Aligarh, blinded by a Hindu nationalist fervour during the Ayodhya agitation, was plunged into horrendous violence. Unlike Calicut's newspapers, which neutralized rumours after investigating them, Aligarh's local newspapers printed inflammatory falsehoods. Two of the largest-circulation Hindi newspapers wrote in lurid detail of Muslim nurses, doctors, and staff of the Aligarh Muslim University (AMU) hospital killing Hindu patients in cold blood.[30] Some Hindus were indeed killed outside the university campus,[31] but nobody was murdered in the AMU hospital.[32] The rumours were believed, however. And gangs of Hindu criminals went on a killing spree. Some of them stopped a train just outside the city, dragged Muslims out, and brutally murdered them. The press under-reported their acts of killing. Although these newspapers were later reprimanded for unprofessional behaviour by the Press Council, the damage had already been done. Gruesome violence rocked the city for several days, leading to nearly seventy deaths and many more injuries.

As in the past, Aligarh's local mechanisms of peace were remarkably inadequate for the task of dealing with an exogenous shock—in this case, the Ayodhya agitation. The criminals who engaged in killings could not be brought to justice. Not only were they protected by politicians, but they also had remarkable journalistic connections—Muslim criminals with the Urdu press, and Hindu thugs with the Hindi press. Effective peace committees could not be formed at the city level in Aligarh, for it was difficult even to get the Hindu nationalists and the Muslim politicians together. Rumours were often started and then exploited by political organizations. Instead of investigating rumours, the press merely printed them with abandon.

Contrast the situation with that in Calicut. Two points were common to all the accounts given by the administrators of Calicut between 1989 and 1992 (as well as those posted there since the mid-1980s) about how the peace was kept. First, politicians of all parties helped establish peace in the city, instead of polarizing communities, as in Aligarh. Second, city-level peace committees were critical to the management of tensions.[33] They provided information to the administration; they became a forum at which all were welcome to speak out and express their anger; they gave a sense of participation to local actors; and they provided links all the way down to the neighbourhood level where, in addition, citizens formed smaller peace committees.

By contrast, those peace committees that did emerge from below in Aligarh often tended to be intra-religious, not inter-religious. They were organized at the neighbourhood level to protect co-religionists from a possible attack by other communities, and did not facilitate communication with those other communities. Rather, the peace committees simply increased the perception of risk and hardened the attitudes of those who participated in them. The members of these committees took turns policing their community. The process resulted in a very different kind of consciousness from what there would have been if the committees had been inter-religious since, by definition, intra-religious committees were based not on inter-religious trust but rather on a lack of such trust. Moving within one's own community, hearing rumours that no one could verify or disprove, staying up in the middle of the night for weeks together, collecting firearms and other small weapons to ensure that retaliation would be swift in the event of an attack—the activities of intra-religious committees fuelled and reflected a communal consciousness, not the consciousness that builds bridges.

The Variety of Civic Networks

Why did the two cities respond so differently? Why did politicians of all kinds cooperate in Calicut but not in Aligarh? Most of all, why did even those politicians of Calicut who stood to benefit from Hindu–Muslim polarization—such as the Hindu nationalists of the BJP—avoid working to inflame communal passions and, instead, cooperated in peacemaking efforts? The BJP leader in Calicut admitted that Hindu–Muslim polarization would be in his party's political interest because it would lead larger numbers of Hindus to vote for the BJP. But he was also convinced that it would not be wise for his party to systematically initiate the polarizing process, because it might then be blamed for undermining the local peace. If, however, the radical Islamic groups were to launch a violent campaign, it would doubtless benefit the party, and the BJP would be happy to respond in kind.[34]

To understand why the BJP was unwilling to engage in polarizing activities in Calicut, one needs to survey the texture of civic life there. Hindu–Muslim civic integration runs so deep in Calicut (and, many would argue, in the state as a whole) that polarization is a highly risky strategy. If a party can be clearly linked to activities destroying the decades-long Hindu–Muslim peace, there is a good chance it will be punished by the electorate. The reverse is true in Aligarh, where the utter weakness of cross-cutting links opens up space for communal politicians to play havoc.

Consider first the quotidian forms of citizen engagement in the two cities. According to our survey, nearly 83 per cent of Hindus and Muslims in Calicut often ate together in social settings; only 54 per cent in Aligarh did.[35] About 90 per cent of Hindu and Muslim families in Calicut reported that their children played together; in Aligarh, a mere 42 per cent reported that to be the case. Close to 84 per cent of Hindus and Muslims in the Calicut survey visited each other; in Aligarh, only 60 per cent did, and not often at that. The Hindus and Muslims of Calicut simply socialize more often and enjoy it much of the time, whereas Hindu–Muslim interactions in Aligarh are comparatively thin. Aligarh's statistics on all of these interactions would have been much lower if we had concentrated only on the violent neighbourhoods. We saw from the few peaceful but integrated neighbourhoods that politics had not destroyed civic interaction in all parts of the town, since some of the neighbourhoods had managed to keep their distance from the hegemonic political trends elsewhere in the town. It should be noted, however, that an overwhelming proportion of respondents over the age of sixty reported that their neighbourhoods in Aligarh had been much more integrated in the 1930s and 1940s.[36] But in the 1930s, as politicians started using thugs to spread violence, migration to communally homogeneous localities began. Neighbourhood-level intimacy was simply unable to withstand the depredations of the emerging politician–criminal nexus.

What about the associational forms of engagement? Much like Tocqueville's New England, Calicut is a place of 'joiners'. Associations of all kinds—business, labour, professional, social, theatre, film, sports, art, reading—abound. From the ubiquitous traders' associations, to the Lions and Rotary Clubs found in almost all towns in India, to the otherwise-rare reading clubs, the head-loaders' (porters) association, the rickshaw-pullers' association, and even something like an art-lovers' association—citizens of Calicut excel in joining clubs and associations. Religion-based organizations also exist, as they do in Aligarh; what is distinctive is the extent of inter-religious interaction in non-denominational organizations.[37]

Consider the economic life of Calicut, which is based primarily on merchandise trade. The city, with a population of about 700,000 in 1995, was dominated by merchants and traders.[38] About 100,000 people depended partially or wholly on trade, and estimates indicated that the city had between 10,000 and 12,000 traders.[39] It was a rare trader who did not join a trade association. These associations—ranging from organizations of traders who deal in food/grains to those who deal in bullion—were, in turn, members of the Federation of Traders Associations (Kerala Vyapari Vyavasayi Ekopana Samithi).

In 1995, as many as eleven out of twenty-six trade associations registered with the federation had Hindu, Muslim, (and Christian) office holders: if the president of the association was from one community, the general secretary was from one of the others.[40] These associations refuse to align with any particular political parties in electoral contests: 'We don't want to enter politics because our unity will be broken. We have debates in our association, so, conflicts, if any, get resolved.' Moreover, the depth of engagement was such that many transactions were concluded without any formal contracts. 'Our relationships with Muslim businessmen are entirely based on trust. Payments as large as Rs 10 to 15 lakhs (equal to \$30,000–\$35,000 in 1995–96) sometimes fall due. We send bills, but there are no promissory notes valid in the courts of law. Payments come in thirty days. We work through brokers. There is no breach of trust.'[41]

Aligarh, too, has a traders' association (Vyapar Mandal). In the late 1980s it had about 6,000 members. In the 1970s it had even acquired a fair number of Muslim members, who emerged on the business map after the Gulf migration. The association, however, began to engage in infighting over whether it should support and work for a political party, the argument being that supporting a party favourable to traders would benefit all of them. In the 1980s, the association finally split into two bodies: a 'secular' organization and a 'non-secular' one, with the non-secular faction joining the BJP and the Muslims turning to the 'secular' faction.[42]

Unlike trade-based Calicut, Aligarh had a significant industrial sector and was among the largest producers of locks in India. The lock manufacturing was mostly on a small scale. Moreover, different units specialized in different parts of the manufacturing process. Yet Aligarh had not developed an economic symbiosis between Hindus and Muslims.

It was impossible to estimate the number of people working in Aligarh's lock industry, as no surveys had been conducted.[43] However, we know from ethnographic work that the workers came from both Muslim and Hindu communities, as did the firm owners. We also know that there was virtually no inter-communal dependence. The informal credit market—normally dominated by Hindu lenders (*mahajan*)—was the only Hindu-run economic activity on which some Muslim manufacturers traditionally used to depend. Over the last few decades, rotating credit societies have emerged.[44] But these are intra-Muslim societies that build trust within communities, not across them.[45]

If the businessmen are not integrated, then, what about the workers? Since they numerically constitute a larger proportion of the city than the businessmen, inter-religious links formed in trade unions could, in principle, more than make up for an absence of such links among the businessmen. But, unlike Calicut, trade unions hardly existed in Aligarh. The decrepit offices of the local branches of national trade unions, with no staff and little data, greet researchers who study labour activities. By contrast, trade unions thrive in Calicut. The largest unions are linked to two major national trade-union federations: the Centre of Indian Trade Unions (CITU), which is associated with the Communist Party (Marxist), and the Indian National Trade Union Congress (INTUC), whose political patron is the Congress Party.[46] Both these unions are inter-communal. Calicut does have a political party of the Muslims—the Muslim League—which regularly wins general elections. It also sponsors a trade union, the Swatantra Thozhilali Union (STU). The STU, however, is neither as large as the local units of CITU or INTUC, nor as vibrant. It is the weakest and smallest of the three. Muslim workers by and large voted in assembly elections for the Muslim League, but they tended typically to join INTUC or CITU for protection of their labour rights. The Marxist and atheistic character of CITU did not stop them from joining CITU's unions, if they thought that CITU would do a better job of fighting for their rights and wages. In the process, they came in contact with Hindu workers, inter-communal links were formed, and a Hindu–Muslim division of the workforce did not take place.

A most unlikely site for unionization—the 'head-loaders' or porters—is worth mentioning, for it shows the associational abilities and success of Calicut workers. Distributed over hundreds and thousands of shops and small business units, porters in Indian bazaars are rarely unionized. But they are in Calicut (and in Kerala). In 1995, there were nearly 10,000 head-loaders in Calicut—about 60 per cent Hindu and 40 per cent Muslim. Most were part of INTUC and CITU trade unions. There are head-loaders in the bazaars in Aligarh but they have no associations.

A final and highly distinctive aspect of associational life in Calicut concerns its social and educational activities. The city has an array of film clubs, popular theatre, and science societies. There is nothing unusual about film clubs—they are popular throughout South India. But societies which are interested in bringing theatre and science to the masses are rather uncommon. Even more uncommon are the reading clubs. The literacy rate in Kerala today is the highest in India. 'Reading rooms', a unique Kerala institution, accompanied Kerala's remarkable rise in literacy and formed deep social networks between the 1930s and 1950s. Young people from most communities would get together several times a week to read newspapers and cultural and political books. Menon tells the fascinating story of the birth of reading clubs:

> The rise in literacy found expression in the numbers of reading rooms that were established both in the countryside and in the towns. . . . One of the novelties in the organization of reading rooms was the [communitarian] drinking of tea, as one person read the newspapers and the others listened. . . . The importance of tea and coffee lay in the fact that they were recently introduced beverages. . . . Tea shops and reading rooms all over Malabar provided [a] common place for people to meet and to drink together regardless of caste [and community].[47]

The cumulative outcome of the reading-room movement is noteworthy. In our Calicut sample, as many as 95 per cent of Hindus and Muslims reported reading newspapers—a statistic that is likely to be even higher than that in most cities of the richer countries of the world. Calicut in 1995, with a population of over 700,000, had twenty newspapers and magazines.[48] By contrast, while most Hindus in the Aligarh sample read newspapers, less than 30 per cent of Muslims did so. Information often travelled in the Muslim community by word of mouth. As links with the Hindu community were minimal, it took only a few people to spread nasty rumours and make them stick.

To sum up, the civic lives of the two cities were worlds apart. So many Muslims and Hindus were interlocked in associational and neighbourhood relationships in Calicut that peace committees during periods of tension were simply an extension of the pre-existing local networks of engagement.[49] A considerable reservoir of social trust was formed out of the associational and everyday interactions between Muslims and Hindus. Routine familiarity facilitated communication between the two communities; rumours were squelched through better communication; and all this helped the local administration keep peace. In Aligarh, however, the average Hindu and Muslim did not meet in those civic settings—economic, social, educational—where mutual trust could be forged. Lacking the support of such networks, even competent police and civil administrators looked on helplessly as riots unfolded.

The other pairs of cities in the project experienced similar processes. The different outcomes, however, resided neither in the absence of religious identities nor in the presence of tensions, provocative rumours, and small clashes. Decisive, rather, was the presence of the inter-communal networks of engagement. Intra-communal networks, by contrast, did not contain, or stop, violence.

Cause or Consequence?

Before we accept the argument about civic engagement, two more questions must be explored. First, how can one be sure that the causation did not flow in the other direction? Did communal violence destroy the Hindu–Muslim civic networks in riot-prone towns, or did the presence of such networks prevent violence from occurring? Have causes and consequences been mixed up here? Second, process tracing can at best establish short-run causality. Are long-term causes different from short-term causes? Are there historical forces that explain the vitality or absence of civic networks?

The city of Surat, paired with Ahmedabad, helps us establish the short-run primacy of civic networks. In Surat (Gujarat) a nasty riot occurred after the destruction of the Ayodhya mosque, the first such riot in nearly seventy years. An overwhelming proportion of violence, however, was confined to the slums; all 192 deaths took place in the shanty towns. The old city, by contrast, witnessed some arson and looting but no deaths. Subjected to the same stimuli, the pre-existing social networks accounted for the variance within the city.

Surat has experienced an industrial boom since the 1970s, becoming the small-industry capital of India. Among cities of more than 1,000,000 people, Surat registered one of the highest population growth rates after 1980. Migrants from within and outside the state poured into the city and settled in the shanty towns. Working in small industrial units and unprotected by the labour laws of the Factory Act, most of these migrants worked exceptionally long hours, returning to the slums and shanty towns only to sleep and eat. There were few institutionalized settings for building civic ties.

When the mosque came down in Ayodhya in December 1992, the slums were the site of awful brutality and violence. In the old city, however, peace committees were quickly formed. The business associations of Surat, whose members live primarily in the old city, were integrated. These Hindus and Muslims, who had lived side by side for years and had participated in the old city's business and social life, were able to come together to lower tensions. They set up neighbourhood watch committees and deployed their own resources and organizations in checking rumours and communicating with the administration. As a result, the local administration was more effective in the old city than in the industrial shanty towns, where civic networks were entirely missing and criminals were free to commit acts of savagery and violence.

What about the long-run causation? Have the Hindu–Muslim civic networks always been robust in peaceful towns, directing their Hindu–Muslim politics and making it possible for them to withstand exogenous shocks? Historical research conducted in the cities demonstrates that civic networks—quotidian and associational—determined the outcome in the short-to-medium run but, in the long run, inter-communal networks were politically constructed. The 1920s were a transformative moment in the nation's politics because it was then that mass politics emerged in India under the leadership of Mahatma Gandhi. Politics before Gandhi had been highly élitist. The Congress party was a lawyers' club that made its constitutional arguments for more rights with the British in the Queen's English.

Gandhi seized control of the movement in 1920 and revolutionized it by arguing that the British were unlikely to give independence to India until the Indian masses were involved in the national movement. Gandhi talked of two intertwined battles of independence (*swaraj*)—one against an external adversary, the colonial power, and the other against an internal enemy, India's social evils. He was interested not only in political independence from the British but also in the social transformation of India, arguing that the former could not be meaningful without the latter. He first concentrated on some key social objectives: Hindu–Muslim unity; abolition of untouchability; *swadeshi* (buy Indian, wear Indian, think Indian). To these were later added other projects of social transformation: women's welfare; tribal welfare; labour welfare; prohibition, and so on. In the process, his followers created a large number of organizations between the 1920s and 1940s. Before Gandhi, the civic structure of India had been quotidian. After the Gandhian moment in the national movement, it became associational.

The biggest organization, of course, was the Congress party, which led the movement politically and developed cadres all over India during the 1920s.[50] The argument about social reconstruction also created a second set of organizations, the voluntary agencies. The Congress party was primarily political, and organizations that dealt with education, women's issues, the welfare of the tribals and the 'untouchables', self-reliance, and the homespun movement were immediately concerned with their social projects.

The civic order that emerged was not identical in different places. The movement had greater success in putting together

Hindu–Muslim unity in towns where a Hindu–Muslim cleavage had not already emerged in local politics. India's towns had been having elections for local governments since the 1880s. If local politics emphasized some other cleavages—for example, caste cleavage among the Hindus or the Shia–Sunni division among the Muslims—then, the Congress party and Gandhian social workers found it easier to bring Hindus and Muslims together in the local civic life. If, however, Hindu–Muslim differences were the dominant axis of local politics, the national movement found it harder to build integrated organizations. Though originally a child of politics, these organizations, depending on how integrated or communal they were, began to create very different pressures in politics. To sum up, the role of inter-communal civic networks has been crucial for peace at a proximate level. In a historical sense, however, a space for them was created by forms of mass politics that emerged in India in the 1920s.

This reasoning suggests a twofold conclusion. If a historical perspective is applied, then, it turns out that a transformative ideological shift in national politics, seeking to address social evils and to reorient the fight for independence, was the cause of a systematic organizational effort. In the short-to-medium run, however, the organizational civic order, instituted by the national movement, began to exercise an influence over politics. Given the thrust of the national movement, the constraint on politics was especially serious if building or destroying bridges between Hindus and Muslims was the object of politicians' strategies.

Concluding Observations

Are the conclusions of this chapter India-specific, or have they resonance elsewhere? Two sets of concluding observations—one on civil society and another on ethnic conflict—are in order.

Putnam has used the term 'social capital' for civic networks.[51]

While civic engagement in Putnam's work rightly includes both formal and informal interactions between individuals and families, the difference between the two forms should also be noted. For ethnic peace, everyday engagement between ethnic groups may be better than no interaction at all, but it is also qualitatively different from the more formal, organized engagement. Everyday interethnic engagement may be enough to maintain peace on a small scale (villages or small towns), but it is no substitute for interethnic associations in larger settings (cities and metropolises). Size reduces the efficacy of informal interactions, privileging formal associations.

My findings also have implications for the literature on ethnic conflict. Although disaggregated statistics on local or regional dispersions of ethnic violence have not been systematically collected for many countries, the data that we do have—for example, for Indonesia, the United States or Northern Ireland[52]—show roughly the same larger pattern that exists in India. On the whole, ethnic violence tends to be highly concentrated locally or regionally, not spread evenly geographically across the country. A countrywide breakdown of ethnic relations—a characteristic of civil wars—is rare: we tend to form exaggerated impressions of ethnic violence, partly because violence, not the quiet continuation of routine life, is what attracts the attention of the media. It is more common to have pockets of violence coexisting with large stretches of peace.

If we systematically investigate the links between civil society and ethnic conflict, there is a good chance of getting a good theory that can explain these local or regional variations. The reason for this intuition is quite simple. Though networks of communities can be built nationally, internationally, and, in this electronic era, also 'virtually', the fact remains that most people experience civic or community life locally. Business associations or trade unions may well be confederated across local units, and business or labour leaders may also have national arenas of operation but, most of the time, most businessmen and workers who are members of such organizations experience associational life locally. The type and depth of these local networks—whether they bring ethnic communities together or pull them apart; whether the interactions between communities are associational or informal—are the variables that have the potential for explaining the observable patterns of ethnic violence and peace.

Darby, for example, studied three local communities in Greater Belfast—Kileen/Banduff, the Upper Ashbourne Estates, and Dunville.[53] All three communities had mixed populations, but the first two saw a lot of violence after the late 1960s, whereas the third remained quiet. Darby found that churches, schools, and political parties were segregated in all three communities, but Dunville had some distinctive features not shared by the other two. In contrast to the segregated voluntary groups in the first two communities, Dunville had mixed Rotary and Lions Clubs, soccer clubs, and bowling clubs, as well as clubs for cricket, athletics, boxing, field hockey, swimming, table tennis, and golf. There was also a vigorous and mixed single-parents club. These results are quite consistent with my Indian findings.

Studies of racial violence in the US are also of interest, but in a different and potentially highly challenging way. There is no good theory emerging from these studies that can explain the city-level variance in racial violence in the 1960s. Why were Newark (New Jersey), Detroit (Michigan), Los Angeles (California)—which, together, accounted for a very large proportion of the deaths in the 1960s riots—so violent? And why did Southern cities, though politically engaged, not have riots?[54] The studies show that economic inequalities between African Americans and white Americans neither explained the *timing* nor the *location* of riots, but no firm alternative explanations have been provided. Lieberson and Silverman's work comes reasonably close to what I am arguing for India: they emphasize local integration, especially African American participation in the local government structures.[55] But, to my knowledge, no scholar has investigated whether civic associations—labour unions, churches, PTAs, and so on—were on the whole racially better integrated in the peaceful cities.[56]

If they were not—and here lies the innovative potential of American race relations in a comparative sense—we might need an initial distinction in our theory between (1) multi-ethnic societies that have a history of segregated civic sites (unions, churches, schools, business associations, and so on)—for example, the United States and South Africa; and (2) multi-ethnic societies where ethnic groups have led an intermixed civic life—for instance, India and Indonesia. Interracial or inter-communal civic engagement may be a key vehicle of peace in the latter, but, given the relative absence of common black–white civic sites in countries like the United States, there may not have been any space historically for interracial associational engagement, leading to puzzles about the precise nature of mechanisms that led to peace in a different historical and social setting.

If we think further about the distinction above, it may actually be more accurate to say that *groups,* not *societies* as a whole, have a history of segregation. In India, where political parties, unions, business associations, film clubs, and voluntary agencies are by and large ethnically quite mixed, segregation has marked relations between the scheduled castes—who were 'untouchable' for centuries—and the 'upper castes'. Historically, there have been no civic or associational sites where the upper castes and the former untouchables could come together.[57] Similarly, Protestants, Catholics, and Jews could eventually find common civic sites in the US, but blacks and whites on the whole could not.[58]

'Self-policing', a mechanism of peace proposed by Fearon and Laitin, may well be relevant to such segregated settings.[59] In the terminology developed in this chapter, it means intra-ethnic, or intra-communal, policing. If exercised by elders, by an ethnic association, or by civic organizations, such as black churches, intra-ethnic policing may lead to the same result as interethnic engagement does. Cross-country research must take such alternative possibilities seriously. Much remains to be learnt.[60]

6

How Has Indian Federalism Done?

Traditional scholarship on federalism has focused on either fiscal or constitutional matters. The literature on fiscal federalism has revolved around resource transfers from the Centre to the states: its logic, equity and quantum. Constitutional scholarship basically has laid out the division of powers between the central and state governments, and debated whether India was a 'centralized federation', a 'quasi federation', a system more unitary than federal, etc.

While not denying that the question of resource transfers or constitutional division of powers is important, this chapter departs from both of these approaches and focuses primarily on the *politics* of Indian federalism. This is so for some obvious reasons. The pattern of resource transfers is embedded in the political currents of the time. So is the question of how to interpret and, more importantly, apply the various constitutional clauses.

These claims can be easily demonstrated. Everyone, for example, acknowledges that the power of the states has been rising in the coalitional era of Indian politics that began in 1989. As a result, it should not be surprising that the use of Article 356 of

India's Constitution—used repeatedly by Delhi to dismiss state governments in the 1970s and 1980s—has dramatically declined over the last decade and a half. Article 356 still exists in the Constitution, but political realities are such that Delhi can now use it to suspend state governments only at its own peril.

While the coalitional era does make the country more federal, India remains quite Delhi-centric. Most of all, Delhi continues to have remarkable control of public resources. Delhi can sometimes indeed be helpless—and a contemporary version of that helplessness, counter-terrorism, will be explored in this chapter—but on the whole, even in the coalitional era, Delhi's powers are enormous.

Does this mean that of late, both states and Delhi have been simultaneously strong? An understanding of the deeper dynamics of Indian nationhood is needed to comprehend more fully the logic of India's Centre–state relations. What kind of a nation is India? Is India, like France, a nation-state? Is it, like the US, a multicultural state? Or is there another conceptualization that is better? And what are the implications of Indian nationhood—however one may characterize it—for its Centre–state relations?

Some recent variants of scholarship on Indian federalism are indeed explicitly political, not simply constitutional or fiscal, and have greatly advanced our understanding.[1] But more needs to be done. In what follows, I begin with a conceptual discussion of how to think about the relationship between federalism and Indian nationhood. Having clarified conceptual matters, the next section will deal with the constitutional clauses pertaining to Centre–state relations. Section three, then, presents an overview of the vast literature on the fiscal dimensions of federalism. Section four concentrates on the reasons that underlie the successes and failures of Indian federalism. The next section turns its gaze towards a contemporary topic, terrorism. It will be argued that national security and India's existing federal structure are in considerable tension in an age of terrorism.

What Kind of Federation? What Kind of Nation?

A fundamental political question has been at the heart of India's freedom movement and post-independence nation-building: How should democracy and ethnic diversity be combined? For Centre–state relations per se, this question takes a specific form: How should democracy and *geographically concentrated* ethnic diversities be brought together? Federalism, after all, is never non-territorial.[2] Federal units are always territorially organized.

India's social diversities have basically taken four forms: caste, religion, language, and tribe. Of these, language and tribe are territorially concentrated. Castes have always been, and continue to be, highly dispersed. Brahmins are to be found everywhere, as are the lower castes or Dalits. Because they are geographically concentrated, language and tribe became the mainstay of Indian federalism.

Before 1947, it was also claimed that Muslims were geographically heavily concentrated. Whatever one thinks about that claim, the formation of Pakistan broke the link between territory and religion. The heavy overlap between Punjab and Sikhs is about the only major exception to the otherwise ubiquitous geographical dispersion of religious groups in India. More importantly, the partition carnage also made it impossible for India's post-independence leadership to privilege religion in politics. Religion came to be seen as India's principal fault line. The immediate post-independence leadership thought it necessary to counter it by delegitimizing religion-based demands for states within the federation. Of course, religion could not be expelled from the politics of a highly religious society, but religion as the foundation of state-making was a different proposition altogether. It was to be discouraged or fought.

Thus, so long as the demand for a state of Punjab in the Indian federation was couched in terms of the distinctiveness of Sikhism vis-à-vis Hinduism, Delhi did not allow a separate Punjab state. Once the argument became linguistic and it was claimed that Punjabi, as a language, was different from Hindi, Haryana and Punjab were born as separate states, one Hindi-speaking, the other Punjabi-speaking.[3] In the end, the safeguarding of religious distinctiveness took the form of freedom of worship, separate 'personal laws' such as the religiously governed codes for property inheritance, divorce and marriage for minorities, and privileges for minority educational institutions. After partition, religion could not be the basis of federal statehood, a principle which has been followed consistently for the more than six decades of Indian democracy regardless of which party ruled in Delhi.

In short, language and tribe became the foundations of Indian federation—partly because of their geographical concentration, and in part because these two identities were not viewed as profound existential threats to India. Nehru was initially ill-disposed towards language as the basis of statehood but, over time, he came around to accepting its legitimacy.[4]

But what sort of federation, based on language and tribe, did Indian leaders construct? How were state powers conceptualized? Did India's founding fathers follow the same federal principles as the USA did? If not, what accounts for the difference?

Following Stepan,[5] it is best to call India a 'holding together' federation, not a 'coming together' federation. The US is the prime example of the latter kind of federation. Stepan also plausibly demonstrates that 'most democratic countries that have adopted federal systems have chosen not to follow the US model'.[6] 'Holding together' federations are more common, and they typically have a stronger Centre than the US does. Unlike the US, pre-existing states did not put together a Centre in India. Rather, it would be more appropriate to say that the Centre created the states as they came to be.

If this is how India's federation can be classified, what can we say about its relationship with Indian nationhood? It is logical to suppose that *the design of Indian federation would have some identifiable linkage with how the nation was to be viewed*. This is not a question normally asked in the vast literature on Indian federalism. Its absence has made the existing arguments needlessly bipolar. Scholars often argue that a strong Centre inevitably means that the states would be weak, and vice versa. Some politicians and bureaucrats also take the same view. Indira Gandhi, in particular, was associated with the claim that India's national unity depended on a strong Centre, and the stronger the states were, the weaker would India be. Roughly in the same vein, it is sometimes argued that, with the rising strength of the states, India is beginning to look like the European Union, as Delhi has become too weak.[7]

The binary, that a strong Centre requires weak states and vice versa, is conceptually flawed. To understand why that is so, we need to ask a deeper question about Indian nationhood. Is India a 'nation-state' in the classical sense of the term? The concept of a nation-state, developed most clearly in recent times by Gellner,[8] essentially represents a coincidence of the territorial boundaries of a state and the cultural boundaries of a nation. France is viewed as the best historical example of such a fusion.

But, in the literature on nationalism, the French model of undifferentiated citizenship is viewed as a nineteenth-century curiosity, to be studied primarily to understand why the Basques and the Bretons did not rebel against the profoundly assimilationist thrust of Paris.[9] As noted earlier, Weber shows that, through conscription armies and public schools, peasants were turned into Frenchmen and the diversities of France were flattened.[10] At the time of the French Revolution, more than 50 per cent Frenchmen did not speak French at all, and 'only 12–13 per cent spoke it correctly'.[11]

Of the current nations in the world, Portugal and some Scandinavian countries approximate the French nation-state model; Germany and France are also nation-states, but in radically different ways.[12] But most of the contemporary world is either 'multicultural' like, for example, the US, or it consists of states that have strong cultural diversity, *some of which is territorially based* and can potentially create demands for independence. In a conceptually novel and highly plausible formulation, Stepan, Linz, and Yadav call the latter political entities 'state-nations', not 'nation-states'.[13] They concentrate on India, Canada, Spain, and Belgium as key examples. The list, of course, can be made longer: Thailand, Pakistan, Nigeria, Sri Lanka, and the Philippines can also be included. Each has geographically concentrated ethnic differences. State-nations are not only different from nation-states, but they are also different from multicultural countries like the United States, where ethnic or cultural diversity is not territorially concentrated.

Nation-states tend to be assimilationist in character. Removal of ethnic or cultural diversities is one of the key features of nation-states. In contrast, state-nation policies work on two levels: the creation of a sense of belonging with respect to the larger political community (in this case, India), while *simultaneously* putting in place institutional guarantees for safeguarding politically salient diversities, such as language, religion, and culturally sacred norms. If territory-specific, federalism is normally a necessary condition for the protection of such diversities. And having two or more political identities is not considered subversive to the nation.[14]

One can thus simultaneously be a Punjabi and an Indian, a Catalan and a Spaniard, a Quebecois and a Canadian. Undifferentiated and singular Indians, Canadians and Spaniards do exist. But a lot of citizens in such countries tend to have multiple, though complimentary, identities. To try to hammer these various identities into a singular national identity would in fact fracture these political communities, not solidify them.

Melting Pots and Salad Bowls

This new formulation of state-nation allows us to interrogate the standard discussions of Indian nationhood. The metaphors of 'melting pot' and 'salad bowl' were widely used in the older discussion.[15] It was argued that mirroring these metaphors, two different versions of Indian nationhood have been in contestation since the 1920s: secular nationalist and Hindu nationalist. The two versions have been discussed at length in Chapter 4. Recalling that discussion, let us briefly look at each of these versions, examine their institutional implications, especially for federalism, and then re-engage the new concept of state-nation.

Secular nationalism, or 'composite nationalism', constituted the basic ideological force guiding the freedom movement under Mahatma Gandhi and Jawaharlal Nehru. The country's Constitution-makers accepted this idea of India after independence. All religions would have an equal place in the national family and, as a principle, none would dominate the functioning of the state. The state would be neutral between the religions. Though the main focus of this narrative was religion, this narrative also emphasized that neither one's language, nor caste or tribe, would determine citizenship in the country and the rights that went with it. Birth in India, or naturalization and acceptance of Indian nationhood, would be the sole criterion. Acceptance of the various forms of diversity as intrinsic to Indian nationhood came to be called the 'salad bowl' view of the nation.

This view accepts pluralism as central to Indian nationhood, and protects it through laws (e.g., personal laws for marriage, divorce and property inheritance, and protection of minority educational institutions) and through political institutions (e.g., federalism). Federalism, in short, ties up neatly with this view of nationhood.

Hindu nationalists have historically disagreed with this narrative of Indian nationhood. A 'salad bowl', according to them, is a recipe for disunity; only a 'melting pot' is capable of producing national cohesion.[16] What does the latter mean?

Hindu nationalism insists on assimilation.[17] Initially, the term covered linguistic assimilation as well, since Hindu nationalists emphasized the centrality of Hindi to Indian nationhood.[18] The realities of political life have led them to drop such insistence. Their view, by now, concentrates primarily on religious minorities who, according to them, must assimilate, which, for all practical purposes, means acceptance of Hindu dominance and/or an abandonment of special privileges such as maintenance of religious personal laws. *Ekya* (assimilation) is the proof of loyalty to the nation.

To begin with, this view was much more in favour of political centralization and not hospitable to federalism. But, as indicated above, political experience has changed Hindu nationalism. Hindu nationalists may not explicitly debate whether federalism is about the multiple identities of Indians. But, at the very least, they have accepted federalism as perhaps the only way to administer India, as a convenient administrative device for running a continent-size polity.

India as a State-Nation

The new concept of state-nation takes the previous discussion significantly forward. In two ways, it adds a new perspective and clarity to arguments about Indian federalism. First, an understanding of India's federalism does not require adherence to the notion of Indian exceptionalism, which is an underlying current in a lot of India-specific literature. Insights from Spain, Canada, and Belgium show that the state-nation is a larger category, not just a single case. India's diversities may be greater than those of Spain, Canada, and Belgium but, essentially, all these countries belong to the same conceptual category. They have territorially centred cultural differences. For stability and unity, state-nations generally require policies that are respectful of such geographically concentrated cultural diversities.

The India–Sri Lanka contrast is worth briefly noting here.[19] Sri Lankan Tamils were heavily concentrated in the North and, for many years, demanded federal autonomy, not independence. Despite the desirability of state-nation policies, such as federalism under such circumstances, Sri Lanka followed nation-state policies à la France, leading to one of the nastiest civil wars in Asia, lasting two and a half decades.

Few significant political leaders in India have made a case for Sri Lanka–style unitary policies: imposition of Hindi, let us say, on the entire population.[20] Even under Indira Gandhi, when Delhi often used its powers to undermine state governments, the argument was never about the imposition of Hindi for the sake of national cohesiveness. Indira Gandhi's argument was about the respective powers of the Centre and states. Similarly, even after they came to power, the Hindu nationalists, generally viewed as centralizers, never attacked the linguistically based federalism.

Second, the concept of state-nation does not simply indicate an institutional safeguarding of diversities, but also *a simultaneous nurturing of commitment to the larger Indian political community.* The 'salad bowl' metaphor does not adequately capture this dualistic dimension of nation-building; it primarily speaks of embracing diversities as a way of building the Indian nation. The concept of state-nation is both about recognizing diversities and building larger all-India loyalties.

In India, the institutions that have played a key role in generating all-India loyalties, historically or currently, include the Congress party; the armed forces; the Indian Administrative Service (IAS); educational institutions such as the Indian Institutes of Technology and Indian Institutes of Management; central high schools; the Supreme Court; and, over the last two decades, the Election Commission. Though no good studies of the film industry and sports are available, the hypothesis that Bollywood and cricket have enlarged the corpus of all-India loyalties has enormous plausibility, and is worth exploring later.

Some might object to the inclusion of the IAS in this list. The IAS has often been criticized for its red tape and for obstructing India's economic progress. That may well be true, but from a nation-building perspective, another side of the IAS deserves fresh scrutiny. Since IAS officers are part of both the Centre and the states—in that they are selected by Delhi but assigned to a state cadre, and they go back and forth between Delhi and the states during their careers—they are in many ways an embodiment of the state-nation concept. They simultaneously belong to a state as well as to the Indian nation. Their incentives are structured in such a way that even when they serve states, Delhi is never far from their consciousness. Had India had a civil service that was entirely state-based, or wholly Delhi-centric, the problems of nation-building would have been far more, not less, serious.

A simultaneous pursuit of recognizing diversity and building unity is not an easy political undertaking. India's record is not perfect, as the secessionism demands in some states—to be discussed later—clearly demonstrate. But it is worth asking how the concept of state-nation has empirically fared so far.

Luckily, survey research provides evidence. Table 6.1 summarizes data, collected in four surveys, on whether Indians are proud of India. The proportion that is 'very proud' or 'proud' adds up to more than 85 per cent in each survey. Table 6.2 presents data on subjective national identity in India, collected between 1998 and 2005. Roughly two-thirds of Indians say that their identity is (a) only Indian; (b) more Indian than state-based; and (c) equally Indian and state-based. Only 20–22 per cent of the random sample says that it has either (d) an entirely state-based identity; or (e) a more state-based than an Indian identity. Comparative research on this question suggests these are very high numbers for commitment to a larger political unit, despite the institutional safeguarding of state-based diversities.[21]

In sum, it would appear that the simultaneous pursuit of nationalism and sub-nationalism has been reasonably successful in India. The commitment to the larger polity has not been achieved by a suppression of diversities.

TABLE 6.1: PRIDE IN INDIA, 1990–2005 (PER CENT)

	WVS1990	WVS1995	WVS2001	SDSA2005
Very Proud	67	66	67	61
Proud	25	19	21	28
Not Proud	8	9	7	3
Don't Know/No Answer	0	6	5	8
(Sample Size)	(2,466)	(2,040)	(2,002)	(5,387)

Notes: 1. WVS is conducted by the Inter-University Consortium for Political and Social Research, headquartered at the University of Michigan, Ann Arbor, USA.
2. SDSA is conducted by the Centre for the Study of Developing Societies, Delhi.

Sources: 1. 1990, 1995, and 2001 rounds of the *World Values Survey* (WVS)
2. The 2005 round of the *State of Democracy in South Asia Survey* (SDSA)

TABLE 6.2: SUBJECTIVE NATIONAL IDENTITY IN INDIA, 1998–2005 (PER CENT)

	NES 1998	SDSA 2005
Only Indian	50	35
More Indian than state identity	NA	12
As Indian as state identity	16	19
More state identity than Indian	NA	10
Only state identity	20	12
Don't know/No answer	14	12
(Sample Size)	(8,140)	(5,385)

Sources: 1. The 1998 round of the *National Election Study (NES)*
2. The 2005 round of *State of Democracy in South Asia Survey (SDSA)*, both conducted by the Centre for the Study of Developing Societies, Delhi

The Linguistic Principle and Constitutional Division of Powers[22]

Of all of India's cultural identities, as already explained, language and tribe are the only geography-based ones. Religion and caste tend to be unevenly spread all over the country.

Because language was the rationale for statehood for most parts of India, the federal scheme came to be called linguistic. Each state has its own official language; the Central government business is conducted either in Hindi or in English. Fifteen languages are spoken by an overwhelming majority of people in their respective states (Tables 6.3 and 6.4). These fifteen form the basis of most Indian state boundaries. With the exception of Hindi (which is the lingua franca in six states), each of the fifteen languages is both the main language in a single state and only marginally spoken outside that state.

TABLE 6.3: INDIA'S PRINCIPAL LANGUAGES

Language	Spoken by Percentage of India's Population
Hindi	39.9
Bengali	8.2
Telugu	7.8
Marathi	7.4
Tamil	6.3
Urdu	5.1
Gujarati	4.8
Kannada	3.9
Malayalam	3.6
Oriya	3.3
Punjabi	2.8
Assamese	1.5

Source: Census of India, 2001

TABLE 6.4: DISTRIBUTION OF LANGUAGES ACROSS
STATES IN INDIA

State	Language	No. of Speakers	Percentage
Arunachal Pradesh	Nissi/Daffla	172,149	19.9
	Nepali	81,176	9.4
	Bengali	70,771	8.2
Andhra Pradesh	Telugu	56,375,755	84.8
	Urdu	5,560,154	8.4
	Hindi	1,841,290	2.8
Assam	Assamese	12,958,088	57.8
	Bengali	2,523,040	11.3
	Bodo/Boro	1,184,569	5.3
Bihar	Hindi	69,845,979	80.9
	Urdu	8,542,463	9.9
	Santhali	2,546,655	2.9
Gujarat	Gujarati	37,792,933	91.5
	Hindi	1,215,825	2.9
	Sindhi	704,088	1.7
Goa	Konkani	602,626	51.5
	Marathi	390,270	33.4
	Kannada	54,323	4.6
Haryana	Hindi	14,982,409	91
	Punjabi	1,170,225	7.1
	Urdu	261,820	1.6
Himachal Pradesh	Hindi	4,595,615	88.9
	Punjabi	324,479	6.3
	Kinnauri	61,794	1.2
Karnataka	Kannada	29,785,004	66.2
	Urdu	4,480,038	10
	Telugu	3,325,062	7.4

Table 6.4 (*continued*)

State	Language	No. of Speakers	Percentage
Kerala	Malayalam	28,096,376	96.6
	Tamil	616,010	2.1
	Kannada	75,571	0.3
Maharashtra	Marathi	57,894,839	73.3
	Hindi	6,168,941	7.8
	Urdu	5,734,468	7.3
Meghalaya	Khasi	879,192	49.5
	Garo	547,690	30.9
	Bengali	144,261	8.1
Madhya Pradesh	Hindi	56,619,090	85.6
	Bhili/Bhilodi	2,215,399	3.3
	Gondi	1,481,265	2.2
Manipur	Manipuri	1,110,134	60.4
	Thado	103,667	5.6
	Tangkhul	100,088	5.4
Mizoram	Lushai/Mizo	518,099	75.1
	Bengali	59,092	8.6
	Lakher	22,938	3.3
Nagaland	Ao	169,837	14
	Sema	152,123	12.6
	Konyak	137,539	11.4
Orissa	Oriya	26,199,346	82.8
	Hindi	759,016	2.4
Punjab	Punjabi	18,704,461	92.2
	Hindi	1,478,993	7.3
	Urdu	13,416	0.1
Rajasthan	Hindi	39,410,968	89.6
	Bhili/Bhilodi	2,215,399	5
	Urdu	953,497	2.2

Table 6.4 (*continued*)

State	Language	No. of Speakers	Percentage
Tamil Nadu	Tamil	48,434,744	86.7
	Telugu	3,975,561	7.1
	Kannada	1,208,296	2.2
Tripura	Bengali	1,899,162	68.9
	Tripuri	647,847	23.5
	Hindi	45,803	1.7
Uttar Pradesh	Hindi	125,348,492	90.1
	Urdu	12,492,927	9
	Punjabi	661.215	0.5
West Bengal	Bengali	58,541,519	86
	Hindi	4,479,170	6.6
	Urdu	1,455,649	2.1

Source: Census of India, 2001

From the national perspective, multiple languages as a basis of state communication were viewed initially as problematic. For greater national cohesion, Article 351 directed the Central government to promote Hindi 'so that it may serve as a medium of expression for all the elements of the composite culture of India', and Article 343 provided for the English language only for a period of fifteen years. In practice, however, the inability to quell the political mobilization that followed attempts to introduce Hindi as an all-India language was decisive. After the bad experiences, the Central government restrained its excessive enthusiasm for Hindi and, every fifteen years, Parliament reinstates English as an official language. Basically, a multilingual India has been accepted as a reality, especially after it became clear that the linguistic formation of states had led to a dissipation of language-based violence.

The discussion of the concept of state-nation might have suggested that the choice of linguistic identities as a basis for statehood in the federation was a principled act of far-sighted statesmanship, but that would not be entirely true. Understanding the nature of Indian diversities as early as 1920, the Congress party did commit itself to a linguistic federation. But doubts about the validity of the idea did develop.[23] Many of India's violent political mobilizations in the post-independence period were organized along linguistic lines. The first linguistic state, Andhra, was created in 1953 following riots touched off by a 'fast unto death' by a linguistic promoter. As it finally emerged, the linguistic basis of federalism was a synthesis of considered principles and learned pragmatism. This principle was given concrete institutional and administrative form only following linguistically based political mobilization in the 1950s. By the late 1960s, India's state boundaries had been fundamentally restructured along linguistic lines.

Constitutional Division of Powers

The debate in India's Constituent Assembly showed a fair degree of consensus on the subject of centralization. The horrors of India's 1947 partition provided the context for such a consensus. Nehru contended that 'it would be injurious to the interests of the country to provide for a weak central authority which would be incapable of ensuring peace, of coordinating vital matters of common concern and of speaking effectively for the whole country in the international sphere'.[24] Ambedkar, chair of the Constituent Assembly, also liked 'a strong united Centre, much stronger than the Centre we had created under the Government of India Act of 1935'.[25]

Eventually, the Constitution created three lists: Union, State, and Concurrent. The Union list of legislative powers includes ninety-nine subjects and the State list, sixty one. The Concurrent powers belonging to the Union and the states extend to fifty-two items.[26] The first list includes defence, external affairs, major taxes, etc.; the second covers law and order, police, agriculture, primary and secondary education, etc.; the third includes economic and social planning and higher education. All the residual powers are vested in the Centre.

The most Delhi-oriented constitutional provisions cover the powers of the national Cabinet and Parliament with respect to the making of states. Articles 2 and 3 of the Constitution enable Parliament by law to admit a new state, increase or reduce the area of any state or change the boundaries or name of any state. The consent of the state is not required.

Articles 352–60 of the Constitution have generated the maximum debate. Under these emergency provisions, the country begins to function more or less like a unitary state. The emergencies are broadly defined as: financial emergency; external threat to the state; and cases of internal disturbance.

In June 1975, Prime Minister Indira Gandhi declared Emergency under Article 352 on grounds of internal disturbance. During the term of the Emergency, lasting till March 1977, the 42nd Amendment was passed, which made the Constitution quite centralized. Later, when Indira Gandhi and the Congress party were electorally defeated in 1977, the 43rd and 44th Amendments corrected the imbalance.

In the event of a state-level breakdown of the constitutional machinery, Article 356 allows for the invocation of 'President's Rule', whereby the president, on the recommendation of the Union cabinet, can assume the normal powers of a state, remove a state government, dissolve the state legislature, and empower the Union legislature to exercise the respective state's power for a temporary period.

In the first five decades of independence, Article 356 was used on more than 100 occasions. A commission appointed by the Government of India—the Sarkaria Commission—to investigate the abuse of this provision found that out of seventy-five cases until then, only in twenty-six was the use clearly justified or inevitable. The pattern, however, changed in the 1990s, when the frequency of President's Rule and the use of Article 356 went down significantly.

In 1994, the Supreme Court ruled—in the S.R. Bommai case—that a proclamation under Article 356 could be judicially reviewed, and the Central government would have to reveal to the court the relevant material justifying its decision to exercise its power under the provisions of this article. In the 1990s, the President also exercised the constitutional privilege to return to the cabinet the executive request to impose President's Rule on a state. Over the past decade and a half, three such requests have either been denied or sent back for review.

These interventions, by the Supreme Court and the President, have seriously reduced the risk of arbitrary central intervention in state politics and begun to restrain central leaders from using exceptional powers for partisan purposes. Another important constraint is simply the coalitional nature of politics. Both major coalitions that have ruled Delhi over the last two decades have depended on regional parties for their survival. Suspending state governments would undermine coalitions and bring about the downfall of national governments. A political consensus that the use of Article 356 should be minimized has emerged in India, which appears to have made federalism deeper and more secure.

Resource Transfers

The literature on fiscal federalism that deals with the transfer of resources from the Centre to states is truly voluminous.[27] Abstracting from details, an overview of the basic edifice of resource transfers is presented below. For the purposes of this chapter, especially important is the question of how, and in what ways, politics influences the distribution of resources.

Resource transfers from Delhi to the states take place in implicit and explicit ways. Not easily calculable for each state but increasingly part of the discourse, the implicit transfers consist of subsidies, especially for food, fertilizer and fuel; tax concessions for special economic zones; and subsidized loans to states from the Central government, the banking system, etc.[28]

The explicit mechanisms of transfer are threefold:

1. Devolution of taxes through the Finance Commission, set up by the Central government every five years under Article 280;
2. Grants and loans given by the Planning Commission for the implementation of development plans;
3. Transfers for various projects wholly funded by the Central government, or for the so-called centrally sponsored schemes, for which the states typically bear a proportion of the cost.

In the early 1950s, only 10–12 per cent of the central tax revenue used to be given to the states. By the 1990s, that share rose to roughly 30 per cent and, since then, has fluctuated between 26 to 30 per cent (Figure 6.1). On the whole, the poorer and bigger states with larger populations receive more, but, if their own tax effort is not substantial and fiscal discipline is lax, the share will be lower than would be justified purely in terms population, area, and income.

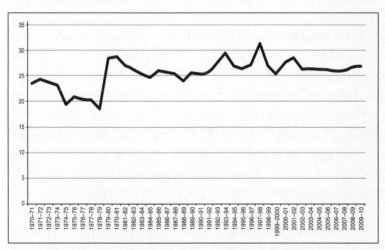

FIGURE 6.1: PERCENTAGE OF CENTRAL REVENUE
TRANSFERRED TO THE STATES

Source: Indian Public Finance Statistics 2011–12, Ministry of Finance, Government of India

'Plan transfers', in the form of grants and loans and routed through the Planning Commission, constitute the second mechanism of resource transfer. The so-called Gadgil formula, approved in 1969, is the cornerstone of plan transfers. Accordingly, India is divided into two types of states: special category states and general category states. Special category states are basically the border states of the North and North-east. They get 30 per cent of all central assistance for their state economic development plans, of which 90 per cent comes in the form of grants and 10 per cent in the form of loans. General category states are the bigger states. They get 70 per cent of the total central plan assistance, of which 30 per cent comes in the form of grants and 70 per cent as loans. On the whole, special category states rely heavily on central transfers, but general category states considerably less so. And within the latter category, the poorer and the more populous states rely on Delhi's transfers more than the richer and less populous states do (Table 6.5).

Transfers made under the third mechanism—central projects and centrally-sponsored schemes—are basically discretionary. Governed neither by the Finance Commission, nor by the Gadgil formula for plan transfers, these resources rose from 12 per cent of the total transfer in the early 1970s to roughly 20 per cent by the end of the 1990s.[29] Since then, they appear to have risen further.

The third mechanism is where, according to the economic bureaucrats and scholars, politics matters most.[30] Which states would get central resources for power plants, higher educational institutions, roads, and ports on the one hand; and which would get bigger shares of centrally sponsored schemes on the other? The answer to these questions has a lot to do with which states and/ or political parties wield power in Delhi. It is widely believed that Tamil Nadu has received a disproportionate amount of discretionary transfers since 1991. While it is hard to clinch this point statistically, the perception is consistent with a political reading of the power structure in Delhi. Ever since coalitions have ruled Delhi, especially

TABLE 6.5: STATE-WISE REVENUES AND EXPENDITURES, 2006–07

State	Per Capita State Domestic Product (Rs)	Poverty Ratio (%) 2004–05	Per Capita Revenue (Rs)	Per Capita Transfers (Rs)	Per Capita Current Spending (Rs)	Own Revenue as % of State Domestic Product 2000–03	Own Revenue as % of Current Spending
High-Income States	**35,249**	**10.9**	**4,287**	**800**	**5,286**	**7.5**	**81.1**
Goa	52,530	1.7	16,798	2,207	17,271	6.5	97.3
Gujarat	27,027	12.5	3,478	926	4,640	7.7	74.9
Haryana	35,779	9.9	4,605	692	5,347	8.3	86.1
Maharashtra	30,750	25.2	4,245	690	4,923	7.8	86.2
Punjab	30,158	5.2	5,138	985	7,339	7.1	70.0
Middle-Income States	**24,773**	**15.7**	**3,177**	**1,170**	**4,562**	**7.4**	**69.6**
Andhra Pradesh	22,835	11.1	3,277	1,245	4,567	7.3	71.8
Karnataka	2,931	17.4	4,211	1,112	3,804	8.3	110.7
Kerala	30,044	11.4	4,268	1,164	6,315	8.1	67.6
Tamil Nadu	27,101	17.8	3,440	1,120	5,337	9.0	64.5
West Bengal	21,953	20.6	1,781	1,178	3,780	4.3	47.1

State	Per Capita State Domestic Product (Rs)	Poverty Ratio (%) 2004–05	Per Capita Revenue (Rs)	Per Capita Transfers (Rs)	Per Capita Current Spending (Rs)	Own Revenue as % of State Domestic Product 2000–03	Own Revenue as % of Current Spending
Low-Income States	**14,211**	**30.8**	**1,449**	**1,514**	**3,134**	**5.8**	**46.2**
Bihar	8,056	32.5	481	1,650	2,774	4.5	17.3
Chhattisgarh	NA	32.0	2,509	1,583	3,262	NA	76.9
Jharkhand	13,984	34.8	1,737	1,608	2,198	NA	79.0
Madhya Pradesh	12,577	32.4	1,661	1,372	3,490	6.5	47.6
Orissa	15,096	39.9	1,487	1,880	4,423	5.8	33.6
Rajasthan	16,401	17.5	2,094	1,238	4,318	6.5	48.5
Uttaranchal	22,178	31.8	2,577	2,651	6,148	NA	41.9
Uttar Pradesh	11,188	25.5	1,389	1,436	2,492	5.9	55.7
General Category States	24,744	19.1	2,535	1,263	3,958	6.9	64.1
Special Category States	20,077	12.0	2,241	3,176	8,233	2.9	27.2
Arunachal Pradesh	20,380	13.4	1,447	5,980	9,513	1.5	15.2

State	Per Capita State Domestic Product (Rs)	Poverty Ratio (%) 2004–05	Per Capita Revenue (Rs)	Per Capita Transfers (Rs)	Per Capita Current Spending (Rs)	Own Revenue as % of State Domestic Product 2000–03	Own Revenue as % of Current Spending
Assam	15,152	15.0	1,289	1,662	5,311	4.6	24.3
Himachal Pradesh	28,236	6.7	3,029	4,472	12,795	5.1	23.7
Jammu and Kashmir	16,817	4.2	3,147	3,534	7,100	4.5	44.3
Manipur	15,047	13.2	837	5,326	10,952	1.2	7.6
Meghalaya	19,292	14.1	1,815	3,506	6,128	3.3	29.6
Mizoram	20,618	9.5	1,085	9,688	12,295	1.0	8.8
Nagaland	NA	14.5	792	6,936	9,531	1.2	8.3
Sikkim	22,167	15.2	3,547	6,274	13,578	4.6	26.1
Tripura	22,987	14.4	1,499	4,884	8,170	2.2	18.4
All States	22,411	15.6	2,263	1,230	3,767	4.9	60.1

Sources: 1. *Public Indian Finance Statistics, 2008–09*, Ministry of Finance, Government of India
2. *Twelfth Finance Commission Report*, Annexure 3, 6, and 10 (Projections for 2005–10)

after 1991, each major regional party of Tamil Nadu has been linked with one national party or the other. As a result, Tamil Nadu has had major ministers in Delhi regardless of whether the coalition was Congress-led, BJP-led or a Third Front–led. No other state has this character. Indeed, politicians of Tamil Nadu have sometimes unhesitatingly announced how much the state has gained from its association with power in Delhi. Just before the 2009 general elections, the DMK-led government of Tamil Nadu placed a front-page colour advertisement in Chennai's leading newspapers entitled 'Benefits Accrued to Tamil Nadu under the UPA Government'. Many benefits were listed, including new institutions of higher education and new railway bridges and lines, but the emphasis was on 'four-lane highways, gigantic flyovers, expansion of sea ports, container terminals and waterways', adding that 'such a huge amount has not been spent so far on infrastructure in Tamil Nadu after independence'.[31]

Some statistical studies have also sought to estimate the role of politics in resource transfers. Rao and Singh review existing econometric work and present their own results. They find 'some evidence for the importance of variables that may proxy bargaining power of the components of Indian federal system'.[32] They also detect 'a positive effect of the proportion of ruling party/coalition MPs on per capita statutory transfers', though they admit that 'econometric results such as these' suffer from 'the general problem of potential fragility'.[33] In her econometric study, Khemani divides up resources into those transferred through the statutory mechanisms—such as the Finance Commission—and those transferred through a non-statutory route.[34] She finds evidence of politics shaping transfers in favour of powerful states in the latter category, but finds the opposite in the former. Larger shares of statutory transfers often go to states not powerful and in need of resources, and she calls these transfers 'non-political'.

However, to call the latter non-political is to unduly truncate the concept of 'the political'. Politics is not simply about the sectional accrual of benefits to states with more ruling MPs or more important ministries.

Another notion of politics is also relevant here. This second notion concerns visions about how to handle geographically centred cultural diversities. Two kinds of states require special economic attention for nation-building: those that are large and poor; and those that are far from the Centre and might feel excluded or neglected. If statutory transfers have gone more in the direction of such states, it gives evidence of the kind of politics that is consistent with the concept of state-nations discussed earlier. Moreover, the fact that, for plan purposes, India has been divided into special category and general category states, and transfers to special category states are primarily grants, not loans, is also consistent with the notion that India is a state-nation, whose policies must pay attention to the diversities and felt exclusions. Both forms of politics—those focusing on sectional benefits and those dealing with larger political visions—appear to have played a role in how the Centre has transferred resources to states.

Successes and Failures of India's Federal Experiment

Though India's federal experiment has on the whole been a success, there have also been some failures. Let me first list the major successes and failures, and then give an explanatory account of how those successes and failures have come about.

Consider the following indices of success or failure:

1. India's 1950 Constitution, which laid down the federal framework, has not been overthrown, and its legitimacy has only occasionally been challenged by states. On the Central side, Indira Gandhi was perhaps the only leader, who sought to challenge the overall principles of federal functioning, but the centralization she attempted has long been reversed. Her

favourite argument that if states became powerful the nation would be weakened has virtually disappeared from the political sphere. Moreover, many Central leaders over the last decade have argued that the more powerful the states became, the fewer would be the governance problems for the nation as a whole. More new states have been voluntarily created, not resisted, by the Centre. In 1957, India had fourteen states; in 1971, the number had grown to seventeen, and in 1981 to twenty-three; by 2001, to twenty-eight states.

2. Language riots, which preceded the formation of linguistic states and continued through the 1960s, have precipitously declined since the emergence of linguistic states. Language is no longer a seriously divisive political force in India. It used to be a source of great conflict in the 1950s and 1960s.

3. Dispute resolution mechanisms between the Centre and the states have become institutionalized. The disputes are settled either in the National Development Council—which is the forum for bargaining over project funds—or in the Finance Commission—which is the forum for distribution of national revenue—or in the highest reaches of ruling political parties. If nothing works, all units of the federation have learnt to accept Supreme Court judgments. In some institutional arena or the other, disputes get resolved, and problems are managed.

4. The failures of Indian federalism must include five separatist insurgencies—Nagaland, Mizoram, and Assam in the North-east, and Punjab and Kashmir in the North. But two facts should be noted. First, none out of the remaining states, currently numbering twenty-three, has ever raised the banner of a secessionary revolt. Second, at no point have more than two insurgencies rocked the polity simultaneously. The worst year was 1990, when the insurgency in Punjab hadn't quite died out, and it had recently burst on the scene in Kashmir. Even at that moment, a mere 3.5 per cent of the national population, spread

over these two states, was directly affected. In other instances, the affected percentages were considerably lower.

After all is said and done, the greatest objective of India's federation was to hold the nation together without giving up the division of powers between the Centre and states. Whatever the other deficiencies, Indian federalism has certainly achieved its paramount objective.[35]

Cross-Cutting Cleavages

A major reason, if not the only one, for the success of Indian federalism has to do with the country's ethnic configuration. As already suggested in Chapters 1 and 2, Indian identities tend to cross-cut, instead of cumulating. (The same factors that help democracy also aid federalism.) As we know from the theory of ethnic conflict, cumulative cleavages create a greater potential for conflict; cross-cutting cleavages dampen them.[36] Sri Lanka is a classic case of cumulative cleavages. Tamils are not only religiously distinct from the Sinhalese, but also linguistically and racially.

Given their geographical concentration, language and tribe could, in principle, have provided states with a firm resolve and a source of great power against the Centre. That did not, however, happen. First of all, in each state, linguistic minorities exist, making a statewide linguistic unity hard to achieve (Table 6.4). Moreover, if one reads Tables 6.3 and 6.6 together, one can see that linguistic and religious groups do not match in most states, with some exceptions discussed later. As a result, religion seriously cross-cuts the political potential that language (or for that matter, tribe) might theoretically create for brinkmanship on the part of a state. Though census data on caste have not been collected since 1931, it is well known that castes also cut across language groups. Thus, both religion and caste often cause splits within a state's boundaries, turning intra-state

issues into a more enduring form of politics than a confrontation
with the Centre.

TABLE 6.6: DISTRIBUTION OF RELIGIONS ACROSS INDIAN
STATES (PER CENT)

States	Hindus	Muslims	Christians	Sikhs
Andhra Pradesh	89.14	8.91	1.83	0.03
Assam	67.13	28.43	3.32	0.07
Bihar	82.42	14.81	0.98	0.09
Goa	64.68	5.25	29.86	0.09
Gujarat	89.48	8.73	0.44	0.08
Haryana	89.21	4.64	0.10	5.81
Himachal Pradesh	95.90	1.72	0.09	1.01
Jammu and Kashmir	32.24	64.19	0.14	2.23
Karnataka	85.45	11.64	1.91	0.02
Kerala	57.28	23.33	19.32	0.01
Madhya Pradesh	92.80	4.96	0.65	0.24
Maharashtra	81.12	9.67	1.12	0.21
Manipur	57.67	7.27	34.11	0.07
Meghalaya	14.67	3.46	64.58	0.15
Mizoram	5.05	0.66	85.73	0.04
Nagaland	10.12	1.71	87.47	0.06
Orissa	94.67	1.83	2.10	0.05
Punjab	34.46	1.18	1.11	62.95
Rajasthan	89.08	8.01	0.11	1.48
Tamil Nadu	88.67	5.47	5.69	0.01
Tripura	86.50	7.13	1.68	0.03
Uttar Pradesh	81.74	17.33	0.14	0.48
West Bengal	74.72	23.61	0.56	0.08
Delhi	83.67	9.44	0.88	4.84

Source: Census of India, 2001

Consider some examples of how the typical Indian stands at the intersection of multiple identities. Depending on where he lives, the first language of a Muslim could be Hindi, Urdu, Bengali, or any of the many others. The same is true of Hindus. Moreover, Hindus are divided into thousands of local castes. For classificatory simplicity, these castes may be aggregated into the five meta-categories— Brahmin, Kshatriya, Vaishya, Sudra, and Dalit—but that is not true experientially. Other than an experience of suffering, as already stated in Chapter 3, a South Indian Dalit has little in common with a North Indian Dalit: Caste names are different, caste histories and traditions are different, and spoken languages are different. Likewise, being a Brahmin in North India is very different from being one in South India. Only a larger social hierarchy—in which the Brahmin is normally at the top and the Dalit always at the bottom—is what is common to this extraordinary social diversity. When politics mixes with such a social landscape, political entrepreneurs mobilize their communities on a whole variety of issues, creating serious internal pluralism in state politics. The state versus the Centre scenario often takes a back seat.

The few Indian states, where identities are cumulated, instead of cross-cutting, have indeed produced the most serious Centre–state clashes, including secessionary movements. The majority community in Kashmir is not only Muslim—otherwise a minority in India—but the region of Kashmir is also linguistically different and geographically distinct from the rest of India. Moreover, caste distinctions do not exist among the Muslims in the same rigid way as in Hindu society. In the state of Punjab, the Sikhs—a minority in the country overall— constitute a majority and their first language is Punjabi, not Hindi. Finally, in North-eastern India, some states, especially Nagaland and Mizoram, are not only tribe-based, but those tribes are linguistically as well as religiously distinct from the rest of Indians. Their respective vernaculars are the first languages of Nagaland and Mizoram, not Hindi, and both are Christian-majority states (Table 6.6).[37]

It is in these states that the attempts at secession have been made. It should also, however, be noted that, with the exception of Punjab, the Congress party during India's freedom movement was not allowed by the British to do its political work in these states.[38] The problem thus may be doubly serious, going a long way towards explaining the drive for secession in them. Identities tend to cumulate in Kashmir and the North-eastern tribal states, and the nation-making enterprise did not reach them.

It is interesting to note how the Indian state has dealt with separatism. Delhi has always had a threefold approach to insurgencies: military, political, and economic. Militarily, Delhi has waged counter-insurgency operations against rebel organizations— as any modern state must, faced with secession. As Weber argued long ago, no modern state gives up its monopoly over the means of coercion. Politically, however, Delhi has always sought to persuade the rebel leaders and organizations to participate in elections and run state governments, if they win power electorally. Finally, Delhi has allocated more fiscal resources for developmental purposes to the disaffected states as a way to deal with the discourse of grievance, undermine the mass base of the rebels (where it exists), and win over the regional political elite. If Delhi's response to separatism had taken only a military form, it would perhaps have had much greater difficulty defending national integrity. With the partial exception of the later years of Indira Gandhi (1980–84), Delhi's fundamental approach has remained one of incorporation, not suppression. To be sure, the idea of incorporation has not been practised perfectly, but the principle itself has never been abandoned.

Cross-Border Terrorism: A New Problem for Federalism

In November 2008, India painfully watched real-life terror on TV and waited for nearly a day for commandos to land in Mumbai after terrorists had captured two leading hotels and attacked several landmark buildings, killing scores of Indians and tourists. Millions of citizens were angered by what appeared to be an inexplicable delay in providing security. Observers of Indian politics, however, were seized by a puzzle: What could possibly have prevented paramilitary counteraction for so long? Interviews and research demonstrate that India's Centre–state laws and practices were the principal culprit. It is also clear that, if not addressed imaginatively, Mumbai-style attacks simply cannot be ruled out in the future. For all its successes, India's federalism now faces a new and extremely serious challenge.

Central to India's internal security are the following laws and practices:[39]

First, public order is *entirely* on India's 'state list', not on the 'Central list' or the 'Concurrent list'. Unlike in the US, 'federal crime' is not a concept in Indian law, and it cannot be introduced unless the Constitution is amended. Its relevance has been debated within government circles since the late 1960s, but the idea of 'federal crime' remains legally elusive.[40] Even when the Indian Airlines flight from Kathmandu was diverted to Kandahar in December 1999, leading to India's External Affairs minister agreeing to a humiliating deal that released well-known terrorists from Indian jails in return for the safety of passengers, the case could not be registered as a federal crime. Indian Airlines reported to the Delhi police that its plane, due to arrive at Delhi airport, was missing. It was registered as a Delhi-based—in other words, state-based—crime.

Second, central agencies—including the national security guards (or commandos) who are especially trained for urban terrorism—simply cannot function without the cooperation of the state government and the state police. Often, they cannot enter a state without the state's request and/or permission. India's commandos were all based in Delhi when Mumbai was terrorized. Since then, hubs have been created in Hyderabad, Chennai, Kolkata and Mumbai. As a consequence, they can be deployed more quickly but, for operations, they still need the cooperation of the state police. They have no knowledge of ground-level specificities.

Third, India's intelligence system is deeply fractured, both vertically and horizontally. The Central Bureau of Investigation (CBI)—the institution often identified as the leading intelligence agency of India—is most unlike America's Federal Bureau of Investigation (FBI). In contrast to the FBI, which combines intelligence and investigative functions, the CBI is primarily an *ex-post* investigation body, not an intelligence-collecting agency. For the latter, it depends primarily on state police, and secondarily on Delhi's Intelligence Bureau (IB). The state police remain the greatest repository of ground-level intelligence in India.

The CBI was established under the Delhi Special Police Establishment Act, 1946. Its direct jurisdiction covers Delhi and the centrally administered Union Territories. Unlike the FBI, again, it cannot pursue investigation at the state level suo motu. To investigate, it must receive state consent, or be ordered to do so by the Supreme Court or a high court. In other words, for it to function well, it depends heavily on the state police. It can also team up with the Intelligence Bureau (IB), but the IB reports to India's Home Ministry, whereas the CBI reports to the Ministry of Personnel. The cooperation is not always forthcoming.[41]

State governments have the constitutional right to deny permission for CBI investigations. Goa, for example, did so during 1996–98. The Maharashtra government did not hand over the cases concerning the Mumbai blasts of 1993 to the CBI for almost a year. Some North-eastern states have often not given permission to the CBI.

At the root of this problem is what might be called the dark underbelly of Indian politics. The story of federalism has been told above in two political ways: one concerning the high principles of a state-nation, namely, the simultaneous pursuit of national integration and protection of cultural diversity; and the other concerning the structure of mundane politics, namely, the disproportionate benefits normally accruing to a state or a party that acquires a lot of power in Delhi.

A third political narrative, relevant here, is about the ignoble, but real, side of Indian politics: corruption and vendetta. The CBI is not trusted by state leaders for they believe it is politically used by Delhi to target adversaries. The adversaries may be accused of corruption, or even murders and kidnappings. It does not matter that such corruption or criminal conduct is often real, not imagined. But over the last twenty–thirty years, as politicians accused of crime, in particular, have risen in politics, the CBI has been caught in a political crossfire. Delhi often wants to use it, but the CBI faces enormous resistance at the state level, especially if the state government is run by a coalition or a political party different from the one ruling in Delhi.

As long as the Congress party was ruling both in Delhi and the states, there was no such resistance. Matters were handled as internal negotiations within the party. The rise of a coalition era might have made Indian politics much more democratic and competitive, but it is possible to argue that national security has suffered as a consequence.

Of late, India's political process has thrown up a potential solution. Via a parliamentary act, the National Investigation Agency (NIA) was created after the Mumbai attacks. In theory, the NIA can become India's FBI, but serious impediments remain.

The NIA Act was created using an entry related to defence of India on the Central list. Of all security matters, only defence of India is handled by Delhi. What is generally called internal, as opposed to external, security is almost entirely under state jurisdiction. The NIA Act is not a constitutional amendment, which would have required the approval of two-thirds of Parliament and of half the states, not easily possible in a coalition era. The concept of a federal crime, requiring a constitutional amendment, has still not been introduced precisely for the same reason. States would not give consent if they believed that the NIA might become a much more powerful CBI. Similar issues have been involved in the debate over the National Counter Terrorism Centre (NCTC) which, according to a number of state governments, gives too much power to Delhi.

Basically, Delhi cannot legally force a state government to accept the dictates of the NIA, or NCTC, unless a constitutional amendment introducing the concept of federal crime is put through. However desirable such a concept might be in the twenty-first century, India's federal polity will not easily allow it to come about.

Conclusion

Three arguments have been made in this chapter. First, India's federalism is fundamentally rooted in two simultaneous pursuits of nationhood: an embrace of state-based cultural diversities and a commitment to the larger Indian political community. This idea was politically implemented through organizations, especially the Congress party, during the long freedom movement, which changed the framework within which India's Centre and states bargained after independence. The same political party ruled both the Centre and the states after independence, and internal federalism was one of its key organizational principles. In the critical early years after independence, India's federalism thus developed a cooperative character. Many political battles were fought by the states against the Centre, but few were taken to the brink of breaking nationhood. Embracing diversities, the Centre, too, did not on the whole seek to obliterate the many identities of Indian citizens, regions, or states.

Second, the dispersed and cross-cutting nature of India's identities has also contributed to the survival of federalism. Had the identity structure been bipolar, reducible to 'the majority' and 'the minority', and had the identities been cumulative in nature, battles over federalism could have acquired deadly political proportions.

There are so many ways to construct a majority in India, both in states and the nation as a whole. As a result, considerable fluidity is lent to the majority–minority framework of politics. In Indian politics, permanent majorities are virtually inconceivable. This gives a certain benign edge to India's federalism.

Third, a coalition era has emerged in Indian politics in the last two decades. It has deepened democracy at one level, but also made national security more cumbersome. The laws concerning India's Centre–state relations—especially those concerning states having exclusive responsibility for public order—are obstructing the evolution of a solid organizational structure to deal with cross-border terrorism. Constitutional amendments may resolve this problem, but such amendments are unlikely to go through in a coalitional political atmosphere. In all probability, on countering terrorism, India will have to muddle through.

7

Two Banks of the Same River? Social Orders and Entrepreneurialism in India

Since 1980, as is well known, India's economy has registered a significant departure from the so-called Hindu rate of growth—3.5 per cent annually—that marked its performance during 1950–80. By now, however, India's South has surged far ahead of the North. In 1960, compared to the North, the South's per capita income was barely higher.[1] By 2007, the South's per capita income was more than twice as high.[2] The acceleration in the South's per capita income has been especially remarkable since 1980, now generally viewed as the starting point of India's economic acceleration, to which the market-oriented reforms of 1991 gave a further push. During the period 1980–2007, per capita incomes in the South grew at an annual rate of 4.32 per cent; those in the North at less than half as rapidly (2.12 per cent).

Accounting for about 20.8 per cent of the national population in 2001 Census, India's South comprises Andhra Pradesh, Karnataka, Kerala, and Tamil Nadu. India's North is not so easily definable. For the sake of tractability, I will use the term to describe the *Hindi-*

speaking North, holding nearly 41.6 per cent of India's population, according to 2001 Census, and comprising four big states: Uttar Pradesh (UP), Madhya Pradesh (MP), Bihar, and Rajasthan. In 1999, Bihar, MP, and UP were broken up, leading to the birth of three new states: Jharkhand, Chhattisgarh and Uttarakhand. Since this chapter tracks down historically rooted politics, I will concentrate on the older units. For my analytical purposes, a post-1999 disaggregation is not required.[3]

Sen has suggested that, if the current trends continue—and this assumption is critical—India will soon be 'part California and part Sub-Saharan Africa'.[4] Though Sen spoke of increasing inequalities amid rising prosperity in general, one of the most obvious ways, as of now, to interpret this comment is to contrast the South (and the West) and the North (and the East). The contrast is not perfect and partial exceptions exist[5] but, on the whole, enormous entrepreneurialism has burst forth in the South, while the Northern lag—though not locked in perpetuity—has been quite noticeable. Indeed, it is quite possible that the lag will be lower in the future years and may even close, but it is important to understand why the South went ahead in the first place.

One of the greatest differences between India's North and South is that lower caste movements opposed to the Hindu caste hierarchy erupted in Southern India as early as the 1910s, and democratic politics—both movement- and election-based—eroded the vertically organized caste system by the late 1960s. The erosion was not deep enough to liberate the Dalits, but it did lift the middle-ranking other backward castes (OBCs), thereby bringing down the political dominance of the upper castes. In contrast, caste hierarchies have come under intense pressure in parts of the North relatively recently. Does this social difference have anything to do with the radically diverging economic trajectory? This is the key question for this chapter.

My central hypothesis is Tocquevillean. In the 1830s, when

Tocqueville visited Kentucky and Ohio, he attributed the former's economic listlessness to the presence of slavery in the state, and the latter's dynamism to the absence of slaves. Analogously, I argue that the undermining of a vertical social order in the South, based on the caste system, has unleashed enormous entrepreneurial energies, while the Northern lag in caste politics has delayed the region's economic transformation.[6] Since there was, traditionally speaking, a neat fit between caste and occupation, entrepreneurship was historically confined only to some castes.[7] The unravelling of the caste order in Southern India means that the relationship between caste and business has broken down. Brahmins as well as the lower castes have turned entrepreneurial. In the North, such developments are more recent and the extent of the social revolution, arguably, not as deep. The breakdown of caste hierarchies appears to be integrally connected to the Southern economic rise, and the converse seems to be true for the Hindi-speaking North. Ascriptive (birth-based) verticality of the social order and entrepreneurialism show signs of an inverse correlation.[8]

Observers of Indian political economy will inevitably point to what appears to be a huge exception to the claim above. Gujarat, part of neither the South nor the North, has been one of India's fastest-growing states for over two decades. But unlike the South, Gujarat has not had any significant or long-lasting lower caste movements.[9] Does that invalidate the basic claim above?

For historically specific reasons, the traditional business communities of Gujarat—the Vaishyas—have enjoyed a remarkable cultural hegemony in the state. The social desire to be an entrepreneur is much more widespread in Gujarat than in any other state in India, and Brahmins and other traditionally non-business castes have followed the social and economic lead of the Vaishyas.[10] An entrepreneurial revolution took place in Gujarat due to the cultural hegemony of the Vaishyas, not because of a lower caste revolution. These are two different routes to the same outcome, but *each relies on breaking the traditional link between caste and occupation.*[11]

It is perhaps incontestable that the long-run economic transformation of a country or region nearly always has multiple reasons. In explaining the Southern turnaround, I will make no attempt to analyse the many factors that could potentially be listed: superior infrastructure, greater public investment, higher mass literacy, superior health indicators, better law and order, etc.[12] The changing caste structure is one of several factors.[13]

There are two conventional ways of explaining economic transformation at low levels of income. Economic growth is either viewed as a function of rising savings and investments rates[14] or explained in terms of growth-inducing economic policies and institutions.[15] The former is often termed factor-driven growth, to be analytically distinguished from efficiency-driven growth normally associated with economic policies such as trade-openness.[16] There is also an alternative line of inquiry that scholars have deployed to explain economic success. In this alternative framework, human development indices, especially education and literacy, are emphasized. Mass literacy can lift skills and give millions greater capabilities which, in turn, allow them to create and/or exploit economic opportunities.[17] Illiterate populations cannot be highly productive in modern times.

In no tradition is the focus on entrepreneurialism and its social foundations. In what follows, I start with the theoretical inspiration behind framing the problem of economic dynamism in terms of social orders. Having outlined the inspiration and analysed its implications, I move on to India and present some economic contrasts between India's North and South. Next, I concentrate on a particular Southern caste, the Nadars, to illustrate the depth of Southern transformation and identify the mechanisms of transformation. The penultimate section explores the commercial implications of the rise of lower castes in UP and Bihar. It is followed by a summarizing section.

Tocqueville and the Two Banks of the Ohio River

Tocqueville's *Democracy in America* does not centrally deal with race, a master narrative of American politics and society. Only one section, 'The Three Races that Inhabit the United States', is devoted to understanding the economic and political implications of racial stratification. Nearly a decade before John Stuart Mill proposed his method of difference in 1843,[18] Tocqueville anticipated that form of reasoning and argued that the settlements of Ohio and Kentucky, on either side of the Ohio River, were identical in all respects except for slavery, and that slavery made all the difference to their landscapes of economic dynamism and listlessness, respectively:

> The stream that the Indians had named the Ohio, or Beautiful River par excellence, waters one of the most magnificent valleys in which man has ever lived. On both banks of the Ohio stretched undulating ground with soil continually offering the cultivator inexhaustible treasures; on both banks the air is equally healthy and the climate temperate; they both form the frontier of a vast state: that which follows the innumerable windings of the Ohio on the left bank is called Kentucky; the other takes its name from the river itself. There is only one difference between the two states: Kentucky allows slaves, but Ohio refuses to have them.
>
> So the traveler who lets the current carry him down the Ohio till it joins the Mississippi sails, so to say, between freedom and slavery; and he has only to glance around to see instantly which is best for mankind.
>
> On the left of the river, the population is sparse; from time to time one sees a troop of slaves loitering through half-deserted fields; the primeval forest is constantly reappearing; one might say that

society had gone to sleep; it is nature that seems active and alive, whereas man is idle.

But on the right bank a confused hum proclaims from afar that men are busily at work; fine crops cover the fields; elegant dwellings testify to the taste and industry of the workers; on all sides there is evidence of comfort; man appears rich and contented; he works.[19]

It may well be that in the 1830s, Kentucky and Ohio were not identical in all respects except slavery.[20] Still, Tocqueville's insight—that slavery impeded economic dynamism and the absence of slavery freed the human spirit and creativity—is to be taken seriously. It stands to reason.

Why should a hierarchical social order inhibit productivity? Following Taylor, we can argue that a hierarchical social order is defined by honour, not dignity.[21] By depriving the toiling masses of dignity and reserving honour only for the slave-owners, slavery stifled the creativity of millions who could have potentially taken control of their own lives, negotiated a legally secure space for political and economic expression, and added substantially to the ideas and productivity of the whole society.

It is, of course, worth probing whether ascriptive hierarchies are always associated with a lack of economic dynamism. Moore gave a widely noted answer four decades back.[22] By focusing on the comparative history of modernity, he identified a way of combining deeply structured hierarchies and economic productivity in the early years of German and Japanese industrialization. An industrial transformation of largely agrarian societies, he argued, was possible if 'labor-repressive agriculture' was imposed upon the peasantry. Exploiting peasants economically but inculcating values of obedience in them (and also drawing their support by arousing intense hatred for 'the other'), both Germany and Japan, despite their hierarchical social orders, managed to go through a massive industrial transformation. But such industrial transformations, according to Moore, are normally accompanied by militant dictatorships, and we know from a comparative theory of democratization that, at high levels of income, dictatorships are not sustainable.[23] The implication is that ascriptive hierarchy and economic productivity can go together, but not for long. Sustained and long-run economic productivity requires the erosion, not maintenance, of ascriptive stratification. In order for economies to continue to do well in the long run, human beings must breathe freely.

Let me now recast Tocqueville's basic argument in the language of modern social science, and suggest that it can be meaningfully extended to India. In his comparison of the two banks of the Ohio river, Tocqueville essentially talked about the negative economic impact of what Horowitz has called a ranked ethnic system, which is to be distinguished from an unranked ethnic system.[24]

Horizontal and Vertical Social Orders

The key to Horowitz's distinction between ranked and unranked ethnic systems is the idea that relations between ethnic groups can have a horizontal or a vertical structure. In a horizontal social order, an ethnic group is more or less randomly distributed over the upper, middle, and lower classes. In such systems, ethnicity, an ascriptive term, does not coincide with class, a term economically or occupationally defined. Think of the Irish in the US today, though one should quickly note that that is not how the Irish were distributed over the various economic class categories in the 1840s and 1850s, when the ancestors of many Irish-Americans arrived on US shores as poor peasants escaping a potato famine in Ireland. Analogously, the Nadars of Tamil Nadu, discussed at length later in this chapter, are now to be found in all sorts of class categories though, until 150 years ago, they were mostly 'toddy-tappers', confined to a 'near-untouchable' and 'unclean' status.

Group relations can also take a radically different, and vertical, form. A vertical social order represents an overlap of ethnicity and class. In such systems, ethnic groups are occupationally confined; inter-occupational mobility is prohibited by custom or coercion; some groups are superordinate and others, subordinate. In the field of comparative ethnicity, racial slavery in the US and the apartheid system of South Africa are viewed as examples of an ideal-typical vertical ethnic order.

How about India's caste system? How does it compare with racial stratification? Just as race is the dark underbelly of American society, caste is India's. This equivalence, not entirely obvious, requires some explanation. Race and caste are not identical, but they share some key conceptual properties.

Let us first note the key differences between racial stratification— as historically observed in the US—and caste stratification—as it traditionally operated in India. First, whatever one may say of ancient times, we have no evidence that, in the late medieval or modern periods of Indian history, the Dalits, untouchable for centuries, and the lower Hindu castes were ever *enslaved as a group*. Slavery existed in modern India, but in pockets. Moreover, no specific ethnic group, or caste, was viewed as a target of enslavement all over India, or in any given linguistic region. Ethnic groups were neither bought and sold as commodities, nor owned as private property, as slaves were. The most recent historical overview of South Asian slavery argues that 'capture in war and impoverishment' were the 'two primary mechanisms of enslavement in South Asia'.[25] Caste was not directly linked to slavery.

Second, caste and skin colour do not overlap perfectly, as they normally tend to do in a racial stratification system. Last names give away the caste in North India, and first names in South India, not the colour of the skin. Darker-skinned Brahmins and lighter-skinned lower castes can be found in all parts of India. Since there are no all-India last names, the caste system is normally defined as national in theory, but regional or local in practice. It is virtually impossible for most South Indian Brahmins to recognize North Indian Brahmin last names, and vice versa. The same is true for other castes. There are Dalits all over India, but there are no all-India Dalit last names. *Each last name makes sense in a linguistic register,* and India has many linguistic regions. As a consequence, conceptually, caste-based stratification is no different from racial stratification but, empirically, its theatre of operation is always local or regional. This is one of the important reasons why national-level, caste-based, political parties do not exist in India. Caste-based parties tend to be regional.

Let us now turn to the commonalities between racial and caste stratification. Two similarities stand out. First, each is an ascriptive and vertical division of labour.[26] Barack Obama, the 44th President of the US, has written about 'the almost mathematical precision with which America's race and class problems (are) joined'.[27] In its pristine form, the caste system also aligned the ascriptive and occupational categories more or less perfectly. The upper castes had the higher professions (priesthood, administration, the military, scholarship, business); the Dalits—'untouchables' until India's independence and scheduled castes (SCs) since then—were placed at the bottom of the social scale and restricted to the 'polluting' professions (cleaning, scavenging, leather-making, alcohol-making, etc.); the 'lower castes', located in the middle, had the menial jobs (mainly farming and artisanship). The 'lower' or 'middle' castes came to be called the 'other backward classes' (OBCs) after independence. In aggregate terms, thus, the caste hierarchy is *tri-modal.* The three modes are: the upper castes, the OBCs, and the Dalits (SCs).[28]

Beyond an enumeration of SCs, no caste census has been taken since 1931. As a result, we do not have precise demographic percentages for the various castes. India's 2011 Census will—when the results are made public—give us reasonably precise magnitudes, but the general belief is that the upper castes are about 15–18 per cent of India today; the OBCs, 45–50 per cent; and the SCs, 17 per cent.[29]

Another similarity between race in the US and caste in India has to do with segregation and denial of human dignity. Like African Americans in the US, Dalits were also socially segregated in all parts of India. There were no common civic sites where Dalits and the lower castes on the one hand and Dalits and the upper castes on the other could come together. Temples, housing, community halls, and, especially in Southern India, even roads were segregated. The story of the Ezhavas, a toddy-tapping caste, described as semi-polluted due to its traditional professional association with alcohol-making, briefly covered in Chapter 3, is worth revisiting. In Kerala, paradoxically India's most socially egalitarian state today, this is how the Ezhavas were treated until roughly the 1930s:

> They were not allowed to walk on public roads. . . . They were Hindus, but they could not enter temples. . . . Ezhavas could not use public wells or public places. . . . An Ezhava should keep himself at least thirty-six feet away from a Namboodiri and twelve feet away from a Nair. . . . He must address a caste Hindu man, as *Thampuran* (My Lord) and woman as *Thampurati* (My Lady). . . . He must stand before a caste Hindu in awe and reverence, assuming a humble posture. He should never dress himself up like a caste Hindu; never construct a house on the upper-caste model. . . . The women folk of the community . . . were required, young and old, to appear before caste Hindus, always topless.[30]

Analogous stories can be culled from US history as well. Slavery ended in the US in 1865, but racial segregation and humiliation did not. A decade and a half after the end of the US Civil War (1861–65), America's South witnessed the rise of Jim Crow laws, which segregated Blacks for housing and education, and in religious and social life; would not allow them access to public spaces and voting rights; and punish them through lynch mobs if they crossed a politically and socially determined line. Interracial marriages were outlawed; interracial sex was criminalized. Lynching of African Americans became quite common.[31] Available studies suggest an annual average of a little over 100 lynchings during 1882–1930 or roughly one lynching every third day during those forty nine years.[32]

Similarly, discrimination, degradation, and violence were written into customary norms of caste relations. The system worked peacefully if the pre-assigned caste roles were accepted. There was upward mobility in the caste system, especially through 'Sanskritization' and 'Westernization', but such mobility was severely limited. Sanskritization meant following the lifestyle and rituals of the upper castes, but such moves by the lower castes were often unacceptable to the upper castes, and force would be exercised to maintain social order. 'Westernization'— speaking English and adopting English lifestyles—became a model of mobility only after the beginning of the British conquest of India in 1757. Bringing England home was, however, never a practical choice for India's masses. At best, it was available in the cities. At the time of independence, no more than 15–16 per cent of India was urban. The literacy rate, too, was a mere 17–18 per cent. English-speakers were a minuscule percentage of the population.

All that I have said above is basically *conceptual*, an attempt to suggest that, in its verticality, if not in other ways, caste is analogous to race. Let me now move towards the *explanatory* side of the problem at hand. The key question is: What economic consequences follow when a vertical caste order is undermined? Tocqueville's argument about Ohio and Kentucky converges on how the absence of slavery led to economic dynamism in Ohio. In Kentucky, 'nature . . . seems active and alive, whereas man is idle'. And in Ohio, which never had slaves, 'men are busily at work; fine crops cover the fields; elegant dwellings testify to the taste and industry of the workers'. Can different caste configurations be similarly linked to the economic dynamism or stagnation of states and regions of India?

The Rise of the South: Some Basic Statistics

To illustrate the divergence between Northern and Southern India, let me present three sets of statistics: state-level economic growth rates as well as state-level growth rates in per capita income; growth rates in the number of what the Government of India calls 'enterprises', both rural and urban; and growth rates of OBC-owned enterprises. The numbers below will make greater sense, if we keep in mind the relative population shares of the two regions. To recap, according to 2001 Census, the four Southern states held about 20.8 per cent, and the four major Hindi-speaking states about 41.6 per cent of India's population.[33]

Table 7.1 captures the annualized economic growth rates of the two regions. During 1960–80, the economic growth rates of the North and the South were not terribly different. The Hindi-speaking North grew at an average of 2.8 per cent per annum, the South at 3.1 per cent. Moreover, both sets of states had a growth rate lower than the all-India average. In the period 1980–2007, the all-India growth rate picked up substantially. The Hindi-speaking North continued to grow below the national average, but the Southern growth has caught up with the national trend line.

Table 7.2 makes the contrast sharper. It presents the growth rates in per capita incomes, a more meaningful category than aggregate growth rates, for it subtracts population growth rates from economic growth rates, providing a better measure of economic welfare. During 1960–80, compared to the North, Southern per capita incomes grew 2.77 times higher per year. During 1980–2007, the South–North ratio in the growth of per capita incomes continued to be an impressive 2.04. In absolute terms, the South–North ratio for the second period is lower than for the first, but it is on a much

TABLE 7.1: NORTH AND SOUTH: ECONOMIC GROWTH RATES, 1960–2007 (PER CENT PER ANNUM)

	1960–80	1981–2007
All-India Average	3.4	5.7
Hindi-speaking North		
Bihar	2.7	4.4
Madhya Pradesh	2.6	4.2
Rajasthan	2.9	5.6
Uttar Pradesh	2.8	4.5
Average	*2.8*	*4.7*
Southern States		
Andhra Pradesh	3.1	6.0
Karnataka	3.7	5.8
Kerala	3.1	5.6
Tamil Nadu	2.3	5.7
Average	*3.1*	*5.8*
South–North Ratio	**1.11**	**1.23**

Source: Tables 7.1 and 7.2 are based on the World Bank statistics on Indian states

higher statistical base by 1980. This effectively means that, compared to the North, per capita incomes in the Southern states have been growing at a much higher rate since 1960.[34] This is perhaps the sense in which we can best interpret Sen's comment that India will become 'part California, part Sub-Saharan Africa' before long.[35] If the North does not catch up—though the chances are it will— Southern incomes will be many times higher than Northern incomes in the next 15–20 years.[36]

Let us now turn to the growth of enterprises in the two regions. The Ministry of Statistics, Government of India, started taking an Economic Census of India in 1977. The aim was to provide a 'complete enumeration of all agricultural (except crop production & plantation) and non-agricultural entrepreneurial activities'. It

TABLE 7.2: PER CAPITA NET STATE DOMESTIC PRODUCT (NSDP) GROWTH RATES (PER CENT PER ANNUM)

	1960–80	1981–2007
Hindi-speaking North		
Bihar	0.6	1.5
Madhya Pradesh	0.1	2.0
Rajasthan	0.2	3.2
Uttar Pradesh	0.7	1.8
Average	*0.4*	*2.1*
Southern States		
Andhra Pradesh	1.0	4.3
Karnataka	1.3	3.9
Kerala	1.0	4.6
Tamil Nadu	0.9	4.5
Average	*1.1*	*4.3*
South–North Ratio	**2.77**	**2.04**

defines an 'enterprise' as 'an undertaking engaged in production and/or distribution of goods and/or services not for the sole purpose of own consumption'.[37] The definition includes non-crop-growing agricultural enterprises, and large-, medium-, and small-scale industries as well as rural enterprises. The data on capital employed in each enterprise is not collected, nor is it perhaps easy to get an accurate measure of it in a largely informal economy. But the census does count the number of enterprises, permitting some fairly meaningful inferences for our purposes.

Contemporary travellers to Southern India invariably note signs of economic dynamism in most parts of the region, whereas vast parts of Hindi-speaking North, like Tocqueville's Kentucky, appear remarkably listless to the naked eye. Tables 7.3, 7.4, and 7.5 provide some statistical evidence for the traveller's visual impressions. Table

TABLE 7.3: GROWTH IN THE NUMBER OF ENTERPRISES

	1980–90	1998–2005
South	33.61%	55.39%
North	21.27%	27.82%

Source: Table 7.3 is based on the Economic Census 1998 and 2005, Department of Statistics, Government of India, available in CD-Rom format

TABLE 7.4: GROWTH OF RURAL ENTERPRISES, 1998–2005

State	1998	2005	Growth (per cent)
Andhra Pradesh	2,007,386	2,847,796	41.87
Karnataka	1.152,092	1,590,152	38.02
Kerala	1,240,685	2,101,075	69.35
Tamil Nadu	1,407,786	2,727,624	93.75
South Total	**5,807,949**	**9,266,647**	**59.55**
Bihar	872,107	1,131,303	29.72
Madhya Pradesh	1,207,195	1,356,340	12.35
Rajasthan	910,625	1,216,060	33.54
Uttar Pradesh	1,478,767	2,403,629	62.54
North Total	**4,468,694**	**6,107,332**	**36.67**
South–North Ratio	**1.30**	**1.52**	**1.6**

Source: Tables 7.4 is based on the Economic Census 1998 and 2005, Department of Statistics, Government of India, available in CD-Rom format

7.3 shows that during 1980–90, while the number of enterprises in the South grew by 33.6 per cent, the North managed a decadal rise of 21.2 per cent. During 1998–2005—the latest period for which data are available—the South went through an explosive boom, as its number of enterprises grew by a massive 55 per cent, while new enterprises in the North added a mere 27.8 per cent to the 1998 base. If the economic census had also given us the capital deployed, and

TABLE 7.5: GROWTH OF URBAN ENTERPRISES, 1998–2005

State	1998	2005	Growth (per cent)
Andhra Pradesh	895,156	1,149,186	28.38
Karnataka	759,539	948,722	24.91
Kerala	323,986	702,753	116.91
Tamil Nadu	1,106,018	1,705,767	54.23
South Total	**3,084,699**	**4,506,428**	**46.09**
Bihar	570,667	584,721	2.46
Madhya Pradesh	917,245	1,016,227	10.79
Rajasthan	619,960	745,405	20.23
Uttar Pradesh	1,564,244	1,942,138	24.16
North Total	**3,672,116**	**4,288,491**	**16.79**
South–North Ratio	**0.84**	**1.05**	**2.7**

Source: Table 7.5–7.7 is based on the *Economic Census* 1998 and 2005, Department of Statistics, Government of India, available in CD-Rom format

not simply the number of enterprises, we would have had a fuller picture. But these statistics, when added to the next two tables, make it clear that compared to the North, many more new enterprises have been born in Southern India right since 1980.

Table 7.4 shows how the rural South has been transformed. During 1998–2005, the number of rural enterprises grew by approximately 59.5 per cent in the South on a base that was higher to begin with, whereas enterprise growth was a mere 36.7 per cent in the rural North. By 2005, the rural South had almost one and a half times as many enterprises in absolute terms as the North did, though in terms of population, the rural South carries only about half as many people as the rural North. During 1998–2005, urban enterprises in the South also grew much more (Table 7.5). 1n 1998, Northern towns and cities had more enterprises than those in the South but, by 2005, the South had surged ahead. In purely numerical terms, then, the rural entrepreneurial boom in the South is very impressive, but the urban enterprise is not far behind.

Theoretically, of course, it is quite possible for the number of enterprises to decline or stay the same, and economic dynamism to rise, provided mergers create economies of scale. No data are available on mergers and acquisitions in India beyond the top tiers of the formal capitalist sector, and most of the enterprises counted in the census are small- and medium-sized in the so-called informal sector.[38]

In short, these statistics do not clearly establish that Southern enterprises are much more efficient than their Northern counterparts, though that may well be true. It is, however, incontestable that by now, *a significantly larger proportion of Southern population is involved in commerce.*

Are the new entrepreneurs randomly distributed across the various castes, or is it that some castes have stood out in the entrepreneurial boom sweeping through much of the South? The business landscape in Eastern, Western, and Northern India has been traditionally dominated by the trading castes, especially the Vaishyas and the Marwaris. In the South, the Chettiars have been the equivalent of Vaishyas.[39] Have the 'lower castes' finally entered commerce in a big way?

The next chapter discusses the rise of Dalit millionaires. Though symbolically significant, their numbers are remarkably small. To the observers of India's political economy, the realistic issue concerning the change in the traditional occupational structure is not whether the Dalits (SCs) have risen as a commercial force, but whether the OBCs have. Dalits were, and still remain, at the bottom of the social hierarchy. The OBCs were always in the middle, and their numbers were also much larger than those of the Dalits. It is therefore theoretically possible to imagine that a combination of political power, facilitated by their numbers in a universal-franchise polity, and an economic base higher than that of the Dalits would engender a massive commercial revolution. The contrast between the trading and the artisan castes is especially relevant here. The artisan castes, placed in the OBC category, were historically unable to scale up. They lacked the initial capital and literacy to transform their small-scale projects into larger units, while the trading castes, placed in the upper-caste category, were able to utilize their connections and capital to dominate business as a profession.

How have the OBCs figured in Northern and Southern commerce? India's Economic Census did not collect caste-based commercial statistics until 1998. We only have two data points—1998 and 2005—so we cannot statistically ascertain the changing social background of business over the long run. However, some indicative inferences can still be drawn.

Table 7.6 shows that in 1998, compared to the North, the OBCs had greater presence in Southern commerce. While 40 per cent of Northern enterprises were OBC-owned, nearly 50 per cent of all Southern enterprises were owned by the OBCs. Among Southern states, at 74 per cent, the OBCs had the highest share of enterprise ownership in Tamil Nadu.[40]

Table 7.7 shows that compared to 1998, OBC ownership rose both in the North and the South, though by a larger percentage in the North. The South continues to be ahead but, compared to 1998, its lead is smaller. At one level, this may mean that, with the rise of lower castes in Northern India, especially in UP and Bihar, a commercial revolution is perhaps in the offing. If so, the emerging trend will be consistent with the Tocquevillean hypothesis. But three points of caution are worth noting.

First of all, there are questions about how governments define OBCs in different states. It is worth exploring whether the term OBC, used in public policy in the North later than in the South, became much more political in the Northern states? The most obvious example is the placement of Vaishyas in the OBC category in Bihar.[41] The Vaishyas are North India's core merchant community

TABLE 7.6: PERCENTAGE OF OBC OWNERSHIP OF ENTERPRISES, 1998

State	Total Enterprises	Urban Enterprises	Rural Enterprises
Andhra Pradesh	44.05%	36.96%	47.21%
Karnataka	29.91%	25.31%	32.94%
Kerala	44.75%	44.32%	44.87%
Tamil Nadu	73.63%	73.30%	73.90%
South Total	**49.50%**	**47.89%**	**50.35%**
Bihar	51.69%	49.76%	52.96%
Madhya Pradesh	43.91%	40.95%	46.15%
Rajasthan	29.23%	24.25%	32.61%
Uttar Pradesh	37.58%	34.52%	40.83%
North Total	**40.16%**	**36.76%**	**42.96%**

TABLE 7.7: PERCENTAGE OF OBC OWNERSHIP OF ENTERPRISES, 2005

States	Total Enterprises	Urban Enterprises	Rural Enterprises
Andhra Pradesh	43.08%	40.67%	44.05%
Karnataka	40.31%	31.22%	45.73%
Kerala	49.76%	55.93%	47.70%
Tamil Nadu	71.69%	73.47%	70.57%
South Total	**53.14%**	**53.48%**	**52.97%**
Bihar	48.62%	44.41%	50.79%
Madhya Pradesh	44.41%	40.29%	47.49%
Rajasthan	44.92%	36.51%	50.07%
Uttar Pradesh	49.18%	43.99%	53.38%
North Total	**47.19%**	**41.87%**	**50.93%**

and normally viewed as an upper caste, but many of them are designated as 'backward' in Bihar. The statistical consequence of this placement is worth pondering: it is likely to have increased OBC business ownership figures by a huge margin. Similarly, the Jats, viewed by scholars as a dominant caste, are included in the list of OBCs in some Northern states. In Rajasthan where, compared to the other states, the growth in OBC ownership was the highest between 1998 and 2005, rising by more than 50 per cent, the Jats were added to the OBC list only in 1999.[42] A large part of the OBC business ownership in Rajasthan in 2005 may well be an artifact of the 1999 legislation.

On the whole, it is not unreasonable to conjecture that in government statistics, the OBC category in the North is substantially inflated. It is possible that the Southern OBC lead is bigger than what the government statistics indicate.

Second, we have no systematic analyses yet of the average size of the business enterprise in the North and South. If it is true, as is often speculated, that OBC enterprises in the North are generally very small, whereas many OBC businesses in the South are reasonably large, then, the lead of Southern OBCs in commerce would be commensurably greater. An example of this phenomenon, the rise of Nadars, is given below, and some cases are also examined in the next chapter.

Third, even if the OBC share of business is not inflated in the North, it would appear that the upper or dominant castes, whose traditional occupation was not business, have become much more involved in commerce in the South. A comparison of Tables 7.3, 7.4, and 7.5—which report the overall numbers of business enterprises—with Tables 7.6 and 7.7—which report the OBC share of these enterprises—makes this inference plausible. By 1998, the overall size of the entrepreneurial community in the South had more than caught up with the North, even though the total population of the North was twice as large, and by 2005, the number of enterprises was greater in the South than in the North. Assuming that Dalit businesses are still few and far between, both in the North and South, the much bigger non-OBC ownership in the South is likely to consist, substantially if not entirely, of upper and dominant castes.[43] A greater disaggregation of data, when available, will clinch this point, but the inference makes sense. This is another sense in which the crumbling of the vertical social order is connected to a commercial revolution. Not only the OBCs, but all castes—regardless of what their traditional professions were—have entered business in large numbers in the South.

To sum up, India's South appears to have stolen an entrepreneurial march over the North, and the earlier and more decisive unravelling of the caste order has played a large part in it. The North has lagged behind. The gap may well have started to close of late, but the historical difference is beyond doubt.

From Toddy-Tappers to High-Tech Businessmen

Statistics give us a clear picture of the aggregate outcomes, but they rarely give us a sense of the process generating the outcomes we observe, nor do they reveal the texture of politics that drives the process.[44] It is the in-depth examination of a representative or a critical case that uncovers the process. Let me, therefore, turn to one of the most remarkable transformations in India's caste history over the last 150 years.

The Nadars of Tamil Nadu are widely recognized as a dynamic business community of Tamil Nadu today. But that was not always so. Until a century back, the Nadars were placed near the bottom of the caste pyramid. Their upward mobility indicates the depth of Southern social transformation. Nothing comparable has happened in the North.

Historically known as Shanars—a term of abuse which they successfully fought to change—the Nadars were traditionally toddy-tappers. They were classified as 'near untouchables', placed at the bottom of the so-called OBC category, slightly above the SCs. Toddy-tapping essentially meant that the Nadar men 'climbed the palmyra (tree) to tap its sap, some of which was fermented to make an alcoholic beverage known in English as toddy. This association with alcohol was one of the primary reasons for the traditionally low social status of the Shanars.'[45]

Like the Ezhavas in Kerala described earlier, the Nadars too had to go through a series of quotidian deprivations and insults, all enforced by violence if the tradition was violated:

> A Nadar must remain thirty-six paces from a . . . Brahmin, and must come no closer than twelve to a Nair. As members of a degraded caste, Nadars were prohibited from carrying an umbrella, and from wearing shoes or golden ornaments. Their houses could not be higher than one storey. . . . Nadar women were not permitted to . . . cover the upper portions of their bodies. They were subjected to heavy taxation, and while they were not enslaved . . . the Nadars were forced to perform corvee labour in service to the state.[46]

In conditions like this, some Nadars embraced Christianity in the middle of the twentieth century, responding—with hope and relief—to the attempts of Christian missionaries doing their religious work under British rule. Christian Nadar women started to cover their breasts, defying tradition.[47] In October 1858, 'Sudras attacked Nadar women in the bazaars, stripping them of their upper garments.'[48] Nadar defiance continued, so did the repressive reaction by castes higher than them. The British government sided with tradition. Considerable violence followed.

> In a village market, a petty official . . . stripped Nadar women of their breast cloths. The incident sparked twenty days of rioting in the district. . . . Rioting soon followed in other districts. . . . On

4 January 1859, some two hundred Shudras, armed with clubs and knives, attacked the Christian Nadars of a village . . . Houses were burned and looted. During the months of rioting between October 1859 and February 1859, nine chapels and three schools were (also) burned.[49]

A second set of vicious riots broke out at the turn of the century. The dispute was over the right of entry to Hindu temples. The Nadars had, for centuries, been denied temple entry. By the end of the nineteenth century, through local trade and commerce, the Nadars had developed a small middle class. Once a middle class emerged, the Nadars began to assert that they had a right to enter Hindu temples. In 1899, in Sivakasi—where the economic rise of the Nadars was the highest—four years of violent confrontations between the Nadars and the higher castes began. When 'the military finally brought riots under control, nearly 150 (primarily Nadar) villages had been attacked, and the reported figures of the number of houses destroyed varied between 1,600 and 4,000'.[50]

Quite in contrast to such conditions a century and a half ago, the Nadars by now have expanded their commercial interests over a variety of sectors, including high-technology products. The greatest success story is that of Shiv Nadar, a billionaire and the founder and chairman of Hindustan Computers Limited (HCL), one of India's most successful computer hardware companies,

Innumerable medium- and small-scale enterprises in Tamil Nadu are also Nadar-owned. The city of Sivakasi, famous for its fireworks industry for a long time, emerged as the heart of the Nadar business community. Initially, the Nadars manufactured matchboxes and matchsticks in Sivakasi. This eventually gave rise to the growth of Nadar-owned chemical plants. Later, members of Nadar community started businesses that used chemicals as the primary inputs—fireworks and art supplies. As these businesses grew, the demand for printed packaging materials increased, and

Nadar-owned printing presses emerged to supply labels. Once established, these printing presses diversified their production by printing greeting cards and chequebooks. An industry that made matches and matchboxes 'has since evolved into a Rs 1000 crore business performing more sophisticated jobs, from printing notebooks, calendars, diaries, greeting cards, and brochures to flight tickets and bank chequebooks'.[51]

Three developments shaped the economic transformation of the Nadars: the creation of a strong community organization in 1910 that survives till now; the growth of a self-respect movement in the 1910s and 1920s that made alliances with other lower castes and shook the politics of the state; and the emergence of an ambitious affirmative action programme in Tamil Nadu in response to the rising pressure from the lower castes. Affirmative action brought lower castes to positions of authority in the government and to institutions of higher education. The Nadars were denied entry to public schools in British India until as late as the first decade of the twentieth century.

The creation of a community organization, called Nadar Mahajana Sangam (NMS), was at the heart of the developments listed above. The NMS not only fought social discrimination, but also became a financial educational and welfare organization. Apart from providing access to financial resources, the NMS regulated and coordinated business activity. It built communal facilities, *pettais*, for conducting business. The organization levied a formal tax, *mahamai*, on its members in exchange for using the communal commercial infrastructure.[52] The revenue from mahamai was used for the association's operations and for the maintenance of communal facilities. The NMS also levied a charity tax, *dharuman*, to provide social services to the poorer members.

Finally, the NMS raised funds to provide educational facilities to its members and the community at large. The NMS manages a range of educational institutions from schools to colleges to polytechnic institutes. Ninety-four educational institutions are listed on the community's website.[53] Especially noteworthy is the number of colleges and training facilities, such as V.A.P. Nadars Accountancy College; C.S.I. Jeyaraj Annapackiam College of Nursing; C.S.I Sri Sivasubraminya Nadar College of Engineering; and MEPCO Schlenk Dental College and Hospital.[54]

Because of the power the lower castes have come to exercise in Tamil Nadu, state institutions have helped the efforts of organizations like the NMS by providing partial funding for their projects. For example, the Government of Tamil Nadu has allocated funds for the construction of school buildings by private groups and also paid teachers' salaries. 'Being relieved of teachers' salaries while receiving substantial grants towards construction of new buildings has helped the associations rapidly to expand their educational services.'[55]

Emerging as a byproduct of the lower caste revolution in politics, a final development should also be noted. Since affirmative action programmes in Tamil Nadu were among the most ambitious in the country—reserving as much as 69 per cent of all government jobs and seats in state-supported, higher educational institutions for lower castes—Brahmins started entering commerce. Brahmins had traditionally dominated the educational sector and the civil service in the South,[56] but with big lower caste quotas during the mid- to the late-1960s, government jobs started drying up. Scholars started noticing the rise of Brahmins in industries in the 1970s.[57] By the turn of the century, Brahmins had come to dominate the knowledge-intensive IT clusters virtually all over Southern India.[58]

In short, the commercial revolution in Southern India appears to be driven to a substantial extent by the flattening of caste hierarchies. It led to the rise of lower castes in business on the one hand and the emergence of Brahmin entrepreneurs on the other. In contrast, the North did not witness a significant caste upheaval for much of the twentieth century.[59] That has begun to change only recently.

A Lower caste Revolution in UP and Bihar?

Of late, two of the Northern states, UP and Bihar, have witnessed a significant lower caste churning. Since the late 1980s, lower caste parties have been in power in both states, substantially or wholly. Indeed, in UP, India's largest state, and home to nearly 200 million people, the Bahujan Samaj Party (BSP), a primarily Dalit political organization, led by Mayawati, a Dalit, and supported substantially by Brahmins, came to power in May 2007. In South India, where the non-Brahmin castes came to power by the late 1960s, the Dalits (SCs) were never in the lead; the OBCs, including those at the bottom of the OBC category, such as the Nadars, were. No Dalit party had ever come to power in India's states.

The BSP was defeated in the 2012 elections, but its return to power cannot be ruled out in the future. Moreover, the party that came to power in 2012, the Samajwadi Party (SP) is also a lower caste party. Whether UP will follow in the footsteps of Bihar, already witnessing a lower caste hegemony in politics, is still to be seen.[60]

Can these political transformations lead to a Southern-style commercial revolution? How does one assess the commercial possibilities of the new political dispensations?

In the South, lower caste social organizations have historically been very significant. These organizations have emphasized not only affirmative action, but also education and commercial activities. They did not rely entirely on the government to uplift their communities. For example, the apex social organization of the Nadars is also among the largest educational organizations in Tamil Nadu, running schools, colleges, and institutes of engineering and medicine.

Lower caste politics in Southern India moved from *movement politics* to *electoral politics*; in the North, lower caste politics has been almost entirely electoral.[61] The Dalits of UP have no significant commercial or educational organizations. Nor do the OBCs, on the whole. If a Dalit bourgeoisie is not developed, a Dalit revolution in politics will not necessarily lead to a commercial revolution. Much will depend on whether the upper castes, pushed out of government jobs, take to commerce in increasingly larger numbers. Alternatively, if the OBCs take to business in large numbers, a commercial revolution is also possible. Tables 7.6 and 7.7 do suggest that this may happen, but a definite conclusion cannot yet be formed. The big difference between the North and the South remains: lower caste empowerment in Southern India was propelled by movements; in Northern India, electoral politics has driven it. The organizational characteristics of movements and election machines tend to be different.

Conclusion

Compared to the North, the greater undermining of the Southern caste hierarchies has released tremendous entrepreneurial energies, as all sorts of castes, with very different occupational traditions, have entered trade and modern businesses in large numbers. India's South has become a Tocquevillean Ohio. While India's Hindi-speaking North may not be trapped in an 1830s Kentucky-like iron grip of vertical hierarchy, the Northern unravelling, especially in Bihar and UP, has taken place decades after the breakdown of caste hierarchies in the South.

In the near future, these patterns are likely to be reinforced. But in the medium and long run, some new issues are worth thinking about. Wages in North India are much lower than in the South. Cities, like Bangalore, are choked with traffic and pollution, and have also become remarkably expensive. Chennai and Hyderabad, too, are headed in the same direction. If caste churning in the North does not lead to greater lawlessness, but instead a new political order is institutionalized, leading to better governance—as was the case in the South by the 1960s—then, it is quite possible that investors will begin to move towards the North due to its wage advantage. Bihar's recent turnaround in governance holds considerable promise, though we still have to watch the longer-run trends in the state. Where such economic processes are not strong enough or not possible, the state may have to midwife a commercial revolution.

8

Caste and Entrepreneurship
in India

(with Lakshmi Iyer and Tarun Khanna)

Focused on the relationship between caste and entrepreneurship, this chapter sheds light on two larger narratives about India's emerging political economy. The first one has to do with India's rapid economic growth rate over the past couple of decades. Whatever one's view on the reasons underlying the fast growth—an international opening of the economy; the demographic dividend arising from a large and growing young workforce; the greater liberalization of economic activity within the country since the mid-1980s[1]—there is concern that not all sections of society have benefited equally from economic growth, and that inequality might be rising after the introduction of economic reforms in the early 1990s.[2] Rightly or wrongly, the narrative—that the rich have benefited more than the poor, the towns and cities more than the villages, the upper castes more than the lower castes—has acquired salience in several quarters.[3] There is also some concern that the levels of entrepreneurship in India lag behind other countries with similar income levels.[4]

The second narrative relates to an important new discourse

232

in Dalit politics, one which concentrates on the need for Dalit entrepreneurs, conspicuous by their absence in India's business history. This narrative has its philosophical and political roots in the so-called Bhopal document of 2002. Getting together in Bhopal, Madhya Pradesh, under the sponsorship of Digvijay Singh, the then-chief minister of the state, some leading Dalit intellectuals argued that 'the imagination of the post-Ambedkar Dalit movement has been shackled ... within the discourse of reservations'.[5] Questioning the adequacy of reservations for Dalit welfare in contemporary India, they articulated an important challenge faced by the Dalit community in a rapidly growing Indian economy:

In the new scenario of the state's retreat, when public employment is shrinking, does it make any sense to simply reiterate the old slogan of reservations—even if it is extended to the private sector—as is now being demanded? Will the Dalits always have to remain content with the demand for such job reservations, which effectively means that they be employed as proletarians in the enterprises owned by others—in primarily upper caste concerns or those owned by the state but nevertheless controlled by the upper castes? Or must they now gird up their loins to play for fundamentally different stakes, making room for themselves in the new, free-market/global dispensation? Should they not also have their own bourgeoisie, their own millionaires and billionaires?[6]

Indeed, Dalit millionaires have been increasingly visible of late. Articles in leading newspapers and magazines have focused on the emergence of such millionaires.[7] In January 2011, the Planning Commission invited these businessmen for a special meeting that discussed both opportunities and constraints that their businesses faced. A separate Dalit Indian Chamber of Commerce & Industry (DICCI) has been formed.

The second narrative notably stands in considerable tension with the first. Case studies show that 'the growth of Dalit entrepreneurship took off . . . during the 1980s and more vigorously after the 1990s'.[8] India's post-1991 reforms are, thus, connected to rising economic inequalities in the first narrative, but they are also linked to the emergence of Dalit entrepreneurs in the second.

Dalit millionaires may have burst on the scene, but how far do they represent the general state of Dalit entrepreneurship in the country? More generally, what is the relationship between caste and entrepreneurship?

This is an important question. As is well known, the caste system was not only a scheme of social stratification, but also a division of labour. With each caste came a traditionally ascribed profession. Historically, there was undoubtedly some flexibility in the system,[9] but the flexibility was limited. It is only with the rise of democratic politics that the process of change was considerably spurred. Substantially because the lower castes constituted a majority of India's populace, democratic politics has been a forceful ally of the lower castes in the twentieth century.[10] Not all the changes have been benign,[11] but there is no doubt that, as far as representation in state assemblies and Parliament is concerned, India has gone through an OBC (other backward classes/castes) revolution.[12] Moreover, the reservations for the scheduled castes (SCs) and scheduled tribes (STs) have ensured that the SC and ST shares are substantial in representative assemblies.

Has this political revolution been accompanied by corresponding changes in the economic sphere? How has the caste map of entrepreneurs changed? On the whole, the relationship between caste and entrepreneurship remains under-researched, though a whole variety of other political economy questions concerning lower caste welfare have been probed. Some studies, for example, have shown an increasing convergence in habits and rituals across caste categories,[13] but others document persistent differences in important development outcomes, like consumption expenditure, education levels, and access to public goods.[14] The effects of affirmative actions for SCs and STs also appear to be mixed. Some scholars suggest that political reservations lead to greater social expenditures and more jobs for the SCs,[15] but not for the STs, while others find very limited effects of such affirmative action on educational outcomes for the SCs.[16]

We examine the role of caste differences using a very different metric of economic development, namely, the ownership of enterprises across the country. We are aware of only a handful of research attempts of this kind.[17] We build upon these studies and go beyond.

To arrive at our conclusions, we use comprehensive data from the Economic Censuses of India, which enumerate every non-agricultural enterprise in the country. Our findings reinforce the persistence of caste differences in important development outcomes. As late as 2005, scheduled castes and scheduled tribes were significantly under-represented in the ownership of private enterprises, and the employment generated by private enterprises. For instance, scheduled castes owned 9.8 per cent of all enterprises in 2005, well below their 16.4 per cent share in the total population. Such under-representation in the entrepreneurial sphere was widespread across all large states of India, and was present in both rural and urban settings. Moreover, despite more than a decade of rapid nationwide economic growth, the share of SCs and STs in firm ownership and employment generation over the period 1990–2005 increased only very modestly.

In addition to these broad measures of entrepreneurship, there are significant differences in firm characteristics across caste categories. Enterprises owned by members of SCs and STs tend to be smaller; they are less likely to employ labour from outside the family, and more likely to belong to the informal, or unorganized, sector. All these differences across caste categories are more pronounced in urban areas compared to rural areas, suggesting that these results cannot be attributed purely to social discrimination, which we might expect to be higher in rural areas. Overall, our results highlight that SC and ST entrepreneurs face significant obstacles in entering entrepreneurship, and in expanding the scale of their enterprises. These differences in entrepreneurship are not significantly correlated with demographic or economic characteristics, such as literacy rates or levels of secondary schooling, or the proportion of the population engaged in farming at the state level. This suggests that we need to think deeper and examine data at a more disaggregated level in order to understand the reasons behind what we observe. We also present preliminary results on the progress of other backward castes (OBCs) in enterprise ownership and employment generation. OBCs are traditionally the 'middle' castes, that is, neither suffering the extreme social and economic discrimination of the scheduled castes, nor enjoying the social privileges of the upper castes. These castes were given access to affirmative action policies at the national level only in the 1990s, though, after independence, they had started receiving reservation benefits in education and government employment at the *state level* in the late 1950s and early 1960s in Southern India. We find that the OBCs appear to be making significant progress in playing an important entrepreneurial role. By 2005, their share in enterprise ownership and employment generation was very much in line with their population share, having risen significantly since the 1998 wave of the Economic Census.

The Economic Census of India

Our main data come from the Economic Censuses of India conducted by the Central Statistical Organisation. The Economic Census is a complete count of all entrepreneurial units located within the geographical boundaries of the country, with the exception of those directly involved in the growing of crops (enterprises linked to agriculture, such as food-processing units, are included). As such, it covers all non-agricultural enterprises in the country. It is different from other enterprise-level data sets in India (such as the Annual Survey of Industries, the National Sample Survey, or the CMIE Prowess database) in that it is a complete census: it covers both manufacturing and services, and it includes information on enterprises in the unorganized, or informal, sector of the economy. The Economic Censuses provide detailed information on the location and industrial classification of each enterprise, the number of workers employed, the mix of family and hired labour, sources of finance, and the caste category of the enterprise owner.

We have access to the micro-data from the 1990, 1998, and 2005 rounds of the Economic Census. The 2005 round covered more than 42 million enterprises, employing around 99 million workers. Thirty-nine per cent of enterprises were located in urban areas, and these urban enterprises employed 49 per cent of all workers.[18] Most of our results are based on the 2005 data, but we will show some of the trends over the period 1990–2005 as well. We focus on the data from nineteen large states of India, which account for 96 per cent of India's population and 95 per cent of all enterprises.[19] *Since the ownership of publicly traded firms or cooperatives cannot be assigned to a specific owner's caste, our analysis focuses on the ownership of private enterprises only. For all practical purposes, thus, we are capturing the smaller firms in the economy,* some of which may have the potential to grow larger in the future. Most international studies of entrepreneurship also focus on smaller or younger firms.

We supplement the data from the Economic Censuses with data on population sizes and the proportion of scheduled castes and scheduled tribes from the 1991 and the 2001 Population Census of India.[20] We also obtained estimates of the proportion of OBCs in each state from the 66th round of the National Sample Survey. These estimates are very close to those in the National Election Study 2009, conducted by the Centre for the Study of Developing Societies.

Caste and Enterprise Ownership

Our first major finding is that members of the scheduled castes and scheduled tribes are under-represented in the ownership of enterprises. The scheduled castes accounted for 16.4 per cent of India's population in 2001, but owned only 9.8 per cent of all enterprises in 2005, which employed 8.1 per cent of all non-farm workers (Table 8.1). We should note that, since the majority of such enterprises are single-person enterprises—as noted in the next section—this measure of enterprise ownership is highly correlated with the extent of self-employment and, as such, might be a relatively crude measure of entrepreneurship.[21] However, there is no universally accepted definition of entrepreneurship and, in future work, we will investigate alternative measures. A similar pattern of under-representation is observed for scheduled tribes, whose members constituted 7.7 per cent of the nation's population but owned only 3.7 per cent of non-farm enterprises, employing 3.4 per cent of the non-farm workforce.

These patterns are not specific to any one region or state of the country. As Figure 8.1 shows, the share of the non-agricultural workforce employed in SC-owned firms is lower than their population share in all states except Assam. It is also not the case that the states which were among the earliest to have progressive movements to end caste discrimination during the first half of the twentieth century (Kerala, Karnataka, Andhra Pradesh, Tamil Nadu, Maharashtra) have a lower degree of under-representation.[22] A similar pattern is seen for ST entrepreneurship, where even states with a particularly high degree of STs in the population appear to be equally under-represented compared to states with a lower proportion of STs in the population (Figure 8.2).

In contrast to the under-representation of SC and ST communities in entrepreneurship, we find that the OBCs are well

TABLE 8.1: SHARE OF ENTERPRISES AND EMPLOYMENT BY
CASTE CATEGORY, 2005

		Caste Category of Enterprise Owner				Number of Private Enterprises
		General	OBC	SC	ST	
Population share		33.2%	42.7%	16.4%	7.7%	
	Rural			18.2%	9.7%	
	Urban			11.7%	2.2%	
Share of enterprise ownership, 2005		42.9%	43.5%	9.8%	3.7%	35,951,686
	Rural	36.9%	46.8%	11.5%	4.8%	31,890,552
	Urban	52.3%	38.4%	7.3%	2.0%	14,061,134
Share of employment, 2005		48.5%	40.0%	8.1%	3.4%	74,754,978
	Rural	40.3%	45.0%	10.1%	4.7%	34,177,965
	Urban	58.2%	34.1%	5.8%	1.9%	40,577,013

Note: SC population share in *NSS 66th Round* was 19.6% and ST population
        share was 8.2%.
Sources: 1. The *Economic Census* 2005
        2. The population shares of SC and ST from the *Population Census*
           2001
        3. The OBC population share from the *National Sample Survey 66th
           Round* 2009–10

represented. The OBCs owned 43.5 per cent of all enterprises in
2005, and accounted for 40 per cent of non-farm employment (Table
8.1). This is very much in line with their overall population share
of 43 per cent. In most states, the share of the workforce employed
in OBC-owned firms was quite close to their overall population
share (Figure 8.3).

Two more points ought to be noted here. The fact that, in
2005, OBC shares of business enterprises in most states roughly

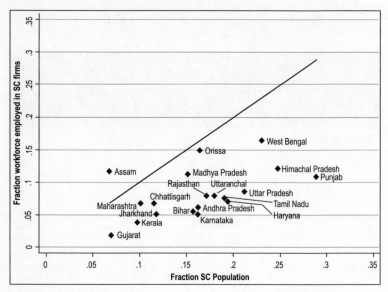

FIGURE 8.1: EMPLOYMENT GENERATION IN SC ENTERPRISES

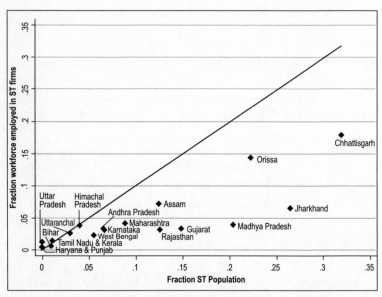

FIGURE 8.2: EMPLOYMENT GENERATION IN ST ENTERPRISES

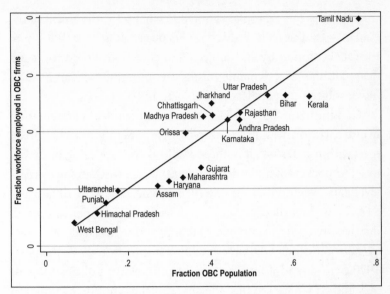

FIGURE 8.3: EMPLOYMENT GENERATION IN OBC ENTERPRISES

corresponded to their estimated shares in the state population does not mean that OBC enterprise shares were also roughly the same across states in the 1970s and 1980s. Given how many studies we have of the changes in the caste structure of Southern India in the twentieth century, it is quite possible that the OBCs entered the business sector sooner in the South, as compared to the North.[23] Unfortunately, there was no economic census taken in the early 1970s, and even after the government started collecting such economic information, the OBC caste category was not recorded separately till 1998. As a result, we cannot be statistically thorough about the hunch that OBCs entered Southern businesses long before they did so in the North, but as Chapter 7 noted, this is quite likely to have happened. Second, the Economic Census does not identify the proprietor's caste for firms whose shares are publicly traded. Southern India has witnessed the phenomenal rise of some OBC communities to the highest corporate reaches of publicly traded firms. For example, as noted in Chapter 7, the ascent of the Nadars—traditionally, toddy-tappers placed at the very bottom of the OBC community and subjected to enormous deprivation and degradation—as a dynamic business community of Tamil Nadu has absolutely no parallels yet in North India.[24]

Coming to the SCs and STs, the pattern of under-representation in enterprise ownership and employment generation is widespread even within states—that is, these results do not appear to be driven by a few pockets of underdevelopment. When we examine district-level data, we find that the enterprise ownership share of SCs and STs is less than their population share in over 80 per cent of all districts. Even in a state like Maharashtra, which had an above-average per capita GDP, reasonably fast growth rates in the post-1990 period, and a long history of progressive policies towards SCs and STs,[25] we see that the share of the workforce employed in SC-owned enterprises is lower than the SC population share in twenty-five out of thirty-four districts; the ST employment share is lower than the population share in twenty-two out of thirty-four districts. Despite the success of Dalit movements in Ambedkar's native Maharashtra—which has made Dalits quite prominent in the political life of the state and pushed all political parties after independence to include Dalit issues in their platforms[26]—they remained under-represented in entrepreneurship in the state as late as 2005. Politics and economics remained mismatched.

Another example is Gujarat, which had an extremely high economic growth rate over the past decade (8.5 per cent growth in gross state domestic product over 1999–2008, compared to 7.2 per cent nationwide), and which showed a large increase in the share of the workforce employed in OBC-owned enterprises over the period 1998–2005 (from 22 per cent to 39 per cent), suggesting that caste barriers were breaking down rapidly in this state. Nevertheless, the share of the workforce employed in SC-owned enterprises remained at 7 per cent in both 1990 and 2005, and only three districts showed an increase in this share over the period 1990–2005, suggesting that the SCs are unable to overcome the barriers to entrepreneurship which the OBCs are able to surmount.

A second major finding is that these differences in entrepreneurship persist across space and time. Table 8.1 shows that the share of SCs and STs in the entrepreneurial sphere is low even in urban areas, where we might expect to have lower levels of explicit caste-based discrimination. The caste differences in entrepreneurship do not appear to be disappearing over time. The share of enterprises owned by SCs in 2005 was the same as it was in 1990, while the employment share in SC-owned enterprises increased by less than one percentage point (Table 8.2). The STs also show a similarly modest increase in their share of entrepreneurship over this long period (share of enterprise ownership rising from 2.6 per cent to 3.7 per cent; employment share rising from 2 per cent to 3.4 per cent).

TABLE 8.2: TRENDS IN ENTERPRISE OWNERSHIP AND EMPLOYMENT GENERATION BY CASTE CATEGORY

	1990	1998	2005
Share of enterprise ownership			
Non SC/ST	87.5%	87.3%	86.4%
of which OBC		37.5%	43.5%
SC	9.9%	8.5%	9.8%
ST	2.6%	4.2%	3.7%
Share of employment			
Non SC/ST	90.6%	89.4%	88.5%
of which OBC		33.8%	40.8%
SC	7.4%	6.9%	8.1%
ST	2.0%	3.8%	3.4%

Source: The *Economic Census* 1990, 1998, and 2005. Data are for nineteen major states of India. *Economic Census* 1990 did not identify OBCs.

In contrast, the OBCs made significant progress over the period 1998–2005, increasing their share of firm ownership from 37.5 per cent to 43.5 per cent, and their share of employment from 33.8 per cent to 40 per cent.[27] However, the population shares for the OBCs are estimated from a sample survey rather than the official Population Census (which, for the first time since 1931, will collect and release such statistics only in late 2013 or 2014), and the 1990 round of the Economic Census does not include this caste category, making these comparisons less reliable than those for SCs and STs.

Caste Differences in Enterprise Characteristics

One reason for the scheduled castes and scheduled tribes to lag behind in employment generation could be difficulties in expanding the size of their enterprises. This can be either because of caste discrimination (members of other castes do not want to work with the SCs) or because of lack of knowledge, or financing constraints. All these factors can also prevent the SCs from entering industries, which have significant economies of scale. In this section, we examine whether firm sizes and other characteristics differ systematically across different caste categories.

Caste and Enterprise Scale

We find that firms owned by SCs and STs are smaller on average than firms owned by the non-SCs/STs (Table 8.3). Note that average firm sizes are very small overall: the average size is 2.13 for enterprises owned by the non-SCs/STs; 1.72 for the SCs; and 1.89 for the STs. The gap between the SCs/STs and other castes in the average firm size is larger in urban areas than in rural areas. This difference is also widespread: the average firm size for SC-owned firms is smaller than the average firm size for non-SCs in all the states.

TABLE 8.3: FIRM SCALE CHARACTERISTICS BY
CASTE CATEGORY

| | | Caste Category of Enterprise Owner | | |
		Non SC/ST	SC	ST
Average size of enterprise	2005	2.13%	1.72%	1.89%
	Rural	1.89%	1.63%	1.79%
	Urban	2.47%	1.93%	2.27%
	1998	2.37%	1.88%	2.09%
	1990	2.59%	1.86%	1.95%
% firms with only one person	2005	56.9%	64.7%	55.9%
	1998	52.1%	58.9%	48.4%
	1990	55.3%	60.8%	50.1%
% firms with institutional finance	2005	3.6%	2.6%	3.6&
	Rural	3.6%	2.5%	3.3%
	Urban	3.7%	2.7%	4.5%
	1998	3.0%	2.4%	2.9%
% unregistered firms	2005	77.4%	88.1%	87.4%
	Rural	86.5%	92.7%	92.6%
	Urban	64.3%	76.7%	67.8%

Source: The *Economic Census* 2005, 1998, 1990

One of the reasons for this difference in the average enterprise size is the relative extent of one-person enterprises. The majority of private enterprises in India are one-person firms, that is, they consist of self-employed people. Fifty-seven per cent of enterprises owned by the non-SCs/STs have only one person, compared to 65 per cent for the SCs. The difference in the proportion of self-employment is particularly pronounced in urban areas (50 per cent vis-à-vis 61 per cent), though the difference is present in both rural and urban areas for SC enterprises. Interestingly, this does not appear to be a major source of the size difference between the ST-owned and non-ST-owned firms.

Employing Outside Labour

Are the differences in enterprise scale driven by differences in the size of networks? For instance, if SC firm owners find it easier to work with SC workers, the smaller size of the worker pool might limit the growth possibilities of enterprises. We examine this by looking at the extent to which firms employ hired labour—that is, labour from outside the family. In the overall data set, we see that 51 per cent of two-person and 26 per cent of three-person firms consisted purely of family labour in 2005, so that employing people from outside the family is a fairly significant step in enterprise growth.

Consistent with the average small size of enterprises, most firms in our study do not employ any labour outside family members. Sixty-eight per cent of enterprises owned by the non-SCs/STs operate with only family labour. This proportion rises to 77 per cent for SC and ST owners. More firms in urban areas hire outside labour, but the differences among caste categories are substantially larger in urban areas. For instance, 77 per cent of non-SC/ST firms and 81 per cent of SC/ST firms hire no outside labour in rural areas, but the corresponding figures for urban areas are 56 per cent for the non-SCs/STs, 67 per cent for the SCs and 61 per cent for the STs. The results for ST owners are particularly interesting because the difference in the proportion of one-person firms was lower for STs as compared to SCs—but these results show that ST firms face similar constraints in moving beyond family labour.

The trends show that, while the average firm size is declining over time for all caste groups, the size gap between SC/ST firms and non-SCs/STs has remained fairly stable over time. For instance, 55 per cent of the non-SC/ST firms were single-person firms in 1990, compared to 61 per cent for the SCs. The corresponding numbers for 2005 were 57 per cent and 65 per cent.

Sources of Finance

The vast majority of enterprises in our data set—more than 90 per cent—do not access outside sources of finance. This is true both in urban and rural areas. Of those who do access outside sources of finance, firms owned by the non-SCs/STs are slightly more likely to access institutional sources of finance (3.6 per cent compared to 2.6 per cent for the SCs), as opposed to accessing government anti-poverty programmes, moneylenders, or NGOs for financing.

More than three-quarters of firms are unregistered with any government agency, and hence belong to the 'unorganized' or 'informal' sector.[28] They are not subject to government regulations such as labour laws or environmental regulations, nor can they access government financing programmes or other institutional sources of finance. Consistent with our results on the accessing of formal finance, we find that while 77 per cent of enterprises owned by the non-SCs/STs are in the unorganized sector, this proportion is more than 85 per cent for the SCs and STs. As with all other differences documented earlier, the caste differences in the extent of informality are much larger in urban areas compared to rural areas, particularly for the SCs.[29]

Industry Mix

Do the factors documented above—the smaller firm size, the higher preponderance of family labour and the informality—prevent SC and ST entrepreneurs from entering certain sectors? Overall, the differences are not large in the types of industries entered by different communities. The SCs and STs are more likely to have been involved in agriculture-related activities and manufacturing, while the non-SCs/STs are more likely to be involved in retail trade, throughout this period. But there have been important changes in the industry distribution over time: both SC and ST enterprises have a greater share in retail trade, and a lower share in manufacturing in 2005 as compared to 1990. In this sense, their industry distribution has become closer to that of non-SCs/STs (Table 8.4). An important implication of this convergence in the industry mix is that the persistent under-representation of SCs and STs documented earlier, and the persistently smaller firm size of SC/ST enterprises, cannot be attributed to underlying economic characteristics of the industries in which these groups are involved.

Why the Gaps and Lags?

What could be the possible reasons for these persistent gaps in entrepreneurial activity across caste categories? We should note that outright discrimination is unlikely to be the *full answer*, since many of these differences in enterprise ownership and enterprise scale are larger in urban areas where, following Ambedkar, one expects discrimination to be lower. On the basis of his studies in Panipat and Saharanpur, Jodhka reports that caste did influence Dalit businesses negatively, but:

> Caste appeared to matter least in procuring supplies. Only 5 per cent of all . . . respondents reported any kind of difficulties in getting supplies because of their being Dalits. 'As long as you can pay, no one cares who you are' . . . A large majority of our respondents . . . faced no caste-related discrimination in getting supplies or raw materials for their businesses. This was so when the suppliers in almost all . . . cases were non-Dalits, mostly from the locally dominant business communities, the Banias, Punjabis or Muslims.[30]

In short, while discrimination does exist, there are likely to be many other factors as well. The existing literature on entrepreneurship suggests a number of possible explanations. Perhaps SC and ST entrepreneurs lack access to the capital needed

TABLE 8.4: PERCENTAGE OF FIRMS IN DIFFERENT INDUSTRIAL
CATEGORIES BY CASTE OF OWNER

2005	Caste Category of Enterprise Owner		
	Non SC/ST	SC	ST
Agricultural activities	15.7%	17.2%	27.0%
Manufacturing	21.0%	23.9%	24.8%
Wholesale trade	4.2%	2.6%	2.1%
Retail trade	38.3%	35.5%	30.8%
Restaurants and hotels	3.8%	2.6%	2.8%
Transport, storage, warehousing, communications	5.2%	7.1%	1.5%
Finance, insurance, real estate, and business services	3.1%	2.0%	1.8%
Community, social, and personal services	4.3%	3.1%	2.8%
Other*	4.6%	5.7%	3.5%
1998	Caste Category of Enterprise Owner		
	Non SC/ST	SC	ST
Agricultural activities	12.3%	12.9%	25.6%
Manufacturing	19.1%	25.0%	25.6%
Wholesale trade	2.6%	1.7%	1.3%
Retail trade	39.0%	31.7%	27.8%
Restaurants and hotels	4.4%	2.7%	2.6%
Transport, storage, warehousing, communications	3.7%	5.8%	3.7%
Finance, insurance, real estate, and business services	2.2%	1.2%	1.3%
Community, social, and personal services	15.6%	17.2%	10.6%
Other*	1.1%	1.8%	1.5%

Table 8.4 (*continued*)

1990	Caste Category of Enterprise Owner		
	Non SC/ST	SC	ST
Agricultural activities	9.2%	14.1%	27.0%
Manufacturing	20.0%	29.0%	28.1%
Wholesale trade	2.3%	1.6%	0.9%
Retail trade	33.1%	23.0%	17.7%
Restaurants and hotels	8.8%	3.7%	6.1%
Transport, storage, warehousing, communications	3.0%	5.0%	2.4%
Finance, insurance, real estate, and business services	1.4%	0.5%	0.3%
Community, social, and personal services	17.1%	16.3%	7.6%
Other*	5.4%	6.9%	9.3%

* 'Other' includes mining and quarrying, electricity, gas, water, and construction
Source: *Economic census* 1990, 1998, 2005

to set up and expand enterprises. Or perhaps they do not have high enough education levels to become successful entrepreneurs. Maybe, the growth of enterprises depends strongly on network effects, both for finding the right workers and for making links with suppliers and customers. The SC and ST enterprise owners might thus be disadvantaged by their relatively smaller networks.

Many of these factors are known to be relevant in India. Banerjee and Duflo show that even formal sector firms are extremely credit-constrained in India;[31] informal firms are likely to be even more so, despite the high rates of return to capital among small enterprises.[32] In terms of caste differences, the SCs and STs have been shown to have lower rates of landownership,[33] as also long-lasting gaps in educational attainment.[34]

Can low levels of landownership and educational attainment

explain the gaps in enterprise ownership at the state or district level? We provide preliminary evidence. After examining the share of SC/ST enterprise ownership in the state against the levels of literacy, urbanization, the fraction of population engaged in farming and the fraction of landless among the farmers,[35] we do not find these latter sets of variables to have much explanatory power in explaining the share of SC or ST enterprise ownership, controlling for the SC or ST population share (Table 8.5, Panel A). Of course, one possibility is that the absence of correlations may be driven by poor measures of the underlying phenomena. For instance, literacy captures only one dimension of educational attainment; perhaps what matters for entrepreneurship is a specific type or a particular quality of education, which cannot be measured accurately.

Further examination at the district level also shows a similar result: the SC/ST enterprise ownership share across districts within a state is not significantly related to access to capital and education (Table 8.5, Panel B). The only exception to this is that higher literacy levels do seem to be a spur to greater ST entrepreneurship.

Entrepreneurship and Social Structure in International Perspective

As we think further about how entrepreneurship might flourish among the SCs and STs, it might be worthwhile to consider, briefly, the experiences of marginalized groups in other socially diverse parts of the world. These collectively validate the difficulty of such groups overcoming the historical barriers to becoming entrepreneurs.

Consider the Malaysian experience recently summarized in Gomez.[36] Malaysia's New Economic Policy (NEP) was the first institutionalized attempt to redress the small economic share of the numerically dominant *bumiputras* ('sons of the soil', referring to ethnic Malays and other indigenous people), and was triggered by the race riots of May 1969, at a time when the *bumi*s held only

TABLE 8.5: DETERMINANTS OF SC/ST SHARE IN ENTERPRISE AND EMPLOYMENT

	Fraction of Enterprises Owned by SCs	Fraction of Workforce Employed in SC-owned Enterprises	Fraction of Enterprises Owned by STs	Fraction of Workforce Employed in ST-owned Enterprises
Panel A: Relationship with state-level characteristics of SCs/STs				
Population SC (ST) share	0.581 ***	0.358 **	0.401 ***	0.413 ***
	(0.162)	(0.155)	(0.106)	(0.121)
% SC (ST) urban	-0.126	-0.155	-0.004	-0.040
	(0.119)	(0.114)	(0.209)	(0.240)
% SC (ST) literate	0.086	0.089	0.049	0.049
	(0.106)	(0.101)	(0.097)	(0.112)
% SC (ST) engaged in farming	-0.056	-0.008	-0.010	-0.011
	(0.080)	(0.077)	(0.0163)	(0.187)
% of landless among SC (ST) farmers	-0.052	-0.050	0.009	0.014
	(0.038)	(0.036)	(0.043)	(0.049)
R-squared	0.61	0.47	0.74	0.70
Observations	18	18	16	16
Panel B: District-level relationship				
Population SC (ST) share	0.398 ***	0.346 **	0.519 ***	0.475 ***
	(0.049)	(0.043)	(0.054)	(0.055)
% SC (ST) urban	-0.018	-0.030*	0.003	-0.003
	(0.017)	(0.016)	(0.021)	(0.022)
% SC (ST) literate	-0.009	-0.030	0.115**	0.100*
	(0.033)	(0.032)	(0.055)	(0.058)
% SC (ST) engaged in farming	-0.034	-0.038	-0.009	-0.004
	(0.024)	(0.022)	(0.027)	(0.029)

Table 8.5 (*continued*)

	Fraction of Enterprises Owned by SCs	Fraction of Workforce Employed in SC-owned Enterprises	Fraction of Enterprises Owned by STs	Fraction of Workforce Employed in ST-owned Enterprises
% of landless among SC (ST) farmers	-0.001 (0.017)	-0.007 (0.017)	0.010 (0.022)	0.014 (0.023)
R-squared	0.68	0.63	0.75	0.70
Observations	516	516	481	481

Note: Standard errors in parantheses, corrected for heteroskedasticity.
***, ** and * indicate significance at 1%, 5%, and 10% respectively.
District-level regressions include state fixed effects; regressions for ST limited to states and districts with non-zero ST population.
Sources: The *Economic Census* 2005; *Population Census* 2001

1.5 per cent of corporate equity. Even after four decades of policy attempts to increase bumi representation in business, the share of bumi ownership never rose above 21 per cent, well short of the 30 per cent mandated target. Most famously, Prime Minister Mahathir Mohamad tried to bet on particular bumi entrepreneurs but managed to create a version of crony capitalism whereby selected bumis flourished, but the bulk were left behind. Further, the empires of many of the chosen few collapsed during the Asian financial crisis of 1997 and, by 2003, Mahathir himself was complaining that policies to favour the bumis had resulted in their having developed a 'crutch' mentality. His successor in 2003, Prime Minister Badawi, changed course and favoured a 'vendor' system, whereby he planned to help small and medium enterprises by connecting them to established corporations. This largely did not work. In 2009, Prime Minister Najib Razak,worried about deterring foreign investment in a moribund economy and the possibility of getting stuck in a so-called middle-income trap. He finally backed away from the long-standing goal of 30 per cent bumi ownership in several sectors.

The Malaysian failure to redress bumi economic marginalization, in a sense, mirrors that of post-apartheid South Africa. The emphasis on Black Economic Empowerment (BEE) has sometimes resulted in the creation of BEE business behemoths, but the empowerment of the disenfranchised has largely not been forthcoming.[37] In response to the criticisms of BEE, the government passed the Broad-Based BEE Act in 2003.[38] Yet, black ascent to the rarefied summits of the economic peaks remains scarce, and white skilled outmigration remains a perpetual fear.[39]

Studies, such as those in Malaysia and South Africa, are largely qualitative analyses of the evolution of a particular marginalized group. In the past decade, economists have tried to quantify some of the barriers to entrepreneurship, influenced by the work of De Soto.[40] While their work generally does not focus on marginalized groups per se, many studies have examined cross-country determinants of entrepreneurship. In general, these studies do show that more onerous regulations deter entrepreneurship;[41] that reductions in the number of procedures required to start a business help entrepreneurs;[42] and that increased growth opportunities lead to increased mobility from informality to the formal sector.[43]

Whether dismantling regulatory barriers helps marginalized groups is a conjecture worth examining in detail.[44] Many studies suggest that marginalized groups get more of a helping hand from their own community, however construed, than they do from the top-down dismantling of generalized regulatory barriers. Munshi's empirical analysis illustrates the importance of social networks in finding jobs or climbing out of poverty; Iyer and Schoar show that community ties influence the types of business behaviour in a controlled setting in India; Kalnins and Chung examine this matter for Gujarati entrepreneurs in the hotel industry in the United States; Vissa demonstrates that in knowledge-intensive industries, entrepreneurs tend to privilege those who are from their own caste group and speak their own language in attempting to form a business.[45] Chinese diasporic ties to particular locales on the mainland are well documented as well.[46] Perhaps the best theoretical treatment of the importance of community is by Portes—he shows how communities invest in public goods to overcome barriers to entrepreneurship, particularly in the informal economy and among disadvantaged communities.[47]

Conclusion

We started with an observation about how the SCs, the STs, and especially the OBCs have made significant progress at the level of political representation in independent India. The evidence we have presented shows that the OBCs have made progress in entrepreneurship, but the SCs and the STs are considerably under-represented in the entrepreneurial sphere. That is, for the SCs and STs, political gains have not manifested themselves in greater entrepreneurial prowess. The rise of Dalit millionaires—driven in part by newer economic freedoms—does not appear representative of the broader swathes of the SC/ST population; at least, until 2005, it did not. Such under-representation appears to persist even in states with very progressive policies towards the SCs and STs, in states where OBCs have made considerable progress in enterprise ownership, and in urban areas where outright discrimination is lower than in rural India. Further, the patterns of SC and ST entrepreneurship are not strongly related to broad measures of educational attainment, access to land, or transition away from farming. Further research, especially at the level of local networks, might yield more decisive results.

III

Economic
Development

9

Why Have Poor Democracies
Not Eradicated Poverty?

In the most meticulous and comprehensive statistical examination yet of the relationship between democracy and development, Przeworski and his colleagues provide compelling evidence for a hunch long held by observers of development. 'The lists of miracles and disasters,' they argue, 'are populated almost exclusively by dictatorships . . . The [economic] tigers may be dictatorships, but [all] dictatorships are no[t] tigers.'[1]

Indeed, Przeworski *et al.* could explicitly have taken another analytic step, a step that can be logically derived as a syllogism from what they say. Moving beyond a bimodal distribution—miracles and disasters—they could have also constructed a third, in-between category. They would have found that democracies tend to fall almost exclusively in the unspectacular but undisastrous middle. No long-lasting democracy in the developing world has seen the developmental horrors of Mobutu's Zaire, but none has scaled the heights of a Taiwan, a Republic of Korea, a Singapore, and, now, a China.

Can this argument be extended from economic growth, which is the focus of Przeworski *et al.* to the poverty-eradicating record of democracies in the developing world? Would it be true to say that, while no democracy has attacked poverty as successfully as Singapore, Korea, Taiwan, or China, none has made economic life as awful for its poor people as Haiti, Chad, Zambia, or Niger, among the worst performers on poverty-alleviation in the developing world?[2]

Surprising as it may seem, not enough is known about the relationship between democracy and poverty. Instead, there is a great deal of literature on the relationship between democracy and economic growth. Unless it is incorrectly assumed that what is good for economic growth is necessarily good for poverty-reduction, we can't really draw any firm conclusions from this literature about poverty.

I argue below that the poverty-eradicating record of democracies in the developing world is, indeed, neither extraordinary nor abysmal. Democracies have succeeded in pre-empting the worst-case scenarios, such as famines,[3] and have avoided a consistent or dramatic deterioration in the welfare of the poor, but they have not achieved the best results—namely, eradication of mass poverty. The performance of dictatorships, by comparison, covers the whole range of outcomes: the best, the worst, and the middling. Some dictatorial regimes have successfully eradicated poverty. In others, the problem has worsened, or no significant change in mass poverty is observable. In still others, the progress has been slow but steady, much as it has been in many democracies. The promise of democracy was greater in the eyes of liberals.

Why should we have expected poor democracies to do better at poverty-alleviation? One reason is sheer numbers. In the United States and Europe, a very small proportion of the population, typically less than 5 per cent of the total, lives in poverty. Their numbers being so small, poor people in these richer economies can hardly leverage themselves into a great electoral or political force in order to push governments to do more for them. If their needs are taken care of, the reasons for that lie elsewhere. But poor democracies, by definition, possess many poor people. In the developing world, the poor constitute a large plurality of the population, sometimes even a majority. Given the 'one person, one vote' principle, poor people in poor democracies, if not in poor dictatorships, ought to experience over time some degree of empowerment by virtue of their numbers alone. They should be able to exercise pressure on the government to address poverty effectively through public policy. A 30 per cent voting bloc can often be decisive, especially in a first-past-the-post electoral system, in which elections are often decided on the basis of a plurality of the popular vote. Election victories in a Westminster-style democratic system often do not require majorities, if the electoral contestation is between more than two political parties, as is often the case. Most stable democracies in the developing world, listed later in this chapter, have a Westminster-style system. Yet, mass poverty remains extensive in them.

Of course, it can be argued that the validity of this conceptual reasoning and expectation depends on whether the poor actually do vote, or vote as much as the richer classes do. If the poor do not vote, or are not allowed to vote because of manipulation or coercion by the local elite, or they vote according to the wishes of the local elite—since the elite are the patrons and the poor their dependent clients—then we should expect poor people to remain as powerless as always, incapable of exerting pressure even on a democratic government.

What do we know about whether, and how freely, the poor vote in the developing world? Disaggregated statistics along the rich–poor divisions are not available for most poor democracies. For India, however, turnout rates have been systematically disaggregated, and it is clear that since the late 1980s, the poor have tended to vote as much as, or more than, the middle and upper classes.[4] We also know that in this period, the patron–client relationships between the upper or dominant castes on the one hand and the lower and generally poorer castes on the other have been considerably undermined across much of India.[5] Though poverty rate in India appears to have declined quite rapidly since 2004–05, substantial poverty still remains.

Voting, of course, is not the only mechanism of influence available to poor people in a democratic polity. The poor can also, at least in theory, be politically mobilized into, let us say, a poor people's movement, and can thereby exercise their weight and push the government to adopt pro-poor policies.[6] Both mobilization and voting are available as options and can be viewed as two forms of *pressure from below* on governments. These mechanisms are not present in the same way in authoritarian systems for, given the absence of political freedoms, opportunities for the mobilization of the poor are significantly fewer, and voting is either perfunctory or non-existent. Of course, in theory, authoritarian polities can feel a significant amount of *pressure from above*—stemming from a commitment of the political elite to reducing poverty—and they may therefore make a significant attempt to eliminate poverty. But dictatorships do not feel a systematic pressure from below, whereas democratic systems can be subjected to both kinds of pressure— from below and above.

In short, as many political theorists have argued since the nineteenth century, universal-franchise democracies ought to empower the poor significantly, if their numbers are large. By extension, there should be a great deal of pressure on poor democracies to eliminate poverty. However, defying this theoretical expectation, poor countries that are viewed as having had long-lasting periods of democratic rule—India, Costa Rica, Venezuela, Colombia, Botswana, Jamaica, Trinidad and Tobago, and Sri Lanka, among others—on the whole still have a substantial proportion of their populations stuck below the poverty line.

This experience raises some questions. Do poor democracies really feel enough pressure from below to remove poverty? And if they do not, then, why not? Are these governments following economic policies that best tackle the problem of mass poverty? If not, why not?

In response to these questions, I make two arguments. First, if we draw a distinction between direct and indirect methods of poverty-alleviation, it is possible to show that in the developing world, democracies find it politically easier to subscribe to the direct methods of poverty-alleviation, despite the by now widely recognized economic inferiority of such methods. Direct methods consist of public provision of income—for example, targeted employment programmes, such as India's National Rural Employment Guarantee Act (NREGA) or food-for-work programmes; credit and producer subsidies for small farmers; or a transfer of assets to the poor—for example, land reforms. Indirect methods are essentially mediated by growth—not any kind of growth, but one that aims at enhancing opportunities for the poor to increase their incomes. Since the early 1980s, the conventional wisdom in economics has moved towards the superiority of indirect methods, suggesting that they are more productive in the use of resources and also more sustainable in the long run. Economic growth, in and of itself, might not be enough to reduce poverty rapidly enough and direct methods might be necessary, but it is widely recognized that without a significant growth rate, it is not even possible to finance direct programmes attacking poverty. The political logic, however, goes in the opposite direction in democracies. Because of electoral and mass pressures, democracies tend to have an elective affinity for direct methods of poverty-alleviation. Not given to the electoral renewal of mandates, authoritarian polities avoid this problem. If indirect methods are better at eradicating poverty, it follows that authoritarian countries—*some, not all*, as argued later—would have greater success with poverty-eradication.

My second argument has to do with the distinction between class and ethnicity. At its core, class is an economic category, but ethnicity is defined in terms of a birth-based (ascriptive) group identity, imagined or real. Ethnic politics of subaltern groups is typically not couched in terms of poverty. Rather, it uses the language of *dignity and social justice*, in which poverty is typically only a component, incorporated in a larger theme emphasizing self-respect, equality of treatment, and an end to everyday humiliation. If the poor, irrespective of the ethnic group they come from, were to vote or mobilize strictly on economic grounds, they would also press the decision-makers to attack poverty a great deal more forcefully. However, at least in multi-ethnic democracies, not only is it easier to mobilize the poor as members of ethnic communities, but that is also how they often vote—along lines of ethnicity, not class. The dignity gains of democracy might be greater than the poverty gains.

That being so, *even with direct methods*, a democratic polity would be better able to attack poverty if (a) ethnicity and class roughly coincided for the poor, instead of clashing; and (b) the subaltern ethnic group was relatively large in size. If the poor belong to very different ethnic groups (defined by caste, language, race, or religion), and no ethnic group is large enough to constitute a significant voting bloc, the pressure on the political elite to ease poverty decreases significantly.

In short, my argument is that no democracy in the developing world has entirely eradicated poverty because, on the one hand, direct methods of poverty-alleviation tend to have greater political salience in democracies, and on the other hand, the poor are typically not from the same ethnic group. The former hurts the poor because it can be shown that direct methods in attacking poverty cannot easily be financed without a reliance on markets for growth, and in addition, growth can generate employment for the poor. And the latter goes against them because a split between ethnicity and class militates against the mobilization and voting of the poor as a class and dilutes the exertion of pro-poor political pressure on governments.

What is Poverty?

The term 'poverty' today is used in two ways. The conventional usage is linked to consumption and, hence, income, focusing heavily though not exclusively on a caloric floor that the human body, on an average, needs to function normally. In this narrow sense, hunger and endemic malnutrition constitute the core of poverty. The original $1-a-day yardstick used by the World Bank substantially, if not entirely, conforms to this hunger-based definition of poverty, sometimes called *income poverty*.

The term 'poverty' is also used more broadly to encompass other fundamental dimensions of human life and development beyond income and consumption—for instance, deprivation with respect to education and health. This is sometimes called *human poverty*. Sen has added a philosophical dimension to this concept by introducing the notion of *poverty as capability deprivation*.[7] I will not use the term poverty in these latter senses. It is not that education and health are not valuable; they undoubtedly are, and Sen's broadening of the concept gives it a deeper philosophical foundation. It is simply that I am clearer about the relationship between democracy and income poverty than about democracy and the broader concepts of poverty.

What is Democracy?

As already argued in Chapters 1, 2, and 3, the most widely accepted conceptualization of democracy has been provided by Dahl, who defines democracy in terms of two basic criteria: contestation and participation.[8] To repeat, the first criterion has to do with how freely the political opposition contests the rulers. The second asks whether all groups—irrespective of social and economic status—or only some groups participate in politics and determine who the rulers should be.

Democracy may have an identifiable impact on poverty, but it should be noted that poverty itself does not enter into the definition of democracy. The best we can say is that if poverty, despite the presence of democratic institutions, obstructs the free expression of political preferences, it makes a polity *less* democratic, but it does not make it *un*democratic. As argued in Chapter 3, so long as contestation and participation are present, democracy is a continuous variable (conceptualized as 'more or less'), not as a discrete or dichotomous variable (framed as 'yes or no').[9]

For analytical tractability, it is necessary, first, to identify which countries have been relatively stable democracies—that is, democracies for a long enough period—in the developing world. An exercise like this is not necessary in the developed world, where democratic stability can be assumed. It is difficult, though not impossible, to analyse the impact of democracy on poverty, if democracy itself is not stable.

If we construe 'long enough' to mean *three-fourths of the period since 1950 or since independence*, then, countries that would meet the criterion of democratic longevity are few and far between.[10] They include India, Botswana, Costa Rica, Venezuela, Papua New Guinea, Sri Lanka (between 1950 and 1983), and the Philippines (between 1950 and 1969, and since 1986). Also included are the former British colonies in the Caribbean (principally Jamaica, Trinidad and Tobago, Barbados, and the Bahamas), along with some other very small states.[11] Some would add Malaysia to this list as well, but it should be noted that Malaysia is by now seen as a long-lasting, consociational-type democracy, where participation may be high but contestation between political parties is limited by consensus, and political competition, by agreement, is designed around ethnic groups rather than individuals.[12] Malaysia, in other words, is a particular kind of democracy, not one in the standard sense.[13] For our purposes here, we can count it as a democracy, given that universal-franchise elections are held regularly, so long as we remember the specific nature of electoral competition and consider its economic implications.

In short, it is the countries above that are critical for analysing the relationship between democracy and poverty. Democracy has come to many more countries than ever before in the so-called 'third wave' that began in the 1970s,[14] but if we enlarge the canvas to include the entire post-1950 period, it will be hard to add many more countries to the small list above. By contrast, the number of countries that remained authoritarian for long periods after 1945 is very large. This asymmetry means that we have only a small number of observations about long-lasting democracies.[15]

Poverty-Eradication: The Broad Picture

Whether democratic systems have reduced poverty, it should be clear, is not a cross-sectional question. We need at least two sufficiently distanced periods for analysis, if not an entire time series. Such data on an inter-country basis do not exist. Global figures for poverty were first calculated for 1985 based on an international poverty line of $1-a-day.[16] Though doubts remain as to the authenticity of such large-N, inter-country statistics, the World Bank's figures are now customarily used for discussion of world poverty.[17]

We simply do not know the numbers of the poor, either globally or in individual countries, for the 1950s or 1960s in any systematic sense. If, to gather such statistics, we rely on the reports available for each country, we find that the criteria used by different countries to define and measure poverty do not match and, often, the criteria have not been consistently used even within the same country. A methodologically tight time series on poverty for the entire developing world is not available, nor is it easy to create figures for the pre-1985 period.

Luckily, some broad conclusions can nonetheless be presented, for they do not depend on statistical accuracy but on statistical reasonableness. Complete data sets would be necessary if we were to make finer judgements—for example, if we were asked to rank-order all developing countries on poverty-eradication, just as the United Nations Development Programme's human development reports rank all countries on the human development index. But, since all we need is categorical judgements, rather than a comprehensive rank-ordering, the available statistics, despite being incomplete, do permit some fairly good conclusions.

On poverty-alleviation, there is a huge variation in the record of authoritarian countries. Spectacular authoritarian successes in attacking poverty (South Korea, Taiwan, Singapore and China) coexist with miserable failures (much of sub-Saharan Africa and Latin America). And many countries also fall in the middle between the two extremes. According to *World Development Report 2005*, the following developing countries still had more than 40 per cent of their populations below the international poverty line of $1 a day in the late 1990s (or later): Burkina Faso, Burundi, Central African Republic, Ghana, Madagascar, Malawi, Mali, Nicaragua, Niger, Nigeria, Sierra Leone, and Zambia.[18] It is noteworthy that these countries have all been mostly authoritarian over the past several decades.[19]

By comparison, long-lasting democracies—India, Jamaica, Botswana, Venezuela, the Philippines, Sri Lanka, Costa Rica, and Trinidad and Tobago— are neither the biggest successes nor the greatest failures. In the early 1960s, South Korea, Taiwan, Singapore and China were roughly as poor, or poorer, than these countries[20] but, by now, the first three have wiped out mass poverty and the last, too, has reduced it very substantially. Indeed, economically speaking (though not politically), Singapore today is a developed country, nearly as rich as the United Kingdom and without the obvious signs of poverty one sees in parts of Britain.[21]

In short, the violent authoritarian fluctuations contrast sharply with a certain middling democratic consistency. Democracies may not necessarily be pro-poor, but authoritarian systems can be viciously anti-poor. Democratic attacks on poverty have simply been slow but steady—unspectacular but undisastrous. Why?

As noted above, there are two main reasons: the political preference in poor democracies for direct rather than indirect methods of reducing poverty; and the salience of ethnicity rather than class in multi-ethnic democratic politics. Let us examine these reasons in detail.

Direct versus Indirect Measures

As is often noted in economic literature, direct methods of poverty-alleviation represent income transfers to the poor (producer and credit subsidies, or targeted employment programmes) and, at a more radical level, asset transfers (land reforms). The indirect methods are growth-mediated. Economic growth, according to mainstream economic wisdom today, is best achieved through trade liberalization and a generally more market-oriented economic strategy than was typically adopted in developing countries until the late 1970s. These trade- and market-oriented policies have also, by implication, become the indirect methods of poverty-eradication in economic thinking.[22]

Two clarifications, however, must be added. First, the emphasis on a growth-mediated strategy does not imply that all growth strategies are good for poverty-alleviation. A labour-intensive growth strategy is better than one that is capital-intensive. There is a difference between South Korea since the late 1960s and Brazil until recently. Both relied heavily on high growth, but the former went primarily for a labour-absorbing, export-oriented strategy in the late 1960s and the 1970s, whereas the latter, during the two decades after the mid-1950s, concentrated mostly on a capital-intensive, import-substitution strategy. South Korea has more or less eradicated mass poverty; despite recent successes under President Lula, Brazil continues to have considerable poverty.

Second, a growth-based strategy of poverty-alleviation does not entail a full-blown external liberalization of the economy, nor does it imply a complete absence of reliance on direct methods. Many consider trade liberalization to be infinitely superior to the liberalization of capital markets,[23] and there are a great many arguments about the ambiguous effects of dramatic privatization as well.[24] Market-based methods may on the whole be better, but not all of them work. What is clear is that so long as growth does not generate enough resources, it may not be possible for public authorities to allocate more for direct measures. Thus, even the sustenance of direct methods relies heavily on growth-generating policies. *Direct measures can often be more effectively implemented in the long run in the framework of growth-enhancing, trade-oriented policies.*[25]

In democratic politics, however, these arguments have a very different meaning. Whether their impact on poverty is lasting or not, direct methods have clearly comprehensible and demonstrable short-run linkages with the well-being of the poor.[26] The impact of indirect methods—exchange rate devaluations; tariff reductions; privatization of public enterprises—on poverty is not so immediate, or intuitively transparent. As argued in the next chapter, long-run and indirect links do not work well in the campaigns and rhetoric of democratic politics: the effect has to be seen to be intuitively graspable, clearly visible, and capable of arousing mass action.[27]

An affinity between electoral democracy and direct methods has on the whole—and so far—limited the ability of democracies to eradicate poverty. A better alignment of the political and the economic may be possible in authoritarian countries, where politicians do not have to carry the masses with them in election campaigns, and where the long-run and indirect methods of poverty removal can simply be implemented by decree (if a political elite is committed to the poor which, of course, may not be true).

Class versus Ethnicity

The argument above does not imply that direct methods will have no impact. To repeat, both approaches can make a dent in poverty; one is simply more effective in the long run. Besides, without growth, which requires reliance on markets, the direct methods are not sustainable.

Within the parameters of direct action, the best results are obtained in societies where class and ethnicity coincide for the poor, not in those where class and ethnicity clash. As argued in Chapter 7, the former are called ranked ethnic systems in literature, and the latter, unranked ethnic systems.[28] If ranked ethnic systems are also democratic, the poor can exert more effective pressure on governments, and the effect on poverty is greater than is normally possible in unranked ethnic systems. Why should this be so? And what kind of evidence do we have to support the claim?

In generating collective action, the greater power of ethnicity vis-à-vis class can be explained in three ways. Two of them treat all kinds of ethnic mobilization together, contrasting them with class mobilization. The third concentrates especially on the ethnic mobilization of the subaltern groups. All three are relevant, the third especially so.

First, developments in collective action theory seek to show why ethnicity solves the collective action problem better than class does. Class action is bedevilled by freeriding: on the whole, individuals would like the benefits of class action, but would not like to pay the costs. As a consequence, collective action based on class is harder and generally weaker. This problem is often illustrated through the so-called prisoner's dilemma game. But the main strategic problem in ethnic collective action is one of *coordination*, not freeriding.[29]

In prisoner's dilemma games, it is rational for individuals to not cooperate with others. Coordination games are different. Instead of privileging individual defection from cooperation, coordination games rely on 'focal points' to facilitate the convergence of individual expectations; hence, they make collective mobilization easier.[30] Ethnicity can serve as a focal point; class cannot, at least not easily.[31] To put it simply, on collective action, ethnicity normally trumps class.

The second line of reasoning, not typically deployed in the political economy literature, has emerged from the theories of ethnicity and nation-building. Compared to class, the shared identities of caste, ethnicity, and religion are more likely to form historically enduring bonds, and to provide common histories, heroes, and villains.[32] Moreover, the poor as a class rarely have leaders from their own ranks. In contrast, a poor ethnic community can give rise to a small middle class, and thereby generate its own leaders. The story of the Nadars, an example of this tendency, has already been narrated in Chapter 7.

A third explanation also comes from the field of ethnicity and nationalism, focusing especially on the ethnic politics of subaltern groups.[33] In subaltern ethnic politics, economic issues dealing with the poverty of the group are typically part of a larger template emphasizing equality of treatment and an end to quotidian insults and humiliation in public spaces—in schools; fields; places of work and worship; and on roads and public transport. In contemporary times, the political equality of democracy clashes with a historically inherited world where group-based hierarchy, humiliation, and degradation continue to exist.[34] The denial of basic human dignity and the practice of discrimination on grounds of one's birth, when added to poverty, constitute a much more powerful font of resistance than poverty alone.

Clearly, such a distinction between ethnicity and class may not be present everywhere. It will certainly not mark the politics of mono-ethnic societies, such as Korea and Taiwan, or societies where the subaltern ethnic group is not only poor but also small and has yet to develop a middle class.[35] For all these reasons, in the literature on ethnicity, East Asia and Latin America have traditionally been considered outliers, though, with the rise of indigenous people's movements, that may have begun to change for Latin America.[36] On the whole, East Asia and Latin America have seen a lot of class politics but not enough ethnic politics, at least not yet. In comparison, in South and South-east Asia, sub-Saharan Africa, and Eastern and Central Europe, ethnicity has often been more politically potent than class.

Ranked Ethnic Systems and Poverty: Malaysia and India

What examples can be cited for the claim that, unless poverty is linked to ethnic identity, it does not necessarily become a great force in democratic politics?

While we know a great deal about the ethnic profiles of most poor democracies, inter-country comparisons on poverty, as already stated, are rendered difficult by the absence of a time series and by lack of consistency in measurement criteria. Still, from what we know, of all poor democracies—consociational or adversarial—Malaysia has shown by far the best results on poverty-reduction. The proportion of population below the poverty line in Malaysia declined from 49.3 per cent in 1970 to less than 2.0 per cent in 1997.[37] We must, however, note two special features of the Malaysian political economy.

First, when democracy was instituted, the Malays, constituting the majority ethnic group, were vastly more rural and poor than the largest minority group, the Chinese. Once inaugurated, democratic politics became ethnically structured, and the Malays acquired constitutionally mandated political hegemony through quotas in the political and bureaucratic structures. Once the majority ethnic group, led by its small upper and middle class, came to power, the political elite undertook a large number of direct measures, in both the countryside and the cities, to increase the incomes of their ethnic group, including allocation of private equity for Malay companies after 1970.[38]

Second, the direct measures were undertaken within the larger framework of a trade-oriented economic policy. Since 1963, Malaysia has been an externally open economy.[39] By comparison, it may be noted that Sri Lanka, often compared to Malaysia in both size and potential (and, one might add, considerably more literate and peaceful than Malaysia in the 1950s and 1960s), used only direct poverty-alleviation measures. It was unable to alleviate poverty as successfully as Malaysia. Unlike Malaysia, open since 1963, Sri Lanka remained a closed economy until 1978.[40] By the late 1970s, the fiscal ability of Sri Lanka to run its direct anti-poverty programmes was seriously in doubt.[41]

Let us now turn to India, where detailed and disaggregated statistics on poverty are available for individual states going back to the 1960s. Patterns of state politics and policy can thus be clearly linked to the outcomes for poverty.

The states of Punjab and Kerala have produced two of the best results.[42] In Punjab, the Green Revolution—an indirect and growth-based method—was the key to poverty-alleviation. In Kerala, the method was direct. Land reforms and extensive job reservations in government employment were the twin strategies.

Was the emphasis on direct methods in Kerala a result of the poor organizing themselves as a class? On the face of it, this would appear to be the case, primarily because the Communist party, repeatedly elected to power after 1957, led the campaign for land reforms and social justice. Its rhetoric was based on class.

However, both social history and electoral data make it clear that there was a remarkable merging of caste and class in Kerala, the former defined ethnically, the latter economically. At the centre of this coincidence is the Ezhava caste, estimated to constitute a little over 20 per cent of the state's population. The Ezhavas were traditionally engaged in 'toddy-tapping' (production of coarse liquor) and were therefore considered 'polluting' by the upper castes.

At the turn of the century, the Ezhavas, experiencing some mobility and developing a small middle class, rebelled against the indignities of the Hindu social order and started fighting for their rights. Led by a famous Ezhava social reformer, Sree Narayana Guru, sometimes called the Gandhi of Kerala, their protest movement aimed at self-respect and education. Self-respect entailed withdrawal from toddy-tapping, a movement into modern trades and professions, and a non-violent attack on the symbolic order. Since they were denied entry to temples and were allowed to worship only 'lower gods and spirits', the Ezhavas, the Guru said, would have their own temples, in which they would worship 'higher gods' to whom they would offer flowers and sweets, not animals and liquor reserved for the lower gods. Meanwhile, to improve their economic and social status, they would educate themselves. And to facilitate all these activities, they would set up an organization. 'Strengthen through organization, liberate by education' was the motto.[43]

These issues, all caste-based, decisively restructured the politics of Kerala in the 1930s. Entry into temples; an attack on the social deference system concerning dress; access to public roads; and more equal access to education—these drove the rights campaign. It was only subsequently that tenancy rights and land reforms spurred the mobilization for economic rights, and it was not until 1940 that the Communist Party of Kerala was born.[44]

If the fit between the Ezhava caste and the rural poor had not been so good in the 1930s and 1940s, class mobilization would have made little headway. Class politics was inserted into the campaign for caste-based social justice.[45] To this day, the Ezhava caste continues to be the principal base of the Communist Party Marxist (CPM).

Historically, people of similar class positions, if Nair, have gone, on the whole, with the Congress Party; if Christian, with the Kerala Congress; if Muslim, with the Muslim League.[46]

Conclusion

Democracies in poor countries have neither attacked poverty as successfully as some dictatorships in the past five decades, nor failed as monstrously as many authoritarian countries have. Dictatorships fall in all categories of performance: some have abolished mass poverty; many have allowed poverty to worsen; and still others, like democracies, have made some progress but have not eliminated mass poverty. By comparison, democracies have avoided the worst-case scenarios on poverty-alleviation, but they have not achieved the best-case scenarios. They have simply been locked in the middle category: slow and not spectacular. Malaysia is about the only exception to this generalization, but there is consensus among scholars of democracy that it is at best a half democracy, never achieving the status of a fully competitive democracy since independence in 1957.

On why have democracies not done better, this chapter has made two arguments. First, democracies have been more inclined towards the direct approach to alleviating poverty. Generally speaking, direct methods are not as effective as some (though not all) indirect growth-based methods, nor are they as fiscally sustainable. When direct attacks on poverty are made in the framework of growth-based strategies, they work much better. Until the era of trade- and market-oriented economic policies began in the1980s, democracies tended not to embrace indirect methods for, while there were clear economic arguments in favour of growth-based methods, their political appeal in democracies was limited. The politics and economics of market-based approaches to eliminating poverty were not in agreement.

Second, the poor have not been a political force in poor democracies because they are often split among ethnic groups. As a result, despite their large numbers, they are rarely, if ever, empowered as an economic class and are unable to pressure democracies as a united force. Only when the poor as a class and the poor as an ethnic group coincide—and this class/ethnic group is also numerically large—has this obstacle typically been overcome, partially or wholly. Such a coincidence, however, is not common. More often than not, ethnicity and class tend to cross-cut each other.

Whether the first equation above has changed with the worldwide rise of market-oriented economic policies is still to be investigated definitively. From what we know, market-driven growth processes have indeed quickened the rate of poverty reduction, but substantial mass poverty still exists in the developing world.[47] It would appear that a key question continues to be how markets—domestic and global—can be made to work for the poor.[48]

10

Democracy and Markets in India

> When economists propose their favored economic policy agendas
> and fret that they are not immediately adopted, or get aborted after
> adoption, because of social instability, one reason for policy failure
> and economists' frustration is the lack of understanding of the
> social and political context in which the policy was implemented.
> . . . Hence the focus on the politico-cultural underbelly of an
> economy does not have to be founded in skepticism of economic
> policy, but in recognition of the fact that this is a complement of it
> and so should assist in the design of better and more appropriate
> economic policy (Kaushik Basu).[1]

Notwithstanding the current short-run growth deceleration and
legitimate macroeconomic concerns, a consensus has for some
time been emerging in the international development and business
community that India's economy has turned a corner. Since 1991—
when market-oriented economic reforms were first systematically
introduced—an inward-looking and over-regulated economy has
been shedding its controls and embracing international openness.
For roughly two decades after 1990, India was the third fastest-

278

growing economy in the world, behind only China and Vietnam, but ahead of Singapore, Malaysia, South Korea, and Thailand.[2] The emergence, first, of an internationally competitive information technology industry, and the prospects that some other industries were also headed in a similar direction brought enormous confidence to India's entrepreneurs. Although there are criticisms that the pace of reforms could be quicker and the growth rate higher, most India observers now believe that the economic reforms are irreversible; India's economic environment has qualitatively changed. Some corporate assessments suggest that China and India are soon likely to make up almost half of the world's economic expansion, up from 13.7 per cent during 1982–87, 25 per cent during 1992–97, and 31.3 per cent during 2002–07.[3]

At 5.8 per cent per annum, the growth rate in the 1980s was also quite considerable. The Indian economy, thus, has been growing at close to 6 per cent per annum for almost three decades, and a trend growth rate of 6 per cent per annum increasingly constitutes the lower bound of expectations about the medium-to-long run. All this is a decisive break from the past. During the period 1950–80, India's economic growth rate was a mere 3.5 per cent per annum. Since the growth rate of the population, compared to 2.5 per cent per annum during the period 1950–80, has slowed down to roughly 1.9 per cent annually since 1980, the growth in per capita incomes shot up from 1 per cent per annum in the first three decades after independence to over 4 per cent per annum since then. The more than six decades of India's independence, economically speaking, split into two halves of remarkably different economic rhythms. Per capita incomes in the second half have grown four times faster than in the first.

India has been a latecomer to the international trends towards market-oriented shifts in economic policy. If we go by the Sachs–Warner index of economic openness, India became an open economy only in 1994, three years after the reforms were introduced.[4] If we apply this index to Asia in general, Thailand has been open right since the 1950s; Malaysia since 1963; Indonesia since 1970; and the Philippines since 1988. (One might note that, according to the Sachs–Warner index, China was not open till 1994.)[5]

Are the market-oriented economic reforms and India's international opening-up since 1991 responsible for improving the growth rate of the Indian economy? Are the higher growth rates in turn responsible for reductions in poverty? Have reforms been good for mass welfare? A vigorous economic debate has raged over these questions.[6] The purpose of this chapter is not to engage this economic debate. Rather, I will concentrate on politics, *assuming* that reforms are causally linked to these economic outcomes, at least substantially if not entirely, and leave to the economists the question of whether or not that is empirically provable. To be more specific, I will ask three questions: Is there, in general, a tension between democracy and markets and is India a specific case of a generic problem? Why were market-oriented reforms introduced successfully in 1991, not earlier? And how does one explain why some reforms have been embraced and others avoided?

More than a decade back, seeking to explain the timing and pattern of the first few years of economic reforms in India, I had argued against a strictly economic view of reforms—the view that reforms were made necessary by the macroeconomic crisis of mid-1991, when India ran into a serious balance of payments problem and had foreign exchange reserves worth only two weeks of imports left in the treasury.[7]

My argument was that this economic view, though necessary, was not sufficient. It had two analytic faults. First, a macroeconomic crisis requires stabilization, not structural adjustment. Stabilization programmes are short-run and macro; they can, in principle, solve a balance of payments crisis. In contrast, structural adjustment, besides being long-run, also covers policies that change the micro environment of firms: how and where to borrow capital; how to price products; where to buy inputs and where to sell outputs; which technology to use, etc. In 1991, India went for both macro stabilization as well as structural reforms.

This is not surprising, some might say. Faced with the standard International Monetary Fund (IMF) conditionalities for the dollar bailout in 1991, one could argue, India had no choice except to adopt a stabilization package as well as to introduce structural reforms. Even if we agree with this view, a purely economic explanation cannot account for why India continued on the path of economic reforms *after* the short-run balance of payments problem was resolved. The IMF's power effectively ends once the macroeconomic crisis is over.[8] India's foreign exchange crisis ended within two years—in 1993.

Second, and more importantly, a basic restructuring of economic policies has to go through a well-defined political process in India, so politics are unavoidable. Some policies can be announced simply as executive decisions but others, by law or the Constitution, require parliamentary approval. A recent case in point was the reform of India's (multi-brand) retail trade in 2012. The government had to seek parliamentary endorsement before the intended reform could become new policy. Similarly, the annual government budget is often, if not always, a key indicator of changes in economic policies. In many countries, the budget simply sums up the health of government finances. In India, given the historically entrenched and highly interventionist role of the state in the economy, the big changes in economic policy—especially those that reduce the role of the government and, therefore, alter taxes, public expenditures, and economic laws—have tended to show up prominently in the budgetary instrument. But it is an instrument over which the executive does not have final authority. The government can only present a budget, it cannot approve it. In the parliamentary system, the legislature must approve the budget. If Parliament does not approve the budget, the government can neither function economically nor introduce market-oriented economic policies. We must, therefore, not only ask why the government introduced reforms, but also why India's parliaments repeatedly endorsed them by approving budgets, especially in the early years of reform when the changes were quite radical.

Identifying thus a non-economic territory of analysis, the alternative explanation I provided was political. Based on the distinction between mass politics and elite politics, I made two principal arguments:

Economic reforms were a big concern in India's elite politics, but a secondary or tertiary concern in the nation's mass politics. Ethnic conflict and identity politics drove India's mass politics. *Paradoxically, it was the nation's preoccupation with identity politics during the 1990s that gave the government enough political room to bring in market-oriented reforms.*[9]

India's decision-makers had greater success in introducing and executing reforms that directly affected the welfare of the elite, and less success touching areas that directly affected mass welfare. Policy arenas, such as trade and exchange rate regimes, capital markets, industrial investment regimes, were examples of the former; and matters, such as food and fertilizer subsidies, agricultural policy, privatization, labour laws, and retail trade were instances of the latter. Counterfactually speaking, if India's policymakers had attacked the economic irrationalities of the latter set of policies in the early years of reform, the politics could well have become impossible to manage. An important reason for the success of economic reforms is that the less politically difficult reforms were embraced first.

Why were these arguments made? How do these arguments fare now, given the developments of the nearly decade and a half since then? And, given my understanding of the politics of reforms, where are India's economic policies headed? This chapter concentrates on these questions.

Democracy and Markets

It is a standard proposition of political economy that there are some built-in tensions between markets and democracy.[10] Such tensions arise due to the well-known difference in the organizing principles of the two systems. For democracies, the masses are citizens; individually, they have the same weight in franchise as those who are privileged or part of the elite. But markets deal with commodities, not citizens. By and large, the masses appear in the markets as consumers of goods, as suppliers of labour, or as small producers of low value–added goods. As consumers, the masses matter if they have purchasing power. And, as suppliers of labour and products, the value of their work is determined by the forces of supply and demand. In a market-based economy, no assumption of the equality of all is made, which is intrinsic to elections, and a vital principle of democracy.

In the West, the tensions between democracy and markets remained manageable for at least three reasons: (1) universal franchise came to the West only after the Industrial Revolution had been completed, which effectively meant that the poor got the right to vote after Western societies had become quite rich; (2) a welfare state, attending to the low-income segments of the population, has been in operation for much of the twentieth century; and finally, (3) those more educated and earning higher incomes tend to vote more often than the poorer sections of society.

The Indian experience constitutes a departure on all three counts. First, India adopted universal franchise at birth, long before the prospects of an industrial revolution could be visualized. India's development experience was thus bound to be different from that of the West. It is also remarkably distinct from that of East Asia. South Korea and Taiwan embraced universal-franchise democracy only between the late 1980s and mid-1990s, which was two to three decades after their economic upturn began. China and Singapore are not yet democratic. One might argue that in countries such as China, too, policymakers have to anticipate what policies might cause serious explosions of discontent and try to deal with them before they arise. But collective action is simply much easier in India. Protest is constitutionally protected, and opposition parties and NGOs exist to lead protests. Mass protest, thus, is more normal in Indian politics and can often be quite consequential.

Second, India does not have an extensive welfare state, though it has been trying to create one of late. The poor have had very few safety nets. Third, and this is critical, defying democratic theory, a great 'participatory upsurge' has marked Indian politics of late. Compared to the upper tiers of society, the so-called plebeian orders have of late participated more vigorously in elections. Indeed, the new conventional wisdom of Indian elections turns standard democratic theory on its head: the lower the caste, the lower the income; and the lower the education, the greater the odds that an Indian will vote.[11]

How do markets deal with the poor? The standard market-based economic perspective is quite straightforward: the expansion of markets will conquer poverty better than any other method. Markets release remarkable entrepreneurial energies, which can be harnessed for the greater good of society, including that of the poor. History shows, say the neo-liberal economists, that societies are unable to banish mass poverty without embracing markets.[12]

All these statements are true, but only in the long run, not in the short-to-medium run. Authoritarian politicians may concentrate entirely on the long run, but, faced with the requirement that election mandates must be periodically renewed, democratic politicians are, of necessity, concerned more about the short and medium run than about the long run. Moreover, how the masses view the markets in the short-to-medium run also depends on whether the markets are gainfully employing them, thereby increasing their purchasing power and welfare.

India's growth over the last three decades has not been employment-intensive. For all practical purposes, at 25–30 per cent of the population, the numbers of those who are the prime beneficiaries of reforms and those who continue to hover below the poverty line roughly match, and the latter have a much higher voting turnout. If one adds to this calculus, the fortunes and dispositions of those not much above the poverty line (let us say those below $2 a day, instead of $1 a day), who also tend to vote more often than the middle classes do, one can see why any reforming government in India will have to think about the tensions between democracy and markets. Democracy and market-oriented reforms are not natural bedfellows.

As elsewhere, India's decision-makers have also had to weigh the long-run welfare promise of markets against the great short-run dislocation they might cause. Whether or not it is possible in an authoritarian system, political leaders in India's highly contentious and adversarial democracy have found it extremely difficult to stake political fortunes on long-run economic gains, when (a) short-run dislocations are substantial; (b) long-run gains, even though likely, are uncertain; and (c) meanwhile, issues, such as identity politics, have occupied the centre of the political theatre, requiring immediate political attention, making or breaking political coalitions.

Mass Politics, Elite Politics

The terms mass and elite politics, with which I explained the origins and patterns of reforms in the 1990s, also require elaboration. What are the key differences between mass politics and elite politics?

The primary arena of mass politics is the street and the ballot box. Voting, agitations, protests, and demonstrations are the principal forms for mass politics; riots are also sometimes a key element. The major theatres of India's elite politics are the English-language press; the Internet; university seminars; corporate conferences; and the corridors of power, where corporate executives, officials of the international financial institutions, foreign government representatives, and lobbies meet with the bureaucrats and politicians. Negotiations, discussions, and bargaining are the typical forms of elite politics. Authoritarian polities, only episodically disrupted by mass agitations and protests, are normally driven by elite politics. Democracies witness both forms of politics, often routinely.

What allows a policy to enter mass politics? Three factors are typically critical: (1) how many people are affected by the policy; (2) how organized they are; and (3) whether the effect is direct and short-run or indirect and long-run. The more direct the effect of a policy, the more people are affected by it, and the more organized they are, the greater the potential for mass politics. *Underlying, long-run, and indirect links do not flourish in mass politics where the basic message has to be simple, intuitive, clearly demonstrable, and capable of arousing mass action.* Elite concerns—investment tax breaks, stock market regulations, tariffs on imported cars—rarely filter down to mass politics.

Within economic policy, following this reasoning, some issues are more likely to arouse mass contestation than others. For example, inflation, by affecting more or less everybody except those whose salaries are inflation-indexed, quickly gets inserted into mass politics. A financial meltdown has a similar effect, for a large number of banks and firms collapse and millions of people lose their jobs. In contrast, capital markets directly concern the shareholders, whose numbers are not likely to be large and who are also not likely to be organized in a poor country. As a result, short of a financial collapse, stock market disputes or fluctuations rarely, if ever, enter mass politics in developing countries.

What of trade liberalization and currency devaluation? They are often integral parts of market-oriented economic reforms. Are they part of mass politics or elite politics? In countries like Mexico, they are known to have seriously affected mass politics. In Venezuela, they were followed by a military coup, and a link between the reforms and the coup was explicitly made.[13]

If a country's economy is heavily dependent on foreign trade, a lowering of tariff walls, a reduction in quantitative trade restrictions, and a devaluation of the currency will indeed be of great concern to the masses, for they will directly affect mass welfare. In 1991, when India's reforms began, trade constituted more than 50 per cent of the GDP of Singapore, Malaysia, Thailand, the Philippines, Mexico, Hungary, South Korea, Poland, and Venezuela, among others. Changes—especially dramatic changes—in the trade and exchange rate regimes of these countries had a clear potential for mass politics. However, if trade is a small part of the economy—as has been true of India and Brazil until recently—changes in trade and exchange rate regimes will be of peripheral, short-run importance to the masses.[14] In 1991, India's trade–GDP ratio was a mere 15 per cent. Of late, this ratio has been rising rapidly, nearing 40 per cent. Trade could well become a matter of mass contestation before long.

One can, of course, argue that even if the trade-dependence of an economy is small, several long-run or indirect linkages can be shown to exist between mass welfare on the one hand and overvalued exchange rates or relatively closed trade regimes on the other. Krueger, for example, has contended that, by discouraging exports and making 'import competing' industrial goods dearer for the countryside, the import-substituting industrialization (ISI), a popular development strategy till the 1970s, systematically discriminated against the countryside.[15] The overvalued exchange rates and trade controls of the ISI period hurt a majority, or a large plurality, of a developing country's population, especially those in the countryside. Thus, even when trade is a small part of the economy, trade regimes can have an effect on mass welfare, not simply on elite welfare.

Why, then, have agrarian politicians in most countries rarely, if

ever, agitated for an open foreign trade regime, focusing instead on
the unfavourable urban–rural terms of trade, which could have, as
Krueger argues, caused less overall damage? The answer should be
clear. If such indirect links were not clear even to the economists—
who continued until the 1970s to look at rural welfare primarily in
terms of internal, urban–rural terms of trade—how can a politician
be expected to mobilize peasants over the underlying and subtle,
though hugely important, links between foreign trade and mass
welfare in a poor country? To repeat, long-run and indirect links
do not work well in mass politics; the message has to be simple,
intuitively graspable and clearly demonstrable. It is easy to contrast
urban privileges and rural misery, but rather hard to make the
connections between foreign trade and exchange rates on the one
hand and rural poverty on the other.[16]

Compared to economic policy, consider now the role of ethnic
conflict in politics. Ethnic disputes tend quickly to enter mass politics
because they isolate a whole group, or several groups, on an ascriptive
basis. They also directly hit political parties—both ethnically based
parties (which may defend, or repel attacks on, their ethnic group)
and multi-ethnic parties (which may fiercely fight attempts to pull
some ethnic groups away from their rainbow coalitions). Because
they invoke ascriptive, not voluntary, considerations, the effects of
ethnic cleavages and ethnically based policies are obvious to most
people and, more often than not, ethnic groups are either organized,
or tend to organize quickly. As explained in Chapter 9, according
to the theorists of collective action, ethnic protest can basically
be likened to a coordination game, whereas economically based
class action is crippled by free-rider problems. The former kind of
collective action is easier, the latter more difficult.[17]

It is intuitively plausible to suggest that the distinction
between mass politics and elite politics would be more relevant
to democracies, given that periodic renewals of mass mandates
are not necessary in authoritarian countries. Compared to China,

India's privatization plans remain slow and halting: the welfare of workers who might lose their jobs continues to be an important political concern, and questions about transparency in sales touch off substantial political storms. To be sure, China was also cautious about privatization to begin with, embarking on it only in the late 1990s, nearly two decades after the market-oriented turn in economic policy had come about. But once Chinese political leaders decided to go for privatization, they did not retrace steps, regardless of what consequences it had for those laid off. A treason or subversion trial against labour leaders protesting job losses is virtually impossible in India's democracy. But in China, this is what a *Washington Post* correspondent observed:

> Under tight security and with an angry crowd holding a vigil in sub-zero temperatures outside, a court in this North-eastern Chinese city (Liaoyang) tried two prominent labor leaders on subversion charges today. . . . Yao Fuxin, 52, and Xiao Yunlinag, 56, were arrested last March for helping organize large-scale protests in Liaoyang demanding aid for workers left jobless by economic reforms and punishment for officials unfairly profiting from the privatization of state industries. The protests, which drew as many as 30,000 people from factories across the city, were among the biggest labor demonstrations in China in years.[18]

In the 1990s, India witnessed both economic reforms and ethnic conflict together. How did their differential political salience play out? In a survey of mass political attitudes in India conducted in 1996,[19] only 19 per cent of the electorate reported any knowledge of economic reforms, even though reforms had been in existence since July 1991. In the countryside, where two-thirds of India still lives, only about 12 per cent had heard of reforms, whereas the comparable proportion in the cities was 32 per cent. Further, nearly 66 per cent of graduates were aware of the dramatic changes in economic policy, compared to only 7 per cent of the poor, who are mostly illiterate. In contrast, close to three-fourths of the electorate, urban and rural, literate and illiterate, rich and poor, were aware of the 1992 mosque demolition in Ayodhya; 80 per cent expressed clear opinions of whether the country should have a uniform civil code or religiously prescribed and separate laws for marriage, divorce, and property inheritance; and 87 per cent took a stand on caste-based affirmative action.

Further, economic reforms were a non-issue in the 1996 and 1998 elections.[20] And in the 1999 elections, the biggest economic reformers either lost or did not campaign on reforms.[21] Ethnic and religious disputes, secularism, and caste-based affirmative action drove India's mass politics, and led to large-scale mobilization, insurgencies, riots, assassinations, and desecrations and destruction of holy places. In comparison, economic reforms aroused very little mass passion.

Did this situation change in the 2004 and 2009 elections? I shall deal with this question later on in this chapter. At this stage, it would be more pertinent to note that the kind of political space I have described above is essentially two-dimensional, with ethnic or identity politics playing itself out on one axis, and reform politics on the other. Scholars of economic reforms, especially the economists, have generally assumed that reforms are, or tend to become, central to politics.[22] That is a one-dimensional view. Depending on what else is making demands on the energies of the electorate and the politicians —ethnic and religious strife; political order and stability; corruption and 'crimes' of the incumbents—the assumption of reform centrality may not be right. The main battle lines in politics may be drawn on issues such as how to avoid (or promote) a further escalation of ethnic conflict; whether to support (or oppose) the political leaders if there has been an attempted coup; whether to forgive (or punish) the 'crimes' of high state officials.

Paradoxically, it may be easier to push through reforms in a context like this, for politicians and the electorate are occupied by matters they consider more critical.[23] Economic reforms may not cause the political opposition they otherwise would. As we shall see later, this insight makes it easier to understand the pattern and evolution of India's economic reforms. But, in order to understand what exactly was reformed and how, we need first an understanding of the key pillars of India's economic strategy before 1991.

India's Initial Economic Strategy (1950–90)

Very much in keeping with the worldwide trends in the days of development planning, India in the 1950s went for central planning, a relatively closed trade regime and an interventionist state. This strategy lasted till 1991, longer than in most developing countries. India's economic strategy—called structuralism by economic theorists—radically departed from a neoclassical view of development, which would have relied on prices for allocation of resources as opposed to quantitative controls of planning; an open trade regime as opposed to import substitution; and a minimal as opposed to an interventionist state. The logic of structuralism is worth revisiting briefly, if only to appreciate why it was so widely adopted by the profession of development economics, with very few dissenters,[24] and what its pitfalls turned out to be, especially in India.[25]

As structuralists, Indian planners believed that prices as a mechanism of rational resource allocation would work if, and only if, the supply of goods was responsive to prices and the adjustment mechanisms worked smoothly.[26] That is, the functioning of the price mechanism depended on the existence of markets. If markets did not exist, or did not work smoothly, the price mechanism was relatively useless. Food production was an arch example of this reasoning. Food production may not increase even if the demand for food goes up because enough fertilizers or enough seeds do not exist. More fertilizers and new seeds can be provided if they can be bought from outside, but there may not be enough foreign exchange to buy fertilizers. Foreign exchange indeed was a 'bottleneck' in the developing world, but it was not the only bottleneck. Structuralists argued that such rigidities and bottlenecks simply abounded in poor countries, making price mechanism relatively useless.

Similarly, structuralists argued, and Indian planners agreed, trade policy based on comparative advantage, instead of facilitating industrialization, would in fact make industrialization difficult. As incomes increase, people spend relatively smaller proportions of their incomes on agricultural goods and primary commodities, more on industrial goods. Thus, agricultural and commodity exports (not sophisticated manufactures), in which the developing countries were likely to specialize, would run into the proverbial terms-of-trade problem. With the exception of commodities, such as oil, there would simply not be enough demand for such goods over the medium to long run. The international terms of trade of agricultural and primary commodity exporters would decline, making it difficult for countries having a comparative advantage in them to earn enough money to industrialize.

Industries, thus, would need to be set up on some other ground. And once set up, the infant industry would require protection from international competition. The state would have to construct tariff barriers, or set up quantitative restrictions, or both. Structuralism was, thus, trade-pessimistic. The idea of import substitution logically followed.

Moreover, import substitution was supplemented by the idea of central planning, which had its roots in the theory of the big push.[27] The basic logic of central planning was simple: if a steel plant was necessary for industrialization, there was also need for other industries that could consume the steel so produced. One solution was to build an auto plant as well as a machine tool plant, both of which could use steel. But how would the cars so produced be sold? Those working in the steel plant, the auto factory and the machine tool factory would buy cars. Building steel plants thus logically required that all these plants be constructed together. Inevitably, the state had to step in to suggest how much steel ought to be produced, given how many cars were likely to be produced, given how many cars were likely to be bought. Poor countries needed an interventionist state, not a minimal state.

In the 1950s and 1960s, these ideas were highly influential in India, which practised a particularly strict form of structuralism. Indian structuralism rested on three pillars: two sets of regulatory regimes—internal and external—and a third pillar consisting of the role of the public sector, which was to take over the 'commanding heights' of the economy.

The internal regulatory regime relied on investment and production controls. Its chief instrument was the industrial licensing system. The controls related not only to plant capacity but also to: what price could be charged for the output; in some cases, where and how the output was to be distributed; how much capital could be used; the quantity and type of inputs permissible and where they had to be procured from; what technology to use; what product lines or sectors would be reserved for small-scale investors; what the debt–equity ratio would be, etc.

The intended goal of this control regime was to ensure that scarce resources were utilized according to a plan that was socially rational, and that investment went into 'strategic' sectors beneficial for the entire society rather than only some sections of it. The actual outcome, however, was very different. Given that there was only a limited number of licences that could be given—the number depending on an assessment of the size of the market for a given product balanced against some normative criterion of whether production in that line was to be encouraged—the early entrants typically reaped stable profits, which were not to be depressed by more new entrants. Moreover, the principle of cost plus pricing ensured profits. In a system like this, the energies of investors were centred not so much on capturing markets and earning via cost reduction or product differentiation—which is normally the case in competitive settings—but on 'licence cornering', or what came later to be called 'rent seeking'.

On the external side, an import substitution strategy ensured that there was no foreign competition. A host of tariff and quantitative controls provided a protected market to domestic producers. Very few scholars would claim that the very initiation of this strategy was wrong. Any country wishing to develop must protect domestic industry in the beginning.[28] But an infant-industry argument cannot hold indefinitely. A child, after all, must grow into maturity: protective care stretched too far impedes the coming of age. Not forcing infant industries to compete in the international market till 1991 had disastrous results. Sectional benefits, accruing to protected industries, overwhelmed the social benefit that was supposed to have resulted from such protection. Profits of the protected industries remained unaffected, while costs did not come down. Lower costs would more easily have been a net social benefit.

Finally, the performance of the public sector was a major source of waste in the economy. There were many aspects to the public sector inefficiency—lag in project completion; low capacity utilization; bad management; lack of managerial autonomy in input choice, pricing, and technology; overstaffing, etc. Management—a reasonably specialized matter in the late twentieth century— was mostly entrusted to the generalist officers of the Indian Administrative Service (IAS), who did everything from diplomacy to development to electronics to fertilizers; and by the time they understood something about fertilizers, they were moved to power, then to shipbuilding, and still later, to telecommunications, and so on.

This overview of the basic structure of India's pre-reform economic strategy should explain why India grew so slowly. The long-run growth rate of the Indian economy over the period 1951–

52 to 1981–82 was 3.5 per cent. At the core of it lay the paradox of an increasing savings and investment rate but a barely changing growth rate. There was considerable consensus among Indian economists in the 1960s that a low savings rate and meagre foreign exchange reserves accounted for the slow growth rate. The situation on both fronts improved dramatically in the 1970s. The savings rate went up from 9 per cent of GDP in the early fifties to 22 per cent by the early eighties and, thanks to remittances from abroad, foreign exchange reserves ceased to be an overriding everyday constraint. Investment rate went up from a mere 11 per cent in the early 1950s to 24 per cent by the early eighties. Yet the economic growth rate barely picked up.

The investment rates might have gone up, but so did the incremental capital–output ratios, reflecting rising economic inefficiencies. By the 1970s, India was using roughly twice as much capital as before to generate the same output. A long period of ISI did produce a broad industrial base, but virtually no industry was internationally competitive.

Why did this industrial strategy last so long? Several explanations are available. The analysis provided by Bardhan is the most widely read.[29] Bardhan argued that three classes—the industrialists, the rich peasantry and the professionals in the bureaucracy—constituted India's 'dominant coalition'. Each class exerted pressure on the state for subsidies and grants, pulling the state in its own direction. As a result, resources that could have gone towards investment were frittered away in grants and subsidies. The rich peasantry got subsidized fertilizers, water, power, diesel, and ever higher support prices; the industrialists got low-interest credit, export subsidies, underpriced public sector services; and the professionals in the public bureaucracy got higher and higher salaries without any reference to productivity. Subsidies on three items alone—food, fertilizers, and exports—were roughly half of the gross investment in the public manufacturing sector in 1980–81. In short, over time, vested interests emerged around the economic strategy and blocked all changes.

Partly disagreeing with an interest-group-based explanation and arguing that the state often had considerable autonomy in decision-making, Weiner added ideological factors to Bardhan's explanation.[30] India's decision-makers simply did not believe in the profit motive and markets. A famous passage of Nehru's *The Discovery of India*, a founding text of Indian nationhood, is always—and rightly—cited to show how anti-business the attitudes at the highest levels of Indian polity were. Nehru, the father of Indian planning, had argued:

> It would be absurd to say that the profit motive does not appeal to the average Indian, but it is nevertheless true that there is no such admiration for it as there is in the West. The possessor of money may be envied but he is not particularly respected or admired. Respect and admiration still go . . . especially to those who sacrifice themselves . . . for the public good.[31]

Right through the 1950s, 1960s, and 1970s, one could argue that this attitude dominated the highest levels of Indian polity. The profit motive and businessmen were distrusted.[32]

Reforms in the 1990s

It is against this thicket of ideologies and webs of control that the reformers began to push hard in 1991. The occasion was a serious balance of payments crisis. 'The current level of foreign exchange reserves', announced Finance Minister Manmohan Singh, 'would suffice to finance imports for a mere fortnight.'[33] But, instead of addressing only the macroeconomic crisis through an IMF stabilization programme, he demonstrated that a serious rethinking on the entire economic strategy had begun. 'Macroeconomic stabilization and fiscal adjustment alone cannot suffice,' he argued; 'they must be supported by essential reforms in economic policy . . . (facilitating) *a transition from a regime of quantitative restrictions to a price based mechanism* . . . Over-centralization and excessive bureaucratization have proved to be counterproductive.'[34]

Thus began a whole series of economic reforms, introduced incrementally. In some areas, the progress has been dramatic; in other areas, moderate; and in still others, little progress has been made. The policy arenas showing maximum progress are: investment liberalization, including rules for foreign investment; trade and exchange rates; and capital market reforms. I deal with these policies first, coming to the non-performing policy areas later.

Investment Liberalization

There has been 'a bonfire of industrial licences' that used to control virtually every aspect of industrial production.[35] Except for a few hazardous industries, industrial licensing has been abolished altogether. Moreover, in the earlier economic regime, eighteen industries—including telecommunications, heavy machinery, air transport, and power—had been reserved for the public sector. But, by the end of the first decade of reforms, only three industries—rail transport, defence, and atomic energy generation—were left for the public sector. More changes have taken place since then, and these industries, too, have been opened up substantially, if not entirely. Private investment in defence, including foreign investment, has been allowed. Private trains now carry goods, if not passengers. Finally, to pre-empt concentration of economic power, the earlier policy had prohibited large business houses from investing beyond a certain capital ceiling. Such ceilings have been lifted, allowing economies of scale.

Rules governing foreign investment, both direct and portfolio, have also been dramatically liberalized. The new policy allows 100

per cent foreign ownership in a large number of industries, and
majority ownership in most industries. Before the reforms began,
annual foreign investment used to be about $80–100 million. In
2012–13, a low year of economic growth, foreign direct investment
(FDI) was a little over $20 billion. In recent years, FDI has routinely
exceeded $30 billion annually. There was no foreign portfolio
investment in India before 1992, when foreign institutions were
allowed, for the first time, to buy and sell stocks. Now, Indian
companies can also issue equity in foreign markets.

Trade and Exchange Rates

A great deal of progress, though less spectacular than in investment
reforms, has also been made in trade and exchange rate policies.
Two devaluations of the Indian rupee were among the initial
macroeconomic moves of the government in July–August 1991.
They brought market realism to the exchange rate, which has been
flexible ever since. Tariff barriers and quantitative restrictions on
foreign trade have also been sharply reduced. The average tariff
has come down from about 72.5 per cent in 1991–92 to roughly
10–12 per cent now. By 2001, all quantitative restrictions on trade
had been lifted.

Capital Market Reforms

Equally important has been a fundamental transformation in
the principles of institutional oversight over capital markets. The
office of the Controller of Capital Issues (CCI) was replaced by a
new institution, called the Securities and Exchange Board of India
(SEBI). The CCI's prior permission used to be required before a
company could issue equity at a given price. It was effectively a
price setter. A long gap between the time of request and the time of
permission would typically introduce unnecessary price distortions

in the stock market. The SEBI is not a price setter, but a 'market-friendly' regulatory body.

Let me now turn to the four policy areas where progress has been minimal, or where no reforms have been introduced at all: fiscal deficits, privatization, agriculture and labour laws.

Fiscal Deficits

India's fiscal deficits continue to be high. The combined fiscal deficit of the federal and the state governments, 9.4 per cent in 1991, has returned by now to roughly the same level as before the reforms. Subsidies accruing due to high support prices for grain and low fertilizer prices and energy subsidies are among the main reasons for the high levels of the fiscal deficit; the others, by now, are the welfare programmes—for poverty-alleviation, education, health, etc. Almost every attempt at lowering support prices and increasing fertilizer prices has led to political opposition on behalf of farmers.

Privatization

On privatization, a beginning was made in 2001, ten years after the reform era began. By creating a separate Ministry of Disinvestment, and then elevating it to the Cabinet level, Prime Minister Vajpayee demonstrated his commitment to privatization. But unions have vigorously resisted privatization. Concerns about the transparency of rules, and the question of whether only the loss-making, or all, public sector units should be sold also continue to cause significant obstacles. Economists, on the whole, are convinced about the desirability of privatization, but India's politically active groups and political elite remain unconvinced. Opinion is changing slowly, and the necessity of building coalitions of support in a democracy slows the process down.

Agriculture and Labour Laws

An argument about ending agricultural subsidies and exposing agriculture to a border (international) price regime has often been intellectually aired,[36] but subsidies continue at fairly high levels. Convincing the large rural populace that subsidies are not in its long-run interests remains a politically daunting task. Labour laws too have not been reformed. No firm, which has more than 100 workers, can fire its workers without government permission, which is almost never granted. India has a lifelong employment system. Once hired as a regular employee, a worker cannot easily be retrenched. This has implications for firm entry as well as exit: the former, because recruitment in new firms cannot be made assuming that the workforce, if necessary, could be restructured later; and the latter, because loss-making firms cannot close down or restructure their labour force. They must find other ways of turning themselves around.

Did Ethnic Conflicts Help India's Economic Reformers?[37]

Why some reforms have been enthusiastically embraced and successfully implemented, others neglected, and still others haltingly pursued? To repeat, economic logic alone cannot explain the selectivity and rhythm of reforms. Reforms that touch, directly or primarily, elite politics have gone the farthest: a large devaluation of the currency; a restructuration of capital markets; a liberalization of the trade regime; and a simplification of investment rules. Reforms that are economically desirable but concern mass politics have been of two types: those that have positive political consequences in mass politics (for example, inflation control), and those that have potentially negative or highly uncertain consequences in mass politics (labour laws, privatization of the public sector, agricultural subsidies). The former have been implemented with considerable determination; the latter have been either ignored, or pursued with less than exemplary policy resolve, or if pursued, have become a casualty of the inability of the government to carry large swathes of political opinion with it.

An important and analytically separable question, however, remains. How were the reforms of trade, exchange rate, investment and capital market policies adopted in the first place? The macro-crisis of 1991 did provide the occasion for reformers inside the government to pursue their market-oriented agenda, but without a political endorsement of their views, either the reforms would have been stillborn or, after the short-run macroeconomic crisis was over—as it was in 1993—India would have wriggled out of the IMF's conditionalities.

As briefly suggested earlier, any major economic policy initiative that has serious budgetary implications must go through parliamentary approval in India. Since India's economy was so heavily state-centric from 1950–90, any market-based restructuring of the economic policy naturally entailed a reduced role of the government in the economy. It also meant a change in the government's tax plans, expenditure profiles, non-tax revenue raising policies, and a change in many economic laws. It is the legislature that has the final authority over many of these matters. Change, especially a fundamental change, is not a matter of executive decree. The executive may present budgets and seek changes in economic laws, but only the legislature can pass them and turn them into actual laws.

The question, then, is: Why did India's elected parliamentarians approve budgets that carried the message of economic reforms, especially in the first three years after 1991 when the magnitude of change, given India's economic past, was the greatest? If India's Parliament had not passed the first few budgets after 1991, the new economic policies would not have emerged, not because of a faulty economic logic but due to the institutional constraints of a parliamentary system.

By now, of course, it has become customary to say that India's reforms are irreversible. It is hard to recall how gloomy the reform prospects were in July 1991. Lacking a majority in Parliament, the Rao government did not even seem stable; only six years back, the Rajiv Gandhi government, despite enjoying a three-fourths majority in Parliament, had found it politically hard to push market-oriented reforms. The country was going through a massive Hindu–Muslim upheaval on the one hand and a serious dispute over caste-based affirmative action on the other. To make matters worse, two insurgencies—one in Punjab, the other in Kashmir—were showing no signs of abatement. The nation's former head of government, Rajiv Gandhi, had just been brutally assassinated. Instead of reform optimism, many commentators were concerned whether India would survive as a nation in the 1990s.[38]

As it turned out, in spite of lacking a clear majority in Parliament, the Rao government was able to push many of the reforms which Rajiv Gandhi's government, even with a three-fourths majority, was unable to put through. Unless we uncover the logic of this paradoxical outcome, we will not be able to understand the political dynamics of economic reforms in India. The key difference was the phenomenal political rise of Hindu nationalism, accompanied by some of the most violent Hindu–Muslim (and caste) riots in the country, during 1989–92. The institutional and political details of how the rise of Hindu–Muslim (and caste) tensions helped the reformers, but their absence hurt Rajiv Gandhi's reform plans between 1985 and 1989, are summarized below.

The Rao government, as already stated, did not have majority support when it came to power in July 1991; it added some more seats to its strength in by-elections in March 1992, but till 1996, when its term ended, it was still short of a majority (Table 10.1). Yet, while Rajiv Gandhi, commanding three-fourths of parliamentary

TABLE 10.1: PARTY POSITIONS IN THE LOWER HOUSE OF
PARLIAMENT, 1984–89 AND 1991–96

Party	Seats 1984–89	Seats 1991–92	Seats 1992–96
I. Congress and Congress Supporters			
Congress	415	220	232
ADMK	12	11	11
II. Hindu Nationalists			
BJP	2	120	120
III. The Left and Other Congress Opponents			
Janata Dal	10	59	59
CPM	22	35	35
CPI	6	14	14
TDP	30	13	13
IV. Others	46	52	53
TOTAL	543	524	537

Notes: 1. Elections were not held in Jammu and Kashmir at all, bringing the total seats in the Lok Sabha down to 537 in the tenth Lok Sabha. J&K has 6 seats in the Lower House.
2. Elections in Punjab (13 seats) were held in February 1992, and results announced in March 1992. Column II does not, therefore, include the seats in Punjab. The figures for 1992–96 include the results of the 1991 elections and the 1992 Punjab elections.
3. Because of a large number of parties, each of them with a small number of MPs, 'Others' are presented in an aggregated manner. Most were traditionally against the Congress party.

majority, delicensed only a few industries, the Rao government delicensed all except a few.[39] Rajiv Gandhi lowered corporate and personal income taxes; the Rao government reduced them further. Under Rajiv Gandhi, capital markets had no foreign investors; under Rao, foreign portfolio institutions were allowed, rules for FDI were liberalized and, in 'key' sectors, such as power, foreign ownership was permitted. Finally, unlike Rajiv Gandhi, the Rao government had to sign a stabilization agreement with the IMF, which is often politically controversial in the developing world. Arguments about the Rao government mortgaging the nation's economic sovereignty could easily be made.

The debate on the first two budgets—in July–August 1991 and March–April 1992—was bitter and charged. Opposition politicians made trenchant arguments in Parliament about the actual or impending loss of economic sovereignty to the IMF and the World Bank. A second set of political criticisms was about the pro-rich and pro-urban orientation of the new policies. Finally, there was the apprehension that reforms would lead to retrenchment in the public sector undertakings.

Opposition politicians vigorously criticized the budgets, but finally did not vote against them. The Rao government had initiated reforms at a time when Hindu nationalism was a rising force. In 1991, with 120 seats in Parliament, the Hindu nationalist BJP was the second largest party in the country. In 1990, it had led the movement for the demolition of the Baburi Mosque, touching off ghastly Hindu–Muslim riots, polarizing the electorate and national politics, and causing a great deal of anxiety about violence and lack of order in the country. Out of a total of 524 elected members in the Lower House in July–September 1991, the Congress party had 220 seats, as also the support of 11 members of a regional party, the Anna Dravida Munnetra Kazhagam (ADMK), bringing the aggregate of its House support to 231, whereas 273 was the halfway—and winning—mark. Similarly, at the time of vote on the next budget in May 1992, the Congress tally of seats had gone up to 232 out of a total of 537 seats. Combined with 13 seats of the pro-Congress regional parties, it had 245 votes in all, 24 short of the majority (Table 10.1). The 1991, 1992 and 1993 budgets would have been blocked and reforms stalled, if the remaining opposition parties had coordinated their moves and jointly voted against the government.

They did not do so because, by 1990, India's politics had become triangular. Between 1950 and 1989, the principal battle lines of politics had been bipolar. The Congress was the party of government, and all other parties were opposed to it. Between 1990 and 1997, a triangular contest developed between the left (both the Marxists and lower caste parties), the Hindu nationalists, and the Congress party. Coalitions were increasingly formed against the Hindu nationalists, not against the Congress. To begin with, the left disliked the reforms, but they disliked Hindu nationalism even more. Having risen from 2 seats in 1984 to 120 seats in 1991, the Hindu nationalist BJP was the rising force in Indian politics. After the Hindu nationalists demolished the mosque in December 1992, the left became even more convinced that the Hindu nationalists had to be contained. A full-floor coordination between the various opposition parties was required to defeat budgets, but the Hindu nationalists and the left simply could not come together. That would have meant unseating the Congress party from power which, in turn, implied the clear possibility that the BJP would march further in the elections that would ensue.

Thus were the first three annual budgets after reforms passed in India's Parliament. India's economic reforms kept progressing because the political context had made Hindu–Muslim relations (and caste animosities) the prime determinant of political coalitions. In 1998–99, a substantial section of the non-Marxist, lower caste left and the BJP came together to form of a National Democratic Alliance (NDA). However, by the time this happened, the reforms were firmly in place. When the BJP finally came out of its isolation, found alliance partners and came to rule, reforms were no longer a break from the past and not a matter of intense political contestation.

The political context in 1985–86 was very different. Rajiv Gandhi did face a Hindu–Sikh cleavage in the state of Punjab, but the Hindu–Sikh cleavage never had the same nationwide intensity as the Hindu–Muslim divide. It was confined to North India. Moreover,

Rajiv Gandhi had already concluded an agreement in 1985 with Sikh politicians for a peaceful resolution of Sikh demands. The agreement would unravel in 1988 and violence would touch dangerous levels. But 1985 and 1986 were years of cooled passions. The BJP had a mere two seats in Parliament; the movement for the demolition of the mosque was still to take off; and the Kashmir insurgency was not on the horizon. In a political context of this kind, when economic reforms were introduced, politicians could easily use the proposed changes in policy as a basis for mass mobilization. The trade unions and the opposition parties first mobilized support, and then, in an expression of factional battle within the ruling party, the factions opposed to the new policies also rebelled.

Thus, economic liberalization became a victim of its splendid solitude on the political agenda during 1985–87. Between 1991 and 1996, economic reforms were crowded out of mass politics by issues that aroused greater passion and anxiety about the nation. Concurrently, during 1991–96, the government touched only those reforms that concerned elite politics, staying away from reforms that would have direct, short-run, serious, and uncertain consequences for the masses.

Reforms and Mass Politics since 2004

Did the 2004 elections end the relative non-significance of economic reforms in electoral politics? The question is relevant because the ruling BJP-centred National Democratic Alliance (NDA) ran an 'India Shining' campaign, and lost the elections. Further, two of the biggest reformers at the state level, Chandrababu Naidu in Andhra Pradesh and S.M. Krishna in Karnataka, also lost power. The former was, in fact, routed.

Studies are unclear as to whether reforms single-handedly accounted for the National Democratic Alliance's election defeat,[40] but it is clear that political pressure is rising on politicians to make reforms relevant to the masses. Reforms are beginning to penetrate areas that matter to the masses: for example, land acquisition for urbanization and industrialization. Many protests against land acquisitions have been launched and, as India grows further, more rural or tribal land will have to be acquired. If viewed as favourable to the businessmen and unfavourable to the masses, these acquisitions are likely to continue to spur mass agitation.

The National Election Study 2004 and 2009 give us the materials to understand how the masses are beginning to view economic reforms.[41] Table 10.2 summarizes some key results. More people believed that the reforms benefited only the rich, not the whole nation, and the more we climbed down the social ladder, the greater was that belief. Upper castes were nearly evenly split on whether the reforms had helped the whole nation or only the rich. But, among those segments placed lower on the socio-economic scale—the OBCs, Dalits, adivasis, and Muslims—a huge plurality or majority held the belief that the reforms had mainly benefited the rich. One should also add that the upper castes constitute an overwhelming proportion of India's middle class. The fit between

TABLE 10.2: PERCEPTIONS OF ECONOMIC REFORMS ACCORDING TO VARIOUS COMMUNITIES, 2004 (PERCENTAGE OF ROW TOTALS)

Economic Reforms Benefited	Upper Caste	OBC	Dalit	Adivasi	Muslim	Other	N
The whole country	38	29	19	20	16	27	6,387
Only the rich	36	42	51	44	53	42	9,755
No one	13	14	14	16	17	13	3,143
No opinion	12	16	16	20	13	19	3,263

Note: N = 22,548
Source: The National Election Study (NES), 2004

the two categories—upper castes and middle class—is not perfect, but it is very substantial.

Further, in a dramatic contrast to 1996—when a mere 19 per cent of the citizens had any opinion on reforms—a little over 85 per cent expressed clear judgements in 2004.[42] It is obvious that in 1996 there had been no understanding of reforms beyond elite levels, but now the reforms were entering mass consciousness.

The first post-2004 government (2004–09), formed by the United Progressive Alliance 1 (UPA-1), had some of the ace reformers of post-1991 India, including Prime Minister Manmohan Singh, Finance Minister P. Chidambaram, and Planning Chief Montek S. Ahluwalia, but two of the biggest initiatives of that government were distinctly anti-market: the National Rural Employment Guarantee Act (NREGA), and the extension of affirmative action to the OBCs in higher education. The first gave a guarantee to every rural household that 100 days of annual work would be given to at least one member of the household. The second sought to reserve 27 per cent of seats for the OBCs in higher education institutions, including the Indian Institutes of Technology and Indian Institutes of Management. Whether these are the right ways to bring benefits to the masses may be debatable, but it should be obvious why the government took these measures.

Did such measures make a difference to the mass perceptions about economic reforms? For the 2009 elections, a similar question was again asked by the National Election Study. The results, summarized in Table 10.3, are not dramatically different from those for 2004. Two points, however, should be noted. The Dalits appeared to be not so heavily aligned in favour of the view that the reforms had benefited only the rich, nor did the Muslims have that view. But, on the whole, those who believe that reforms have benefited only the rich continue to outnumber those who think reforms have helped the entire country. In short, significant pressure remains in the polity to include the excluded.

TABLE 10.3: PERCEPTIONS OF ECONOMIC REFORMS
ACCORDING TO VARIOUS COMMUNITIES, 2009
(PERCENTAGE OF ROW TOTALS)

Economic Reforms Benefited	Upper Caste	OBC	Dalit	Adivasi	Muslim	Other	N
The whole country	27	24	24	19	32	26	1,854
Only the rich	35	36	37	35	31	34	2,541
No one	11	8	7	9	8	8	640
No opinion	27	32	32	37	29	32	2,229

Note: N = 7,264
Source: The *National Election Study (NES)*, 2009

It is now clear that India's remarkable growth since 1991 has generated a new political economy triad. India today has: (i) the fifth largest concentration of listed dollar billionaires in the world (after the US, Russia, China, and Germany);[43] (ii) the third largest middle class (after China and the US); and (iii) the single largest concentration of the poor. Historically, India's economic structure had the massively wealthy princes at the top, whose incomes were based on inherited wealth and land; a tiny middle class; and a huge mass of the poor. Billionaire businessmen and a huge middle class constitute a historical novelty for India. Together, current downturn notwithstanding, these two factors make an internationally attractive place for business.

But the political implications of the triad are very different. The middle classes—no more than 30 per cent of India's population—are electorally not as attractive to political parties as the poor. As already noted, the fit between the upper castes and the middle class is not complete, but considerable.[44] The number of votes in the other two categories—the OBCs and the other lower segments (SCs, STs, and Muslims)—is much higher and these strata, by and large below the middle classes, also tend to have higher turnout rates.

Thus, in the pure arithmetic of votes, unless India's middle classes—the principal beneficiaries of economic reforms—begin to participate more in elections and/or become roughly 50 per cent of the electorate, they will be less than fully consequential in electoral politics. The middle classes control the press, especially the English-language press, and have a preponderant presence in the corporate sector. As a result, they can still generate a vigorous debate in the country, strengthening the public sphere of democracy. But their electoral significance does not match their power over instruments of public criticism.

It should also be noted that the BJP—should it return to power in an alliance—cannot entirely escape these inclusionary pressures. In search of votes, the BJP also has to move downward for support. That is where the biggest numbers of votes exist. Unsurprisingly, the BJP did not oppose the NREGA, nor did it resist the 2006 affirmative action plan, nor the right to education and food security bill. All parties are subject to the rise of inclusionary pressures.

Conclusion

India has come a long way since independence in 1947. To be sure, India's independence was a moment of joy, 'a tryst with destiny', as Nehru, India's first prime minister, memorably put it. But it was also a moment of pain and agony. Partition violence killed a large number of people; India's literacy rate was a mere 16–17 per cent; and roughly half of the population was below what we have come to call the poverty line. Beyond the princes and the maharajas, the middle class was very small, and the manufacturing sector minuscule. A half-century of virtual economic stagnation had preceded independence.

Over the last two decades, India has gone through an economic boom. Mass poverty has come down; the literacy rate has crossed 72 per cent; the middle class numbers anywhere between 250 to 300 million people, the exact magnitude depending on the indicator chosen. Finally, with great confidence, India's corporate leaders are acquiring major firms abroad, creating new international synergies in their supply chains.

But a lot of Indians, and certainly most of India's political leaders, including those who champion market-oriented economic reforms, believe that poverty and deprivation have not come down rapidly enough. *What is an acceptable rate of decline in poverty is not, fundamentally, an economic question.* A nation's politics decides what is acceptable. The impression that India's boom has mainly benefited the upper Hindu castes, the cities, and the Southern and Western states, is inescapable. On the whole, the lower Hindu castes, the STs, the large Muslim minority, the villages, and the Northern and Eastern states have lagged behind. India's post-independence leadership had undertaken to abolish mass poverty. That pledge remains only partially redeemed.

Under such circumstances, a universal-franchise democracy, where the deprived—defying standard democratic theory—have come to vote at least as much as, if not more than, the privileged, is bound to feel inclusionary pressures. Many more would like the fruits of the economic boom to come to them. The greatest challenge for India's policymakers today is to balance the new growth momentum with inclusionary policies.

Notes on Chapters

Chapter 2, 'Why Democracy Survives', was first published in the *Journal of Democracy* in July 1998.

Chapter 3, 'Is India Becoming More Democratic?', was first published in the *Journal of Asian Studies* in February 2000.

Chapter 4, 'Contested Meanings: India's National Identity, Hindu Nationalism, and the Politics of Anxiety in the 1980s and 1990s', first appeared in *Daedalus* in Summer 1993.

Chapter 5, 'Ethnic Conflict and Civil Society: India and Beyond', was first published in *World Politics* in April 2001.

Chapter 6, 'How Has Indian Federalism Done?', was first published in *Studies in Indian Politics* in July 2013.

Chapter 7, 'Two Banks of the Same River? Social Orders and Entrepreneurialism in India', first appeared in the *Anxieties of Democracy: Tocquevillean Reflections on India and the United States*, edited by Partha Chatterjee and Ira Katznelson, and published by Oxford University Press in 2012.

Chapter 8, 'Caste and Entrepreneurship in India', was first published in the *Economic and Political Weekly* in February 2013.

Chapter 9, 'Why Have Poor Democracies Not Eradicated Poverty?', first appeared in *Measuring Empowerment*, edited by Deepa Narayan, and published by the World Bank in 2005; and 'Why Have Poor Democracies Not Eliminated Poverty? A Suggestion' in *Asian Survey* in 2000.

Chapter 10, 'Democratic Politics and Economic Reforms in India', was first published as 'Mass Politics or Elite Politics? India's Economic Reforms in Comparative Perspective', *Journal of Policy Reform* in December 1998; 'Battles Half Won: The Political Economy of India's Growth and Economic Policy Since Independence' (with Sadiq Ahmed) in *The Oxford Handbook of the Indian Economy*, edited by Chetan Ghate, and published by Oxford University Press; and 'India's Democratic Challenge' in *Foreign Affairs* in 2007.

Endnotes

Chapter 1
Yogendra Yadav's comments on an earlier version of this chapter are highly appreciated.

1. See Huntington (1991) for the magnitude of the democratic reversals.
2. See especially Bardhan (2010); Dreze and Sen (2013); Kohli (2012); Weiner (1991).
3. Even before the new statistical arguments were made, Kohli (2001) and Weiner (1989) had proposed this line of reasoning. We need a fuller development of the argument.
4. In 2009, the National Commission for Enterprises in the Unorganized Sector (NCEUS), also known as the Arjun Sengupta Committee, found that between 1993 and 2004, as much as 77 per cent of India lived on less than Rs 20 (or $0.50) per day.
5. See Nehru (1947). The sections cited below are from the same reference.
6. Nehru held the defence portfolio three times, mostly briefly: February 1953–Janaury 1955; January–April 1957; 31 October–14 November 1962.

7. The concepts of mass and elite politics are discussed in Chapter 10.
8. Tellis (2012).
9. Jalal (1995). Chapter 3 has a longer discussion. Also see Macpherson (1977).
10. See Heller (2000). Chhibber (2001) too has an associational critique of Indian democracy, but does not deny that India is a democracy.
11. For a new argument about the depth of Kerala democracy, its evolution and its welfare impact, see Singh (2011).
12. Dahl (1971).
13. Dahl (1989, p. 253).
14. See Dahl (1971, 1989); Huntington (1968, 1991); Khilnani (1997); Kohli (2001); Weiner (1989). Also see the essays in the special issue of the *Journal of Democracy*, April 2007, entitled 'India's Unlikely Democracy': Ganguly (2007); Sinha (2007); Jenkins (2007); and Mehta (2007).
15. Przeworski *et al.* (2000). It should, however, be noted that of the two Dahl principles, they pick only contestation, not participation. That conceptual issue, however, does not affect the argument about Indian exceptionalism.
16. Since Lipset (1959), the relationship between democracy and income has been extensively debated. Przeworski *et al.* take it in a new, highly rigorous direction.
17. Przeworski *et al.* (2000, p. 79).
18. Przeworski *et al.* (2000, p. 87).
19. Ibid.
20. Przeworski *et al.* (2000, p. 109)
21. The endogenous view is related to the decades-old modernization theory, according to which, as societies become richer, political, social and economic structures become complex. In traditional societies, at low levels of income, it is possible for a tribal chief to rule, legislate as

well as adjudicate. All these roles begin to get differentiated at higher levels of income. Democracies emerge under such conditions, that is, with institutional differentiation witnessed at high levels of income. In political science, besides Lipset, Gabriel Almond and Lucian Pye were among the leading advocates of the modernization theory in the 1960s and 1970s. See Almond and Powell (1966); and Pye (1966).

22. This view, thus, questions the foundations of an influential book that emerged later. Acemoglu and Robinson (2005) develop an argument about the economic origins of both democracy and dictatorship. Also widely noted in this vein was Boix (2003). Boix and Stokes (2003) directly critique the exogenous view of Przeworski *et al.* That critique, however, does not change the claim about Indian exceptionalism. Both on endogenous and exogenous grounds, India has had a highly improbable democracy.

23. Przeworski *et al.* (2000, p. 101).

24. In an ambitious attempt, Huntington (1991) sought to investigate the reasons, but he said he was unable to come up with a parsimonious theory.

25. Indeed, it might be argued that all social science theories are probabilistic, or stochastic, not deterministic.

26. Keohane (2003). Also see Keohane (2005, 2010). With reference to India, Guha says something similar: 'Political scientists have written with insight and depth about the functioning of parties and the process of voting in India, but less so about Indian political leaders' (Guha 2010, p. 289).

27. Kohli (2001, p. 1).

28. This is as true of the classic work of Moore (1966) as of the more recent and influential work of Acemoglu and Robinson (2005). Also see O'Donnell (1973), and Boix (2003).

29. It should, however, be noted that Moore (1966) did not

add inequalities to his analysis, only class structures and coalitions. Moore's point that the nature of *rural* class relations remains central to the rise of modern democracies is both original and still noteworthy.

30. Dahl (1971, ch. 7).

31. Capoccia and Ziblatt (2010).

32. Horowitz (1985).

33. However, under some conditions, it can be deeply threatening to national integrity. See Chapters 2 and 4.

34. Horowitz (1985); Gubler and Selway (2012).

35. See Chapter 6 for a larger discussion.

36. Guha (2007) calls India an 'Unnatural Nation'. He perhaps means an 'improbable nation'. As later discussion will show, modern history of nationalism argues that all nations were constructed. There are no 'natural' nations. In premodern times, there were no nations, only three kinds of political formations: city states, empires, or ecclesiastical communities (Anderson 1983).

37. Mill (1975, p. 384). If what he called 'an inveterate spirit of locality' prevails, then 'portions of mankind may be unqualified for amalgamating into even the smallest nation' (Mill 1975, p. 204). All citations in this section are from *Representative Government*, originally published in 1861.

38. 'Free institutions are next to impossible in a country made up of different nationalities. Among a people without fellow feeling, *especially if they read and speak different languages*, the united public opinion, necessary to the working of representative government, cannot exist' (Mill 1975, p. 382, emphasis added).

39. Mill (1975, p. 402).

40. Mill (1975, pp. 408–09).

41. Mehta (1999) is seminal.

42. An inveterate admirer of Mill could still find plausibility in

his second claim and suggest that many decades of British tutelage lifted India's civilizational standards. Mill, after all, wrote his arguments about civilizational standards in 1861: India became a democracy in 1947. Eight decades of tutoring must have had some effect! India's democracy can, thus, be made logically consistent with Mill's civilizational analysis.

43. Huntington's well-known argument about civilizations is not about democracy, but about international conflict after the Cold War. See Huntington (1997).

44. The most important argument was by Almond and Verba (1963).

45. Stepan (2001, ch. 11).

46. Cited, most recently, in Guha (2007, p. 3).

47. Gellner (1983, p. 42).

48. Twain (1899, p. 146).

49. Weber (1976).

50. Colley (1992).

51. The writing of the history of Indian nationhood awaits its Colley or Weber. The widely noted intellectual creativity of the subaltern school had mostly to do with how peasants and other subaltern groups were not fully penetrated by Indian nationalism and how they put their own interpretations on what the leaders were saying. Fewer attempts have been made to investigate how the ideas of nationhood were carried across the very diverse elite and middle classes and, perhaps, some peasants. Nation-building is not simply a vertical project; in a highly diverse society, it is also horizontal. Antonio Gramsci was the principal intellectual interlocutor for the subaltern school, not Benedict Anderson.

52. The exceptions were the Hindu nationalists, who wanted European-style nationhood. Within the Congress, the biggest challenge to Gandhi's concept of nationhood came from Subhash Chandra Bose. Neither challenge was able to

subdue Gandhi's control over the ideology of the national movement. See Khilnani (2010).

53. On the differences between nationalism in India and the West, also see Kaviraj (2010). A seminal account of the struggle to define Indian nationhood is Chatterjee (1986).

54. Gandhi (1921, p. 170).

55. Gandhi (1909, p. 45).

56. Gandhi (1909, p. 59).

57. See the discussion in Varshney (1990).

58. For a new argument about the foundations of Nehru's world view, see Vajpayee (2012, Ch. 4).

59. Brown (2003, chs 10–12, 14); Gopal (1979); Kohli (2001, ch. 1); Rudolph and Rudolph (1987, ch. 3); Weiner (1967, 1989: chs 3, 12).

60. Patel's commitment to democracy is seriously in doubt. The biggest hurdle was his wavering on minority rights. See Gopal (1979, ch. 4).

61. Gopal (1979, p. 150).

62. Huntington (1968); Weiner (1989; chs 3, 12); Kohli (2001, ch. 1).

63. Some former Congressmen, such as Jayaprakash Narayan, Ram Manohar Lohia, and C. Rajagopalachari, did leave the party. Documents that bring out their disagreements and reasons for departure have been put together in Part IV of Guha (2010).

64. Kothari (1964).

65. Gopal (1979, ch. 8).

66. Brown (2003, p. 198). Though Brown captures the mood of the time, her claim is imprecise on two counts. First, Sri Lanka, also part of the British Empire, had 'gained freedom'. Second, one election is perhaps not equivalent to 'taking root'. The latter requires many more elections, which India did have, but only later.

67. Yadav (2010, 351).

68. The imprisonment of Sheikh Abdullah and the suspension of the Kerala government remain shrouded in controversy and doubt. Neither case was clear-cut.

69. Nehru's *Letters to Chief Ministers*, 20 September 1953, reproduced in Guha (2011, p. 335).

70. For the difficult relationship between Nehru and Patel, India's deputy prime minister, on the attitude towards minorities, see Gopal (1979, ch. 8).

71. Nehru, *Letters to Chief Ministers*, 15 October 1947, reproduced in (Guha 2010, p. 329).

72. SDSA Team (2008).

73. O'Donnell (1973).

74. Huntington (1968).

75. Harrison (1960).

76. Laitin (1989). Also see Laitin (1997).

77. Stepan *et al.* (2011).

78. The sons of the soil politics of Mumbai have kept the language issue alive in that city.

79. This argument is more fully developed in Varshney (2011b).

80. Lokniti (2010).

81. The distinction between the OBCs and SCs is not always understood, especially in urban India.

82. One should note that at no point has this policy been extended to Muslims as a principle. Only the socio-economically 'backward' sections of the Muslim community have been brought into the ambit of the policy in some states. Muslims as a religious community are not eligible for affirmative action. Muslims and other religious groups have been given cultural and religious rights, not reservations in legislature and administration. This was in reaction to the British policy of providing political and administrative reservations to the Muslim minority, which India's freedom fighters viewed as

a divide and rule policy, and as a precursor to the partition of India.

83. Rudolph and Rudolph (1967).

84. Dunning and Nilekani (2013); Chauchard (2012); Rao and Sanyal (2010).

85. Jaffrelot (2003); Jaffrelot and Kumar (2009).

86. Ahuja (2008).

87. Kapur *et al.* (2010).

88. Mehta (2003).

89. See Barnett (1976); Subramanian (1999).

90. For the early shrillness in the politics of the Bahujan Samaj Party (BSP), see Chandra (2007); for later moves towards a cross-caste alliance, see Verma (2007).

91. On how the changing power of groups affects public institutions, see Jayal (2006).

92. Nehru had focused heavily on poverty in his 'Tryst with Destiny' speech. The ambition of the father of the nation, he said, was 'to wipe every tear from every eye. That may be beyond us, but as long as there are tears and suffering, so long our work will not be over' (Nehru 1947).

93. See Bardhan (2010).

94. Hirschman (1981).

95. Sachs and Warner (1995).

96. In the 1980s, small steps towards markets were taken, but central planning was dismantled only in the 1990s.

97. For two different views about how to embrace markets and pursue growth, see Bhagwati and Panagariya (2013) and Dreze and Sen (2013)

98. Some argue that Narendra Modi, chief minister of Gujarat state, is one such contemporary leader. That may well be true of his performance in his state. It is still to be seen whether that is portable to the national level.

99. Yadav (2010, p. 351).

100. Yadav (2000). However, on a related problem—why scholars may be misunderstanding the reasons for lower urban vote compared to the villages—see Ramanathan *et al.* (2013).

101. Ahuja and Chhibber (2012).

102. The ideas here and in the next paragraph were briefly presented in Varshney (2011a).

103. For the US, see Huntington (1981); Morone (1998); Smith (1997).

104. Tolnay and Beck (1995).

105. In the end, Parliament did pass a bill dealing with sexual violence.

106. These issues were first discussed in Sinha and Varshney (2011) and in Varshney (2012b).

107. Plunkitt and Riordon (2007, pp. 3–6).

108. See Gowda and Sridharan (2012).

109. Ibid.

110. Huntington (1981, p. 262).

Chapter 2

1. This essay engages in a dialogue the theoretical works—all in the liberal democratic tradition—of Robert Alan Dahl, Samuel P. Huntington, Seymour Martin Lipset, Barrington Moore, and Dankwart A. Rustow. The best summary of liberal democratic theory and its problems is Huntington (1984). The magnum opus is Dahl (1989).

2. Kohli (1991).

3. Huntington (1968).

4. Some may also wish to add Sri Lanka (1948–78) to this list, but Sri Lanka, too, has been richer than India right since its independence. For a list of stable democracies using different criteria, see p. 12, Chapter 1, point 2.

5. Dahl (1989, p. 253). Dahl uses the terms 'democracy' and 'polyarchy' interchangeably.

Endnotes

6. 'India, despite the steady erosion of democratic institutions...
continues to stand as the most surprising and important
case of democratic endurance in the developing world.'
Diamond *et al.* (1989, p. 1).

7. Moore (1966, p. 314).

8. For example, see Eldersveld and Ahmed (1978); Kohli
(2001); Kothari (1970); Manor (1990b); Rudolph and
Rudolph (1967); Weiner (1989).

9. Weiner (1989, p. 78). The essay first appeared in 1985.

10. The Indian nation, to be sure, is not perfect; there have been
secessionist challenges. But it should be noted that India has
faced its strongest separatist challenges in areas *not* penetrated
by the Congress party during the freedom movement—
especially the North-east and Jammu and Kashmir.

11. See Gellner (1983, p. 42).

12. See Weber (1976).

13. The 'subaltern' historians argue that peasants and other
marginalized groups had their own ways of interpreting the
freedom movement's message. These scholars admit the
popularity of Gandhi and Nehru, but insist that different
sections of society viewed things through different lenses.
See, for example, Amin (1989). As collective action theory
explains, a multiplicity of motivations is true of most large-
scale mobilizations and may even be a requisite of success.
Participation in collective action can lead to new collective
units and identities, original motives notwithstanding.

14. This crucial historical background is overlooked by
Arend Lijphart when he contends that India has been a
consociational democracy since independence. See Lijphart
(1996). This is also a gap in Jalal (1995). In Jalal's analysis,
there is not only no distinction made between democracy
and socialism, but also no difference drawn between liberal
and consociational democracies.

15. See Tudor (2013).

16. See the fascinating account of the diaries of Police Commissioner Curry in Dalton (1993). Having to hit non-violent protesters was making it hard to police India, once the movement gained popularity. Dealing with violent protesters, says Curry, was easy; non-violence made the life of administrators tougher. Gandhi had assumed that this might happen, and had reckoned it would be more effective than a violent assault on the British.

17. Lipset (1959). For a different perspective, see Rueschemeyer *et al.* (1992).

18. Moore (1966).

19. Lewis (1954).

20. Moore (1966, p. 422).

21. Krishna and Raychaudhuri (1982).

22. Dominguez (1994).

23. Even sections of the left have recognized the emerging primacy of ethnic (or national) over class conflicts. Among the most iconoclastic statements from the left are Anderson (1983); Nairn (1977).

24. Horowitz (1985).

25. Census of India, 2001.

26. State-level numbers are from the 2001 Census. Data on the religious composition of population had not been published for 2011 while research for this book was being carried out.

27. See Chapter 5 for a detailed examination.

28. See, for example, Diamond *et al.* (1989).

29. Weiner (1989).

Chapter 3

For comments on the original article on which this chapter is based, I am grateful to Hasan Askari-Rizvi, Jagdish Bhagwati, Kanchan Chandra, Robert Hardgrave, Pratap Mehta, Philip

Oldenburg, Vibha Pingle, Sanjay Reddy, Alfred Stepan, the late
Myron Weiner, Yogendra Yadav, and two anonymous reviewers
of the *Journal of Asian Studies.*

1. Basu (2013); Hansen and Jaffrelot (1998); Jaffrelot (1993);
    Varshney (1993).
2. For example, Baruah (1999); Singh (2000); Subramanian
    (1999).
3. Of the three, Dalit politics has been much more analysed
    than the other two. See Chandra (2007); Pai (2002); Ahuja
    (2008). On OBC politics, see Jaffrelot (2003). On the
    relationship between regional parties and OBC politics, see
    Palshikar (2013). On the OBC politics of Bihar, see Witsoe
    (2013).Work on southern OBC politics is listed in detail
    later. For intra-southern comparisons, see Manor (2004);
    Kennedy (2005). Also relevant is the work on 'third force'
    politics: see Ruparelia (forthcoming).
4. See Dirks (1997); Varshney (2002). The prominent southern
    exception was the former princely state of Hyderabad
    (Varshney 1997). To see how British rule may have turned
    caste into a master narrative of South Indian politics,
    paralleling the Hindu–Muslim narrative in North India, see
    Dirks (1997). In strictly political terms, Dirks says, Hindu
    Brahmins can be described as 'the Muslims of South India'
    (1997, p. 279).
5. Beteille (1996); Dirks (1997); Kothari (1970); Rudolph and
    Rudolph (1987, 1967); Weiner (2001).
6. Weiner (1962).
7. Hardgrave (1965); Subramanian (1999).
8. See Nossiter (1982). In the two other South Indian states,
    Karnakata and Andhra Pradesh, the *lower caste* thrust of
    politics, though present, has been less pronounced. For
    Karnataka, see Manor (1990b); for Andhra, Reddy (1990).

9.   Hardgrave (1969).
10. Rajendran (1974, pp. 23–24).
11. Rudolph and Rudolph (1967).
12. Weiner (1967).
13. Based on the Election Commission 1996, pp. 40–51, Election Commission 1998, pp. 49–56, Election Commission 2004, pp. 110–121, and Election Commission 2009 (available at http://pib.nic.in/elections2009/default.asp). The explicitly *lower caste* parties include: JD (various versions), RJD, LJP, SP, BSP, JP, ADMK, DMK, MDMK, PMK, BJD, and RPI. If we increased the number of parties belonging to this category, the overall vote would increase slightly, but not substantially.
14. Nossiter (1982).
15. Strictly speaking, the arguments in this essay apply only to North and South India but they can, in a modified form, be extended to the western states of Gujarat and Maharashtra too. *Lower caste* parties may not have played a similar role in the West, but a *lower caste* churning from below has affected politics seriously (Wood 1996; Omvedt 1993; Ahuja 2008). It is, however, not clear how far these arguments will apply to states east of Bihar.
16. Though technically, scheduled tribes are not part of the Hindu caste system, there has been a consensus in political circles that, along with the scheduled castes, they were historically the most deprived group in India.
17. Based on *Provisional Population Totals 2011*, published by the Census of India (available at http://www.censusindia. gov.in/2011census/hlo/PCA_Highlights/pca_highlights_ file/India/4Executive_Summary.pdf).
18. Non-Hindu OBCs are about 8.40 per cent of India's population. Thus, in all, the OBCs constitute 52 per cent of the country (Mandal Commission 1980, pp. 1–56).

19.   There is some dispute over whether the Mandal Commission overestimated the size of the OBCs, but the nature of that dispute does not change the professional consensus that these three groups together constitute a majority of India's population. Since the population growth rates, according to demographers, are typically higher at lower ends of the economic scale, it also means that the OBC proportion of the electorate is likely to be higher than its percentage in the population.

20.   In 2009, the BSP went ahead of the CPI (M) in vote share. Earlier—in 1996, 1998, 1999, and 2004—the CPI (M)'s share of the national vote, at 5 to 5.5 per cent, was higher than that of the BSP. But the CPI (M) each time won many more seats than the BSP, for the BSP's vote was not as geographically concentrated as that of the CPI (M).

21.   In the 2009 elections, the Congress did much better. It is, however, not clear that that signifies an upward trend, as opposed to a one-shot revival. In the 2012 state assembly elections, the Congress was far behind the BSP.

22.   It is arguable that if Indira Gandhi had not been assassinated barely three–four months before the 1984 national elections, the *lower caste* upsurge would have shaken national politics in 1984 itself, instead of waiting till 1989. Her assassination changed the issues entirely in the 1984 elections.

23.   Chandra (2000). Later, Chandra (2007) developed the argument at greater length.

24.   For further analysis of the reasons for the BSP's high level of support in Uttar Pradesh, and moderate success in Punjab, also see Chandra (2007).

25.   Chandra (2000); Jaffrelot (2013).

26.   Verma (2007).

27.   In November 2000, eighteen districts were carved out of the southern part of Bihar to create the new state of Jharkhand.

28.   Corbridge (2000).

29.   Corbridge (2002).

30.   Jaffrelot (2000).

31.   Jaffrelot and Kumar (2009).

32.   For further details, see Varshney (1995).

33.   Lohia (1964).

34.   Witsoe (2013).

35.   See Sheth (1996); Nandy (1996); Weiner (2001); Yadav (1996b, 1996c, and 1999).

36.   See Mehta (2003); Jayal (2013).

37.   Sandel (1996); Taylor (1998).

38.   *The Wall Street Journal,* 3 November 1998.

39.   Huntington (1991, p. 10).

40.   Jalal (1995).

41.   Bonner *et al.* (1994); Brass (1991); Lele (1990); Shah (1990); Vanaik (1990).

42.   Jalal (1995, pp. 249–50).

43.   Jalal (1995, p. 99).

44.   Jalal (1995, p. 48).

45.   For a detailed treatment, see Dahl (1989), Chapter 19.

46.   Gramsci (1971).

47.   Mosca (1939).

48.   Dahl (1998, 1989, 1981, 1971).

49.   Dahl (1971, ch. 1).

50.   Dahl (1971, p. 29).

51.   Measuring income distribution in a society, the Gini coefficient ranges between 0 and 1. The closer a country is to 1, the more unequal it is, and the closer to 0, the more equal. Given similar Gini coefficients, countries with higher per capita incomes (the USA) would have far less poverty than those with lower per capita incomes (India).

52.   Jalal (1995, p. 205).

53.   Also see Shah (1990); Lele (1990).

54. Srinivas (1966).
55. This, however, would not be true of the *Ryotwari* areas, where the Marathas, Reddys, Kammas, and Patels have been dominant for a very long time.
56. Ravallion and Datt (1996); The World Bank (1997). One can work with later figures on poverty, but these figures are closest to the year Jalal made her argument—1995. They thus provide a good test for her argument.
57. The World Bank (1997, p. 3).
58. The Sengupta Committee gives a much higher figure.
59. See Visaria and Sanyal (1977). These proportions did not significantly change for the next two decades, which makes them relevant for assessing Jalal's claim for the same reasons outlined in Endnote 56. At any rate, these figures did not change for larger holdings which, if true, would have changed the conclusions of this paragraph.
60. Only in Punjab has it been possible to generate a surplus on a 2–3-acre farm until recently (Chaddha 1986).
61. Government of India (2012); *The Economic Survey of India 2011.*
62. Jalal (1995, pp. 209–10). See also Gokhale (1990); Sachchidananda (1990).
63. Katzenstein (1979).
64. And the faculties of Science and Engineering in many American universities, as well as US software companies, have a lot of South Indian Brahmins!
65. Mendelsohn and Vicziany (1998, p. 224).
66. Ibid.
67. Jalal (1995) argues the opposite. During the colonial period, the non-elected institutions were indeed more powerful than the institutions based on limited elections. The reason was simply that the former institutions were British-dominated, whereas the latter saw many elected Indians at the top.

Universal-franchise democracy has reversed the colonial relationship between the elected and the non-elected institutions in India.

68. Chandra (2000).
69. Bouton (1985).
70. Frankel (1990); Omvedt (1993); Jaffrelot and Kumar (2009).
71. Mendelsohn and Vicziany (1998).
72. Yadav (1996b, 1996c, and 1999).
73. Kohli (1991).
74. Dreze and Sen (1995).
75. Bhagwati (1993); Weiner (1991, 1986).
76. Bhagwati (1993); Sachs *et al.* (2002); Weiner (1986).
77. The shift in India's agricultural policy in the mid-1960s is an example (Varshney 1995); so is affirmative action enshrined in India's Constitution. Both came into force without a popular movement in favour of either.
78. For agricultural policy, see Varshney (1995); for affirmative action, see Galanter (2002).

Chapter 4

For comments on the original article, I am grateful to Jorge Dominguez, Robert Frykenberg, Stanley Hoffmann, Donald Horowitz, N.K. Jha, Atul Kohli, T.N. Madan, John Mansfield, Uday Mehta, Pratap Mehta, Vibha Pingle, and the late Myron Weiner.

1. Madan (1987).
2. Nandy (1988).
3. Naipaul (1990, pp. 517–18).
4. The insurgency in Punjab, after a decade of brutal violence, died down after the early 1990s. State assembly elections after 1992 saw turnouts between 60 and 70 per cent, suggesting that the time when militants could shape politics by staging

electoral violence was well past. See '60 Per Cent Voter Turnout in Punjab', *The Hindu*, 14 February 2002.

5. Gellner (1983, p. 1).

6. See Berlin (1992) as well as Hampshire's review of Berlin's views (1991).

7. Some would like to separate religion from this list, letting ethnicity incorporate the other attributes. From the viewpoint of political identities and group solidarity, it is not entirely clear that this separation is justified in principle. It does become critical, however, when ethnicity and religion clash (East and West Pakistan; Kashmiri Hindus and Muslims; Irish Protestants and Catholics; black and white American Christians). See Horowitz (1985).

8. I borrow this way of distinguishing models from Nandy (1992).

9. Savarkar (1989, pp. 110–13), originally published in 1925.

10. Deshmukh (1989).

11. One only had to hear the speeches of Sadhvi Rithambhra, a prominent Hindu activist repeatedly allowed by the BJP to make speeches during 1990–92, to appreciate how much hatred the right wing had for the Muslims.

12. Savarkar (1989); Golwalkar (1992).

13. Sikander Bakht's position on the demolition of the Baburi Mosque is explained in an interview in *Saptahik Hindustan* (Delhi), 23–30 December 1992.

14. The RSS does not participate in elections. The best study of the RSS is Anderson and Damle (1986).

15. The three main proponents of Hindu nationalism within the national movement were Bal Gangadhar Tilak, Sardal Patel, and P.D. Tandon.

16. For a brief view of Gandhi's position on religion, see Gandhi (1962, 1978). See also Chatterji (1983).

17. Gandhi (1909, p. 45).

18. A government investigation committee found that the RSS was not directly involved in the assassination; some RSS individuals were. In the eyes of the populace, this was not an important distinction. For details, see Graham (1990, ch. 3).

19. For a detailed analysis of the Ayodhya movement, see Varshney (1993).

20. For an analysis of Mahatma Gandhi's assassination, see Nandy (1981).

21. For earlier scholarly attempts at defining India's national identity, see Kothari (1970: chs II, VII, VIII); Kumar (1989); Embree (1989).

22. Hobsbawm (1990); Smith (1985).

23. See Laitin (1986).

24. Hoffman (1993, 1994). For a comparison of French and German national identities, see Brubaker (1992).

25. Huntington (1981, ch. 2).

26. Miller (1991).

27. Huntington (1981, p. 16).

28. Eck (2012).

29. Also see Embree (1971).

30. Currie (1989); Bayly (1985).

31. A clear distinction between three terms—pluralism, syncretism, and assimilation—should be made here. Pluralism would indicate a coexistence of distinctive identities. Syncretism would signify not a tolerant coexistence of distinctions but a merging of cultures/religions, leading to a new form of culture/religion. In its interaction with Hinduism, Islam—especially Sufism—developed forms of piety and culture that represented the Indian, as opposed to the Arab, version of Islam (for example, worship at the graves of great Sufi saints). Syncretism should also be distinguished from assimilation. While assimilation means absorption into the dominant culture/religion, syncretism means give

and take between cultures and religions.

32. Some historians disagree. They argue that a Hindu identity
is at best a creation of the last 200–300 years. Before that,
there were different sects, but no Hindu identity as such. See
Thapar (1989); Frykenberg (1993).

33. Golwalkar (1947), originally published in 1939.

34. Savarkar and many other Hindu nationalists contest that
Hindutva is a religious term. For them, it has a cultural
meaning.

35. Savarkar (1989), originally published in 1925.

36. Nehru (1989, p. 62).

37. In a similar vein, Rajni Kothari writes: 'In contrast to the
great historical empires, the unity of India owed itself not
to the authority of a given political system, but to the wide
diffusion of the cultural symbols, the spiritual values, and
the structure of roles and functions characteristic of a
continuous civilization. The essential unity of India has not
been political but cultural' (1970, p. 251). A contrast with
another large multi-ethnic nation, the United States, can be
drawn here. Several commentators argue that the unity of the
United States lies in the political principles that founded the
nation, while different communities evolved their distinctive
cultures. See Walzer (1992).

38. Of these, some are past rulers, others, purely cultural figures.
Kabir and Nanak were saints who inspired syncretistic
beliefs, and preached inter-religious understanding and
love. See Hawley and Juergensmeyer (1988).

39. Nehru (1989, p. 270).

40. Gopal (1980, pp. 647–48).

41. Nehru (1989, p. 63). Also see Nehru's discussion of the role
of *Dharti* (land) in the peasant conception of *Bharat Mata*
(Mother India) (1989, pp. 57–60).

42. Shourie (1987, pp. 91–124).

43. Anderson (1983).

44. Brown (1991).

45. Deshmukh (1989); Seshadri *et al.* (1990).

46. Seshadri *et al.* (1990, p. 30).

47. Interview with L.K. Advani, *Sunday* (Calcutta), 22 July 1990.

48. Frykenberg (1993).

49. Interviews in Lucknow with Hindu nationalists, December 1991.

50. Ashis Nandy (1988) has suggested the distinction between faith and ideology.

51. Weber (1976).

52. The United States is perhaps the most successful case of multi-ethnic nation-building in the world. See Walzer (1992).

53. Connor (1994, pp. 1–42, 128–71).

54. On whether Indira Gandhi was a prisoner of social forces, not someone who led her party's decline, see Kohli (1991).

55. Nandy (1988, p. 155)

56. Madan (1987, p. 749)

57. For literature, see Kundera (1986); for philosophy, see Berlin (1980), and Kolakowski (1990); and for natural sciences, see Einstein's essays on science and religion (1954).

58. Einstein (1954, pp. 36–53).

59. Bayly (1985).

60. Distinctions have so far been drawn between the secularism of Nehru (a religious tolerance) and the secularism of Gandhi (an inter-religious tolerance based on religiosity). See, for example, Rudolph and Rudolph (1983). Distinctions within the modernist secularism, as opposed to that between modernist and 'traditional' secularisms, have not yet been drawn.

61. Tully and Jacob (1985).

62. Brass (1975).

63. There were other ways to deal with the problem: the Rajiv Gandhi government later flushed out its targets by constructing a siege around the temple, not by desecrating it.

64. See Smith (1963).

65. For a historical perspective on the Shah Bano case, see Rina Verma Williams (2006).

66. Based on numerous field interviews conducted from 1990–92.

67. *India Today,* 15 February 1993. Javed Habib, a member of the Baburi Masjid Action Committee, was perhaps the only Muslim politician to have publicly demonstrated a keen appreciation of the problem. He was, however, no match for the senior and more prominent Muslim politicians. See Javed Habib, 'Main Bhi Ram ko Maryada Purushottam Manta Hun' (I too accept Ram as a symbol of moral excellence.), *Dharmayug* (Bombay), 16 January 1991.

68. For further implications, see Weiner (1989), Chapter 7. On how the term 'minority' is used in India, see Weiner (1989), Chapter 2.

69. Gopal (1992, pp. 17–20).

70. Interview with Atal Behari Vajpayee, 'Mere Advaniji se matbhed hain' (I have differences with Advani), *Dharmayug* (Bombay), 16–31 January 1991. Vajpayee was the leader of the moderate faction, and was prime minister of India in 1996 and again from 1998–2004.

71. Interview with Vajpayee, *India Abroad,* 19 December 1992. Also, see Varshney (1993).

Chapter 5

For comments on the original article, I would like to thank Hans Blomkvist, Kanchan Chandra, Partha Chatterjee, Pradeep Chhibber, Elise Giuliano, Donald Horowitz, Gary King, Atul Kohli, David Laitin, Scott Mainwaring, Anthony Marx, Bhikhu

Parekh, Robert Putnam, Sanjay Reddy, Susanne Rudolph, Jack Snyder, James Scott, Manoj Srivasatava, Alfred Stepan, Steven van Evera, the late Myron Weiner, Yogendra Yadav, Crawford Young, and three anonymous reviewers of *World Politics.*

1. For an analysis of why, on the basis of a myth of common ancestry, ethnicity can take so many forms (language, race, religion, dress, diction), see Donald Horowitz (1985, pp. 41–54). One might add that this definition, though by now widely accepted, is not without problems. If all ascriptive divisions can be the basis of ethnicity, can the landed gentry or women's groups be called ethnic? So long as we equate ascriptive identities with ethnic identities, there is no clear answer to such questions.

2. Indeed, such conflict may be inherent in all pluralistic political systems, authoritarian or democratic. Compared with authoritarian systems, a democratic polity is simply more likely to witness an open expression of such conflicts. Authoritarian polities may lock disaffected ethnic groups into long periods of political silence, giving the appearance of a well-governed society, but a coercive containment of such conflicts also runs the risk of an eventual and accumulated outburst when an authoritarian system begins to liberalize or lose its legitimacy.

3. Inglehart (1997).

4. For the early history of the idea, see Adam Seligman (1992).

5. Habermas (1989). For a debate built around the publication of the English translation, see Calhoun (1994).

6. See also Charles Taylor (1990); Michael Walzer (1991); Jean Cohen and Andrew Arato (1992).

7. The debate generated by Putnam's work is finally leading to empirically based scholarship. See, inter alia, Sheri Berman (1997); the special issue on social capital of *American*

Behavioral Scientist 39 (April 1997); Narayan and Woolcock (2000).

8.   Gellner (1995) is a good summary of a large number of Gellner's writings on civil society, written in both the reflective and the activist mode. Many of these writings, including some polemical essays, have been put together in Gellner (1994).

9.   For a similar argument, see Shils (1997).

10. For pioneering work on the modernist uses of ethnicity, see Rudolph and Rudolph (1967); Weiner (1978).

11. See the brief but thoughtful discussion in Boyte (1994).

12. Starting with Thompson (1968), many such historical works exist by now. For a quick review of how they relate to Habermas, see Ryan (1994); Elly (1994).

13. Habermas (1994).

14. Scott (1976).

15. For an argument along these lines, see Putnam (1996, 1995).

16. Among the exceptions are Horowitz (1985); Weiner (1978); Young (1976).

17. For an elaborate argument for the need for variance in social science research, see King *et al.* (1994). To find why discovering commonalities may matter even in a world where variance exists, see Rogowski (1995).

18. The data set on Hindu–Muslim violence was put together in collaboration with Steven I. Wilkinson of Yale University (available at http://www.icpsr.umich.edu/icpsrweb/ICPSR/studies/4342).

19. The cities, as Table 5.1 (column d) shows, are Ahmedabad, Bombay, Aligarh, Hyderabad, Meerut, Baroda, Calcutta, and Delhi. The last two are not normally viewed as riot-prone. But because they have had so many small riots and some large ones in the 1950s, they are unable to escape being included in the list of worst cities in a long-run perspective

(1950–95). In a 1970–95 time series, however, Calcutta is unlikely to figure and Delhi too may disappear.

20. Rudolph and Rudolph (1987, p. 196).
21. L.K. Advani, leader of the BJP, interviewed in *Sunday*, 22 July 1990.
22. Syed Shahabuddin, a prominent Muslim leader, has often made this argument in lectures, discussions, and political speeches.
23. Rudolph and Rudolph (1987, p. 195).
24. Srinivas (1979).
25. These connections can be proven social scientifically, not legally. The latter requires establishing individual culpability, not obvious links between politicians and gangs as groups.
26. Brass (1997).
27. In a democratic system, political parties would be part of civil society, for all of them may not be linked to the state. In one-party systems, however, parties, even when cadre-based, tend to become appendages of the state, losing their civil society functions. India is a multiparty democracy.
28. For a debate on process and causality, see George and Bennet (2005); Gerring (2007).
29. Calicut also has a small Christian population.
30. *Aaj*, 10 December 1990; *Amar Ujala*, 11 December 1990.
31. 'For an Aligarh of Peace', interview with District Magistrate A.K. Mishra, *Frontline*, 22–23 December 1990.
32. Author's interviews with the vice chancellor of Aligarh Muslim University (AMU), M. Naseem Farooqui, Delhi, 15 July 1994; several AMU professors, August 1994; and local journalists, August 1994. For a thoughtful review of all such reports appearing in local Hindi newspapers, see Namita Singh, 'Sampradayitka ka khabar ban jana nahin, khabron ka sampradayik ban jana khatarnak hai', *Vartman Sahitya*, September 1991.

33. Author's interviews in Trivandrum with Amitabh Kant, District Collector, Calicut, 1991–94, 20 July 1995; Shankar Reddy, Police Commissioner, Calicut, 1991–94, 22 July 1995; Siby Matthews, Police Commissioner, Calicut, 1988–91, 21 July 1995; K. Jayakumar, Collector, Calicut, 21 July 1995; Rajeevan, Police Commissioner, Calicut, 1986–88, 21 July 1995. Politicians of the Muslim League and the BJP confirmed their participation in peace committees. The political leaders interviewed were Dr Muneer, Muslim League member of Kerala Legislative Assembly since 1991, 23 July 1995; K. Sreedharan Pillai, President, BJP, Calicut District BJP Committee, Calicut, 25 July 1995.

34. Author's interview with K. Sreedharan Pillai, President, BJP, Calicut District BJP Committee, Calicut, 25 July, 1995.

35. Unless otherwise stated, the statistics here and below are from the survey conducted in Calicut and Aligarh.

36. Forty per cent of the sample was older than sixty years in age, which allowed us to gather recollections of the 1930s and 1940s.

37. It may be asked why people in Calicut join inter-religious associations in such large numbers. Since violence and peace constitute the explanandum (the dependent variable) in this analysis, and civic networks, the explanans (the independent variable), I only ask whether causality is correctly ascribed to civic networks or, alternatively, whether it constitutes a case of endogeneity. The question of why people join inter-religious associations in Calicut but not in Aligarh is analytically different. To answer it requires a research design different from the one that investigates why violence or peace obtains in the two places, for the explanandum is violence in one case and associational membership in the other. That said, it is quite plausible to hypothesize that Calicut citizens have greater faith in the 'rational–legal'

functioning of the state and, therefore, instead of seeking to change the behaviour of the state by capturing state power, they are confident they can exercise enough pressure on it through associations. It may also be that Calicut citizens identify less with caste and religion today than do the citizens of Aligarh though, historically, there is no doubt that caste played an enormously important role in generating struggles for social justice there. For an account of the caste basis of such struggles, see Dilip Menon (1995). Finally, integrated civic networks conceivably achieve much more than the prevention of communal riots. They may, for example, be related to the better provision of social services in Calicut (and Kerala), but such outcomes are not the main object of analysis in this paper. Only communal violence is.

38. Calicut has no industry except tiles. It is small in size, with nine factories and about 2,500 workers in all.

39. These numbers and the information below are based on extensive interviews with the president and general secretary of the Kerala Federation of Trade Associations (Kerala Vyapari Vyavasayi Ekopana Samithi, hereafter, the Samithi). The Samithi is a powerful all-state body, based in all towns of Kerala. The Samithi keeps records and statistics and has a professionally run office. It is rare to find a traders association run so professionally in North India.

40. Data supplied by the Samithi, Calicut branch, July 1995.

41. Author's interview with V. Ramakrishna Erady, wholesale rice dealer, Calicut, 25 July 1995.

42. Author's interview with Mohammed Sufiyan, former president, Vyapar Mandal, Aligarh, August 1995.

43. It pays to under-report how much labour an industrial unit employs for, under Indian law, the small, informal sector does not have to pay pension and other benefits to its workers. Official statistics are thus entirely useless. Foucault's concept

of 'popular illegality', as one keen observer puts it, has caught
the fascination of Aligarh's lock manufacturers (Mann 1992).

44.   Mann (1992).

45.   Ibid.

46.   The exact number of unionized members and their religious
distribution are almost impossible to come by. Estimates
based on the interviews are the best one can do. The
description below is based on interviews with labour leaders
in Calicut, especially a long and detailed interview with M.
Sadiri Koya, state secretary, INTUC, 4 August 1993.

47.   Menon (1995, pp.145–49).

48.   And the state of Kerala has 'a library or a reading room
within walking distance of every citizen' (Isaac 1994).

49.   It may be suggested that this finding is close to being a
tautology: a city is not riot-prone because it is well integrated.
This claim, however, would not be plausible for two reasons.
First, a conventional explanation—which has long defined
the common sense of the field—suggests that, for peace,
multi-ethnic societies require consociational arrangements.
Consociationalism is an argument about segregation at the
mass level and bargaining at the elite level, not integration at
either level. My argument is very different. Second, religious
fundamentalists have often fought violently to 'purify' their
communities of influences from other religions in society.
Islamic fundamentalists have often sought to undermine
Sufi Islam, which has traditionally combined the practice
of Islam with the incorporation of neighbouring influences.
Communally integrated lives and belief systems have often
been seen as a source of tension and conflict rather than
peace. For the North American version of the debate, see
Forbes (1997).

50.   It should, however, be pointed out that in Calicut and the
neighbouring areas, it is the left wing of the Congress party,

later splitting from the parent organization and becoming the Communist Party of India (CPI), that engaged in the most systematic association building.

51. Putnam (1993). It should be noted, however, that, since writing *Making Democracy Work*, Putnam has introduced the notions of bridging and non-bridging civic networks. Putnam acknowledges the distinction further in *Bowling Alone* (2000).

52. For Indonesia, see Varshney (2010); for the US, see Lieberson and Silverman (1965); for Northern Ireland, see Poole (1990).

53. Darby (1986).

54. Horowitz (1983).

55. Lieberson and Silverman (1965).

56. The Kerner Commission Report had an excellent chance to give us an explanation. It missed the chance because it studied only the riot-affected cities, not the peaceful ones.

57. In UP, the Bahujan Samaj Party (BSP) appears to have broken this pattern to some extent in recent years. The party seeks to put Brahmins and the former untouchables together.

58. Glazer (1996).

59. Fearon and Laitin (1996).

60. For recent accounts of Hindu–Muslim relations in the various cities of India, see Gayer and Jaffrelot (2012).

Chapter 6

This chapter has been presented in seminars at the National Institute of Advanced Study, Indian Institute of Management (Bangalore), Delhi University, Azim Premji University, Institute of Social and Economic Change, and Asia Society (Mumbai). For comments, I am grateful to the many participants in these seminars as well as an anonymous reviewer of *Studies in Indian Politics*; and to Bala Posani for research assistance.

1. Nooruddin and Chhibber (2008); Sridharan (1999); Stepan *et al.* (2011); Tillin (2007); Yadav and Palshikar (2003, 2009a, 2009b). Also see Rudolph and Rudolph (2010a, 2010b).

2. For what is sometimes called non-territorial federalism, see Lijphart (1977).

3. See Brass (1973).

4. Gopal (2011)

5. Stepan (1999).

6. Stepan (1999, p. 21). Stepan argues that only Australia and Switzerland approximate the US federal model.

7. Interview with a senior IAS officer from the Maharashtra cadre, Delhi, March 2009. Some of the recent scholarly analysis also discusses this point. See Tillin (2007); Yadav and Palshikar (2009b).

8. Gellner (1983).

9. See, for example, Kymlicka (1996).

10. Weber (1976).

11. Hobsbawm (1990, p. 61).

12. The nationhood in Germany and Japan is conceptualized as *jus sanguinis* (community based on bloodlines), not as *jus solis* (community based on birth in the territory), as in France. See Brubaker (1992).

13. Stepan *et al.* (2011).

14. See also Rudolph and Rudolph (2010a, 2010b).

15. Ashis Nandy popularized these metaphors. For a detailed discussion, see Varshney (1993); Varshney (2002, ch. 3).

16. See Deshmukh (1989); Sheshadri *et al.* (1990); Upadhyay (1992).

17. There is another streak in Hindu nationalism, certainly in its original versions. It drew heavily upon the Europe-based racial notions of nationhood current in the 1930s. See Golwalkar (1947).

18. See Graham (1990).

19. Also worth noting is the comparison with Pakistan. See Ayres (2009).

20. In an interview given to me in 1985, the late Chaudhry Charan Singh, India's prime minister briefly during 1979, argued that imposition of Hindi outside North India would have made India a stronger nation. It was, in his view, badly required.

21. Stepan *et al.* (2011).

22. The discussion in this section builds upon Stuligross and Varshney (2002).

23. For a description of Prime Minister Nehru's vacillations, see King (1997).

24. See Bhattacharya (1992, p. 96).

25. As in Bhattacharya (1992, pp. 88–89).

26. For a full-length treatment of the division of powers between the central and the state governments, see Austin (1999).

27. The most comprehensive treatment of India's fiscal federalism is in Rao and Singh (2005). Some of the discussions and figures below are based on the book.

28. Interview, Vijay Kelkar, Chairman, Finance Commission, Delhi, June 2009.

29. Rao and Singh (2005, p. 196).

30. Interviews with secretaries of finance, industry and planning in Mumbai, Chennai and Bangalore; Indian government economists in Delhi; joint secretaries in the Prime Minister's Office; senior members of think tanks in Delhi. All interviews conducted in April, May and June 2009.

31. *The Hindu*, Chennai, 6 May 2009. This pattern broke only after the DMK left the United Progressive Alliance (UPA) in 2013. Also, one might add that this celebration of Delhi providing ample resources to Tamil Nadu was dramatically in contrast to the dominant sentiment in the state in the late 1960s and early 1970s. M. Karunanidhi, who proudly brought

out the above advertisement, was chief minister in 1969 too. He had, then, set up an expert committee to 'consider in what manner the powers of the states should be increased to ensure them complete autonomy'. The recommendations of the committee are available in the Government of Tamil Nadu (1971).

32.   Rao and Singh (2005, p. 277).

33.   Ibid., p. 278.

34.   Khemani (2003).

35.   One could also argue that the making of the Indian nation during the freedom movement benefited the post-1947 working of federalism. See Ahuja and Varshney (2005).

36.   Horowitz (1985).

37.   However, the differences between the Mizoram and the Nagaland insurgencies are worth noting. For a succinct discussion, see Stepan *et al.* (2011).

38.   This makes the 1980s insurgency in Punjab especially analytically complex. See Singh (2000); Brass (1973). Assam is another state which has witnessed a separatist insurgency. It appears to be a special case, in which migration has played a decisive role. See Weiner (1978).

39.   This section is based on interviews with high-ranking police officers and home secretaries in Mumbai, Chennai, Bangalore and Delhi.

40.   A 1970 debate between two attorney generals, one outgoing, the other incoming—C.K. Daphtary and Niren De, respectively—is legendary in several government circles.

41.   Moreover, the IB does not have the same intelligence-gathering machinery as the states do.

Chapter 7

For comments on the original essay, I am grateful to John Harriss, Lakshmi Iyer, Tarun Khanna, Ramana Nanda, and K.C. Suri; two anonymous reviewers of Oxford University Press: interlocutors at the Shimla and Harvard meetings of the American Political Science Association (APSA)—Tocqueville project; commentators at a Lokniti workshop in Pune; and participants in a seminar at the National Law School, Bangalore. I would also like to thank Sana Jaffrey and Serban Tanasa for research assistance.

1. In 1960 (at 1971 constant prices), the per capita incomes for the North and the South were Rs 467.25 and Rs 530.75, respectively. The South was higher by a factor of 1.14.

2. In 2007, the Southern states had a per capita income of Rs 15,146.75, and the Northern states, Rs 7,140.25 (at 1993 constant prices). The Southern per capita income was 2.12 times higher.

3. I will not go separately into the question of whether the three new states have a very different structure of politics, compared to when they were part of the larger unit. For some purposes, that question would be critical, but not for the issues raised here.

4. Sen (2007).

5. If one examined Delhi as part of the North, the Northern lag would not be as large. Over the last three decades, Greater Delhi (the so-called National Capital Region), consisting of the cities of Delhi, Gurgaon (formally in the state of Haryana) and Noida (formally in UP), has witnessed an astronomical boom, making Delhi one of the richest cities of India. I am not including Delhi in my analysis of the North for two reasons. First, to call Delhi a state is analytically imprecise. Much like Washington, DC, Delhi is basically a metropolitan city, not a state. Second, even if one were to view Delhi as a state, it would be hard to call it a Hindi-speaking one. Hindi–Urdu used to be Delhi's traditional language but, since 1947, the character of Delhi has dramatically changed. A large number

of migrants from Pakistan arrived after India's partition, making Delhi, for many, a Punjabi city. More recently, all linguistic communities of India—from Bengal to Tamil Nadu—have been able to make a home in Delhi. Delhi has become a microcosm of India's many diversities. See Miller (2009). It should also be noted that, unlike Mumbai, Delhi has never witnessed a sons-of-the-soil movement. Finally, Haryana could also be viewed as an exception, for it has done economically well and is today a Hindi-speaking state. But, historically, it was part of Punjab, not part of the Hindi-speaking North.

6. The analogy is not empirically exact. Ohio did not have slaves, so it did not have to undermine slavery . Conceptually, however, the analogy would hold. See the later discussion in terms of vertical and horizontal social orders.

7. In parts of India, especially where Hindu business castes were absent for some reason, Muslims and Christians often performed the role of businessmen. This is especially true of Kerala and Tamil Nadu.

8. Viewed in an interpretive framework, this negative correlation can be called an argument. But viewed in a strictly positivist framework, my claim would have to be phrased differently and called a hypothesis. The existing statistics about caste and business in India are sufficiently indicative to take the Tocquevillean argument seriously, but they are not entirely conclusive. In order to estimate the current, as well as historically varying, caste backgrounds of entrepreneurs in the North and the South, several thousand observations would have to be collected.

9. The KHAM (Kshatriya–Harijan–Adivasi–Muslim) movement of the 1980s was strong for a brief time, but it did not last long. Moreover, it was also sponsored by the Congress party, not by a *lower caste* party. The Congress was trying to incorporate the

lower castes in its vertical mobilization model, not to trigger a horizontal *lower caste* revolution.

10. See Varshney (2002, chs 9–10). It is the only place in India where the term 'merchant prince' was used. The term culturally expresses the hegemony of the business community. Merchants were rarely, if ever, princes in traditional India.

11. For Gujarat's economic development, see Sinha (2005).

12. Bihar, widely viewed as an ungovernable Northern state for three decades after the late 1960s, has of late demonstrated high economic growth rates, but a *lower caste* churning in the state has been followed by better law and order and significantly greater public investment. It is unclear whether the upward growth trajectory has something to do with changing social bases of entrepreneurialism.

13. In short, we are in a multivariate explanatory space. Later work will have to wrestle with the question of which factor accounts for how much of the transformation, if it is at all possible to handle such a question in a statistically rigorous fashion. My focus here will be on a conceptually significant matter whose importance in economic explanations is not explicitly recognized. Social foundations of entrepreneurialism are rarely included in economic explanations of success.

14. A classic statement is Lewis (1954).

15. See Bhagwati and Srinivasan (1985) for the impact of trade on development, and North and Thomas (1973) for the impact of institutions.

16. Relying, as it did, on very high investment and savings rates, the enormous, though unsustainable, Soviet industrialization during the first four Soviet Plans was a classic example of factor-driven growth. In contrast, China and India appear to have combined efficiency and mobilization of the factors

of production. Both became trade-oriented, China more so than India, plus their recent investment/GDP ratios have of late been among the highest seen in the last century.

17. See Sen (1988) and Dreze and Sen (2013).

18. Mill originally proposed the method in *A System of Logic* in 1843. The book has been published many times since then. For the latest version, see Mill (2011).

19. Tocqueville (2003, pp. 345–46).

20. The possibilities of a natural experiment in social sciences have always been viewed as quite limited. Though experimental methods have yet again risen beyond psychology (where they have always maintained a stronghold), even the most enthusiastic exponents of the method have not been able to reject the idea that fully controlled, laboratory-like experiments are inherently hard to come by for a whole range of deeper political, economic or social questions. It is easier to have experimental research designs to sort out which poverty programmes work better than to understand the causes of civil wars and breakdowns of democracy. Moreover, even when experimental designs to ascertain the effectiveness of development programmes do approximate laboratory-like conditions, their external validity—potential for generalization to society at large—has been a matter of considerable doubt. This is now a familiar criticism of the method of randomized experiments, extremely popular in development economics and quite noticeable in political science as well.

21. Taylor (1994), or for a critique, see Krause (2002).

22. Moore (1966).

23. See Przeworski *et al.* (2000).

24. Horowitz (1983, pp. 21–24).

25. Eaton (2006, p. 5).

26. Also see Verba *et al.* (1971).

27. Obama (1995, p. 121).

28. Caste inequalities have been substantially transformed in politics, but not so much in education. Some recent calculations show a substantial, if not one-to-one link, between caste and educational attainment in contemporary India. Compared to their proportions in India's populations, the OBCs and the Dalits are highly under-represented in higher education (along with Muslims), and the upper castes are substantially over-represented (along with Sikhs and Christians). See Deshpande and Yadav (2006).

29. In this formulation, the upper castes include the so-called dominant castes, which were not ritualistically upper but acquired enormous power and status over time (Marathas, Patels, Kammas, Reddys, Jats, etc.).

30. Rajendran (1974, pp. 23–24).

31. This is how Obama describes the 1960 biracial marriage of his parents, a black African father from Kenya and a white mother from Kansas: 'In 1960, the year that my parents were married, miscegenation was still described a felony in over half of the states in the Union. In many parts of the South, my father could have been strung up from a tree for merely looking at my mother the wrong way; in the most sophisticated of northern cities, the hostile stares, the whispers, might have driven a woman in my mother's predicament into a back-alley abortion—or at the very least to a distant convent that could arrange for adoption' (Obama 1995, p. 12). This description is quite similar to what normally used to happen, when a Dalit crossed a sexual boundary by trying to marry into the upper caste. Even today, lynching can take place in rural India, though the incidence does not appear to be large.

32. See Howard (2007). American lynching statistics look quite gory, but some other cases are more horrific. For the mind-boggling contemporary Indonesian numbers on lynching,

see Varshney (2008, pp. 343–45). Indian data on lynching have not been systematically put together, but if press reports are anything to go by, the incidence of lynching in contemporary India does not appear to be large.

33. As reported earlier, three Northern states—Bihar, MP and UP—were broken up into smaller states in 1999. I will continue to use the historical names for the sake of simplicity. The post-1999 statistics summarized later will include the split-off states, when I compare pre- and post-1999 Bihar, MP and UP.

34. In per capita terms, even Kerala, normally viewed as a laggard state in terms of growth (but not in terms of human development), has done very well. One should, however, note that it is not because Kerala's economic growth rate has been exceptional. Rather, Kerala's internationally renowned success in bringing the population growth rate down has been decisive. Demographically, India is a predominantly young country, but Kerala's population growth rate—like that of much of Europe and Japan—has reached below replacement levels.

35. It should be parenthetically added that, since the beginning of economic reforms in 1991, the relative position of Punjab, a non-Hindi speaking Northern state, has also suffered a decline. Driven by a green revolution in agriculture, Punjab used to be an economic powerhouse in the 1970s and 1980s. The Green Revolution is now exhausted, the water tables have sunk because of over-irrigation, the soil is increasingly losing its fertility due to over-salination, and an agrarian revolution has yet to transform itself into an industrial revolution (see Ahluwalia 2009).

36. It is also worth pointing out that the distribution of foreign direct investment (FDI), too, hugely favours the South. India did not have much FDI until 1990. Since then, with

the exception of Kerala, Southern states have attracted a lot of FDI. Indeed, Tamil Nadu and Karnataka have been the leaders in attracting foreign investment, their attractiveness eclipsed only by that of the West Indian state of Maharashtra. More germane to our discussion here, Southern states have left the Northern states behind by a huge margin. Since 1991, the Southern states have together received over three times the investment that the Northern states have.

37. As quoted on the MOS website: http://mospi.nic.in/mospi_ec.htm.

38. Indeed, according to the 1998 Economic Census, 98 per cent of all firms in India were in the so-called informal sector, which tends to be small in size. See more on this in the next chapter.

39. See Rudner (1994). In addition, unlike in the North, Muslims have been a trading community in Southern India.

40. We should note that these numbers, to be more meaningful, would require a denominator. We need to know how much of each state's population can be classified as OBC. But we don't have that information for sure—until the 2011 Census gives us those figures. As a result, we can't fully judge whether the OBC proportion of the number of business firms is the same as their proportion in the population.

41. Robin (2009).

42. Jaffrelot and Robin (2009).

43. In addition, Muslims would be significant in Kerala and Tamil Nadu.

44. For a fuller methodological statement on these lines, see Gerring (2007).

45. Templeman (1996, p. 20).

46. Hardgrave (1969, p. 57).

47. About 10 per cent of the Nadar community is Christian today, the rest, overwhelmingly Hindu.

48. Hardgrave (1969, p. 64).
49. Ibid., pp. 65–66.
50. Ibid., pp. 117–18.
51. The passage is from Damodaran (2008, p. 187). Rs 1,000 crore would, at today's exchange rate, be roughly equal to $160 million.
52. Damodaran (2008, p. 182).
53. A complete list of Nadar-managed educational institutions can be found at http://nadar.kuttyjapan.com/nadar-institutions.asp.
54. This pre-occupation with educating the community is not peculiar to the Nadars. Associations of other OBC and SC groups have also made remarkable progress in the education of their communities.
55. Templeman (1996, p. 171).
56. Washbrook (1989).
57. Nafziger (1978).
58. See Täube (2004); Damodaran (2008).
59. The rise of Charan Singh in UP politics is sometimes read as an example of lower caste assertion (Hasan 1989). Jaffrelot (2003) convincingly demonstrates that it should be interpreted as a rise of the peasantry, not a rise of the lower castes.
60. Witsoe (2013).
61. See Ahuja (2008).

Chapter 8

1. See, among others, Ahmed and Varshney (2012); Ahluwalia (2002); Rodrik and Subramanian (2004).
2. India's Gini coefficient of income inequality increased from 29.6 in 1990 to 36.8 in 2004, based on data from the World Income Inequality Database 2010. (http://www.wider.unu.edu/research/Database/en_GB/wiid/_files/79789834673192984/

default/WIID2C.xls, accessed July 2011).

3. Varshney (2007).

4. Ghani *et al.* (2011).

5. As reported in Nigam (2002, p. 1190).

6. We cite this key paragraph from a well-known report on the Bhopal Conference published in the *Economic and Political Weekly* (Nigam 2002, p. 1190). It should also be noted that the rise of African American entrepreneurs in post-1965 US has served as an important political economy template for these intellectuals.

7. See (Aiyar 2011). Between 19 July and 22 July 2011, *The Economic Times* published many stories under the series entitled, 'The Rise of Dalit Enterprise'.

8. Jodhka (2010, p. 43).

9. Srinivas (1966).

10. Rudolph and Rudolph (1967); Varshney (2000); Weiner (2001).

11. Mehta (2003).

12. Jaffrelot and Kumar (2009).

13. Kapur *et al.* (2010).

14. Desai and Dubey (2011); Banerjee and Somanathan (2007).

15. Pande (2003).

16. See Cassan (2011). A new book by Deshpande (2011) goes over all these questions afresh, summarizing the earlier studies as well.

17. See Damodaran (2008); Thorat, Kundu and Sadana (2010); Jodhka (2010); Varshney (2012b). Damodaran (2008) provides narratives of how caste and business have interacted in the rise of new business families in India. Jodhka (2010) studies Dalit entrepreneurs in Panipat, Haryana, and Saharanpur (UP). Varshney (2012b) asks whether the earlier breakdown of caste hierarchies in South India, compared to North India, are connected to the Southern economic

resurgence since 1980. Thorat *et al.* (2010) look at all-India patterns in the caste background of business owners. We disaggregate the all-India data in newer categories.

18. *Provisional Results of Economic Census 2005,* Central Statistical Organization, Ministry of Statistics and Programme Implementation, Government of India, p 11. Obtained from http://www.mospi.gov.in (March 2010).

19. These states are Andhra Pradesh, Assam, Bihar, Chhattisgarh, Gujarat, Haryana, Himachal Pradesh, Jharkhand, Karnataka, Kerala, Maharashtra, Madhya Pradesh, Orissa, Punjab, Rajasthan, Tamil Nadu, Uttar Pradesh, Uttarakhand and West Bengal. The excluded states are Arunachal Pradesh, Goa, Jammu and Kashmir, Manipur, Meghalaya, Mizoram, Nagaland, Sikkim and Tripura.

20. The Population Census of India is conducted every ten years. These dates do not coincide with the conduct of the Economic Censuses. The results of the 2011 Census with regard to caste composition of the population had not been released as of June 2011.

21. Ghani *et al.* (2011).

22. To be more precise, one should speak about the Madras Presidency parts of the Southern Indian states and the Bombay Presidency parts of Maharashtra. The states of Andhra Pradesh, Karnataka and Maharashtra also inherited the territories of the princely state of Hyderabad, where no such policies were instituted.

23. For the erosion of the Tamil caste structure, see Hardgrave (1969); Rudolph and Rudolph (1967); Subramanian (1999).

24. See Damodaran (2010); Varshney (2012b).

25. Gross state domestic product in Maharashtra grew at an annualized rate of 6.6 per cent over the period 1999–2008, slightly slower than the nationwide rate of 7.2 per cent. Maharashtra extended political reservations in district and

village councils to SCs and STs as early as 1961, while most states of India implemented this only after the Panchayati Raj constitutional amendment in 1993.

26. Ahuja (2008).

27. Note that these increases are not merely a result of certain communities being granted OBC status between 1998 and 2005, such as the Jats in Rajasthan and UP. Even if we exclude UP and Rajasthan, the OBC share of enterprise ownership increased from 37.2 per cent in 1998 to 41.6 per cent in 2005, and the employment share increased from 33.6 per cent to 38.3 per cent. Jats were granted OBC status in Rajasthan in 1999, except for the districts of Bharatpur and Dholpur (http://timesofindia.indiatimes.com/india/OBC-list-shot-up-by-90-since-Mandal-I/articleshow/1561919.cms, accessed August 2010).

28. Formally, these enterprises are not registered under or recognized by any of the following: the Factories Act of 1948; the State Directorate of Industries and Commerce; Khadi and Village Industries Commission; the Development Commissioner for Handicrafts, Powerlooms or Handlooms; the Textile or the Jute Commissioner; the Coir Board of India; the Central Silk Board; the Central Board of Excise and Customs; the Sales Tax Act of 1956; the Shops and Establishments Act; the Cooperative Societies Act; the Labour Act, or any other agencies.

29. We are not able to examine the pattern of informality over time, since the questions on firm registration in the 1998 survey were different from those in 2005; this information is not present at all in the 1990 survey.

30. Jodhka (2010, p. 47).

31. Banerjee and Duflo (2012).

32. McKenzie et al. (2008).

33. Desai and Dubey (2011).

1

58

Endnotes

34. Gomez and Jomo (1999); Gomez (2011).
35. As proxied by the share of agricultural labour in the farming sector, as opposed to cultivators.
36. Gomez (2011). Also see Gomez and Jomo (1999).
37. The term 'Black' here refers to Africans, Coloureds and Indians. Companies were more likely to win government contracts if they shared ownership with blacks, helped develop their human capital, and hired more of them, among other actions.
38. The government gazette of January 2004 referring to the new act can be found here: http://www.info.gov.za/view/DownloadFileAction?id=68031, accessed October 2011.
39. 'The president says it has failed', *The Economist*, 31 March 2010. http://www.economist.com/node/15824024 accessed October 2011.
40. De Soto (1989). See Djankov *et al.* (2002); the Doing Business Indicators of the World Bank for these measures (http://www.doingbusiness.org).
41. Klapper *et al.* (2006).
42. Bruhn (2010).
43. See the introductory chapter in Lerner and Schoar (2010).
44. In an interview, Milind Kamble, President of the Dalit India Chamber of Commerce and Industry, takes some steps in this direction (Saxena 2011).
45. See Munshi (2003, 2011); Iyer and Schoar (2010); Kalnins and Chung (2006); Vissa (2011).
46. See Pan (1999).
47. See Portes and Sensenbrenner (1993).

Chapter 9

For comments on the original essay, I am grateful to Jagdish Bhagwati, Amitava Krishna Dutt, Raghav Gaiha, Ronald Herring, Peter Houtzager, Phil Keefer, Atul Kohli, Mick Moore, the late

Guillermo O'Donnell, and anonymous reviewers of *Asian Survey*. Research assistance by Bikas Joshi and Xavier Marquez is also greatly appreciated.

1. Przeworski *et al.* (2000, p. 178).
2. World Bank (2000, pp. 282–83).
3. Sen (1989).
4. See Yadav (2000, 2004). Also see Ahuja and Chhibber (2012).
5. See Chapter 3 in this volume; Weiner (2001).
6. It can be argued following Olson (1965) and Bates (1981) that large numbers of the poor would in fact impede, rather than facilitate, collective action. But this is truer in authoritarian countries than in democratic ones. See Varshney (1995, pp. 193–200).
7. Sen (1999).
8. Dahl (1971, 1989).
9. Another important conceptual issue should be clarified. In the advanced industrial countries, democracy is a stock variable, but in the developing world, it is a flow variable. In the poorer countries, a military coup or a wanton suspension of the legislature by the executive can dramatically alter the democratic score of a country, as it were. That is to say, on a 0–1 scale, the values of democracy in poorer countries can easily fluctuate between 1 and 0, but richer countries typically don't have coups and their governments don't normally suspend legislatures.
10. The year 1950 is a convenient starting point for, besides Latin America—independent since the early nineteenth century—the decolonization of non-white colonies began with Indian independence in 1947, and more and more developing countries became independent after that.
11. See Huntington (1983); Weiner (1989). Przeworski *et al.* use a different criterion, and have a slightly different listing that

includes Mauritius, the Solomon Islands, and Vanuatu. See Przeworski *et al.* (2000, pp. 59–76).

12. Lijphart (1977). Political parties in India and Sri Lanka may also seek to represent specific ethnic groups, but there has been no constitutional pact, or political requirement, that they must do so. Parties are free to build cross-ethnic alliances if that aids their political fortunes.

13. According to Przeworski *et al.* (2000), Malaysia has never been a democracy. They do not recognize countries with consociational democracy as democracies, hence their categorization. In this chapter, I use Malaysia as an example of limited democracy.

14. Huntington (1991).

15. See parallel discussion in Przeworski *et al.* (2000, ch. 2).

16. World Bank (2000).

17. For example, see Reddy and Pogge (2009).

18. World Bank (2004, pp. 258–59). With the exception of the Central African Republic (1993), Mali (1994), and Sierra Leone, poverty data in these countries were collected after 1995.

19. Przeworski *et al.* (2000, pp. 59–69).

20. Adelman and Morris (1973).

21. In 2011, Singapore's per capita income was $46,241, compared to $38,818 for the United Kingdom (World Bank, 2011).

22. For the latest elaboration, see Bhagwati and Panagariya (2013).

23. Bhagwati (1998); Stiglitz (2002).

24. Stiglitz (2002).

25. In the current debate in India, both Dreze and Sen (2013) and Bhagwati and Panagariya (2013) would agree on this point. Their differences are about (a) whether the indirect and direct measures should be pursued simultaneously, or sequentially;

(b) whether for direct welfare provision, the state should be relied upon, or one should think of alternatives that rely more heavily on non-state organizations and/or markets; and (c) whether state investments in public health and mass education at a very early stage in development are necessary for sustaining high growth.

26. On land reforms, my argument is slightly more complicated. Precisely because the direct linkages are so attractive, all democracies have had land reforms on the policy agenda, which is not true of all authoritarian countries. But few democracies or dictatorships have implemented land reforms. If land reforms are implemented, argue some scholars, they can successfully attack poverty (Herring 1982; Kohli 1987). For why this may be true only under very specific conditions—not generally—see Varshney (1995, ch. 1; 2000, pp. 733–35). It should also be noted that land reforms are typically implemented at the time of, or soon after, revolutions, or by foreign occupiers. Neither democracies nor authoritarian systems seem to have the political capacity to implement them.

27. Varshney (1999).

28. Horowitz (1985).

29. Hardin (1995).

30. Coordination games proceed according to the following logic. So long as others in the group are cooperating, it is rational for me to cooperate—for, if all cooperate, the likelihood of the group gaining power (or realizing group objectives) goes up tremendously. Hardin (1995, pp. 36–37) observes that 'power based in coordination is super-additive, it adds up to more than the sum of individual contributions to it'. He notes that all one needs to keep the coordination game going is a 'charismatic leader', a 'focus', and a mechanism through which information about others cooperating is provided to

each individual. 'Coordination power is . . . a function of reinforcing expectations about the behaviour of others.'

31. For a more detailed explanation, see Varshney (2003).

32. Anderson (1983).

33. Varshney (2003).

34. Taylor (1994).

35. Or, as sociologists have often reminded us, societies where the hegemony of the privileged groups is yet to be broken.

36. For East Asia, see Horowitz (1985); for Latin America, see Dominguez (1994).

37. World Bank (2004, p. 259).

38. Jomo (1990).

39. Sachs and Warner (1995, p. 21).

40. With the exception of two brief periods, 1950–56 and 1977–83 (Sachs and Warner 1995, p. 23).

41. Bruton *et al.* (1992). Malaysia illustrates the point that direct attacks on poverty work best, when pursued in the larger framework of trade- and market-oriented policies. There may be serious concerns today about whether Malaysia's economy can start producing higher value-added goods, move up the value chain, and avoid the so-called middle income trap, but that is an analytically separable matter. Malaysia's poverty-alleviation record is beyond doubt. See Kharas and Kohli (2011) for the concept of the middle income trap.

42. For a quick overview of all states, see Ravallion and Datt (1996).

43. For a detailed analysis, see Rao (1979).

44. In a disarmingly candid statement, E.M.S. Namboodiripad (1994), a Kerala-based politician who was the greatest Communist mobilizer of twentieth-century India, admitted before his death that the inability of the decades-long class mobilization in Kerala to overwhelm the religious divisions

of the state might be rather more rooted in historical realities than the Marxists had expected.

45. For a compelling argument that this merger facilitated the emergence of a Communist movement, see Menon (1995). While talking about the peasants and the workers, the Communists would repeatedly use caste issues, which had great resonance in Kerala.

46. Nossiter (1982, pp. 345–75).

47. Houtzager and Moore (2003).

48. Narayan *et al.* (2000).

Chapter 10

For comments on the original essay, I am grateful to, Robert Bates, Steven Block, Jorge Dominguez, John Echeverri-Gent, Jeffry Frieden, Chetan Ghate, Stephan Haggard, James Manor, Baldev Raj Nayar, Arvind Panagariya, Vibha Pingle, Lloyd Rudolph, and Roberto Zahga.

1. Basu (2004, p. 5)

2. Comparative data summarized in Ahmed and Varshney (2012).

3. Giles and Allen (2013).

4. Sachs and Warner (1995). The Sachs–Warner index judged a country to have had a closed economy if one of the following conditions was met with: non-tariff barriers (NTBs) covered 40 per cent or more of trade; the average tariff rate was 40 per cent or more; the official exchange rate was overvalued by 20 per cent or more; a state monopoly controlled major exports; and a socialist economic system à la Kornai existed. For the János Kornai view of a socialist economic system, see Kornai (1992).

5. Of the developing countries covered in the Sachs–Warner data set (1950–94), eight were open since independence

(Thailand, of course, was never colonized); forty-three out of seventy-eight that were inward-looking outside the Soviet bloc had opened by 1994, but thirty-five, including China, remained closed; and of the twenty-six post-Communist countries, sixteen were open by 1994, and ten were closed.

6. See Bhagwati and Panagariya (2013); Dreze and Sen (2013); Ghate and Wright (2011); Rodrik and Subramanian (2004).

7. Varshney (1999); Sachs, Varshney, and Bajpai (1999).

8. Stiglitz (2002).

9. Jenkins (1999) goes roughly in the same direction, though the details of his argument and mine are constructed differently. Other works on the relationship between Hindu nationalism and neo-liberalism are Corbridge and Harriss (2000); Ruparelia *et al.* (2011). For a different explanation, see Mukherji (forthcoming).

10. See, for example, Lindblom (1977); Polanyi (2001); Przeworski (1991).

11. Yadav (2004).

12. Bhagwati and Panagariya (2013). This point may be generally valid, but the obvious exception of Cuba exists. Moreover, significant pockets of poverty remain in a heavily market-oriented United States.

13. Naim (1993, ch. 5).

14. The overall size of an economy complicates the meaning of low trade–GDP ratios. Smaller economies tend generally to have a high trade–GDP ratio, making trade very important to their political economies. With the striking exception of China, however, the largest economies of the world—the US, Japan, Germany—are less trade-dependent. Still, trade politics, as we know, has aroused a great deal of passion in the US and Japan. The meaning of the same ratios can change, if the leading sectors (autos, computers) or 'culturally significant' sectors (rice for Japan, agriculture in France) of

the economy are heavily affected by trade.

15. Krueger (1992).

16. For a detailed argument on these lines, see Varshney (1995), Chapter 5, Appendix 1.

17. See the formulations on these lines in Russell Hardin (1995), and their critical evaluations in Varshney (2003). It should, however, be noted that ethnic conflict is not the only competitor of economic reforms on the political stage. In countries where military coups are not uncommon, considerations of order and stability can motivate mass politics, allowing greater room for reforms even though the short-run consequences of reforms are difficult. In Peru, President Fujimori's popularity in polls survived a three-and-a-half-year economic downturn after 1990. Susan Stokes argues: 'Economic policy was the cleavage that starkly separated the two major presidential candidates in 1990, and we might have expected after the campaign that Fujimori's term would be judged on his economic performance. But it was only partially so. Instead, an event occurred during the term that was unanticipated in the prior campaign . . . The April 1992 coup d'état was an extraordinary event . . . that ratcheted the president's approval upward. . . . (W) hen Peruvians had thrust on them the evidence that their president was creating order out of chaos, they rewarded him with approval ratings any chief executive would envy. . . . (T)he range and protean quality of standards . . . shielded the popularity of Peru's president from (economically) hard times' (Stokes 1996, p. 545).

18. Excerpt from Pan (2003). For a general discussion of labour–State relations in contemporary China, see Gallagher (2005). For a comparison of Indian and Chinese capitalism, see Huang (2008); Bardhan (2010).

19. The survey was conducted by the Centre for the Study of

Developing Societies (CSDS), under the leadership of Yogendra Yadav and V.B. Singh. For the larger audiences, the findings are summarized in *India Today*, 15 August 1996.

20. McMillan and Yadav (1998); Yadav (1996b).

21. Sachs, Varshney and Bajpai (2000).

22. Bhagwati and Panagariya (2013); Haggard and Kaufmann (1995); Przeworski (1991).

23. This argument, of course, does not mean that an ethnic civil war is the best context for reforms. A distinction between ethnic conflict and ethnic breakdowns is required. It is the latter which is being highlighted above. National anxieties about increasing ethnic violence or declining ethnic relations may provide a niche for reformers to push measures that might otherwise generate considerable political resistance.

24. Hirschman (1981).

25. Bhagwati and Desai (1970).

26. For the most systematic treatment of the ideas developed here by a key Indian planner, see Chakravarty (1987).

27. Rosenstein-Rodan (1943).

28. South Korea, which 'opened' in 1968 and became the most successful case of trade-based growth in the developing world, continued to protect its infant industries even after its 'opening'. For how it did so, see Pack and Westphal (1986); Amsden (1989); essays in Woo-Cummings (1999).

29. Bardhan (1984).

30. Weiner (1986).

31. Nehru (1989, 554).

32. Needless to add, this has begun to change over the last two decades, though not quite radically.

33. Lok Sabha Debates, Series 10, 24 July 1991, p. 272.

34. Lok Sabha Debates, Series 10, 24 July 1991, p. 276, emphasis added.

35. The phrase is from Bhagwati (1993)

36. Pursell and Gulati (1993).

37. This part relies on, extends and updates Varshney (1999).

38. For an analysis of the anxiety of the times and its causes, see Varshney (1993).

39. For a detailed political analysis of how Rajiv Gandhi's reform programme faltered, see Kohli (1987).

40. Yadav (2004); Varshney (2007).

41. The National Election Study project has been led by Lokniti, and is headquartered at the Centre for the Study of Developing Societies, Delhi.

42. Only 3,263 people out of a sample of 22,500 had no opinions.

43. Based on annual Forbes listings.

44. For details, see Deshpande and Yadav (2006).

References

Acemoglu, Daron, and James A. Robinson. 2005. *Economic Origins of Dictatorship and Democracy*. Cambridge, UK; New York: Cambridge University Press.

Adelman, Irma, and Cynthia Morris. 1973. *Economic Growth and Social Equity in Developing Countries*. Stanford, CA: Stanford University Press.

Ahluwalia, I.J. 2002. 'Economic Reforms in India Since 1991: Has Gradualism Worked?' *Journal of Economic Perspectives* 16 (7): pp. 67–88.

———. 2009. 'Challenges of Economic Development in Punjab'. In *Arguments for a Better World: Essays in Honor of Amartya Sen*, eds Kaushik Basu and Ravi Kanbur, pp. 303–26. Oxford, UK: Oxford University Press.

Ahmed, Sadiq, and Ashutosh Varshney. 2012. 'Battles Half Won: The Political Economy of India's Growth and Economic Policy since Independence'. In *The Oxford Handbook of the Indian Economy*, ed. Chetan Ghate, pp. 56–104. New York: Oxford University Press.

Ahuja, Amit. 2008. 'Mobilizing Marginalized Citizens: Ethnic Parties Without Ethnic Movements'. PhD dissertation. Ann Arbor: University of Michigan, Department of Political Science.

Ahuja, Amit, and Pradeep Chhibber. 2012. 'Why the Poor Vote in India: "If I Don't Vote, I Am Dead to the State"'. *Studies in*

Comparative International Development 47 (4): pp. 389–410.

Ahuja, Amit, and Ashutosh Varshney. 2005. 'Antecedent Nationhood, Subsequent Statehood: Explaining the Success of Indian Federalism'. In *Sustainable Peace: Power and Democracy after Civil Wars*, eds Phillip G. Roeder and Donald Rothchild, pp. 241–64. Ithaca, NY: Cornell University Press.

Aiyar, Swaminathan S. 2011. 'The Unexpected Rise of Dalit Millionaires'. *Economic Times*, 31 July.

Almond, Gabriel, and Sidney Verba. 1963. *The Civic Culture: Political Attitudes and Democracy in Five Nations*. Princeton, NJ: Princeton University Press.

Almond, Gabriel, and Bingham Powell. 1966. *Comparative Politics: A Developmental Approach*. Boston, MA: Little, Brown and Co.

Amin, Shahid. 1989. 'Gandhi as Mahatma'. In *Subaltern Studies*, vol. 3, ed. Ranajit Guha. Oxford, UK: Oxford University Press.

Amsden, Alice. 1989. *Asia's Next Giant: South Korea and Late Industrialization*. New York: Oxford University Press.

Anderson, Benedict. 1983. *Imagined Communities*. London: Verso.

Anderson, Walter, and Shridhar Damle. 1986. *The Brotherhood in Saffron: The Rashtriya Swayamsevak Sangh and Hindu Revivalism*. Boulder, CO: Westview Press.

Austin, Granville. 1999. *The Indian Constitution: Cornerstone of a Nation*. Delhi: Oxford University Press.

Ayres, Alyssa. 2009. *Speaking Like a State: Language and Nationalism in Pakistan*. New York: Cambridge University Press.

Banerjee, Abhijit, and Esther Duflo. 2012. 'Do Firms Want to Borrow More? Testing Credit Constraints Using a Directed Lending Program'. MIT Working Paper. Cambridge, MA: MIT.

Banerjee, Abhijit, and Rohini Somanathan. 2007. 'The Political Economy of Public Goods: Some Evidence from India'. *Journal of Development Economics* 82 (2): pp. 287–314.

Bardhan, Pranab. 1984. *The Political Economy of Development in India*. New Delhi: Oxford University Press.

————. 2010. *Awakening Giants, Feet of Clay: Assessing the Economic Rise of India and China*. Princeton, NJ: Princeton University Press.

Barnett, Marguerite Ross. 1976. *The Politics of Cultural Nationalism in South India*. Princeton, NJ: Princeton University Press.

Baruah, Sanjib. 1999. *India against Itself: Assam and the Politics of Nationality*. Philadelphia: University of Pennsylvania Press.

Basu, Amrita. 2013. 'The Changing Fortunes of the Bharatiya Janata Party'. In *Routledge Handbook of Indian Politics*, eds Atul Kohli and Prerna Singh, pp. 81–90. London: Routledge.

Basu, Kaushik, ed. 2004. *India's Emerging Economy: Performance and Prospects in the 1990s and Beyond*. Cambridge, MA: MIT Press.

Bates, Robert. 1981. *Markets and States in Tropical Africa: The Political Basis of Agricultural Policies*. Berkeley: University of California Press.

Bayly, Chris. 1985. 'The Pre-History of Communalism? Religious Conflict in India, 1700-1860'. *Modern Asian Studies* 19 (2): pp. 177–203.

Berlin, Isaiah. 1980. 'The Counter-Enlightenment'. In *Against the Current: Essays in the History of Ideas*, ed. Henry Hardy, pp. 1–24. Oxford, UK: Oxford University Press.

————. 1992. 'The Bent Twig: On the Rise of Nationalism.' In *The Crooked Timber of Humanity: Chapters in the History of Ideas*. New York: Vintage Books.

Berman, Sheri. 1997. 'Civil Society and the Collapse of the Weimar Republic'. *World Politics* 49: pp. 401–29.

Beteille, Andre. 1996. *Caste Today*. Delhi: Oxford University Press.

Bhagwati, Jagdish. 1993. *India in Transition*. Oxford, UK: Clarendon Press.

————. 1998. 'The Capital Myth'. *Foreign Affairs* 77 (3): pp. 7–12.

Bhagwati, Jagdish, and Arvind Panagariya. 2013. *Why Growth Matters: How Economic Growth in India Reduced Poverty and Lessons for Other Developing Countries*. New York: Public Affairs.

Bhagwati, Jagdish, and Padma Desai. 1970. *India: Planning for Industrialization*. New York: Oxford University Press.

Bhagwati, Jagdish, and T.N. Srinivasan. 1985. 'Trade Policy and Development'. In *Dependence and Interdependence* by Jagdish Bhagwati, pp. 88–122. Delhi: Oxford University Press.

Bhalla, Surjit S., and Paul Glewwe. 1986. 'Growth and Equity in Developing Countries: A Reinterpretation of the Sri Lankan Experience'. *World Bank Economic Review* 1 (1): pp. 35–63.

Bhattacharya, M. 1992. 'The Mind of the Founding Fathers'. In *Federalism in India: Origins and Development*, eds N. Mukarji and B. Arora, pp. 87–104. New Delhi: Vikas Publishing House.

Bhargava, Rajeev, ed. 1998. *Secularism and Its Critics*. Delhi: Oxford University Press.

Boix, Carles. 2003. *Democracy and Redistribution*. New York: Cambridge University Press.

Boix, Carles, and Susan C. Stokes. 2003. 'Endogenous Democratization'. *World Politics* 55 (4): pp. 517–49.

Bonner, Arthur, Kancha Ilaiah, Suranjit Kumar Saha, Ashgar Ali Engineer, and Gerard Hueze. 1994. *Democracy in India: A Hollow Shell*. Washington, DC: American University Press.

Bouton, Marshall. 1985. *Agrarian Radicalism in South India*. Princeton, NJ: Princeton University Press.

Boyte, Harry. 1994. 'The Pragmatic Ends of Popular Politics'. In *Habermas and the Public Sphere*, ed. Craig Calhoun, pp. 340–58. Cambridge, MA: MIT Press.

Brass, Paul. 1973. *Language, Religion, and Politics in North India*. London: Cambridge University Press.

———. 1975. *Language, Religion, and Politics in North India*. Cambridge, UK: Cambridge University Press.

———. 1991. 'Pluralism, Regionalism and Decentralizing Tendencies in Contemporary Indian Politics'. In *Ethnicity and Nationalism: Theory and Comparison*, pp. 114–66. New Delhi: Sage.

———. 1997. *Theft of an Idol: Text and Context in the Representation of Collective Violence.* Princeton, NJ: Princeton University Press.

Brown, Judith M. 1991. *Gandhi: Prisoner of Hope.* New Haven, CT: Yale University Press.

———. 2003. *Nehru: A Political Life.* New Haven, CT: Yale University Press.

Brubaker, Rogers. 1992. *Immigration and Citizenship in Germany and France.* Cambridge, MA: Harvard University Press.

Bruhn, Miriam. 2010. 'License to Sell: The Effect of Business Registration Reform on Entrepreneurial Activity in Mexico'. *Review of Economics and Statistics* 93 (1): pp. 382–86.

Bruton, Henry, Gamini Abeysekera, Nimal Sanderatne, and Zainal Aznam Yusof. 1992. *The Political Economy of Poverty, Equity and Growth: Sri Lanka and Malaysia.* New York: Oxford University Press for the World Bank.

Calhoun, Craig, ed. 1994. *Habermas and the Public Sphere.* Cambridge, MA: MIT Press.

Capoccia, Giovanni, and Daniel Ziblatt. 2010. 'The Historical Turn in Democratization Studies: A New Research Agenda for Europe and Beyond.' *Comparative Political Studies* 43 (8–9): pp. 931–68.

Cassan, Guilhem. 2011. 'The Impact of Positive Discrimination on Education in India: Evidence from a Natural Experiment'. Working Paper. Paris: Paris School of Economics.

Chaddha, G.K. 1986. *The State and Rural Economic Transformation: A Study of Punjab.* New Delhi: Sage.

Chauchard, Simon. 2012. 'Can Descriptive Representation Change Beliefs about a Stigmatized Group? Evidence from Rajastan'. Paper presented at the Brown-India Seminar, Rajasthan, 2 November. Brown University, Providence, RI. Forthcoming in *American Political Science Review.*

Chakravarty, Sukhamoy. 1987. *Development Planning: The Indian Experience.* New Delhi: Oxford University Press.

Chandra, Kanchan. 2000. 'The Transformation of Ethnic Politics in

India: The Decline of Congress and the Rise of the Bahujan Samaj Party in Hoshiarpur'. *Journal of Asian Studies* 59 (1): pp. 26–61.

———. 2007. *Why Ethnic Parties Succeed: Patronage and Ethnic Head Counts in India.* New York: Cambridge University Press.

Chatterjee, Partha. 1986. *Nationalist Thought and the Colonial World: A Derivative Discourse?* Minneapolis: Zed Books.

Chatterji, Margaret. 1983. *Gandhi's Religious Thought.* London: MacMillan.

Chhibber, Pradeep K. 2001. *Democracy without Associations: Transformation of the Party System and Social Cleavages in India.* Ann Arbor: University of Michigan Press.

Cohen, Jean, and Andrew Arato. 1992. *Civil Society and Political Theory.* Cambridge, MA: MIT Press.

Colley, Linda. 1992. *Britons: Forging the Nation, 1707-1837.* New Haven, CT: Yale University Press.

Connor, Walker. 1994. *Ethnonationalism: The Quest for Understanding.* Princeton, NJ: Princeton University Press.

Corbridge, Stuart. 2000. 'Competing Inequalities: The Scheduled Tribes and the Reservations System in India's Jharkhand'. *Journal of Asian Studies* 59 (1): pp. 62–85.

———. 2002. 'The Continuing Struggle for India's Jharkhand: Democracy, Decentralization, and the Politics of Names and Numbers'. *Commonwealth and Comparative Politics* 40 (3): pp. 55–71.

Corbridge, Stuart, and John Harriss. 2000. *Reinventing India: Liberalization, Hindu Nationalism and Popular Democracy.* Cambridge, UK; Malden, MA: Polity Press.

Currie, P.M. 1989. *The Shrine and Cult of Muin-al-Din Chishti of Ajmer.* Delhi: Oxford University Press.

Dahl, Robert Alan. 1971. *Polyarchy: Participation and Opposition.* New Haven, CT: Yale University Press.

———. 1981. *The Dilemmas of Pluralist Democracies: Autonomy vs. Control.* New Haven, CT: Yale University Press.

————. 1989. *Democracy and its Critics*. New Haven, CT: Yale University Press.

————. 1998. *On Democracy*. New Haven, CT: Yale University Press.

Dalton, Dennis. 1993. *Mahatma Gandhi: Nonviolent Power in Action*. New York: Columbia University Press.

Damodaran, Harish. 2008. *India's New Capitalists: Caste, Business, and Industry in a Modern Nation*. New Delhi: Palgrave Macmillan.

Darby, John. 1986. *Intimidation and the Control of Conflict in Northern Ireland*. Dublin: Gill and Macmillan.

De Soto, Hernando. 1989. *The Other Path: The Invisible Revolution in the Third World*. New York: Harper Collins.

Deaton, Angus, and Jean Dreze. 2002. 'Poverty and Inequality in India, a Re-examination'. *Economic and Political Weekly* XXXVII (36): pp. 3729–48.

Desai, Sonalde, and Amaresh Dubey. 2011. 'Caste in 21st Century India: Competing Narratives'. *Economic and Political Weekly* 46 (11): pp. 40–49.

Deshmukh, Nanaji. 1989. *Rethinking Secularism*. Delhi: Suruchi Prakashan.

Deshpande, Ashwini. 2011. *The Grammar of Caste: Economic Discrimination in Contemporary India*. Delhi: Oxford University Press.

Deshpande, Satish, and Yogendra Yadav. 2006. 'Redesigning Affirmative Action: Castes and Benefits in Higher Education'. *Economic and Political Weekly* XLI, no. 24 (17 June): pp. 2419–24.

Diamond, Larry, Juan J. Linz, and Seymour Martin Lipset, eds. 1989. *Democracy in Developing Countries: Asia*. Vol 3. Boulder, CO: Lynne Rienner.

Dirks, Nicholas. 1997. 'Recasting Tamil Society: The Politics of Caste and Race in Contemporary Southern India'. In *Caste Today*, ed. C.J. Fuller, pp. 263–95. Delhi: Oxford University Press.

————. 2001. *Castes of Mind: Colonialism and the Making of Modern India*. Princeton, NJ: Princeton University Press.

Djankov, Simeon, Rafael La Porta, Florencio Lopez-de-Silanes and Andrei Shleifer. 2002. 'The Regulation of Entry'. *Quarterly Journal of Economics* 117 (1): pp. 1–37.

Dominguez, Jorge, ed. 1994. *Race and Ethnicity in Latin America.* New York: Garland.

Dreze, Jean, and Amartya Sen. 1995. *India: Economic Development and Social Opportunity.* Oxford, UK: Oxford University Press.

———. 2001. *India: Economic Development and Social Opportunity.* Oxford, UK: Oxford University Press.

———. 2013. *An Uncertain Glory: India and its Contradictions.* London: Allen Lane.

Dunning, Thad, and Janhavi Nilekani. 2013. 'Ethnic Quotas and Political Mobilization: Caste, Parties, and Distribution in Indian Village Councils'. *American Political Science Review* 107 (1): pp. 35–56.

Eaton, Richard M. 2006. Introduction to *Slavery and South Asian History*, eds Indrani Chatterjee and Richard M. Eaton, pp. 1–16. Bloomington, IN: Indiana University Press.

Eck, Diana. 2012. *India: A Sacred Geography.* New York: Three Rivers Press.

Einstein, Albert. 1954. 'Religion and Science: Irreconcilable?' In *Ideas and Opinions.* New York: Crown Publishers.

Eldersveld, Samuel James and Bashiruddin Ahmed. 1978. *Citizens and Politics: Mass Political Behavior in India.* Chicago: University of Chicago Press.

Election Commission of India. 1996. *Statistical Report on General Elections.* Vol. 1. Delhi: Election Commission of India.

———. 1998. *Statistical Report on General Elections.* Vol. 1. Delhi: Election Commission of India.

———. 2009. *Statistical Report on General Elections.* Vol. 1. Delhi: Election Commission of India.

Elly, Geoff. 1994. 'Nations, Publics, and Political Cultures: Placing Habermas in the Nineteenth Century'. In *Habermas and the*

Public Sphere, ed. Craig Calhoun, pp. 289–339. Cambridge, MA: MIT Press.

Embree, Ainslie Thomas, ed. 1971. *Alberuni's India.* New York: W.W. Norton.

Embree, Ainslie Thomas, and Mark Juergensmeyer. 1989. *Imagining India: Essays on Indian History.* Delhi; New York: Oxford University Press.

Fearon, James, and David Laitin. 1996. 'Explaining Interethnic Cooperation'. *American Political Science Review* 90: pp. 715–35.

Forbes, H.D. 1997. *Ethnic Conflict: Commerce, Culture, and the Contact Hypothesis.* New Haven, CT: Yale University Press.

Frankel, Francine. 1988. 'Middle Castes and Classes'. In *India's Democracy: An Analysis of Changing State-Society Relations,* ed. Atul Kohli, pp. 225–61. Princeton, NJ: Princeton University Press.

———. 1990. 'Conclusion: Decline of a Social Order'. In *Dominance and State Power in Modern India: Decline of a Social Order,* ed. Francine R. Frankel, and M.S.A. Rao. Delhi: Oxford University Press.

Frykenberg, Robert Eric. 1993. 'Hindu Fundamentalism and the Structural Stability of India'. In *Fundamentalisms and the State: Remaking Polities, Economies, and Militance,* pp. 233–55. Chicago: University of Chicago Press.

Galanter, Marc. 2002. 'The Long Half Life of Reservations'. In *India's Living Constitution: Ideas, Practices, Controversies,* ed. E. Sridharan, Z. Hasan, and R. Sudarshan, pp. 233–55. Delhi: Permanent Black.

Gallagher, Mary. 2005. 'China in 2004'. *Asian Survey* 35 (1): pp. 21–32.

Gandhi, Mohandas K. 1909. *Hind Swaraj.* Ahmedabad: Navajivan Trust.

———. 1962. *My God.* Ahmedabad: Navajivan Trust.

———. 1978. *Hindu Dharma.* New Delhi: Orient Paperbacks.

Gandhi, Mohandas K., ed. 1921. *Young India*. Vol. 3. Ahmedabad: Navajivan Trust.

Ganguly, Sumit. 2007. 'Six Decades of Independence'. *Journal of Democracy* 18 (2): pp. 30–40.

Gayer, Lauren, and Christophe Jaffrelot, eds. 2012. *Muslims in Indian Cities, Trajectories of Marginalization*. Delhi: Harper Collins.

Gellner, Ernest. 1983. *Nations and Nationalism*. Ithaca: Cornell University Press.

———. 1994. *Conditions of Liberty: Civil Society and Its Rivals*. New York: Penguin.

———. 1995. 'The Importance of Being Modular'. In *Civil Society: Theory, History, Comparison*, ed. John Hall, pp. 32–55. Cambridge, MA: Blackwell.

George, Alexander L., and Andrew Bennett. 2005. *Case Studies and Theory Development in the Social Sciences*. Cambridge, MA: MIT Press.

Gerring, John. 2007. *Case Study Research: Principles and Practices*. Cambridge: Cambridge University Press.

Ghani, Ejaz, William Kerr, and Stephen O'Connell. 2011, 'Promoting Entrepreneurship, Growth and Job Creation'. In *Reshaping Tomorrow: Is South Asia Ready for the Big Leap*, ed. Ejaz Ghani, pp. 168–217. New Delhi: Oxford University Press.

Ghate, Chetan, and Stephen Wright. 2011. 'The "V-Factor": Distribution, Timing and Correlates of the Great Indian Growth Turnaround'. *Journal of Development Economics* 99 (1): pp. 58–67.

Giles, Chris, and Kate Allen. 2013. 'Southeastern Shift: The New Leaders of Global Growth'. *Financial Times*, 5 June.

Glazer, Nathan. 1996. *We Are All Multiculturalists Now*. Cambridge, MA: Harvard University Press.

Gokhale, Jayshree. 1990. 'The Evolution of Counter-Ideology'. In *Dominance and State Power in Modern India: Decline of a Social*

Order, vol. 2, eds Francine R. Frankel and M.S.A. Rao, pp. 212–77. Delhi: Oxford University Press.

Golwalkar, M.S. 1947. *We or Our Nationood Defined*. Pune: Kale.

———. 1992. *Rashtra (The Nation)*. Delhi: Suruchi Parakshan.

Gomez, E.T., and Jomo K.S. 1999. *Malaysia's Political Economy: Politics, Patronage and Profits*. Cambridge: Cambridge University Press.

Gomez, E.T. 2011. 'The Politics and Policies of Corporate Development: Race, Rents, and Redistribution in Malaysia'. In *The Politics and Policies of Corporate Development: Race, Rents, and Redistribution in Malaysia*, eds E.T. Gomez and Hall Hill. London: Routledge Publications.

Gopal, Sarvepalli. 1979. *Jawaharlal Nehru: A Biography*. Vol. 2. London: Oxford University Press.

———. 1992. *Anatomy of a Confrontation*. London: Zed Books.

———. 2011. *Jawaharlal Nehru: A Biography*. Vol. 2. Reprint, Delhi: Oxford University Press.

———, ed. 1980. 'Will and Testament'. In *Jawaharlal Nehru: An Anthology*. Delhi: Oxford University Press.

Government of Tamil Nadu. 1971. *Report of the Centre-State Relations Inquiry Committee 1971*. Madras: Director of Stationery and Printing.

Gowda, M.V. Rajeev, and E. Sridharan. 2012. 'Reforming India's Party Financing and Election Expenditure Laws'. *Election Law Journal* 11 (2): pp. 226–40.

Graham, Bruce. 1990. *Hindu Nationalism and Indian Politics: The Origins and Development of the Bharatiya Jana Sangh*. Cambridge, UK: Cambridge University Press.

Gramsci, Antonio. 1971. *Prison Notebooks*. Vol. 1. New York: International Publishers.

Gubler, Joshua R., and Joel Sawat Selway. 2012. 'Horizontal Inequality, Crosscutting Cleavages, and Civil War'. *Journal of Conflict Resolution* 56 (2): pp. 206–32.

Guha, Ramachandra. 2007. *India after Gandhi.* London: Pan Books.

———. 2010. 'Political Leadership in Independent India'. In *The Oxford Companion to Politics in India*, eds Niraja Gopal Jayal and Pratap Bhanu Mehta, pp. 288–98. Delhi: Oxford University Press.

———. 2011. *Makers of Modern India.* Cambridge, MA: Harvard University Press.

Habermas, Jurgen. 1989. *The Structural Transformation of the Public Sphere: An Inquiry into the Category of Bourgeois Society.* Trans. Thomas Burger and Frederic Lawrence. Cambridge, MA: MIT Press.

———. 1994. 'Further Reflections on the Public Sphere'. In *Habermas and the Public Sphere*, ed. Craig Calhoun, pp. 241–61. Cambridge, MA: MIT Press.

Haggard, Stephan, and Robert Kauffman. 1995. *The Political Economy of Democratic Transitions.* Princeton, NJ: Princeton University Press.

Hampshire, Stuart. 1991. 'Nationalism'. In *Isaiah Berlin: A Celebration*, eds Edna Ullmann-Margalit and Avishai Margalit. Chicago: University of Chicago Press.

Hansen, C., and Christophe Jaffrelot, eds. 1998. *The BJP and the Compulsions of Politics in India.* Delhi: Oxford University Press.

Hardgrave, Robert. 1965. *The Dravidian Movement.* Bombay: Popular Prakashan.

———. 1969. *The Nadars of Tamilnad: The Political Culture of a Community in Change.* Berkeley: University of California Press.

Hardin, Russell. 1995. *One for All: The Logic of Group Conflict.* Princeton, NJ: Princeton University Press.

Harrison, Selig. 1960. *India: The Most Dangerous Decades.* Princeton, NJ: Princeton University Press; London: Oxford University Press.

Harriss, John. 1999. 'Comparing Political Regimes across Indian States'. *Economic and Political Weekly* 34 (48): pp. 3367–77.

Hasan, Zoya. 1989. 'Power and Mobilization: Patterns of Resilience and Change in Uttar Pradesh Politics'. In *Dominance and State*

Power in Modern India: Decline of a Social Order, vol. 1, eds Francine R. Frankel and M.S.A. Rao, pp. 133–203. Delhi: Oxford University press.

Hawley, John Stratton, and Mark Juergensmeyer. 1988. *Songs of the Saints of India.* New York: Oxford University Press.

Hay, Stephen, ed. 1991. *Sources of Indian Tradition.* Vol. 2. 2nd ed. New York: Penguin.

Heath, Anthony, and Yogendra Yadav. 1999. 'The United Colours of Congress: Social Profile of Congress Voters, 1996 and 1998'. *Economic and Political Weekly* XXXIV (34–35): pp. 2518–28.

Heller, Patrick. 2000. 'Degrees of Democracy: Some Comparative Lessons from India'. *World Politics* 52 (4): pp. 484–519.

Herring, Ronald. 1982. *Land to the Tiller.* New Haven, CT: Yale University Press.

Hirschman, Albert O. 1981. *Essays in Trespassing: Economics to Politics and Beyond.* Cambridge, UK; New York: Cambridge University Press.

Hobsbawm, Eric. 1990. *Nations and Nationalism since 1870.* Cambridge, UK: Cambridge University Press.

Hoffman, Stanley. 1993. 'Thoughts on the French Nation Today'. *Daedalus* 122 (3): pp. 63–79.

———. 1994. 'The Nation, Nationalism and After: The Case of France'. In *Tanner Lectures on Human Values,* vol. 15. Salt Lake City: University of Utah Press.

Horowitz, Donald. 1983. 'Racial Violence in the United States'. In *Ethnic Pluralism and Public Policy,* eds Nathan Glazer and Ken Young. Lexington, MA: Lexington Books.

———. 1985. *Ethnic Groups in Conflict.* Berkeley: University of California Press.

Houtzager, Peter, and Mick Moore, eds. 2003. *Changing Paths: International Development and the New Politics of Inclusion.* Ann Arbor: University of Michigan Press.

Howard, Marilyn K. 2007. 'Lynching'. In *Encyclopedia of American Race Riots*, eds Walter Rucker and James Nathaniel Upton. Westport, CT: Greenwood Press.

Huang, Yasheng. 2008. *Capitalism with Chinese Characteristics.* New York: Cambridge University Press.

Huntington, Samuel P. 1968. *Political Order in Changing Societies.* New Haven: Yale University Press.

———. 1981. *American politics: The Promise of Disharmony.* Cambridge, MA: Harvard University Press.

———. 1984. 'Will More Countries Become Democratic?' *Political Science Quarterly* 99 (2): pp. 193–218.

———. 1991. *The Third Wave: Democratization in the Late Twentieth Century.* Norman, OK: University of Oklahoma Press.

———. 1997. *The Clash of Civilizations and the Remaking of the World Order.* New York: Simon and Schuster.

Inglehart, Ronald. 1997. *Modernization and Postmodernization: Cultural, Economic, and Political Change in 43 Societies.* Princeton, NJ: Princeton University Press.

Isaac, K.A. 1994. 'Library Movement and Bibliographic Control in Kerala: An Overview'. Paper presented at the International Congress of Kerala Studies, Trivandrum, India, August.

Iyer, Rajkamal, and Antoinette Schoar. 2010. 'Are There Cultural Differences in Entrepreneurship'. In *International Differences in Entrepreneurship*, eds Josh Lerner and Antoinette Schoar, pp. 209–42. Chicago: University of Chicago Press for National Bureau of Economic Research.

Jaffrelot, Christophe. 1993. *The Hindu Nationalist Movement in India.* New York: Columbia University Press.

———. 2000. 'The Rise of Other Backward Castes in North India'. *Journal of Asian Studies* 59 (1): pp. 86–108.

———. 2003. *India's Silent Revolution: The Rise of Lower Castes in North India.* Delhi: Permanent Black.

———. 2013. 'Caste and Political Parties in India'. In *Routledge*

Handbook of Indian Politics, eds Atul Kohli and Prerna Singh, pp. 107–18. London: Routledge.

Jaffrelot, Christophe, and Sanjay Kumar, eds. 2009. *Rise of the Plebeians? The Changing Face of Indian Legislative Assemblies.* London; New Delhi: Routledge.

Jaffrelot, Christophe, and Cyril Robin. 2009. 'Towards Jat Empowerment in Rajasthan'. In *Rise of the Plebeians? The Changing Face of Indian Legislative Assemblies*, eds Christophe Jaffrelot and Sanjay Kumar, pp. 164–87. London; New Delhi: Routledge.

Jalal, Ayesha. 1995. *Democracy and Authoritarianism in South Asia: A Comparative and Historical Perspective.* Cambridge, UK: Cambridge University Press.

Jayal, Niraja Gopal. 2006. *Representing India: Ethnic Diversity and the Governance of Public Institutions.* Basingstoke: Palgrave Macmillan.

———. 2013. *Citizenship and Its Discontents: An Indian History.* Cambridge, MA: Harvard University Press.

Jenkins, Rob. 1999. *Democratic Politics and Economic Reform in India.* Cambridge, UK; New York: Cambridge University Press.

———. 2007. 'Civil Society Versus Corruption'. *Journal of Democracy* 18 (2): pp. 55–69.

Jodhka, Surinder S. 2010. 'Dalits in Business: Self Employed Scheduled Castes in Northwest India'. *Economic and Political Weekly* XLV (11): pp. 41–48.

Jomo K.S. 1990. *Growth and Structural Change in the Malaysian Economy.* London: Macmillan.

Kalnins, A., and W. Chung. 2006. 'Social Capital, Geography, and Survival: Gujarati Immigrant Entrepreneurs in the U.S. Lodging Industry'. *Management Science* 52 (2): pp. 233–47.

Kapur, Devesh, Chandra Bhan Prasad, Lant Pritchett, and D. Shyam Babu. 2010. 'Rethinking Inequality: Dalits in Uttar Pradesh in the Market Reform Era'. *Economic and Political Weekly* 45 (35): pp. 39–49.

Katzenstein, Mary.1979. *Ethnicity and Equality: The Shiv Sena Party and Preferential Policies in Bombay.* Ithaca, NY: Cornell University Press.

Kaviraj, Sudipta. 2010. 'Nationalism'. In *The Oxford Companion to Politics in India,* eds Niraja Gopal Jayal and Pratap Bhanu Mehta, pp. 317–32. Delhi: Oxford University Press.

Kennedy, Loraine. 2005. 'The Political Determinants of Reform Packaging: Contrasting Responses to Economic Liberalization in Andhra Pradesh and Tamil Nadu'. In *Regional Reflections: Comparing Politics across India's State,* ed. Rob Jenkins, pp. 29–65. New Delhi: Oxford University Press.

Keohane, Nannerl. 2005. 'On Leadership'. *Perspectives on Politics* 3 (4): pp. 705–22.

———. 2010. *Thinking about Leadership.* Princeton, NJ: Princeton University Press.

Keohane, Robert O. 2003. 'Disciplinary Schizophrenia: Implications for Graduate Education in Political Science'. *Qualitative Methods* 1, no. 1 (Spring): pp. 9–12.

Kharas, Homi, and Harinder Kohli. 2011. 'What Is the Middle Income Trap, Why Do Countries Fall Into It, and How Can It Be Avoided?' *Global Journal of Emerging Market Economies* 3, no. 3 (September): pp. 281–89.

Khemani, Stuti. 2003. *Partisan Politics and Intergovernmental Transfers in India.* Washington, DC: World Bank Publications.

Khilnani, Sunil. 1997. *The Idea of India.* London: Hamish Hamilton.

———. 2010. 'Politics and National Identity'. In *The Oxford Companion to Politics in India,* eds Niraja Gopal Jayal and Pratap Bhanu Mehta, pp. 192–204. Delhi: Oxford University Press.

King, Gary, Robert O. Keohane, and Sidney Verba. 1994. *Designing Social Inquiry: Scientific Inference in Qualitative Research.* Princeton, NJ: Princeton University Press.

King, Robert D. 1997. *Nehru and the Language Politics of India.* Delhi: Oxford University Press.

Klapper, Leora, Luc Laeven, and Raghuram Rajan. 2006. 'Entry Regulation as a Barrier to Entrepreneurship'. *Journal of Financial Economics* 82 (3): pp. 591–629.

Kohli, Atul. 1987. *The State and Poverty in India: The Politics of Reform.* New York: Cambridge University Press.

———. 1991. *Democracy and Discontent: India's Growing Crisis of Ungovernability.* New York: Cambridge University Press.

———. 2012. *Poverty amid Plenty in the New India.* Cambridge, UK; New York: Cambridge University Press.

Kohli, Atul, ed. 2001. *The Success of India's Democracy.* Cambridge, UK; New York: Cambridge University Press.

Kolakowski, L. 1990. *Modernity on Endless Trial.* Chicago: University of Chicago Press.

Kornai, János. 1992. *The Socialist System: The Political Economy of Communism.* Princeton, NJ: Princeton University Press.

Kothari, Rajni. 1964. 'The Congress System in India'. *Asian Survey* 4 (12): pp. 1161–73.

———. 1970. *Politics in India.* New Delhi: Orient Longman.

Krause, Sharon. 2002. *Liberalism with Honor.* Cambridge, MA: Harvard University Press.

Krishna, Raj, and G.S. Raychaudhuri. 1982. 'Trends in Rural Savings and Capital Formation in India, 1950-1951 to 1973-74'. *Economic Development and Cultural Change* 30 (2): pp. 271–98.

Krueger, Anne O. 2002. *Economic Policy Reforms and the Indian Economy.* Chicago: University of Chicago Press.

Krueger, Anne O., ed. 1992. *The Political Economy of Agricultural Price Policy.* Vol. 5. Baltimore, MD: The Johns Hopkins University Press.

Kumar, Ravinder. 1989. 'India's Secular Culture'. In *The Making of a Nation.* Delhi: Manohar Publishers.

Kundera, Milan. 1986. 'The Depreciated Legacy of Cervantes'. In *The Art of the Novel.* New York: Grove Press. Originally delivered as the Jerusalem Lecture, Spring 1985.

Kymlicka, Will. 1996. *Multicultural Citizenship*. Oxford, UK: Oxford University Press.

Laitin, David D. 1986. *Hegemony and Culture: Religion and Politics among the Yoruba*. Chicago: University of Chicago Press.

———. 1989. 'Language Policy and Political Strategy in India'. *Policy Sciences* 22 (3): pp. 415–36.

———. 1997. 'The Cultural Identities of a European State'. *Politics and Society* 25 (3): pp. 277–302.

Lele, Jayant. 1990. 'Caste, Class and Dominance: Political Mobilization in Maharashtra'. In *Dominance and State Power in Modern India: Decline of a Social Order*, eds Francine R. Frankel and M.S.A Rao, pp. 115–211. Delhi: Oxford University Press.

Lerner, Josh, and Antoinette Schoar, eds. 2010. *International Differences in Entrepreneurship*. Chicago: University of Chicago Press for National Bureau of Economic Research.

Lewis, W. Arthur. 1954. 'Economic Development with Unlimited Supplies of Labor'. *The Manchester School of Economic and Social Studies* 22 (2): pp. 400–49.

Lieberson, Stanley, and Arnold Silverman. 1965. 'The Precipitants and Underlying Conditions of Race Riots'. *American Sociological Review* 30 (December): pp. 887–98.

Lijphart, Arend. 1977. *Democracies in Plural Societies: A Comparative Exploration*. New Haven, CT: Yale University Press.

———. 1996. 'The Puzzle of Indian Democracy: A Consociational Interpretation'. *American Political Science Review* 90 (2): pp. 258–68.

Lindblom, Charles. 1977. *Politics and Markets: The World's Political Economic Systems*. New York: Basic Books.

Lipset, Seymour Martin. 1959. 'Some Social Requisites of Democracy: Economic Development and Political Legitimacy'. *American Political Science Review* 53 (2): pp. 69–105.

Lohia, Rammanohar. 1964. *The Caste System*. Hyderabad: Lohia Samta Vidyalaya Nyas.

Lokniti. 2010. *State of the Nation Survey*. Delhi: Centre for the Study of Developing Societies.

Macpherson, C.B. 1977. *The Life and Times of Liberal Democracy*. Vol. 3. Oxford, UK: Oxford University Press.

Madan, T.N. 1987. 'Secularism in Its Place'. *Journal of Asian Studies* 46, no. 4 (November) 747–59.

Mandal Commission. 1980. *Report of the Backward Classes Commission*. Delhi: Government of India.

Mann, Elizabeth A. 1992. *Boundaries and Identities: Muslims, Work and Status in Aligarh*. Delhi; Newbury Park, CA: Sage.

Manor, James. 1990a. 'How and Why Liberal and Representative Politics Emerged in India'. *Political Studies* 38 (1): pp. 20–38.

———. 1990b. 'Karnataka'. In *Dominance and State Power in Modern India: Decline of a Social Order*, eds Francine R. Frankel and M.S.A. Rao, pp. 322–61. Delhi: Oxford University Press.

———. 2001. 'Center-State Relations'. In *The Success of India's Democracy*, ed. Atul Kohli, pp. 204–26. Cambridge, UK: Cambridge University Press.

———. 2004. 'Explaining Political Trajectories in Andhra Pradesh and Karnataka'. In *Regional Reflections: Comparing Politics across India's State*, ed. Rob Jenkins, pp. 255–84. New Delhi: Oxford University Press.

McKenzie, David, Suresh de Mel, and Christopher Woodruff. 2008. 'Returns to Capital: Results from a Randomized Experiment'. *Quarterly Journal of Economics* 123 (4): 1329–72.

McMillan, Allistair, and Yogendra Yadav. 1998. 'Results: How India Voted'. *India Today*, 16 March.

Mehta, Pratap Bhanu. 2003. *The Burden of Democracy*. New Delhi: Penguin.

———. 2007. 'The Rise of Judicial Sovereignty'. *Journal of Democracy* 18 (2): pp. 70–83.

Mehta, Uday Singh. 1999. *Liberalism and Empire: A Study in*

Nineteenth-Century British Liberal Thought. Chicago: University of Chicago Press.

Mendelsohn, Oliver, and Marika Vicziany. 1998. *The Untouchables: Subordination, Poverty and the State in Modern India.* Cambridge, UK: Cambridge University Press.

Menon, Dilip. 1995. *Caste, Nationalism and Communism in South India: Malabar 1900-1948.* Cambridge, UK: Cambridge University Press.

Mill, John Stuart. 1975. 'Representative Government'. In *Three Essays,* pp. 5–106. Oxford; New York: Oxford University Press.

———. 2011. *A System of Logic.* Toronto: University of Toronto Libraries.

Miller, Judith. 1991. 'Strangers at the Gate'. *The New York Times Magazine,* 15 September.

Miller, Sam. 2009. *Delhi: Adventures in a Megacity.* London: Jonathan Cape.

Moore, Barrington. 1966. *Social Origins of Democracy and Dictatorship: Lord and Peasant in the Making of the Modern World.* Boston, MA: Beacon.

Morone, James A. 1998. *The Democratic Wish: Popular Participation and the Limits of American Government.* New Haven, CT: Yale University Press.

Mosca, Gaetano. 1939. *The Ruling Class.* New York: McGraw Hill.

Mukherji, Rahul. Forthcoming. *Political Economy of Reforms in India.* New Delhi: Oxford University Press.

Munshi, Kaivan. 2003. 'Networks in the Modern Economy: Mexican Migrants in the U.S. Labor Market'. *Quarterly Journal of Economics* 118: pp. 549–97.

———. 2011. 'Strength in Numbers: Networks as a Solution to Occupational Traps'. *Review of Economic Studies* 78: pp. 1069–101.

Nafziger, E. Wayne. 1978. *Class, Caste and Entrepreneurship: A Study of Indian Industrialists.* Honolulu: The University of Hawaii Press for the East West Centre.

Naim, Moises. 1993. *Paper Tigers and Minotaurs: The Politics of Venezuela's Economic Reforms*. Washington, DC: Carnegie Endowment for International Peace.

Nairn, Tom. 1977. *The Break-Up of Britain: Crisis and Neo-nationalism*. London: New Left Books.

Namboodiripad, E.M.S. 1994. 'Presidential Address'. In 'Addresses and Abstracts', *Proceedings of the International Congress on Kerala Studies*, vol. 1, pp. 27–29. Thiruvananthapuram, India: AKG Centre for Research and Studies. Presented at the First International Congress of Kerala Studies, August.

Nandy, Ashis. 1981. 'The Final Encounter: The Politics of Gandhi's Assassination'. In *At the Edge of Psychology: Essays in Politics and Culture*, pp. 70–98. Delhi: Oxford University Press.

———. 1988. 'The Politics of Secularism and the Recovery of Religious Tolerance'. In *Alternatives* 13, no. 2 (April): 177–94.

———. 1992. 'The Ram Janmabhumi Movement and the Fear of the Self'. Paper presented at the CFIA South Asia Seminar, Harvard University, April.

———. 1996. 'Sustaining the Faith'. *India Today*, 31 August.

Narayan, Deepa, and Michael Woolcock. 2000. 'Social Capital: Implications for Development Theory, Research and Policy'. *World Bank Research Observer* 15 (2): pp. 225–49.

Narayan, Deepa, Raj Patel, Kai Schafft, Anne Rademacher, and Sarah Koch-Schulte. 2000. *Voices of the Poor: Can Anyone Hear Us?* New York: Oxford University Press for the World Bank.

National Commission for Sector Enterprises in Unorganised (NCEUS). 2009. *Arjun Sengupta Committee Report*. New Delhi: NCEUS, Government of India.

Nehru, Jawaharlal. 1947. *Tryst with Destiny*. Speech presented to the Indian Constituent Assembly on the eve of India's independence, Delhi, August 14.

————. 1989. *The Discovery of India.* New Delhi; New York: Oxford University Press.

Nigam, Aditya. 2002. 'In Search of a Bourgeoisie: Dalit Politics Enters a New Phase'. *Economic and Political Weekly* 37 (13): pp.1190–93.

Ninan, T.N. 2004. 'The Colours of the Rainbow'. *Seminar* 533 (January).

Nooruddin, Irfan, and Pradeep Chhibber. 2008. 'Unstable Politics: Fiscal Space and Electoral Volatility in the Indian States'. *Comparative Political Studies* 41 (8): pp. 1069–91.

North, Douglass, and Robert Paul Thomas. 1973. *The Rise of the Western World: A New Economic History.* Cambridge, UK: Cambridge University Press.

Nossiter, Tom. 1982. *Communism in Kerala: A Study in Political Adaptation.* Berkeley: University of California Press.

Obama, Barack. 1995. *Dreams from My Father: A Story of Race and Inheritance.* New York: Three Rivers Press.

O'Donnell, Guillermo A. 1973. *Modernization and Bureaucratic-Authoritarianism: Studies in South American Politics.* Berkeley: Institute of International Studies, University of California.

Olson, Mancur. 1965. *The Logic of Collective Action: Public Goods and the Theory of Groups.* Cambridge, MA: Harvard University Press.

Omvedt, Gail. 1993. *Reinventing Revolution: New Social Movements and the Socialist Tradition in India.* Armonk, NY: M.E. Sharpe.

Pack, Howard, and L.E. Westphal. 1986. 'Industrial Strategy and Technological Change'. *Journal of Development Economics* 22 (1): pp. 87–128.

Pai, Sudha. 2002. *Dalit Assertion and the Unfinished Democratic Revolution: The Bahujan Samaj Party in Uttar Pradesh.* New Delhi: Sage.

Palshikar, Suhas. 2013. 'Regional and Caste Parties'. In *Routledge Handbook of Indian Politics,* eds Atul Kohli and Prerna Singh, pp. 91–104. London; New York: Routledge.

Pan, Lynn. 1999. *The Encyclopedia of the Chinese Overseas.* Cambridge, MA: Harvard University Press.

Pan, Philip P. 2003. 'China Tries Labor Leaders Amid Protest'. *Washington Post,* 16 January.

Pande, Rohini. 2003. 'Can Mandated Political Representation Increase Policy Influence for Disadvantaged Minorities? Theory and Evidence from India'. *American Economic Review* 93 (4): pp. 1132–51.

Riordon, William L., and Plunkitt. 1995. *Plunkitt of Tammany Hall: A Series of Very Plain Talks on Very Practical Politics.* New York: Signet Classic.

Polanyi, Karl. 2001. *The Great Transformation: The Political and Economic Origins of Our Time.* 2nd ed. Boston, MA: Beacon Press.

Poole, Michael. 1990. 'Geographical Location of Political Violence in Northern Ireland'. In *Political Violence: Ireland in Comparative Perspective,* eds John Darby, Nicholas Dodge, and A.C. Hepburn, pp. 88–110. Belfast: Appletree Press.

Portes, Alejandro, and Julia Sensenbrenner. 1993. 'Embeddedness and Immigration: Notes on the Social Determinants of Economic Action'. *American Journal of Sociology* 98 (6): pp: 1320–50.

Przeworski, Adam. 1991. *Democracy and the Market.* New York: Cambridge University Press.

Przeworski, Adam, Michael Alvarez, Jose Antonio Cheibub, and Fernando Limongi. 2000. *Democracy and Development: Political Institutions and Well-Being in the World, 1950-1990.* Cambridge, UK: Cambridge University Press.

Pursell, Gary, and Ashok Gulati. 1993. 'Liberalising Indian Agriculture: An Agenda for Reform'. World Bank Working Paper 1172. Washington, DC: Policy Research Department.

Putnam, Robert. 1993. *Making Democracy Work: Civic Traditions in Italy.* Princeton, NJ: Princeton University Press.

———. 1995. 'Bowling Alone'. *Journal of Democracy* 6 (1): pp. 65–78.

————. 1996. 'The Strange Disappearance of Civic America'. *American Prospect* 7, no. 24 (December 1): pp. 34–49.

Pye, Lucian W. 1966. *Aspects of Political Development: An Analytic Study*. Boston, MA: Little Brown.

Rajendran, G. 1974. *The Ezhava Community and Kerala Politics*. Trivandrum: Academy of Political Science.

Ramanathan, Ramesh *et al.* 2013. 'Urban Voter, Not on a Roll'. *Indian Express*, 3 March.

Rao, M. Govinda, and Nirvikar Singh. 2005. *Political Economy of Federalism in India*. Delhi: Oxford University Press.

Rao, M.S.A. 1979. *Social Movements and Social Transformation: A Study of Two Backward Classes Movements in India*. Delhi: Macmillan.

Rao, Vijayendra, and Paromita Sanyal. 2010. 'Dignity through Discourse: Poverty and the Culture of Deliberation in Indian Village Democracies'. *The Annals of the American Academy of Political and Social Science* 629 (1): pp. 146–72.

Ravallion, Martin, and Gaurav Datt. 1996. 'India's Checkered History in Poverty Alleviation'. *Economic and Political Weekly* XXXI (35-36-37): pp. 2479–85.

Reddy, Ram G. 1990. 'The Politics of Accommodation: Caste, Class and Dominance in Andhra Pradesh'. In *Dominance and State Power in Modern India: Decline of a Social Order*, vol. 1, eds Francine R. Frankel and M.S.A. Rao, pp. 265–321. Delhi: Oxford University Press.

Reddy, Sanjay G., and Thomas W. Pogge. 2009. 'How Not to Count the Poor'. In *Measuring Global Poverty*, eds Sudhir Anand and Joseph Stiglitz. New York: Oxford University Press. Text available at http://www.socialanalysis.org/.

Robin, Cyril. 2009. 'Bihar: The New Stronghold of OBC Politics'. In *Rise of the Plebeians? The Changing Face of the Indian Legislative Assemblies*, eds Christophe Jaffrelot and Sanjay Kumar, pp. 65–102. London; New Delhi: Routledge.

Rodrik, Dani, and Arvind Subramanian. 2004. 'From "Hindu Growth" to Productivity Surge: The Mystery of the Indian Growth Transition'. NBER Working Paper 10376. Cambridge, MA: National Bureau of Economic Research.

Rogowski, Ronald. 1995. 'The Role of Theory and Anomaly in Social-Scientific Inference'. *American Political Science Review* 89 (2): pp. 467–70.

Rosenstein-Rodan, Paul. 1943. 'Problems of Industrialization of Eastern and Southern Europe'. *Economic Journal* 53: pp. 202–11.

Rudner, David. 1994. *Caste and Capitalism in Colonial India: The Nattukottai Chettiars*. Berkeley: University of California Press.

Rudolph, Lloyd I., and Susanne Hoeber Rudolph. 1967. *The Modernity of Tradition: Political Development in India*. Chicago: University of Chicago Press.

———. 1983. *Gandhi: The Traditional Roots of Charisma*. Chicago: University of Chicago Press.

———. 1987. *In Pursuit of Lakshmi: The Political Economy of the Indian State*. Chicago: University of Chicago Press.

———. 2010a. 'Federalism as State Formation in India: A Theory of Shared and Negotiated Sovereignty'. *International Political Science Review* 31 (5): pp. 1–21.

———. 2010b. 'The Old and New Federalism in Independent India'. In *Routledge Handbook of South Asian Politics*, ed. Paul Brass, pp. 147–61. London: Routledge.

Rueschemeyer, Dietrich, Evelyn Huber Stephens, and John D. Stevens. 1992. *Capitalist Development and Democracy*. Cambridge, UK: Polity Press.

Ruparelia, Sanjay. Forthcoming. *Divided We Govern: The Paradoxes of Power in Contemporary Indian Democracy*. New York: Columbia University Press.

Ruparelia, Sanjay, Sanjay Reddy, and John Harriss, eds. 2011. *Understanding India's New Political Economy: A Great Transformation?* Abingdon, Oxon; New York: Taylor & Francis.

Ryan, Mary. 1994. 'Gender and Public Access: Women's Politics in Nineteenth Century America'. In *Habermas and the Public Sphere*, ed. Craig Calhoun, pp. 259–88. Cambridge, MA: MIT Press.

Sachchidananda. 1990. 'Patterns of Politico-Economic Change among Tribals in Middle India'. In *Dominance and State Power in Modern India: Decline of a Social Order*, vol. 2, eds Francine R. Frankel and M.S.A. Rao, pp. 278–320. Delhi: Oxford University Press.

Sachs, Jeffrey D., and Andrew Warner. 1995. 'Economic Reform and the Process of Global Integration'. *Brookings Papers on Economic Activity* 1: pp. 1–118.

Sachs, Jeffrey D., Ashutosh Varshney, and Nirupam Bajpai, eds. 2002. *India in the Era of Economic Reforms*. New Delhi: Oxford University Press.

Sandel, Michael. 1996. *Democracy's Discontent: America in Search of a Public Philosophy*. Cambridge, MA: Harvard University Press.

Sartori, Giovanni. 1976. *Parties and Party Systems: A Framework for Analysis*. Vol. 1. Cambridge, UK: Cambridge University Press.

Savarkar, V.D. 1989. *Hindutva*. Bombay: Veer Savarkar Prakashan.

Saxena, Shobhan. 2011. 'Caste and Capital Can't Coexist'. Interview with Milind Kamble, *Times of India*, October 2.

Scott, James. 1976. *The Moral Economy of the Peasant: Rebellion and Subsistence in Southeast Asia*. New Haven, CT: Yale University Press.

SDSA Team. 2008. *State of Democracy in South Asia Survey*. Delhi: Oxford University Press.

Seligman, Adam. 1992. *The Idea of Civil Society*. Princeton, NJ: Princeton University Press.

Sen, Amartya. 1988. 'The Concept of Development'. In *The Handbook of Development Economics*, eds Hollis Chenery and T.N. Srinivasan, pp. 10–26. New York: North Holland.

———. 1989. 'Food and Freedom'. *World Development* 17 (6): pp. 769–81.

———. 1999. *Development as Freedom.* New York: Knopf.

———. 2007. 'Can Life Begin at 60 For the Sprightly Indian Economy?'. *Financial Times*, 14 August.

Shah, Ghanshyam. 1990. 'Caste Sentiments, Class Formation and Dominance in Gujarat'. In *Dominance and State Power in Modern India: Decline of a Social Order*, vol. 2, eds Francine R. Frankel and M.S.A. Rao, pp. 59–114. Delhi: Oxford University Press.

Sheshadri, H.V., K.S. Sudarshan, K. Surya Narain Rao, and Balraj Madhok. 1990. *Why Hindu Rashtra?* Delhi: Suruchi Prakashan.

Sheth, Dhirubhai. 1996. 'The Prospects and Pitfalls'. *India Today*, 31 August.

Shils, Edward. 1997. *The Virtue of Civility: Selected Essays on Liberalism, Tradition, and Civil Society.* Indianapolis, IN: Liberty Fund.

Shourie, Arun. 1987. *Religion in Politics.* Vol. 5. New Delhi: Roli Books.

Shukla, R.K., S.K. Dwivedi, and Asha Sharma. 2004. *The Great Indian Middle Class: Results from the NCAER Market Information Survey of Households.* New Delhi: NCAER and Business Standard.

Singh, Gurharpal. 2000. *Ethnic Conflict in India: A Case Study of Punjab.* New York: St Martin's Press.

Singh, Prerna. 2011. 'We-ness and Welfare: A Longitudinal Analysis of Social Development in Kerala, India'. *World Development* 39 (2): pp. 282–93.

Sinha, Aseema. 2005. *The Regional Roots of Developmental Politics in India: A Divided Leviathan.* Bloomington, IN: Indiana University Press.

———. 2007. 'Economic Growth and Political Accommodation'. *Journal of Democracy* 18 (2): pp. 41–54.

Sinha, Jayant, and Ashutosh Varshney. 2011. 'It Is Time for India to Rein in Its Robber Barons'. *Financial Times*, 6 January.

Sisson, Richard, and Ramashray Roy, eds. 1990. *Diversity and Dominance in Indian Politics: Changing Bases of Congress Support.* Vol. 1. New Delhi: Sage.

Smith, Anthony D. 1985. *The Ethnic Origins of Nations.* Oxford, UK: Blackwell.

Smith, Donald Eugene. 1963. *India as a Secular State.* Princeton: Princeton University Press.

Smith, Rogers M. 1997. *Civic Ideals: Conflicting Visions of Citizenship in US History.* New Haven, CT: Yale University Press.

Sridharan, E. 1999. 'Toward State Funding of Elections in India: A Comparative Perspective on Policy Options'. *Journal of Policy Reform* 3 (3): pp. 229–54.

Srinivas, M.N. 1966. *Social Change in Modern India.* Berkeley: University of California Press.

———. 1979. *The Remembered Village.* Berkeley: University of California Press.

Stepan, Alfred. 1999. 'Federalism and Democracy: Beyond the US Model'. *Journal of Democracy* 10 (4): pp. 19–34.

———. 2001. *Arguing Comparative Politics.* Oxford, UK; New York: Oxford University Press.

Stepan, Alfred, Juan J. Linz, and Yogendra Yadav. 2011. *Crafting State-Nations: India and Other Multinational Democracies.* Baltimore: The Johns Hopkins University Press.

Stiglitz, Joseph. 2002. *Globalization and its Discontents.* New York: W.W. Norton.

Stokes, Susan. 1996. 'Economic Reforms and Public Opinion in Peru, 1990-1995'. *Comparative Political Studies* 29 (5): pp. 544–65.

Stuligross, David, and Ashutosh Varshney. 2002. 'Constitutional Design and Ethnic Pluralism in India'. In *The Architecture of Democracy: Constitutional Design, Conflict Management, and Democracy,* ed. Andrew Reynolds, pp. 429–58. New York: Oxford University Press.

Subramanian, Narenda. 1999. *Ethnicity and Populist Mobilization:*

Political Parties, Citizens and Democracy in South India. Delhi: Oxford University Press.

Suri, K.C. 2004. 'Democracy, Economic Reforms and Election Results in India'. *Economic and Political Weekly* 39 (51): pp. 5404–11.

Täube, Florian. 2004. 'Proximities and Innovation: Evidence from the Indian IT Industry in Bangalore'. DRUID Working Paper Series 04–10. Copenhagen: Copenhagen Business School, Department of Industrial Economics and Strategy.

Taylor, Charles. 1990. 'Modes of Civil Society'. *Public Culture* 3 (1): pp. 95–118.

———. 1994. *Multiculturalism and 'The Politics of Recognition'.* Princeton, NJ: Princeton University Press.

———. 1998. 'The Dynamics of Democratic Exclusion'. *Journal of Democracy* 9 (4): pp. 143–56.

Tellis, Ashley J. 2012. 'Between the Times: India's Predicament and its Grand Strategy'. India in Transition. Accessed on 6 June 2013. http://www.carnregieendowment.org/2012/12/03/between-times-india-s-predicaments-and-its-grand-strategy/eppe.

Templeman, Dennis. 1996. *The Northern Nadars of Tamil Nadu: An Indian Caste in the Process of Change.* Delhi; New York: Oxford University Press.

Thompson, E.P. 1968. *The Making of the English Working Class.* Harmondsworth, UK: Penguin.

Thorat, Sukhadeo, Debolina Kundu, and Nidhi Sadana. 2010. 'Caste and Ownership of Private Enterprises'. In *Blocked by Caste: Economic Discrimination in Modern India,* eds Sukadeo Thorat and Katherine Newman, pp. 76–95. New Delhi: Oxford University Press.

Tillin, Louise. 2007. 'United in Diversity? Asymmetry in Indian Federalism'. *Publius* 37 (1): pp. 45–67.

Tocqueville, Alexis de. 2003. *Democracy in America.* New York: Penguin Classics.

Tolnay, Stewart E., and E.M. Beck. 1995. *A Festival of Violence: An*

Analysis of Southern Lynchings, 1882-1930. Chicago: University of Illinois Press.

Tudor, Maya. 2013. *The Origins of Democracy in India and Autocracy in Pakistan.* New York: Cambridge University Press.

Tully, Mark, and Satish Jacob. 1985. *Amritsar: Mrs Gandhi's Last Battle.* London: J. Cape.

Twain, Mark. 1899. *Following the Equator.* Vol. 2. N.p.: Harper Collins.

Upadhyay, Deen Dayal. 1992. *Akhand Bharat aur Muslim Samasya* (Undivided India and the Muslim problem). Noida: Jagriti Prakashan.

Vajpayee, Ananya. 2012. *Righteous Republic: The Foundations of Modern India.* Cambridge, MA: Harvard University Press.

Vanaik, Achin. 1990. *The Painful Transition: The Bourgeois Democracy of India.* London: Verso Books.

Varshney, Ashutosh. 1995. 'Mahatma Gandhi'. In the *Encyclopedia of Democracy,* ed Seymour Martin Lipset, pp. 520–22.

———. 1993. 'Contested Meanings'. *Daedalus* 122, no. 3 (Summer): pp. 227–61.

———. 1995. *Democracy, Development and the Countryside: Urban–Rural Struggles in India.* New York: Cambridge University Press.

———. 1997. 'Postmodernism, Civic Engagement and Ethnic Conflict: A Passage to India'. *Comparative Politics* 30 (1): pp.1–20.

———. 1999. 'Mass Politics or Elite Politics? India's Economic Reform in Comparative Perspective'. In *India in the Era of Economic Reforms,* eds Jeffrey Sachs, Ashutosh Varshney, and Nirupam Bajpai, pp. 222–60. New York: Oxford University Press.

———. 2000. 'Why Have Poor Democracies Not Eliminated Poverty? A Suggestion'. *Asian Survey* 40 (5): pp. 718–36.

———. 2002. *Ethnic Conflict and Civic Life: Hindus and Muslims in India.* New Haven, CT: Yale University Press; New Delhi: Oxford University Press.

————. 2003. 'Nationalism, Ethnic Conflict, and Rationality'. *Perspective on Politics* 1 (1): pp. 85–99.

————. 2005. 'Democracy and Poverty'. In *Measuring Empowerment: Cross-Disciplinary Perspectives*, ed. Deepa Narayan, pp. 382–402. Washington, DC: The World Bank.

————. 2007. 'India's Democratic Challenge'. *Foreign Affairs* 86: p. 93.

————. 2008. 'Analyzing Collective Violence in Indonesia: An Overview'. *Journal of East Asian Studies* 8 (3): pp. 341–59.

————. 2011a. 'India's Battle for Democracy Has Just Begun'. *Financial Times*, 29 August.

————. 2011b. 'Rethink the Communal Violence Bill'. *Indian Express*, 16 July.

————. 2012a. 'Two Banks of the Same River? Social Order and Entrepreneurialism in India'. In *Anxieties of Democracy: Tocquevillean Reflections on India and the United States*, eds Partha Chatterjee and Ira Katznelson, pp. 225–56. Delhi: Oxford University Press.

————. 2012b. 'Growth and Graft'. *Indian Express*, 26 October.

————, ed. 2010. *Collective Violence in Indonesia*. Boulder; London: Lynne Rienner Publishers.

Verma, A.K. 2007. 'Mayawati's Sandwich Coalition'. *Economic and Political Weekly* 42 (22): pp. 2039–43.

Visaria, Praveen, and S.K. Sanyal. 1977. 'Trends in Rural Unemployment in India'. *Economic and Political Weekly* 12 (4): pp. 240–49.

Vissa, Balagopal. 2011. 'A Matching Theory of Entrepreneurs' Tie Formation Intentions and Initiation of Economic Exchange'. *Academy of Management Journal* 54 (1): pp. 137–58.

Walzer, Michael. 1991. 'The Idea of Civil Society'. *Dissent* 38 (2): pp. 293–304.

————. 1992. *What It Means to Be an American*. New York: Marsilio.

Washbrook, David A. 1989. 'Caste, Class and Dominance in

Modern Tamil Nadu: Non-Brahmanism, Dravidianism and Tamil Nationalism'. In *Dominance and State Power in Modern India: Decline of a Social Order*, vol. 1, eds Francine R. Frankel and M.S.A. Rao, pp. 204–64. Delhi: Oxford University Press.

Weber, Eugen. 1976. *Peasants into Frenchmen: The Modernization of Rural France*. Stanford: Stanford University Press.

Weiner, Myron. 1962. *The Politics of Scarcity: Public Pressure and Political Response in India*. Chicago: University of Chicago Press.

———. 1967. *Party Building in a New Nation: The Indian National Congress*. Chicago: University of Chicago Press.

———. 1978. *Sons of the Soil: Migration and Ethnic Conflict in India*. Princeton, NJ: Princeton University Press.

———. 1986. 'The Political Economy of Industrial Growth in India'. *World Politics* 38 (4): pp. 596–610.

———. 1989. 'Institution Building in India'. In *The Indian Paradox: Essays in Indian Politics*, ed. Ashutosh Varshney, pp. 77–95. New Delhi: Sage.

———. 1991. *The Child and the State in India*. Princeton, NJ: Princeton University Press.

———. 2001. 'The Struggle for Equality: Caste in Indian Politics'. In *The Success of India's Democracy*, ed. Atul Kohli, pp. 193–226. New York: Cambridge University Press.

Williams, Rina Verma. 2006. *Postcolonial Politics and Personal Laws: Colonial Legal Legacies and the Indian State*. New Delhi; New York: Oxford University Press.

Witsoe, Jeffrey. 2013. 'A View from the States: Bihar'. In *Routledge Handbook of Indian Politics*, eds Atul Kohli and Prerna Singh, pp. 619–31. Routledge.

Woo-Cummings, Meredith, ed.1999. *The Developmental State*. Ithaca, NY: Cornell University Press.

Wood, John. 1996. 'At the Periphery but in the Thick of It'. In *India Briefing: 1996*, eds Marshall Bouton and Philip Oldenburg, pp. 33–54. New York: M.E. Sharpe.

World Bank. 1997. *India: Achievements and Challenges in Reducing Poverty*. Washington, DC: World Bank.

———. 2000. *World Development Report 2000-2001: Attacking Poverty*. New York: Oxford University Press.

———. 2002. *World Development Report 2002: Building Institutions for Markets*. New York: Oxford University Press.

———. 2004. *World Development Report 2005: A Better Investment Climate for Everyone*. New York: Oxford University Press.

———. 2011. *World Development Indicators Database 2011*. Database updated on 27 September 2012. http://data.worldbank.org/data-catalog/world-development-indicators/wdi-2011.

Yadav, Yogendra. 1993. 'Political Change in North India: Interpreting Assembly Election Results'. *Economic and Political Weekly* 28 (51): pp. 2767–74.

———. 1996a. 'Reconfiguration of Indian Politics: State Assembly Elections, 1993-5'. *Economic and Political Weekly* 31 (2–3): pp. 95–104.

———. 1996b. 'How India Voted'. *India Today*, 31 May.

———. 1996c. 'The Maturing of Indian Democracy'. *India Today*, 31 August.

———. 1999. 'Politics'. In *India Briefing: Looking Back, Looking Ahead*, eds Marshall Bouton and Philip Oldenburg, pp. 24–48. New York: M.E. Sharpe.

———. 2000. 'Understanding the Second Democratic Upsurge: Trends of Bahujan Participation in Electoral Politics in the 1990s'. In *Transforming India: Social and Political Dynamics of Democracy*, eds Francine R. Frankel, Zoya Hasan, Rajeev Bhargava and Balveer Arora, pp. 120–145. Delhi: Oxford University Press.

———. 2004. 'The Elusive Mandate of 2004'. *Economic and Political Weekly* 39 (51): pp. 5383–98.

———. 2010. 'Political Representation in Contemporary India'.

In *The Oxford Companion to Politics in India*, eds Niraja Gopal Jayal and Pratap Bhanu Mehta, pp. 347–60. Delhi: Oxford University Press.

Yadav, Yogendra, and Suhas Palshikar. 2003. 'From Hegemony to Convergence: Party System and Electoral Politics in Indian states'. *Journal of Indian School of Political Economy* 15 (1–2): pp. 5–44.

———. 2009a. 'Revisiting Third Electoral System: Mapping Electoral Trends in India, 2004-09'. In *Electoral Politics in Indian States*, eds Sandeep Shastri, K.C. Suri, and Yogendra Yadav, pp. 393–429. New Delhi: Oxford University Press.

———. 2009b. 'Ten Theses on State Politics in India'. In *Electoral Politics in Indian States*, eds Sandeep Shastri, K.C. Suri, and Yogendra Yadav, pp. 46–63. New Delhi: Oxford University Press.

Yadav, Yogendra, and V.B. Singh. 1997. 'The Maturing of a Democracy'. *India Today*, 31 August.

Young, W. Crawford. 1976. *The Politics of Cultural Pluralism.* Madison, WI: University of Wisconsin Press.

Zerinini-Brotel, Jasmine. 2009. 'The Marginalization of the *Savarnas* in Uttar Pradesh?'. In *Rise of the Plebeians? The Changing Face of Indian Legislative Assemblies*, eds Christophe Jaffrelot and Sanjay Kumar, pp. 27–64. New Delhi; London: Routledge.

Copyright Acknowledgements

India and Beyond'. This article was first published in *World Politics* 53, no. 3 (April 2001): pp. 362–98;

6. The *Economic and Political Weekly*, Mumbai, Tarun Khanna and Lakshmi Iyer for 'Caste and Entrepreneurship in India'. This article was first published in the *Economic and Political Weekly* XLVIII, no. 6 (February 2013);

7. Sage Publications India Pvt. Ltd for 'How Has Indian Federalism Done?'. This article was first published in *Studies in Indian Politics* (July 2013);

8. Oxford University Press, India, for 'Two Banks of the Same River? Social Orders and Entrepreneurialism in India'. This article was first published in *Anxieties of Democracy: Tocquevillean Reflections on India and the United States*, edited by Partha Chatterjee and Ira Katznelson, 2012.

Every effort has been made to trace copyright holders and obtain permission; any omissions brought to our attention will be remedied in future editions.

Index